complete me

SPECIAL EDITION

JENN PLUMMER

WildLupine

Complete Me

Aspen Ridge Book 5

Published by Wild Lupine Books LLC

Editing by Katie Ducharme - Between the Covers Editorial

Cover Art by Qamber Designs

Copyright © 2025 by Jenn Plummer

All rights reserved.

This is a work of fiction. All characters, places, incidents, and dialogue were created from the author's imagination. Nothing in this story should be construed as real. Any similarities between persons living or dead are entirely coincidental.

contents

join jenn plummer's readers' group

Stay up to date with Jenn Plummer by joining her Facebook readers' group, Jenn's Harlots. Ask questions, get first looks at new books/series, and have fun with other book lovers!

https://www.facebook.com/groups/jennsharlots/

a note from the author

Dear readers,

Complete Me is book five in a five-book, interconnected standalone series. You do not have to read them in order, but for the best experience, I recommend that you do.

Themes include content that may be triggering for some readers including: explicit language, kidnapping, on page flashbacks to death and rape of a family member, on page murder, discussion of rape (not by a main character), violence, and drug use.

Sexually explicit content including: virgin FMC, breath play, and reckless behavior on a motorcycle.

Please remember that the perception of the Hayes brothers is from the view of their younger sister. They are slightly villainized because that is her story. This is not a reflection on who these men are at their core.

Please read responsibly. If you have any questions about this list, please don't hesitate to reach out to me directly.

Sending you all love.

playlist

Soulmate - Chanin
Perfect for Me - Bradley Marshall
Bad Dreams - Teddy Swims
I Feel Like I'm Drowning - Two Feet
Devil You Know - Tyler Braden
Blink Twice – Shaboozey
Must Be Doin' Somethin' Right – Billy Currington

For everyone wading through the darkness, keep going; your light will come.

For all of my Reid lovers. It's time for our man to get his happy ending.

Rogue
/rōg/

noun

an elephant or other large, wild animal driven away or living apart
from the herd and having savage or destructive tendencies.

REID TEN YEARS AGO

"Take me with you! Please! You can't leave me to Mom and Dad's snoozefest tonight!" my sister begs as she grips my bicep with both hands, pulling me to a stop. She's two years younger than me, and we've been attached at the hip since she was born. She also hates being told no and being left behind when she'd rather go out and have fun with me.

"Hell no, Lena. This is no place for you, and you know it. I mean it, stay home."

"What? Why? I've been to the clubhouse plenty of times before! They like me!"

"That's because you followed me, brat. What was I supposed to do? Leave you outside the gate? You're too curious for your own good and you know it." Lena is notorious for sneaking out and finding trouble, and it's been my job for as long as I can remember to keep her out of it.

When I went in for my first tattoo appointment four years ago and met Ink, the owner of the shop, who's also a member of a motorcycle club, an entirely new world opened up for me. One with open roads, family, and freedom. The only expectation is that your loyalty is given freely to the club, which I happen to have in spades when something is worth it. I skipped college and started my tattoo apprenticeship with him not long after, much to my father's dismay.

A few motorcycle clubs call Washington State home, but I had never been intrigued until I was spending all my time with Ink at Heathen Tattoo.

"I wouldn't have to follow you if you just took me with you. Reeeeeid, c'mon!" she begs, her hands clasped in front of her, bottom lip pushed out in a pout. For a moment, I don't see my twenty-year-old sister; I see the little girl she used to be. Her brown hair falls around her face in large, beachy waves, and green eyes that are identical to my own stare back at me, bright and pleading, and I almost give in. *Almost.*

But I know tonight I've got club business, and I'm finishing some tattoo work on a member's sleeve. I can't bring my sister along for that because I wouldn't be able to watch her like the personal bodyguard she needs when she's there. As much as it pains me to leave her behind, I've got to think about myself from time to time.

"Sorry, brat, not tonight."

"Ugh. Fine. Whatever. I'll just have to find something to do to occupy myself," she says in a tone that is more of a threat than a statement. I roll my neck, trying to ease some of the tension she's putting there.

"Stay out of trouble, k? Tomorrow we can do whatever you want," I try as a way of a bribe, hoping like hell it's enough to keep her from doing anything other than staying put tonight.

"Wait, you mean it? I can plan the entire day?" she squeals in excitement, and I can't help but laugh at her. When Lena smiles, it fills her entire face, her eyes crinkling, lips tugging upward, all toothy and genuine. It's the same smile that gets her in and out of trouble. She didn't get her nickname without a reason.

"I'm good with that. We can even go to the coast if you want to." The first thing Lena and I did when I got my license at sixteen was take the top off my old, rusted-up jeep and drive to the coast. I spent a few years before she could drive toting her and her friends around, but I didn't mind. Anything to make her happy. I know how lucky we are to be best friends on top of siblings, and I want to always keep it that way.

"Yes! Okay, okay. I'm excited to have you all to myself! No club business?"

"No club business," I promise.

My sister's arms bound around my waist in a huge hug, her head resting against my chest. I wrap my arms around her in return, dropping my cheek to the top of her head.

"Be good, brat. I'll see you tomorrow."

"K. You be safe!"

"Always."

I slide my arms into my cut at the front door, *Hell's Heathens* stitched on the back, before walking out of my parents' house and heading to my bike. It's nothing fancy, but it's mine and I love it. I throw my leg over my motorcycle, settling into the leather seat, my fingers flexing over the grip of the handlebars. The engine purrs to life under me as I start it up, loving the vibrations and the weight of it in my hands. The first time I was on a bike, it became part of me, gave me a freedom I hadn't yet learned existed at eighteen. Now, I can't imagine my life without it. It's therapeutic on my bad days, energizing on my good, and all I need in life can be found on the back of it.

Before heading out, I take one last glance up at my spitfire sister standing in her bedroom window, flipping me off like the little shit she is. I chuckle under my breath as I pull out of the driveway, ready to start my night with my brothers at the clubhouse.

My sister and I have always been close. We were inseparable as children, and even though I've long since moved out of our parents' house, I still hang out with her multiple times a week. I've managed to keep the motorcycle club separate from my parents over the last four years to preserve our relationship, but Lena was harder since she's stuck to me like glue.

Unbeknownst to my parents, Lena's been to the clubhouse a

few times for some BBQs and when I was patched in, but I try to keep her from it, especially since the members are all a bunch of horny bastards and throw parties that are filled with debauchery everywhere you look.

Even if they know Lena is off-limits and they respect that fact, she thrives under their attention, and I don't like it one bit. She may be twenty, but she's still my little sister, and I'm not down for letting her have free rein of the clubhouse. It's too much work to bring her with me. There's no unwinding, it's all big brother mode, and the need to keep her safe is front and center—even from my club brothers, whom I trust with my life.

The night air is cool on my skin as I ride through our small town of Amberwood, Washington. I love riding alone, always have, and the road conditions in this small part of our state provide me with exactly what I need. I coast through town, but as soon as the road opens up and it's just me, the purr of my bike and the late summer air, I gun it. I've always enjoyed the solitude of the open road, and this evening is no different.

I lean into every curve, feeling free and untouchable. My dad is a big shot lawyer and had hopes and dreams that I would do something just as prestigious as him, and even though his disappointment is strong, his love for me is fierce. At least he isn't a prosecution attorney because that would make for some tense family dinners. While all the businesses the club is involved in are legit, some of the shit we get pulled into is more seedy and questionable. Especially lately.

The dim lights up ahead signal my approach to the Hell's Heathens' compound. The perimeter is surrounded by a fence with a dozen or so prospects doing twenty-four-hour checks with four guards at the main gate—our only entry point at the moment. We've had an ongoing turf war with another club that has been flexing its strength lately, and our new president has put us all on guard and ready to be prepared for an attack.

The Iron Wolves deal in the flesh and drug trade, and they're looking to take over our territory and push us out of business.

We're not going to let it happen. Their club is run by a monster named Damon—road name: Grim—and he runs it by instilling fear. He picks up the lowest of the low of society, preying on addicts and convicts to fill his ranks. His club is full of sick fucks, and it's clubs like theirs that give the rest of us a bad rap. As one-percenters, they don't live by the same rules as us. They're outlaws.

Hell's Heathens may not look like it from the outside, but we're a family. We live and die together. We have core values that each of us believes in, and when we patch in, it's for life—because we choose it. Not because someone is forcing our hand, not out of desperation or coercion. It's a deep, unwavering loyalty to the club, its values, and each other.

After passing through the gates, my bike rolls to a stop, the music blaring from inside, and a steady thump of bass that consumes your heartbeat and throbs between your ears reaches me as I cut my engine.

It's a typical Friday—the boys looking for a reason to celebrate, and the patch bunnies looking to spend their night in someone's bed with hopes of becoming an old lady.

The doors are pushed open, and people spill out onto the porch, drinks in hand and having a good time. The open room is filled with leather cuts and half-naked women. Brothers play pool and darts, letting loose and having a good time, while others are already getting their dicks wet with patch bunnies out in the open.

I head to the bar to show my face before I need to set up in the back. Tonight, I'm tattooing instead of partying, which is much more my style anyway. Any activity that I can do that empties my head and frees my soul, I'd prefer. Despite my large size, I've never been the loudest in the room, preferring to keep to the back in the quiet. That's not to say that I don't know how to have a good time, given the right circumstances.

"Hey, Rogue. What can I get ya?"

"Hey," I say in greeting to one of our prospects working the bar tonight. "Jack and Coke. Tattooing tonight and gotta keep my head straight. You want anything done? Know you've been itching to add some more."

"Nah, Prez has got me working the bar all night, then I'm on cleanup duty."

I wince on his behalf. Cleanup duty sucks after a rager. "Damn, man. I feel for you. I hear the vote is soon, though, so keep doin' what you're doin'. You'll be patched soon enough, and all the shit duty will be in the past and for some new prospect to deal with."

"You think?"

I give him a nonchalant shrug, but my face is all smiles as I sip on the cool liquid he set in front of me. He's a good guy, and I have a feeling the vote will go in his favor. The noise is thunderous all around me, and I know I need to head to the back to get set up before I get pulled into it.

I stand up and adjust my cut before walking through the main part of the house, trying to avoid any patch bunnies who will be giving it their best shot to convince me to claim them as mine for the night. Most of them are fun, sexy things that satisfy a completely primal urge, but tonight I'm working and need to focus; the last thing I need is the distraction of pussy.

Just as I'm about to step into the hallway off the main area, my path is blocked by a blonde bombshell in a red dress and heels.

"Hey, Rogue," Callie purrs as she drags her manicured nails down my chest. Nails I know all too well, having felt them rake down my back in the past. Maybe my focus can wait. I bend my knees so I can wrap my arm around her back, my free hand grabbing her jaw as I move us to the closest wall. She hitches her leg around my hip as I grip her ass hard with my palm, squeezing just enough around her throat with my other to get her attention.

I've hooked up with Callie on more than a few occasions, and I know she's hoping I'll make her my old lady someday, but it's not going to happen. She's hooked up with me enough to know that I have two rules: no kissing on the mouth, and I won't be making you my old lady. After a few failed attempts, she no longer tries. Which makes things easier on me.

A hard hand slaps the back of my shoulder, pulling Callie's mouth from my neck, where she's sucking on me like a fuckin' vampire.

"Rogue. I'm ready, let's get going."

I drop Callie's leg to the ground, her face pinching into a pout as she whines.

"Sorry, babe, duty calls. Maybe next time," I say with a wink, taking a step back and putting space between us.

"Don't worry, sweet thing, I'll keep you warm," Noose chuckles as he wraps an arm around Callie's shoulder. She perks right up, her glassy eyes shining bright and looking at him like he hung the moon.

When I was brought into Hell's Heathens, I learned real quick that sharing the patch bunnies was common. All of them are here of their own free will and can come and go as they please. Most of them sleep with patch members, and none of us have ever given it much thought. We're all clean and test regularly, and there's no jealousy. It's not a bad setup when you don't have the time or energy to date.

But that's a huge reason why—those of us who care—won't make one of them our old lady. It's the same reason I don't kiss any of them on the mouth. I reserve that right for the person I'm in a relationship with, whenever that time comes. There's something more intimate about kissing than fucking. I'll fuck someone one of my brother's has been inside before me, but I'm not going to kiss her or make her mine permanently.

Sin and I head to the backroom where Ink and I have set up a makeshift studio for the club. While he works the majority of his time at Heathen Ink, one of the club's legitimate businesses, I tattoo here. I'd love to own my own shop one day and am saving every extra penny to make that dream happen.

"You ready to get this sleeve finished?" I ask him. We've been working on a long-term project of fine line work that covers every inch of his arm, fingers to pec, and the next several hours should finish him up. The guy is about my size—six-four and 260 pounds—and is one of the toughest assholes here, but he hates needles. We should have had this work done in two eight-to-ten-hour sessions, but here we are, session six.

Sin shrugs, looking slightly green as he takes off his cut and hangs it on one of the hooks on the wall.

"Let's get this shit over with."

I laugh at him. "Why even do it if you hate it so much?"

"Love the ink, you know what it means to me. Just hate the process. Any chance Stitch got his hands on some Propofol?"

"Believe it or not, he couldn't. You're gonna have to stay awake for this." I continue to shake my head and laugh at him. I move through my routine, opening new tools and setting up my ink, getting the green soap ready, and opening a new roll of towels. The room is painted deep black with my tattoo table in the center, and overhead lights pour directly over us, giving me the lighting I need.

I lay out all my supplies on the black rolling table and grab my pens and markers to get started.

"Ready?" I ask him after everything's been drawn on and prepared for me to make permanent.

"Get it over with, Rogue."

I swipe some Vaseline over the area and get started, focusing on my task and losing myself to the steady vibrations that hum through my hand, and the resistance as I press the needle into his skin. I fall into a hypersensitive trance as I work my way through the project. I'm attuned to his every movement and the quiet grinding of his molars as I work over the sensitive area on the inside of his wrist.

I lose track of time, progressing further and further, checking in with Sin periodically as he scrolls his phone and fights for his life.

Just as I'm about to wipe Sin down, the door to the room slams open, the force bouncing it off the wall. Sin and I both jerk up, wondering what the hell is going on. Chaos stands in the doorway, his face void of the stony features he typically wears, and I'm immediately on guard.

"Reid," he gasps in a hurry. My body is on high alert at his use of my legal name. It's rare and reserved for situations that call for it. "It's Lena. I'm so fucking sorry, I didn't know."

My blood turns to ice in my veins as I quickly stand, dropping my machine to the table, a feeling deep in the pit of my stomach that almost brings me down to my knees. A whoosh of lightheadedness passes through me. His tone is all wrong. His typical, stoic calmness is missing, and putting me on edge. The anger and fear in his voice are palpable.

"What do you mean it's Lena? Where is she?"

"Reid . . ." he says my name like he's delivering a death announcement, but that's impossible. My heart stops as the breath is stolen from my lungs, and Sin grips my bicep.

"No. No, you're wrong. She's at home. Camden, tell me you're fucking wrong."

"She was with Lucas. They've been sneaking around. I didn't know."

Was.

My thoughts race with explanations. Lena and I don't hide things from each other, and she's been seeing Lucas? For how long? I knew I should never have brought her here to begin with. What the fuck was I thinking? She's twenty, for fuck's sake; she doesn't need to be around a motorcycle club with a bunch of testosterone-fueled men, no matter how well-behaved they are or how deep their loyalty runs.

"Where's your brother then? Where the fuck are they?"

My president's face falls further, and I know it's worse than I could have imagined.

"The Iron Wolves have them. We need to go. Now."

Fear like I've never felt before clutches me. There's no love lost between Hell's Heathens and the Iron Wolves, and hurting one of our females is a line none of us will allow to be crossed. The fact that they just did means war.

"I want wheels on the pavement in less than ten minutes!" Chaos yells into the open room, sobering everyone quickly. Everything else happens in a blur. My gun is strapped in its holster behind my back, and we're all on our bikes, a massive show of force as we head to the last place the Iron Wolves have been known to hide out.

We don't have the element of surprise; we don't have a plan or coordinated attack. Just going in guns blazing on a hope and a prayer that we can get Lena and Lucas out of their clutches. We ride in formation, only the loud rumble of our bikes to be heard. Anxiety and fear roll through me in equal measure, my hands shaking as I grip my handlebars. My brain wars with itself, unable to comprehend that my sister could be anywhere but home right now.

She has to be okay.

She's okay.

What feels like hours later, but in reality was under thirty minutes, we roll up to a shitty neighborhood on the outskirts of a town I've never been to. At the end of a long cul-de-sac sits a rundown, decrepit house with fire erupting from the first-floor windows. I skid my bike to a hard stop at the front of the house as Camden is jumping off his and racing inside with other members hot on his tail. I pull my gun and move to rush in when Malice and Wrath grab my shoulders, hauling me backward.

"Let me fucking go! I need to get to her!" I do my best to fight them off, but they hold strong.

"Nope, not happening, brother. Prez' order. We're to keep you back. We don't know what awaits inside, and it looks like their crew is long gone."

I know he's not wrong; the lack of bikes out front was the biggest clue. Whatever happened inside, they've left it and tried to torch the evidence. But that doesn't mean Lena is in there. She could have been taken by them as a hostage, or something worse.

Minutes go by but it feels like fucking hours as I stand by my bike and fucking wait. Wrath and Malice each hold me back by an arm, like they don't trust that I won't book it inside the moment they release me. They aren't wrong.

I should have been with her. I should have fucking taken her with me. She would have been safer if I had just given in and kept her by my side. She fucking begged me to bring her with me tonight. I put my own selfish wants above hers, and now I'll live with that. Regret pulls me under, suffocating and debilitating me.

She has to be okay.

She's okay.

I repeat the words out loud, unintentionally. A mantra, a prayer.

The front door is kicked wide open as fire rages behind Camden. He walks out of the house with my sister's limp body cradled in his arms. Her head hangs back at an angle that's all wrong, arm hanging lifeless toward the ground, the clothes left on her body ripped and dirtied, and I know the truth before they get any closer.

All the life drains out of my body. I crumble to my knees, an animalistic wail echoing through the night as my soul is torn in two and my heart shatters into a million pieces. Like the devil himself plunged his cold, dead hand into my chest and obliterated everything good that was once there, I'm left empty and devoid of any light, any good.

She can't be gone. My sweet Lena. So full of life. Her sweet, infectious smile. The laugh that could turn anyone's mood around. She had her entire life ahead of her. My vision is clouded, darkness creeping in at the edges as he walks toward me. Everything is silent around me, moving like a slow-motion picture, while I spiral out of control. I heave in lungfuls of air, my knuckles rubbing the spot where my heart used to beat.

Camden's leather boots stop in front of me, and he drops to one knee as he places her in my arms. I sink further into the hard ground as I hold my sister close. My eyes trace over her lifeless body, taking in the bruises marring her once-flawless skin, the blood that tracks down her thighs, the cuts, her busted lip. I push the wet strands of hair out of her face, looking into familiar green eyes that life no longer dances behind.

I run my hand over her eyelids to close them. Screams rip from my body as I rock her in my arms. Begging, praying to whoever will listen to take me instead. For whatever being that exists above to bring her back to this plane. To let her live. She deserves to live.

The fear she must have felt as they raped and beat her before stealing her precious life from her slams into me. Sobs wrack from my body. I was too fucking late. Too preoccupied with my own shit to realize she had gone out. I didn't even know she was with Camden's brother; I would have stopped it.

I could have prevented this.

Why didn't I prevent this?

How did I not protect the one person on Earth I would gladly die for?

"Wh-where's Lucas?" I don't recognize my own voice as the words struggle to come out between labored breaths.

Camden's face pales further as he finally stands, but he holds stoic in his position as our leader, even though it's his brother I'm asking about.

"He can't be recovered. They burned him alive."

"FUCK!" I scream until my voice runs hoarse.

Tears continue to pour down my face, dripping onto Lena's, the wet droplets leaving track marks over the dirty flesh of her body.

"We need to move, Rogue. We gotta get out of here before the police arrive."

Camden moves to reach for Lena, and I jerk out of his way with a snarl, pulling her closer to me, an inhuman growl leaving my chest. He puts his hands up defensively, and I know he means no harm, but no one will take her from me. No one. Camden squats down to my level again, and I know what he's gonna offer before he says it.

"We've got two options, and you need to make a decision quick or I'll make it for you. One, we take her with us, we give her a proper burial on our grounds or somewhere pretty, but she's just gonna be a missing person from here on out. No one will know what happened to her but us. Two, we leave her here for the cops to find, and your parents will get closure and eventually find peace. But they'll know every terrifying, brutal detail of what happened to her tonight."

I look down at my sweet little sister, and I know I would rather die than leave her in the hell that took her life from us. I also can't bear my mom's pain of knowing the truth about her only daughter's fate. I would rather her live with hope in her heart that someday Lena would be found. It wouldn't bring them closure; it would kill both of my parents just like it killed me.

Forcing my legs to work is a strength I pull from some unknown place as I cradle her close. Chaos helps me get situated on my bike with her wrapped tight in my arms. It takes all my strength and balance, but I follow the rest of our crew out of this shithole and back to our clubhouse on autopilot, holding my life-less sister—my best fucking friend—in my arms. I'll never recover from this.

I feel like I'm drowning, the weight of Lena's death holding me under the water like an anchor, knowing I'll never be able to come up for air again, but not putting me out of my misery and ending it. I walk into church and am thankful to find that it's only me and Chaos right now.

I drop my cut onto the table in front of him, and the serious-ness and finality of what that represents sucks the air from the room.

"I want out."

Chaos stands, resting his hands on the table as he peers down at my cut.

"You'll never be out, Rogue. You know what you joined. You're a Hell's Heathen. Only way out is through Hell's gates, and you're not dying today."

"Camden . . ."

"No!" he snaps loudly, slamming his fist down onto the table. "In here, I'm your president. You aren't the only one who lost a sibling that day. I feel the weight of that shit every single moment. Lucas was . . . fuck!" His spine straightens as he pushes his hair out of his face.

I know this eats up Camden every day, but he and I both know it's different. We all know it could have been any one of us. Lucas had earned his cut, and he knew the risks just as each of us does. But Lena? Lena was innocent. Lena was pure light and everything good in the world.

"You'll never be *out,* Rogue. Ever."

"Chaos . . ." I plead.

"When I gave you your road name, I didn't think it would mean what it's about to. You're not out, but I'm letting you go. Show up for church when I need you, be there when we call, but you can leave," he says, pushing my cut back into my arms.

My eyes widen in shock; I was prepared to put up a harder fight. I nod my head in agreement, the emotion choking me up and preventing words from forming. I knew it was a long shot that I'd be released, and I was prepared to beg. I can't live here anymore, not when it serves as a constant reminder of how I lost everything. The reason all the light was sucked from my life, shrouding me in complete darkness.

The only girl who would ever mean anything to me is gone, and it's all my fault. If I hadn't been involved with Hell's Heathens, Lena would never have been exposed to this world. If I had just taken her with me that night, she wouldn't have been out alone with Lucas. I turn to walk out of the room, reaching for the heavy wood doors as Chaos' voice rings out.

"Oh, and Rogue? Don't stray too far from your family. We're here for you."

CHAPTER 1

Kinsey

"HOLY SHIT, I'M ACTUALLY FREE!" I YELL WITH MY ARMS spread wide as I spin and collapse on top of my mattress. The mattress that is officially moved into my brand-new studio apartment.

"Like hell you are, Kins. One of us will be checking on you constantly."

"Oh, to hell with that, Sawyer Hayes! This is my place! You will not have a key, and trust me, you don't want to just pop on by."

My oldest brother looks down from where he's towering over me at the edge of the bed, pointing his stupid finger at me like I'm a child. His face is pinched in irritation and disgust, which makes me roll my eyes and laugh at his absurdity. He's the sweetest, but man, if he doesn't have a protective side.

"No men, Kins!" he snaps, as if he has any right to tell me what to do.

"Did she seriously just allude to having men over? The fuck, Kins?"

That would be my second-oldest brother, Dallas, chiming in with more overprotective, overbearing, meatheaded opinions. Now we just need the other two, and it'll be a party.

Three.

Two.

One.

"Did I seriously just hear that correctly? Kinsey!"

"The hell? There will be absolutely no men in this apartment! We'll slaughter anyone who tries."

Bingo. Enter the other two Neanderthals, Liam and Carter. Being the youngest with four older brothers has its perks, but it also comes with walls so high they make Mount Rainier look like an ant hill. I sit up on my bed, slamming my hands down next to me, exasperated that we're going to have this talk again. But, like the dutiful sister that I am, I have to constantly school these dumb-dumbs on boundaries, respect, and double standards.

"Listen to me you thick-skulled, ass clowns, I can screw whoever I want, whenever I want, and there's nothing you can do to stop me anymore."

"Did she just call us ass clowns?" Dallas says in feigned indignation, slapping a hand to his chest and stumbling backward like a big oof.

"Kinsey!" Sawyer snaps, making me roll my eyes again. At this rate, I may just let them roll in a constant loop. I may be five foot two compared to each of their six-plus feet, but I'm not afraid of these huge dinks. I've been learning how to handle them since the day I was born.

"Oh, poor Sawyer," I mock, further goading him. "Man enough to scold his sister and sex shame her, but can't handle talking about her actually having it."

"That's . . ." He runs his palm over his stubbled jaw, clearly uncomfortable. "I'm not slut shaming you, Kins. I just don't like the idea of men near you. They're selfish assholes and I don't want you to get hurt."

My face falls slightly, knowing his words are true. My brothers are amazing men, and I consider myself extremely lucky to have them in my corner. They just love with their entire beings, and sometimes . . . okay, most of the time . . . that makes them exceptionally overbearing and protective. Their partners are all completely comfortable with that behavior, but as their little sister? It blows.

"Sawyer," I start, keeping my voice calm but steady. "It would do me good to feel some hurt. At least then I'd be feeling something. Can we not do this again? You four are more protective than Dad is, and that's saying something. I'm a responsible twenty-two-year-old. I've got a good head on my shoulders, I have a career that I love, and now I'm living on my own. Like an adult. I'm going to have experiences, and you four are not going to stand in my way any longer. Or I meant what I said a few weeks ago; I'll leave Aspen Ridge and start my life somewhere without this pressure on me. Now give me back my freedom that wasn't yours to take away to begin with."

The air is thick with tension, both of us caught in this game of tug-of-war where our hearts are on the line. I love him, love all of them, but I have to win this one.

"She's not wrong, shithead," my brother, Carter, says. He's been the only one to have my back lately, and that might have to do with the fact that he's had some eye-opening experiences recently that have made him realize there's a lot out there to learn about ourselves when we lean into possibilities.

"Oh, yeah? How's that bruise healing on your eye? You still look like shit, by the way. Want me to make the other one match?" Sawyer threatens him. Two weeks ago, when I told my brothers I was moving out of our parents' house and into an apartment above Sawyer's best friend's tattoo studio downtown, Carter defended me and took one of Sawyer's haymakers to the face. He's lucky nothing was broken.

My brothers have been boxing together since I was little, forcing me to take self-defense lessons at a minimum, since I never showed any interest in getting in the ring with them until recently.

But lately, I've been feeling the pull. They pummel each other's brains out for stress relief, and I'm feeling the urge to knock their teeth down their throats. Not very kindergarten teacher of me, but hey, I'm the product of them all, and it might do us some good to get in there and duke it out. What are all those years of practice doing for me if I can't use it to whoop their asses?

I'm the youngest of five and the only girl. Comes with its perks, but mostly it just comes with a pack of overbearing meathead brothers who love me so suffocatingly much they want to keep me as sheltered as possible.

Did I mention I'm a virgin? Twenty-two and never met a guy strong enough to want to cross them. I've never been worth the effort to any man I've pursued. Once they find out I have four older brothers, they run away screaming. And while that's probably for the best, I'm not asking for a marriage proposal, I'm asking for a hookup. For fun. For experiences. For freedom.

It seems like everything works against me—four older brothers and a small-ass town that makes it nearly impossible to keep anything from them. As much as it pains me to put distance between us, if they don't start backing off, I'm going to have to move to plan B—leaving Aspen Ridge and starting a life somewhere new. Someplace no one knows me, and the suffocating expectations and protection from my brothers don't exist.

I yearn for freedom, to meet new people, and forge connections that are real and raw. I want experiences and to soak up everything life has to offer. As much as I love Aspen Ridge and my family, I'm exhausted of being their "baby" sister. I'm desperate to find friends and a man who looks at me as Kinsey.

I had friends growing up, but once we hit middle school and boys suddenly became interesting, my friends all had heart eyes for my brothers. Our family name and well-known business make them town royalty, and combined with their looks? It's a recipe for heartbreak. While they never went for any of my friends, it still stung to have the girls I thought liked me for me, only want to use me to get closer to them.

"Don't you boys have work to do? Families to go home to?" I

ask, ready to shoo them out of my apartment so I can finish unpacking alone and finally soak up some independence and quiet. They all took the day off to move furniture that Carter's boyfriend, Finn, gave to me, into my new place.

It's a studio with a small kitchenette and a bathroom, so I couldn't fit much, but the queen-size bed from my room at my parents' house, coupled with the small loveseat and coffee table, is perfect for just me. It's not like I'm going to be entertaining here, as much as I like to threaten my brothers otherwise.

Liam looks down at his watch before removing his backwards hat and running his hands through his sweaty hair. It's the dead of summer in Washington, and my new apartment—like most places here—lacks air conditioning. I make a mental note to run out and purchase a fan or two.

"I need to go pick up Charlie from Hailey and Graham's. Hannah is slammed at Bean Haven. You good here, sis?"

"I'm good. Squeeze her for me." Charlie is technically Liam's stepdaughter, but he's been helping raise her since the day she was born. His wife, Hannah, has been in my life since I was a toddler, and I'm so happy they finally figured out they were supposed to be together. I've never seen him happier since making those two girls his.

It's been a crazy year for our family as each of my brothers has found their soulmates, and I love it for them more than anything. I hope I can find the same someday. Living this life alone would be exceptionally lonely. I'd love to experience what Sawyer has with Ivy, or Dallas with Blaire, Liam with Hannah, or Carter with Finn. Until a man comes along who is strong enough to stand up to them and realize I'm worth it, I'll continue to live vicariously through the romance novels I've gotten lost in since I was a teenager.

"We'll head out, too, let you unpack and do your thing."

"You mean video chat with Piper and have a bottle of wine by myself?" I quip, self-deprecation leaking into my tone, doing my best to make him feel a little guilty.

"Kins . . ." Sawyer says as if he's the one who is exasperated.

"Sawyer . . ."

"I love you. I'm sorry it's so suffocating, but you'll thank us someday."

"Yes, I'll be sure to thank you when I'm a spinster that has to move in with you and your family because I haven't found a love match of my own."

"Want me to find one for you?"

Dallas snaps his fingers loudly, pulling our attention to where he's leaning against the small counter in my kitchen. "That's a good idea, shithead. You don't have 'em often, but I'll give you this one. We can set her up on dates!"

"Nope. No! Not happening. I let you do that one time! It was a nightmare!"

"Only because you walked out!" Sawyer snaps back.

"Ugh! Are you insane? He was twenty minutes late, then spent the entire time talking about how he got drunk during spring break and got crabs!"

Dallas busts out laughing, and I hide my smile with my hand. "That's right! Crabby Calvin! Hopefully he got that cleared up."

"Okay, I admit, not our finest pick, but we can do better. I have faith, Kinsey-Kins."

"Don't call me that. And this isn't Bridgerton! You can't pick who I'm dating and going to marry. Get out of my apartment, you freaks!" I laugh.

"Whoa, whoa, whoa!" Sawyer says as I shove him toward the back door. "No one said anything about marriage."

"No dating at all then!" Dallas adds.

"Yeah? We'll see about that."

"Well, you idiots have really done it now," Carter says mockingly, only slight concern lacing his tone.

"Yep. Way to go, you two. Now I'm going to date even harder."

"What's that supposed to mean, Kinsey?" Sawyer asks. His eyebrows are pinched, and I know he's dead serious, even though

I'm trying like hell to laugh all of this ridiculousness off before I go absolutely insane.

"You heard me. I've just entered my dating era, so I hope you're ready."

"Kins—"

"Nope!" I cut him off. "Don't make me call Ivy, because I will. Give me space or I'll leave and go somewhere you don't have power over me anymore."

Sawyer and Dallas—the twins—stand by the door looking so similar as their faces fall in unison, immediately making me feel guilty. I know they only act this way out of fear of something happening to me. It's especially over the top lately, and I try to understand where they're coming from. After all, they've both experienced trauma over the last year with the events that took place with Ivy and Blaire. My heart clenches at the thought of what each of them went through.

But I'm not them. This is Aspen Ridge, my home, and I'm not going to let fear hold me back. I just hope I can find my people, who want to fight for me and love me for me.

Later that night, after I've grabbed my favorite pizza from North Pass Market and Deli, I sit on my new-to-me little couch, and video call my best friend, Piper. We met at the University of Washington, were roommates for four years, and became inseparable. She even spent an entire summer break with me here in Aspen Ridge. After we graduated, Piper got accepted to medical school on the other side of the country. Living apart this last year has sucked, but we video chat constantly despite the time difference.

My best friend's glowing face appears as she connects the call just in time to watch me take my first bite of warm, delicious pizza.

"Hey, my girl! Ugh. Is that North Pass pizza?"

"Mhm," I mumble through a mouth full of food.

"Barbeque chicken?" she says with a desperate whine, knowing the answer already since it's my favorite.

I swallow the bite and smile brightly at her. "You know it is. Mouthwatering perfection."

"I hate your face."

"Rude," I say, stuffing another bite in my mouth with a moan.

"Ugh. I still haven't found a place here that comes close to as good as that damn pie. I'm jealous."

"As you should be. You could be here with me, eating pizza and binging trashy reality TV. Instead, you're in Maryland, becoming some hotshot pediatric surgeon."

"Well, that's the end goal at least. Thanks for the support."

"Oh, shut it, you know I'm your biggest fan."

"I know. I wouldn't have survived my first year here if it weren't for you telling me to keep going. Now, tell me about what it's like to spend your first night in your own freaking place?"

"Mhmm!" I mumble over a mouthful of food. I wipe my mouth with my napkin before talking. "All settled. Not like I had much to unpack, but I love it. It's obviously only been a few hours, but for the first time in my life, I have no parents. No big brothers. Silence. I'm going to love living here. Today is the first day of my new life!"

"You deserve it, boo-boo. Now, my real question: what's it like living above that sexy beast of a tattoo artist?"

"Reid?"

"Do we know any other sexy man-beast tattoo artists? Because if another one was hired, I may consider a transfer."

I laugh at her. Not to toss them all into the same box, but Piper is no different than the majority of the other women who live here or who've visited Aspen Ridge. One look at the quiet, brooding Reid Knight and they're tossing their panties at him. I'm not immune, I know he's gorgeous, but he's best friends with my oldest brother, Sawyer, and close to the other three. I'm not interested, unlike the rest of the population. He can be just as overbearing as they can, and that's the last thing I need in my life.

"I've only been here for a few hours, P. It's not like I've had time to find out if I can even hear him downstairs or not."

"Hmm. Whatever. I guess you're right. I thought you'd have more juicy details for me."

I pick up another slice, holding it up in front of the camera like a showcase model on *The Price is Right.*

"You're the worst."

"Yeah, yeah. But you're stuck with me, so bite me." A door slams in the background, and Piper rolls her eyes, signaling her roommate's arrival.

"You could be here," I whisper.

She flicks off the camera before giving me a cheeky smile. "I've gotta get some studying in before I crash. It's so freaking late already. Talk tomorrow?"

"Yep. Night! Love you, P."

"Love you more, KiKi."

After closing out the video chat, I pull up my playlist for some noise and crack open my latest book on my e-reader, letting myself get lost in the comforting silence of my apartment. I take a deep breath, and the smile that spreads across my face is huge and genuine. I've got this. Something tells me that everything is about to change and that I'm on my path to finally living, finding myself, and being free.

Bring it.

reid

Unknown: Time to pay up.

I HOLD MY PHONE LIKE A HAND GRENADE, STARING down at it like it's personally offended me. The text glares back, threatening to detonate. I knew the terms when I called in help a few months ago to eliminate a threat against an innocent woman I've come to care for.

I was prepared to pay my dues, but now that the time has come? Being a ranked member of Hell's Heathens is a privilege that I'm proud to have, but the turf wars have picked up again after nearly ten years of quiet, and my peaceful life away from the compound is rapidly changing. The club's gotten too comfortable, too lax, and the enemies that once lurked in the dark have started to crawl from their holes and push back.

I'm not eager to find out which club has been causing issues, but I know I'll find out soon enough, whether I want to or not.

I'm one of the best shots in the club, and while our president, Chaos, doesn't call me in unless he needs the backup, we both know that when something needs to be taken care of discreetly and quickly, I'm who's gonna get it done. This time feels different, though. A black hole settles in the pit of my stomach, a dark, ominous feeling of foreboding creeping in that I can't shake. Dread is a feeling I haven't known in a while, and it settles in deep, digging in its claws.

The gate opens for me, and I clock the side eyes from some of the newer members. I know they don't agree with the agreement I'm living under. We all know what we signed up for. Hell's Heathens is for life. They don't need to understand why I'm afforded to live a normal life outside of the compound, away from the businesses and day-to-day of the club. I show up every week for church, and I answer the call when needed. They can fuck off if they have an issue with something they'll never understand.

A fresh wave of pain grips my heart as I ride up the long dirt driveway, gravel and rocks kicking up from my tires. At least I'll be able to visit Lena while I'm here for an impromptu visit. The large barndominium that's been converted into a clubhouse towers in front of me. With its all-black exterior and large, double-bay doors, it functions as the main house for our meetings, parties, and bedrooms for ranked members.

I shut off my bike and roll my shoulders and neck to ease the tension settling there. After adjusting my cut, I walk up the steps to the large deck. The double-bay doors are open, industrial fans pointing inside to cool off the large, open room from the rare summer heat we're getting. My boots hit the cement floors, my eyes scanning the room, looking for Chaos or Sin. Two pool tables sit on the far side of the room where a few members are playing a game, patch bunnies draped over their arms, trying to steal their affection.

I find a prospect at the bar with a woman on his lap, her mouth sucking at the side of his neck. He doesn't register my entry, which is a fucking problem. My hand connects roughly with the back of his head before he whips in my direction.

"Oh! Hey, Rogue!"

"What the hell are you doing, Bran? If Prez sees you with her, you're gonna be in real shit."

It's at that moment the devil himself appears, walking through the two heavy wooden doors, shooting a look so fierce at Bran, it has the patch bunny on his lap wincing and scurrying off to the back of the house, murmuring an apology to Chaos as she goes.

"There's our boy! What? No smile for us, Rogue?" he chastises, his arms held wide, welcoming me in for a hug. I lean in, clapping his back twice with one hand as he reciprocates. Our president and I go way back, both of us too young and not ready for the shit life was gonna throw at us. We bonded over it. He was a brand-new president, and while he grew up in club life, stepping into the role and having everything go to shit the same month hardened him.

"I'm here, aren't I? Let's get this over with." I shrug.

"That's no way to greet me. I've missed you," he jests in a smooth, confident tone.

"It's barely been a week, Chaos," I deadpan.

"Feels like longer," he says as he throws an arm around my shoulder, slapping my back. "C'mon, I've gotta job for you."

I follow him through the large, ornate, double doors to our meeting room where church is held, the place all important conversations and decisions happen. Chaos takes his seat at the head of our prominent, custom table, and I take one off to his side.

"Just us?" I ask, arching a brow at him. Instead of answering the obvious as the doors shut behind us, he goes right into business mode.

"Wrath will be in your ear. Malice and a prospect will go with you. Malice already knows the details, but I wanted to talk to you privately."

"Well, that sounds ominous. Who's the hit, Chaos?"

His eyes say it all, and I take turns cracking my knuckles

against my palms while working to keep my breathing even. Chaos doesn't need to know I'm rattled, but I can't shake the doomsday feeling that has infected me like a virus.

"The Iron Wolves."

I shake my head, knowing his answer before he said it, but hearing the confirmation forces the anger I keep buried to the forefront. This explains the feeling in the pit of my stomach. The Iron Wolves are responsible for my sister's death. For taking the only good thing in my life away from me. For ending her precious life before it had barely begun. After her and Chaos' brother's murder, we hit them hard. Blew up their compound, decimated their trading routes, took over their strip club, and cleaned out their dismal bank accounts. We killed everyone we could find.

They never retaliated. Never hit us again. We thought we had wiped them from existence. Guess not.

"Thought they were all dead? It's been almost ten years."

"Nine years, eleven months, sixteen days."

Like I didn't already know that. Lena and Lucas' deaths haven't left either of us. At least we recovered Lena's body. Lucas couldn't be recovered, and his final resting spot is a shithole that was burned to the ground the night they were murdered. I'm surprised Chaos isn't going with me, but our sergeant at arms, Malice, and I work well together. Even if he is a little unstable.

"You gonna make me beg for the details?"

"The club was hit a few nights ago. Bouncers said four guys in cuts came in, a howling wolf on the back. They didn't think anything of it, 'cause why would they? No one's heard from the Iron Wolves in a long-ass time. Two of the bastards asked for a private dance, cut up the girls real good, raped 'em and left them for dead before walking out like nothing happened."

"Where the fuck were the bouncers outside the door?"

"Paid off."

"And where are they now?"

"Dead." Good. I would have ended them if he hadn't. No man should be allowed to continue to breathe if he has any part in harming an innocent woman. "Looks like they're gaining in numbers, slowly building back up what they once were. They were sending a message to us by hitting the club, and we need to send one back."

"Agreed. Do you know who their leader is?"

We killed their former leader, Damon, but when you cut off one head, two more will grow in its place. Chaos shakes his head.

"He's laying low, keeping his identity hidden."

"Alright. So we're just hitting these assholes who carved up the girls?"

"They're crashing at an abandoned house in Amberwood, staying close. They must be using it as an outpost because it's certainly no compound. Should just be a few of them."

Amberwood is Heathen territory. My eyes must reveal my shock that they have the balls to stay local because Chaos nods his head in agreement.

"Alright, we rollin' out tonight?"

"Yep. You got this?"

I know what he's asking, and it isn't whether or not I can get the job done, because he knows I can. I always do. He's asking because of who they're affiliated with. That the Iron Wolves have come back to haunt us. Too bad I'm not the same person I was when I was twenty-two.

"Yeah, I got it."

With the information I need gathered, I stand and head for the door, pulling it open and ready to go find Malice and Wrath to get our plan together. Chaos' voice stops me from leaving.

"Rogue?"

I look over my shoulder at him, waiting.

"Make sure you leave a message that this is Heathen territory, and we won't stand for this."

With a nod, I'm out the door, ready to level these assholes for daring to come out of hiding to cross us.

. . .

A few hours later, I'm crammed into the back of an empty van with a prospect at the wheel and Malice and Wrath next to me.

"Feeds on loop. You're good to go. Get in and get out, I wanna get home."

"You want pussy and a drink," Malice corrects, always trying to push buttons that will get him a reaction.

"So shoot me." Wrath shrugs, not playing into his games.

Malice's eyes get big, glinting with excitement as he wiggles his thick eyebrows at him. "Don't tempt me with a good time, buddy." Malice has always been a little trigger-happy. He's the most unhinged of all of us. He's just over six feet tall but well under two hundred pounds, with a lean frame, wild brown hair—that I'm almost certain he cuts himself—is covered in random-ass tattoos, and has at least two personalities. He's either batshit fuckin' crazy or completely sane and coherent.

"Alright, you dumb fuckers, I actually do want to get this over with, so if you're done flirting . . ."

"Rogue just wants to get back to going rogue. We should draw this one out, Wrath, so he has to stick around a little longer. Maybe he won't be so grumpy."

"I'm not grumpy."

"Lonely then. Maybe you should get a pet," Malice adds.

"Got any leashes I can borrow then?" I quip, knowing that his bedroom at the clubhouse is nicknamed the dungeon for a reason.

Malice's face goes from amused to heated, a lethal glint dancing around his irises, and I brace myself in case he lunges for me. I've never been on his bad side, but a few in our club have—with the scars to prove it.

"You want me to put you on a leash, Roguey, all you have to do is ask," he snarls in a psychotic, amused way that is completely unhinged and wholly him.

I roll my eyes, a genuine smile lifting my lips. It's hard not to miss my brothers.

"I'm heading in," I say, over being stuck in the back of this hot-ass truck with two other huge men in the middle of summer with no AC. I open the back of the truck, stepping out of it as the cool, summer night air hits my damp skin.

Pulling my gun from its holster at my side and holding it between my hands, I move forward in the direction of the house. Malice follows me, flanking me on my left, while Wrath stays back to watch our backs from his drone footage.

The lights flicker from the streetlamps, the moon high in the sky as we skirt the tree line at the side of their shit hovel. The one-story house they're camped out in is falling apart. The roof is partially caved in, windows missing, graffiti and stains from age and fuck knows what else covering every inch of space.

My eyes connect with Malice as we stand on opposite ends of a window. I glance inside, finding three assholes sitting in what looks to be a living room. They're too relaxed for a bunch of criminals who just beat and raped a few women, but then again, that's probably a normal fucking day for them. What sends me over the edge and fills me with a deep sense of outrage is seeing the club patch—an insignia that will forever be burned into my mind—a wolf howling up at the moon.

I had almost convinced myself on the way here that Chaos was wrong. That there was no possible way the Iron Wolves could be regrouping, and strong enough to coordinate a hit on us to let us know they've woken from their slumber. Rage and vengeance take over all other coherent thoughts.

I hold up three fingers for Malice so he knows. There's no way for us to know exactly how many to expect when we go in, so we have to be on guard. We move in sync, keeping to the edge of the house, walking up the rotting deck, and flanking the front door. It's the only part of the house that seems to have held up. With full clips and an intense desire to get in there and kill these assholes, I hold up three fingers between us, counting down silently.

Three.

Two.

One.

I lift my leg and kick the center of the door with all my strength, the wood splintering upon impact and shattering as it busts open with a loud bang and falls off its hinges. Malice is the first one in, with his gun held out in front of him. I'm right behind him, stepping into the decaying house.

The stench immediately assaults my face, my eyes burning from the choking scent of ammonia—fucking urine. It's soaked into the warped floors, yellow stains mixing with the green and blacks of mold climbing up the peeling wallpaper. I hold back the wave of bile wanting to purge itself from my body, doing whatever I can to not breathe in this putrid shit.

"What up motherfuckers? Heard you like to beat on pretty little dancers?" Malice hisses.

The three men are wearing their cuts, standing up and looking at the two of us like they're genuinely shocked to see us here, but not reacting as they should be.

"Surprised, boys?" I ask. "You made a mistake hitting Hell's Heathens. You realize you're still in our territory?"

The three of them are too fucking high to do much but sway on their feet, looking around like they don't have any clue who we are, and what we're asking. That won't do at all.

Malice has the same idea as he shoots first, a bullet landing true, right through one of their kneecaps. I wince as he howls like the little pup he is, grabbing his knee and collapsing to the ground.

"Who's your leader?" I ask, taking a step closer to them, immediately regretting my decision when a wave of unwashed filth from their bodies crashes into me like toxic sludge.

"We don't know."

I shake my head in disappointment. "Impossible. Try again. Who's your leader?"

"We don—" He doesn't get to finish his sentence as I take the shot this time, putting a bullet right between his eyes. His body crumbles to the ground in a heap of useless bones and muscles, blood spreading across the floor from the back of his head.

"Let's try again, huh? Who the fuck is your leader?" I try one last time before I let Malice work the remaining two over. The last man standing looks down at his brother before looking back at us.

"We don't know his name. Only ranked members do. We're just grunts. Told to do a job, and we do it."

Malice stands next to me, moving from foot to foot, cracking his neck from side to side, and I know this wild fucker is barely hanging on by a thread. He's practically rabid, ready to get into the fight.

I hear the footsteps a second before the release of a gun, and the bullet flies between us, causing Malice to jerk. I know he's been hit, but I'm fairly certain it was his arm, and I've seen him take worse, so I push my worry back to deal with it after we take care of this shit.

Malice turns eerily slow in the direction of our shooter, his eyes freakishly wide, a scary-ass grin filling his face.

"Fuck," I curse under my breath. I fire two shots in quick succession, one in the head of the asshole wailing on the floor for his mom, the other in the knee of the dickhead still standing. He drops to the ground with a loud groan, flinging every curse word in my direction.

"That wasn't very nice, now was it?" I hear Malice say before a loud, high-pitched scream ricochets off the walls. Not turning my back on the one in front of me, I let Malice handle our shooter, knowing there won't be much of him left when he's done.

I take several steps in the direction of the one I just shot, planting my foot to his chest and pushing him onto his back. He holds his knee up to his chest, tears falling from his hollowed-out eyes.

His pant leg is drenched in blood, but I know it wasn't a kill shot. I read the name off his cut and chuckle. I watch as his eyes dart all over me, either trying to remember my features or reading my road name on my cut, it doesn't matter either way.

"Well, Scab, it's your lucky fuckin' day. You're gonna live and you're gonna take a message back to your compound." Screeches and maniacal laughter mix in the other room, and I cock my head down at the lowlife piece of shit at my feet. "Or do you want my friend here to play with you next?"

"Nnnn-no," he sputters, spit dribbling from his cracked lips.

"Let your president know that Hell's Heathens isn't going to tolerate you in our territory or bringing harm to our people. We'll cut down every single one of you until there's nothing fucking left." I fire one more shot into his shoulder for good measure before walking backward to the front door. Malice returns from the other room, the screaming silenced, leaving only the heavy panting of my brother walking toward me.

"Jesus Christ, the fuck did you do to him?" I ask as I take in his bloodied body. Dark red blood drips down his naked torso from under his cut, his arms covered, a handprint on his cheek like he was slapped with red paint.

"I wanted to make a coat, but it wouldn't fit."

My eyes bug out of my skull. "Did you fuckin' skin 'em?" I ask incredulously. Malice shrugs, and I take one last look at our new messenger. "You want that to be you, asshole?"

"No!" he pleads.

"Then you make sure your prez gets the message. Get out of our territory and don't fuckin' come back."

Malice and I retreat from the building, the humid summer air a welcome reprieve as I heave in lungfuls of fresh air. "Fuck, man, how were they just chillin' in there? I could barely stand there without dry heaving."

Malice gives me a look that conveys he didn't notice, and I shake my head as we sneak back to the waiting van. Wrath opens the back door and takes one look at Malice before laughing, knowing he isn't covered in his own blood. The gunshot wound to his arm luckily looks like it's just a graze.

"What the fuck happened?"

"Apparently he wanted to make a coat," I deadpan.

"A coat? Like a human one?" he asks, slightly revolted.

"Unfortunately."

Wrath gives me a look that says, 'what the fuck' and I just shake my head to let it go. I grab a towel and some bandages to take care of the flesh wound, blood getting all over me in the process.

"You're a crazy sonofabitch, you know that right?" Wrath challenges.

Malice throws his head back in a maniacal laugh that startles both of us.

"What the hell's wrong with you, dude?"

"You two idiots think I would actually skin someone?"

Wrath and I share a look that conveys our feelings. You never know with him. Wrath beats me to the punch, though. "You do know what your road name means, yeah? And how you got it?"

"Yeah, but I wouldn't skin anyone." Malice stops and his eyes do a weird thing where he's looking up and to the side, his lips pursed like he's trying really hard to think and failing miserably at it. "Yeah, no. I couldn't. I stabbed him in the neck and hit an artery. Or two. Shit erupts like a geyser." He motions an explosion with both of his hands as he talks animatedly. "There's no stopping it once it starts. Did you know hearts are slippery?"

"Oh, for fuck's sake. Get in the damn van!" Wrath says in exasperation.

Malice may pull some absolutely crazy shit, but he's one of us and he loves fucking hard. He'd only ever hurt someone who came after one of his brothers, and only if provoked. The club is his family, just as it is to each of us.

We pack up, Wrath grumbling about Malice not getting blood on his shoes, and head back to the compound. It's late and I should probably crash in my room in the clubhouse, but I want to get home and back to my normal. I have to balance the two lives I live carefully, because if I don't, they could easily cross, and I won't make the same mistakes I made before. I can't.

· · ·

The hot spray of the shower beats down on my body as I relax further, letting the water wash away the blood on my hands, both figuratively and metaphorically. I watch as it swirls down the drain and replay Wrath's words. He's not wrong. I'm lonely. Even if I'm surrounded by my brothers at the club, and my brothers here in Aspen Ridge. Even if I have my studio and I'm doing a job that I'm passionate about. Nights like this are lonely. When the exhaustion settles in bone deep, when all the hope evaporates. I wonder what it would be like if my life were different. If I had a good woman to come home to who loves me.

As the blood continues to swirl at the bottom of the tile, I know that will never happen. How would she be okay with this? Plus, my heart died a decade ago and hasn't beat since. I'd have nothing to give her in return but a warm bed and loyalty. Surely that can't be enough?

After my shower, I lay down on my bed, exhausted in every way, and without any light, I wait for the darkness to finally consume me.

kinsey

I RELAX IN THE STUDIO APARTMENT THAT I WANTED SO badly and wonder for a split second why I wanted to leave my parents' house in the first place. It's been a full week on my own, and I know this is good for me, that it's exactly what I was desperately craving. I need my independence like I need air to breathe. But the quiet between these small walls is starting to get to me. It's too quiet.

My entire life, I've had roommates. Born into a family with four older brothers and two parents who thrive amongst the chaos of a large family, I've never known such a novelty. Even when I went off to college, I had roommates. I spent so much time wishing for a place of my own to relish in the peace and quiet, but now that it's here, it's eerie and brings me whatever the opposite of peace is. Even with music on, it's the lack of hushed chatter, the shuffle of movement, the snicking of doors, and clicks of locks that are missing. The noiseless space between these four walls just may drive me crazy.

I flip aimlessly through my Kindle library, trying to find something to do. Ivy and Blaire are obsessed with romance novels and have stocked my Kindle with their favorites. They have no idea I've been reading these babies for years. I appreciate their recommendations, though, even if I have read some of them already. I love escaping into a book and living out a love story vicariously through the characters.

Not able to find one that feels right at the moment, I toss my Kindle aside and grab my phone, bringing up my group chat with my brothers. The one that is constantly going off. Boundaries weren't something the five of us learned, and we are ridiculously close. They may be overbearing and protective, but they love so hard and are the best people to be around.

Me: Anyone free?

Dallas: ….we're working?

Dallas: Or did you forget we all have normal day jobs with no summers off?

Shit. I forgot it was a random weekday, of course no one is going to be around to hang out with. Only teachers have summers off, and since that's me, now that I've completed my first year teaching kindergarten at our local elementary school, I have to find something to fill my time for the next two months.

Sawyer: Everything ok little sis?

Me: Yeah. Just bored.

Liam: Call one of your friends?

Me: They're either on vacation or shocker, also working.

Dallas: Sounds like a personal problem sis

Me: Why are you a dickhead?

Sawyer: We've been asking this question for years

Carter: Let us know if you find the answer

Seeing my brother Carter's name, I'm instantly hit with an idea. I quickly add his boyfriend, Finn, to our group chat, hoping like hell he will be free since he works from home full time.

Finn was added to the chat

Me: Finny! Are you free? I'm bored out of my mind

Finn: Hey? Are you all sure I'm cool enough to be in this inner Hayes sibling club?

Sawyer: Wtf? You all removed Ivy from it!

Dallas: Out with you!

Liam: Han's not even in here.

Carter: Fuckin' watch it you animals

Finn: It's okay, I can bounce. I don't want to know the inner workings of your five brains. Scary shit happens here

Me: Hello!! Wait! Are you free? No one will hang out with me!

Finn was removed from the chat

Me: You all are seriously the worst

Carter: For fuck's sake

Dallas: You love us

Sawyer: We're your favorite

Liam: It's better this way

Me: Middle finger emoji

My phone vibrates with a new chat, and I smile.

Finn: Should I be concerned?

Me: They're harmless. Like bears. You need to get big and it'll scare them away. Have they taken you boxing yet?

Finn: No, but Carter said soon

Me: I'll give you some tips so you can go in there and knock them on their ass

Finn: You sure that's the best idea? Pissing them off seems like the last thing I should do.

Me: Nah, it'll make them respect you more. They're animals, gotta treat them like it.

Finn: What am I getting myself into?

Me: Carter's worth it, you'll be fine.

Me: Want to hang?

Finn: I can't today but I'm free tomorrow? Want to grab some lunch?

Me: Yes! Please!!

Finn: Sounds like a plan

Unsure what to do with the rest of my day, I throw on a hoodie, pull some scrunchie socks over my leggings, and trot down the back stairs that lead to the tattoo shop to see what Reid is up to. He works nearly every day, and usually late into the evening, so I'd bet my meager teacher bank account that he's there.

While I've known Reid for the last almost decade, he's always been Sawyer's quiet, brooding best friend. I would have to be completely blind if I didn't notice how absolutely gorgeous he is, though. My sister-in-law, Ivy, nicknamed him Drogo, and she is spot on. You can't unsee it. His dark green eyes are set against even darker eyebrows and long eyelashes that would make even the most confident girl jealous. His deep, chocolate brown hair hangs around his shoulders when it's left down, and the way his giant, tattooed hand pushes it out of his face sends shivers to all the right places.

I'm only human. Every inch of exposed skin is covered in tattoos, and I've always been so curious to get a closer look, but have never had the courage to ask.

Hey, Reid, got a minute so I can ogle your tattoos? Nope. Cringe. That would be weird and extremely invasive. Boundaries, Kinsey, no matter how gorgeous that man is or how intriguing his ink is.

My socked feet pad across the sleek cement flooring, eyes scanning the empty, open room. His tattoo shop is gorgeously curated. He's the only permanent artist here right now, but has guest artists come from all over the world to tattoo next to him. The walls are decorated as if it were an art gallery instead of a tattoo shop. Ornate frames hang over brick walls that showcase gorgeous hand-drawn artwork on nearly every inch of available space. There's a small reception area at the front of the store, just on the other side of a gigantic fishbowl interior, which holds several stations. The floor-to-ceiling glass windows make it so anyone in reception can see directly onto the floor to watch people work.

I find Reid sitting in his office, reclined comfortably with a tablet in his hand, a look of concentration and peace over his features. I use the element of my unnoticed visit to watch him for a moment. I don't know a single thing about drawing or tattoos, but I'm mesmerized watching Reid work. His large, tattooed hand holds the tablet pencil as he delicately flows across the screen. His glasses fall down the bridge of his nose, and I'm so surprised to see that he wears them to begin with that my mouth falls open slightly.

He's so ruggedly handsome, but there's an anguish that he can't completely hide. I've always wondered if Reid's broody persona wasn't a persona at all, but rather the effects of a tortured soul or broken heart. Where happiness can only be felt so deep because his heart, his soul, the marrow of his bones, were wrapped in something dark that haunts him, and he can't break free. As if he's wading through darkness without any light to lead his way. My heart pangs at the thought.

As I'm lost to studying him, his vibrant green eyes peek up over the rim of his glasses. Caught me.

"Hey, Reid, you busy?" I ask hesitantly, walking further into his doorway and playing with the drawstrings of my hoodie.

Reid drops the tablet into his lap, pulling the glasses off his face as his eyes trace over every inch of me. I feel the warmth of his stare like a caress, and I'm stunned by the action as heat pools at my core. I've never been on the receiving end of a look like this from Reid. As quickly as he takes me in, he shakes his head and meets my eyes like he's suddenly regained control of his actions and come back to Earth.

"Hey, Kins, need anything?" The deep timbre of his voice only adds to the throbbing currently happening between my legs. How do I even answer his question when I'm so distracted? *Well, I'm kind of hot and bothered after you just undressed me with your gorgeous eyes, but I'm not about to ask you to help with that.* I'm sure that would go over real well.

"I'm bored out of my mind. Would it bother you if I hung out down here?"

He combs those thick, tattooed fingers through his long hair, pushing it out of his face. I track the moment and nearly moan. Remember when I said I wasn't interested in him? My brain clearly knows Reid is off-limits and not at all what I need, but my girl parts are screaming "fuck me! Fuck me!"

"I have a client coming in soon, but he's a regular and he won't mind if you hang out. You wanna watch?"

My day just got way cooler, if I could pull myself together long enough to stick around and enjoy it.

"Are you kidding? I would freaking love to watch you work. I've never actually seen anyone get a tattoo before."

"You still want one?"

"Are you offering?"

He tsks and shakes his head slowly while running his fingers through his hair again, pushing it out of his face and flipping it off to the side. Jesus, why is that move so devastatingly sexy? I swear I can feel my heartbeat throbbing between my legs when he does that.

"You want me dead, sweetheart?"

Sweetheart. Yep. I'm wet. Lovely. I feel the flash of heat warm my cheeks, and I hope to God he can't tell.

"Maybe we keep it our secret?" I try.

"Can't do it. As much as I would be honored to tattoo you, Kins, Sawyer would kill me."

Aaand I deflate. A bucket of ice water crashes over me and cools me off. Probably for the best. I'd most likely erupt into flames if his hands were on me. Even doing something as professional and innocent as a tattoo.

"It's fine. Trust me, I get it. I've heard it plenty of times before. I'm used to it." I shrug.

His head cocks to the side as he takes in what I said. "What do you mean?"

I take a seat in the sleek leather loveseat opposite him and pull my knees up to my chest. His eyes track my movement and settle on my feet, squinting slightly as he takes them in.

"You really should have shoes on down here, Kins."

I look down at my sock-covered feet and wiggle my toes.

"Oops. I'll remember next time."

"So? Going to elaborate?"

"C'mon, don't act like you don't know. They're overbearing to the extreme. You're just like them sometimes. You're telling me you don't remember carrying me out of a bar when I tried to leave with some cute guy at the beginning of the year?"

"You mean when you were drunk and trying to give your virginity away to the first bidder?"

My head bops back in surprise. I don't quite remember it that way, but I guess that is technically what happened. All my brothers had been up north at Mount Baker for their annual trip, and I decided I was done playing by their stupid, outdated rules. All I wanted was some attention. For one night, I didn't want to be Kinsey Hayes. I wanted to be someone that no one was scared to get close to out of fear of my brothers pummeling their brains all over the sidewalk.

"You wanna get out of here and go have some fun? I want to show you a good time," Theo says as he leans in close to my ear, his hands all over my hips and waist. The attention feels so good, and this is exactly what I wanted. A night free from my brothers staring down any man who comes within five feet of me. Lucky enough for me, dumb-dumb Cole brought his out-of-town friend to The Night Owl tonight, and he has no idea I have four overbearing brutes for brothers.

Theo grasps my hand as I nod my agreement to leave with him and pulls me away from the bar just as Blaire stands in front of me, causing me to sway on my feet.

"Hey, you. You seem like you're ready to go home. Want to crash at my place?" she asks me. While she's incredibly beautiful, I would much rather go somewhere with Theo. Theo seems nice. Theo will happily take away my V-card.

"I'm going to go back with Theo," I whisper-yell, leaning in close. "It's time I get laid; I want this shit over with." Because how many twenty-two-year-old virgins are there? Even if I've used my vibrator on myself plenty of times, it's not the same and doesn't count. I want to know what being with a real man is like and not a damn toy.

Blaire's eyes get really big as she takes a step away from me. Weird. I lean back toward Theo to leave when, before I can even grasp what's happening, Reid steps between us and squats down in front of me, picking me up like a caveman and tossing me over his shoulder. I screech loudly, and the sudden shift in gravity makes everything spin around me.

"Oh, no you don't. Fuck that, Kins. You think I'm going to let you go home with some out-of-town stranger? Not fucking happening."

"Screw you, Reid! Put me down!" I scream, my fists pounding into the hard mass of his back as he walks toward the exit of the bar with me over his shoulder like I'm some misbehaving, naughty child.

"Not a chance, sweetheart. You want to get me killed? Your brothers will have my ass six feet under by lunch tomorrow without breaking a sweat. Time to go home. Alone."

"You're just like my stupid overbearing brothers, you dick!" I scream. "Just let me get it over with!"

The chilly winter air hits me like a thousand knives as he stomps outside and to the side of the building, slowly dropping me to my feet, pressing me against the cold brick. His huge hands frame my face, feeling so warm against the unforgiving onslaught of the *cold Washington winter air. Reid bends down significantly to be at my level, his emerald eyes piercing and genuinely concerned, but behind them, I swear I see desperation and feral possessiveness. I've seen it in the way Sawyer looks at Ivy. But that could be the alcohol talking because there's no way Reid Knight is looking at me like that right now.*

"What do you think you're doing?" he asks me.

"I just want it over with, Reid! I don't want to be twenty-two and a virgin. No one will touch me, so if this dude will, he can have the damn thing!" His fingers tighten ever so slightly against my face, as if they involuntarily spasmed, before relaxing, his thumb swiping back and forth across my cheek.

"Your virginity is fucking precious, sweetheart. Don't you dare just give that shit away. You're trashed, and that's not when we make huge decisions like this. It's time to go back to Ivy's." His words come out softly, but there's no confusing the demand in them. The low timbre of his voice is gravelly, like he's trying hard to keep his composure. It sobers me quickly, and I stand there dazed and confused as Blaire walks over with my coat. Maybe he's right, maybe I should wait for the right guy to come along. Too bad that won't be him.

"My point . . . is that I'm used to people disappointing me out of fear of what my brothers will do. Or having fake relationships with women because they just want to get close to my brothers and use me as their way in."

His face falls, his shoulders slumping, but his eyes never leave mine.

"I'm sorry if I've made you feel that way. That night, I wouldn't have been able to live with myself if I let you leave with someone you just met when I knew you had been drinking. Your brothers just want to protect you, and so do I. But like with everything in life, there should be balance. As far as tattooing you . . ."

He pauses and releases a rough exhale while I wait impatiently for him to finish. "I'll think about it. Okay?"

I want to snap at him like I would my brothers. Like I have in the past, when he's pushed into territory that he shouldn't be in. It's no one's job to protect me. I don't need protection. When I look at his face, though, I'm met with such genuine care and concern that something stops me, my typical fight response retreating. He doesn't deserve the wrath that I keep in spades for my brothers. Plus, he said he'd consider tattooing me, something I really want done. I could go somewhere else, and my sister-in-law, Hannah, said she would help me find an artist since Reid did all of hers, and up until this moment, he has been adamant that he isn't doing it. But if I'm going to get a permanent piece of art on my body, I want the best. He just happens to be sitting in front of me and is best friends with dickhead number one.

"Thanks, Reid, I—" I'm interrupted by the front door chiming, but Reid doesn't take his attention off me. His eyes are so serious as he looks at me, easily making me feel like the most important woman in the world, like everything around has disappeared, and I'm the center of his focus. It's a heady feeling; one I've never truly been on the receiving end of from someone before. My heart does a funny thing in my chest, but I ignore it. This is just Reid. He's close to my sister-in-law, Ivy, and has gone above and beyond with other women to make them feel comfortable and safe. He just has a way about him that makes you feel special and seen. It's not like I actually am. Special, that is.

"You what, Kins?" he asks, urging me to go on as if he didn't have his client waiting at reception. Something that should be more pressing and more important than listening to me ramble.

"Nothing," I say with a smile. "You really don't mind me watching you work?"

He looks at me for a silent moment, like he wants to press but is holding himself back, something I appreciate.

"I don't mind at all. Neither will Rhys."

I follow Reid out of his office and into the big room set up for tattooing. He leads me to his station and pulls over a big chair for me.

"Need anything?" he asks, his voice a deep, gruff baritone that nearly growls out of him when he speaks. How is this man so masculine but sweet in equal measure?

"Nope," I chirp, popping the 'p.' "I can always go upstairs if I'm a distraction or getting in the way."

Reid's eyes glance over my body in what would be a flattering, heated stare, but it's more like he was checking to see if I would truly be a distraction.

"I'm gonna go grab him and I'll be right back."

Reid retreats from the room, pulling open the glass doors and leaving me alone as he moves to the small reception area. I take a second to look around at the artwork he's framed around the shop, and make a mental note to ask if he was the one who created it all. He seems to really enjoy being an artist, and it shows.

I love being a kindergarten teacher, and I knew from a very young age that it was exactly what I wanted to do. Having summers off is a massive perk that I am one hundred percent for having, but I also miss the structure and routine of being in my classroom with all my students. Next year, I hope to have my niece, Charlotte, in my classroom. She's such a smart little girl, and it would be so much fun to teach her.

I'm lost in thought and don't hear the two gigantic beasts until they're towering above me at Reid's station. I look up from where I'm sitting cross-legged in the leather chair, and my mouth falls open slightly at the sight of the two of them next to each other.

The other man is Reid's size, possibly bigger, which can't be right since Reid is already the size of angry Hulk. I blink a few times, hoping the image of the two of them in front of me will become clearer because there's no way I'm seeing what I am.

Nope. Still barbarian sized men. Are they from Earth? Maybe

they're aliens. There's no way two men this uncommonly large actually know each other. A convention for giants?

Jesus. Fucking. Christ.

My mouth gapes open, and there's nothing I can do but own it. These two men are gorgeous. Sexy. Reid would never touch me, but this one? I would climb him like a tree . . . if I knew how.

reid

I DON'T LIKE THE WAY KINSEY IS LOOKING AT RHYS, and something inside me roars to life, wanting to shut this down before it's begun. And it has nothing to do with the fact that she's my best friend's sister. I can't explain it, but having Kinsey in my space is different from any of the other female friends I have. *She's different.* I've always chalked it up to the fact that I'm projecting big brother behavior because that's how I would treat Lena. But based on how my cock stirs behind my jeans every time she walks into a room, I'd wager that is most definitely not the goddamn reason.

Rhys is the only member of Hell's Heathens who's welcome to visit me in Aspen Ridge, and it's because he's willing to come as Rhys and not Sin. He leaves his cut at home, drives down here in his truck, and we get to hang out as two people instead of members of the club. He knows I toe this line of separation, and it's worked well for me for almost a decade. I'm not about to ruin it now. Reid and Rogue are going to stay two different people with two different lives for as long as I can help it.

When I look away from Kinsey, I see red, my hands clenching into fists. I warned him outside that she was in here and that he needed to be on his best behavior, but I should have known better. Kinsey is gorgeous and behaves like she has no fuckin' clue just how pretty she is. In my thirty-two years on Earth, I can say I've never met a woman as beautiful as she. It's difficult to look at her without the breath leaving my lungs, and I'm not stupid enough to notice that she has the same effect on every other male that meets her.

Her hair is light brown with bright blonde highlights placed throughout. Right now, she has it piled on top of her head in an untamed, messy bun that showcases her sexy, delicate neck and the beautiful features of her face. I know Rhys sees exactly what I do.

Kinsey Hayes is fucking perfect.

I know I'm walking on a tightrope by telling her I'd think about tattooing her. Her brothers don't want her to get one, but I think that's bullshit. She's a big girl, and if she wants permanent ink on her body, that's her call. The truth of it is that, regardless of where she wants it placed, I don't know if I could handle being so close to her, touching her. I've never looked at a client as anything more than flesh and meat, but I'm so attracted to Kinsey that my body wouldn't be able to separate the client from *her*.

Rhys is clearly affected as his eyes look her over appreciatively. I turn my body to the side, driving my elbow into his gut as I do, hoping he pulls his shit together. Before I can make the introductions I don't fuckin' want to make, Rhys sticks his hand out in her direction, her petite hand dwarfed in his paw.

"I'm Rhys, Reid's brother. You are?"

I rub my hand over the back of my neck, cracking it from side to side, pressure building at the top of my spine. Fuckin' hell, now she's gonna ask questions I can't answer. Asshole.

"Brother?"

"It's complicated," I interject, shrugging it off before Rhys can speak up. I really should be setting up for the tattoo, but I'm not leaving these two together. Not with the way he's holding her little hand in his, his thumb swiping back and forth across the smooth skin on the top.

Wrath bubbles to the surface. He shouldn't be touching her, she's too fuckin' good for him, for all of us. Plus, she's extremely off-limits. Sawyer would kill me if someone I knew got close to her. *If I got close to her.*

"You gonna give me your name, kitten?"

Kinsey removes her hand quickly, as if she was burned, and I brace, wanting to know what the hell he just did. I'll kill him if he just hurt her, and Rhys knows it. Before I can question him, Kinsey speaks up, her voice strong and full of venom.

"You really gonna call me kitten when you know nothing about me? Nice first impression," she says with that fierce Hayes attitude she's perfected. I smile proudly at her.

Give him shit, sweetheart. He deserves it and can take it.

"Ooo. She's got claws, Reid, just like a little—"

"Don't fuckin' say it," she snaps, and he chuckles under his breath.

Kinsey's eyes are no longer doe-eyed and glassy, they're squinted into slits as she glares at him. I laugh under my breath, slapping the back of my hand into his stomach.

"Quit messin' with her, dumbass. Sit your ass on the table."

Rhys moves to remove his shirt, and I slap him again, knocking his hands out of the way.

"What are you doin', brother?"

"Changed my mind, let's finish my chest today," he says while giving Kinsey a wink.

"She doesn't want to see your fuckin' chest, quit being an idiot," I tell him before giving Kins my full attention. "Don't mind him, he's harmless"—an image of Rhys straddling a man and beating him with his fists until his face was unrecognizable flashes through my mind—"most of the time. Rhys, this is Kinsey. Show her some respect."

"Kinsey, it's a pleasure to meet you. I'm just messin' around."

"Mhmm," she hums, her lips pursed together as her tiny figure sits in the big chair comfortably. She looks so fuckin' cute in her lounge clothes, hair piled on the top of her head, face free of makeup, like she doesn't have a care in the world. Rhys clears his throat, which pulls me from staring at her. I feel like an asshole because I'm usually so good about keeping my actions and expressions in check, and I just lost myself admiring how beautiful she is.

Kinsey is a temptation I don't need.

When I was first dragged to Aspen Ridge by Sawyer almost a decade ago, he took me under his wing, never pried, just stuck to me like glue. I didn't talk much, too lost in my sorrow and grief to let anyone in. He got me set up with a bunch of his stuff in a makeshift bedroom at the distillery, and I finally had to ask, the weight of his kindness gnawing at me.

"Why are you helping me?"

"Like attracts like," was his answer, as if it were as simple as that. I recognized it, though, his grief was different than mine, but he still had experienced some type of loss. It bleeds from your pores like a virus.

"Goddamn rain needs to quit!" I scream into the night as I pull my motorcycle over to the side of the road, the gas gauge letting me know I'd be a lucky sonofabitch if I could make it another measly mile. My boots clomp into the sodden earth as I get off my bike and take stock of where I am. I don't remember the last time I saw a road sign. The deserted two-lane highway stretches endlessly in front of me, tall trees leading the way into the abyss.

A single car passes me with no notice, which is all the same to me. This is my penance anyway, and if Lena won't ever feel rain fall on her skin again, the least I can do is stop bitchin' about it and keep pushin' on.

Her young, sweet face flashes in my mind and then is immediately marred by the last time I looked at her—badly beaten, bruised, and cut up. Bile turns in my stomach, and I roughly kick the stand down on my bike, bending over and retching the contents of my stomach onto the side of the road.

After purging my stomach lining and burning up my esophagus, I wipe my mouth with the sleeve of my flannel, pushing my rain-slicked hair out of my face and tying it off. I reach into my satchel to pull out a bottle of water, rinsing my mouth out before chugging some back.

The rumble of a truck comes from behind me, slowing down as it approaches, then pulling off in front of me. Not having any idea what part of Washington I've traveled into, I look down, making sure my gun is easily reachable, just as a man jumps down out of the driver's side of the truck.

He looks to be roughly my age, a few inches shorter than me, with broad shoulders and an athletic shape. I wouldn't have an issue taking him, but he looks like he'd put up one hell of a fight based on the size of his arms.

"Need a lift?"

"Nah." I shake my head, putting the water bottle back and flipping the bag closed. "I'm good. Thanks."

"C'mon, man, it's pouring rain, your bike break down?"

"Yeah, but I'm good, don't mind pushin' it to the nearest town."

The guy chuckles. Actually chuckles at me. The fuck?

"Sorry to tell ya, brother, but next town over isn't for twenty miles. I'm on my way home for break."

Fuck.

"What town?"

"Aspen Ridge."

Never been there. But it sounds nice. I know I've got to be close to the coast; the air is faint with salt even against the earthy scent of wet dirt and motor oil from my bike. The rain suddenly pulls back while I'm contemplating whether or not I want to spend the rest of the day pushing my bike into town or take him up on his offer for a lift.

I hold my breath as the clouds slowly start to glow, the sun *fighting to break through in brilliant streams of gold. It reminds me so much of Lena. Her good always pushing through the bad. If this isn't a sign, I don't know what is.*

"Aspen Ridge, huh?"

I pull my bike into the parking lot of Knockout Boxing Gym and put down my kickstand. A few times a week, I come here to lift weights, sometimes by myself, other times with the owner, Dom, or Liam Hayes—Sawyer's younger brother. Other times, I'm sparring with Sawyer. He's the only one that I'll truly go hand-to-hand with without feeling too bad. He's trained in boxing, MMA, and Krav Maga. We've both only gotten bigger and stronger over the last ten years. The Hayes have grown up in this gym. Their dad forced them all to learn how to fight and protect themselves . . . and handle their disagreements. It's a stress reliever, and I've taken part in it on more than one occasion.

To my surprise, Kinsey is here. Her long hair is pulled back tight in a ponytail, and she's wearing tight black leggings and a pink sports bra, her toned stomach on full display. She's in the ring with Dallas, and it looks like she's using him to work through some shit that has pissed her off. In typical Dallas fashion, he's not letting her get far, blocking every single one of her punches.

I walk up to Sawyer, who's leaning against the ropes of the ring, watching the two of them. He nods at my arrival, not taking his eyes off his siblings.

"She seems pissed."

"He's just not taking it easy on her, and it's getting her riled up. She needs to keep her head in the fight and not take shit so personally."

I want to bite back at his words, argue with him. Kinsey is strong as fuck, and taking things personally isn't a bad thing, it just means she feels deeply. That's admirable and not a weakness.

I watch as she bounces on the balls of her bare feet, Dallas being a dick and not even keeping his gloved hands up to protect his face, taunting her and running his mouth. Dallas loves just as hard as Sawyer does, but man if he doesn't know how to push buttons and piss people off. Which he's doing to his sister right now.

"Fuck you, Dallas!" she screams in frustration, but Dallas just keeps fuckin' with her, making my molars grind together. My hands grip the ropes until my knuckles turn white, but before Sawyer can notice my irritation and desire to get in there and help Kinsey, I drop them to my sides.

"You fightin'?" I ask him, feeling the itch to get in the ring now that I'm watching.

"Already beat dickhead here to a pulp, now he's making himself feel better by taking it out on Kins. Can't let his ego get too bruised," he replies loud enough for Dallas to hear.

"Shut the fuck up, shithead! You wanna go again?" Dallas yells.

The distraction gives Kinsey the opening she needed, and she throws a punch. It lands true, directly on the left side of Dallas' face, splitting his lip, blood pooling immediately.

"Take that, you dumb fucker!" Kinsey whoops. I can't help but smile watching her. She's good on her feet, and she takes everything Dallas has thrown at her without so much as a wince. Fuck, she's amazing. "Damn, that felt good! I should get in here more often with you, Dal. That was cathartic!"

An image of Kinsey on the back of my bike flashes in my mind unwarranted, and I wonder what else would make her feel good. Sawyer laughs from next to me, pulling me from my thoughts and making me feel like shit. He'd bury my ass if he knew how attracted I was to his sister, how dirty my thoughts have been—especially lately—but worst of all, how my cold, dead heart stirs to life and beats when she's near.

"You got me, Blaire's gonna love this shiner. I'll wear it proudly."

"Good one, Kins!" Sawyer shouts.

"Come on, big brother, you next?" she asks Sawyer, who shakes his head.

"Nah, gotta get home to Ivy and Grace. Been away from them too long."

"It's been an hour!" she counters, walking up to us at the ropes. Dallas climbs out, and Kinsey's shoulders deflate.

"You're both leaving?"

"Wives call, baby sis!" Dallas shouts back to her.

"She's not your wife yet, you big idiot."

Dallas whips around and points at Kinsey. "Hey, Blaire is my wife in every way that matters."

"Does she know that?" Sawyer asks, poking at him.

"Oh, she knows," Dallas replies, wiggling his eyebrows.

"Gross, Dallas Hayes! I don't want any ideas of what you two do in your free time."

"Love you, sis, you were amazing in there, proud of you," Sawyer praises her.

"You made me work for it, Kins, I may put on a good show, but you're tough as shit when you want to be," Dallas adds, making a gorgeous, bright smile fill her face at their praise.

"Love you, too, you big oofs." Kins moves to climb out, but I make an offer I'm sure to fuckin' regret.

"You wanna fight some more?"

Sawyer pats my chest and looks back at his sister, offering an apologetic smile and then laughing with Dallas as they walk away.

"You'd get in here with me? Heard you're picky about who you spar with."

"I am. So, you want to or not?"

Her resulting smile is so fuckin' pretty.

"Get in here, big guy."

Damn there are definitely some places I'd like to get into, sweetheart. If you only knew.

I put on some gloves, not bothering to wrap up my wrists, knowing I have no plans to strike her. I could never hurt her, never hurt any innocent female. Climbing into the ring, I don't know what the hell I'm expecting, but it sure as hell isn't where my thoughts have gone—tangled with Kinsey on the mat, her legs spread, and my face buried in her pussy.

I shake my head, willing my cock to calm the hell down. For the most part, I've always been in complete control of my desires, but this newly developed one about Kinsey? My mind seems to be fighting me on what's right and wrong. And Kinsey Hayes? She is definitely wrong, even if everything feels right when I'm with her.

I stretch out my arms and neck, watching her pretty face transform from a smile to stone-cold serious. Good. If she takes this seriously, it'll make being this close to her easier.

"Alright, little fighter, show me what you got," I say as I do a come-hither motion with my gloves. She gives me the cutest fucking smirk, her eyes lighting up, and I know right now that it doesn't matter what happens in this ring, I won't regret a fuckin' thing.

Her body is fucking tiny, and if I had to guess, her waist is smaller in circumference then one of my thighs. Based on her size alone, you'd think all I had to do was flick her and she'd fall to the ground, but not Kinsey. It's clear based on the confident way she moves around me, the strength in each of her punches, her calculated movements—she's been training just like her brothers have. After a few rounds, she bends forward over one of the ropes, taking a break.

"I should feel bad for hitting you when you're only playing defense," she says, her voice revealing she's out of breath and getting tired.

"But you don't?" I ask as she stands back up and faces me. Her face is flushed pink, hair that has escaped her ponytail clinging to her crown in thin, wet wisps.

"Nope," she pants, her chest rising and falling harder, the swell of her breasts pushing out the top of her sports bra and glinting with perspiration. My mouth salivates as I think about hauling her up and lapping it with my tongue.

"Violent little fighter," I tease.

Instead of shooting a quip back at me, she surprises me, jumping up and throwing a quick jab toward my face. She's so much goddamn shorter than me that the jump gives me time to respond. I block her punch, hauling her body against mine, spinning her around with her arms crossed at her waist like a strait-jacket. I hunch forward over her, our bodies lined up, and I hope like hell she can't feel how hard I'm getting from being close to her. Kinsey doesn't fight back, her body melting against mine.

Instead of letting her go, instead of doing anything rational, I whisper into her ear, "Like I said, violent little fighter."

"Don't forget it."

I release her with a smile, climbing out of the ring and grabbing two towels, tossing one at her.

"You feel better?" I ask.

"Yeah. Thanks for giving me your time. I appreciate it."

"Anytime. I'm here if you ever need someone to talk to," I offer, even if for the first time in a decade I'm offering to listen to someone for partially selfish reasons. I like having her around.

"Thanks, Reid. You're a good man. Even if you do keep shitty company."

I bark out a genuine laugh that surprises both of us. "You mean your brothers?"

"Who else?" She smirks. "See you later, Mr. Knight!" Kinsey saunters off, and I'm left standing alone in the gym, wondering how the hell no man has been strong enough to lock her down.

After my long drive across town to my secluded house on Lupine Lane, I do the one thing I've been able to keep myself from doing for months—jerk off to visions of Kinsey.

I barely make it through my front door before I'm resting my back against the cool wood, shoving my athletic pants down, and gripping my cock in my fist. I stroke it from base to tip, beads of precum weeping from the slit. My mind conjures images of Kinsey, her tiny body, and how easily I could pick her up, hold her legs over my shoulders, and eat her pussy. Fuck, I want to taste her. Want her tight, virgin hole to clench around my fingers as her clit swells against my tongue.

For years, she's been Sawyer's sister. But now? That's just one part of her. To me? She's Kinsey, my little fighter. And in my private thoughts, alone in my house, I lose myself to an addiction I have to keep under control. It can never leave here. Here in my head, she's safe. If she was anything more? Shit. I couldn't put her in that position. I don't deserve her. No. My perfect Kinsey will stay my fantasy and nothing more. No matter how right she feels and how badly I'm starting to want her.

kinsey

ASPEN RIDGE IS GORGEOUS IN THE SUMMER. THE TALL Sitka spruce trees tower over our town, lush and gorgeous, the Olympic Mountains cocooning us in a little bubble that is so far removed from every other place in the state. It's a quintessential small town, and I love every minute of living here. I just wish my brothers would back off and let me live a little. I know I've threatened to leave Aspen Ridge if they don't stop smothering me, but the thought of doing that makes me feel physically ill.

The sun is shining today, the clouds giving our town a small reprieve from the near-constant cloud cover, so I throw on my favorite midi-dress. It has a deep plunge in the front, and since I can't wear a bra with it, I stick on some pasties so the restaurant doesn't get a free show of my perky nipples when the air conditioning inside chills me. I lace up my sandals, tying off the ends at my calf before taking a look at myself in the mirror. I've always felt confident about my looks. Sure, I have similar insecurities to every woman I know, but overall, with all the love my huge family has showered me with for the last twenty-two years, I feel good about myself.

After securing my headband and fluffing up my waves, I grab

my bag, ready to head out to meet Finn for lunch at Barrel House. My parents live on the outskirts of town, about fifteen minutes from all the downtown shops and dining, and my god, has it been a game changer to live right in the center of it all. Reid's tattoo studio has a prime location directly in the middle of Main Street. Instead of going down the stairs that lead to his shop, I take the outdoor stairs that dump me out in a small parking lot. I have to walk around the building through a small alley to get to the cobblestone sidewalks that line our two-lane Main Street on the other side, but it's better than waltzing through Rogue like I own the place.

Aspen Ridge could easily feel like a cage for some, but the only one I've ever felt is the one I was placed in by my brothers. I've always loved living in Aspen Ridge and plan on taking full advantage of living downtown. Especially since the only one who lives down here is Carter, and he seems to be mostly on board with me living for myself. I know twenty-two is still young, but I'm not a little kid any longer, and it's past time they all start treating me like the grown-ass woman I am.

The sun beats down on my fair skin, and I know it won't take much before the light dusting of freckles I have right under my eyes and on the tops of my shoulders starts to become more visible. I inhale a deep breath of pure, mountain air before skipping around the corner to head down the street. I'm immediately met with a wall—two large hands reaching out to grab my shoulders, steadying me from falling flat on my ass as I bounce backward.

"Ooph!"

"Whoa, sweetheart. Where are you goin' in such a rush?"

I arch my head back as if I'm looking up at the sky, the large body in front of me blocking the sun. Reid looks down at me with a half smirk, his hands still on my arms, the warmth radiating from the contact rivaling the sun.

He towers over me by at least a foot, the top of my head just barely meeting the bottom of his shoulders. He really is a giant. Or I'm just tiny in comparison.

"Hey you," I offer as a greeting as his thumbs slowly swipe back and forth on my bare skin before dropping away. "Off to meet Carter's boyfriend, Finn, for lunch. Have you seen him since he confused you for Sawyer?"

Reid barks out a laugh and rubs his thick fingers through his beard before moving to his heavily tattooed neck, rotating his hand back and forth like he's loosening an invisible noose.

"Still can't believe that happened. Don't think Sawyer will ever let the poor guy forget it either."

Now it's my turn to laugh. When Carter brought his boyfriend to family dinner to meet us all for the first time, Finn may have been slightly overzealous and saw Reid standing next to Ivy. Assumptions were made, and he's lucky Sawyer didn't knock his head clean off his shoulders.

"Eh. He'll get over it. Finn is awesome, and I desperately need a friend who isn't trying to get into my brothers' pants."

Reid arches a brow at me, and I throw my head back in a laugh. "Pretty sure he's well acquainted with what's in your brother's pants, Kins."

"Eww! Reid Knight! Did you just make a joke? Gross! I don't need to think about that. Finn and I are saints, both virgins and pure as freshly fallen snow."

Reid's face morphs from amused to something much fiercer that I can't decipher. His dark pupils are blown, making his eyes look almost black. It's not like he didn't already know I was a virgin. He's the one who kept me from losing it in February. Maybe he assumed I would have checked that box by now, but sadly for me and my inexperienced girl parts, I'm still untouched by anything other than my own fingers and my trusty vibrator. Whatever. If he's uncomfortable with my joke, that's on him.

I reach forward, patting his chest with the flat of my hand. Jesus Christ, he's hard; muscular in a way that I've never felt before. What the hell is he made of? Steel?

"Alright, big guy, I'm going to head to lunch, I'm starving. See you later?"

"Yeah, Kins. I'll see you later."

As I walk away from Reid, I can't help but shake how he said his last words to me. They almost sounded like a promise.

Finn is standing next to the steps that lead down to Barrel House—the only real sit-down restaurant in Aspen Ridge—as I arrive. He's deep in conversation with another man I've never seen before, and I slow my steps to give them time to finish talking, not wanting to interrupt.

As I approach, the mystery friend glances over Finn's shoulder, his eyes slowly perusing my body from head to toe. It's flattering, and a smile pulls at my lips.

"Hey, Finn!" I chirp as I sidle up next to him, giving him a friendly mini hip-check. He slings his arm around my shoulders in a quick side hug.

"Hey, glad you made it!"

"Aren't you pretty? I'm Trey, this one's best friend, although, since he spends all his time with your brother, I'm looking to replace him," he says, his voice smooth like butter. He must get along well with the ladies. His name rings a bell, though, I just can't place why. I put my hand in his outstretched one to be polite.

"Kinsey. But I guess you already know that?" His smile stretches across his face. I'll give it to him, Trey is cute as hell and seems like a mega flirt.

"I do. I've heard a lot about you."

That surprises me, and he must read that on my face because he clarifies.

"Your brothers hired me at the distillery. This was my first week."

My shoulders relax, but the tension doesn't dissipate. I'm sure those four goons have already drilled it into his head to stay far away from me. That's what they do. Last year, when they hired their intern, Marcus, he was thoroughly warned not to even look in my direction. Not that I was interested in Marcus, which they never seem to take into consideration.

We move indoors, ordering our food, and I start to relax a little more. I haven't spent much time with Finn yet, but the few times I've been around him, I can't help but smile. His personality is infectious, and I get the appeal he had to my brother.

"So, how's living with my brother?"

Finn's eyes get all mushy—like fairytale sparkly in love kind of mushy, and I laugh at him. "That good, huh?"

"He's everything, Kinsey. My favorite person in the world." He says the words so ardently, and my heart pangs in my chest, both from happiness and jealousy. To be loved like that is such a gift. I chew on my bottom lip and wonder if I'll ever meet someone who falls in love with me in a way that nothing else matters. To be the center of someone else's world must be a heady feeling.

Lunch goes amazingly well. Finn and Trey together are quite a duo, and it makes me miss Piper so much. We laugh so hard tears pour from our eyes, share appetizers, and eat way too much. The food at Barrel House is incredible. My sister-in-law, Ivy, is the head chef here, and even though she is still on maternity leave with my niece, she's clearly trained her staff well. The conversation between the three of us is easy, and I really hope I've found some new friends here.

As we're walking outside, Trey grasps my elbow, pulling me to a stop to talk. He's average height, but like most people, taller than me, so I arch my head back slightly to look at him.

"I know we just met, but is there any chance you'd let me take you out for dinner?"

"You want to take me out? Like on a date?" I ask, surprised. Even though Trey wasn't holding back by flirting with me before and during lunch, I thought it was just playful, harmless flirting.

"Of course I do. What gives you the impression that I don't?"

"My brothers," I answer like it's the most obvious thing in the world. Is he well?

"They mentioned something about staying away from you, and I'll be honest with you, I don't want to ruffle feathers; I really want to work at the distillery. But you're gorgeous, Kinsey, and funny, and I'd like to get to know you better."

I'm not sure how to take his words. Is he saying that I'm worth putting up with my brothers' shit to take that chance on me? Or is he saying we would need to keep it a secret? Deeply rooted insecurities rise to the surface, and I'm unsure what to do. As if he can tell, Finn speaks up, trying to save the conversation.

"How about he gives you his number, and if you decide you want to take him up on it, you can give him a call?"

I smile at Finn, appreciating him jumping in.

"That works. I'd like that."

We part ways, and even though I'm cautious, it felt good to be asked out. Trey is good-looking, but I'm not overly attracted to him, and I definitely am not jumping for joy that he works at the distillery for my brothers. I love them so much, and they really are the best humans, but they really lack boundaries. I suppose we all do, though. We're all too close for our own good.

I walk up Main Street, enjoying the sun on my skin, and decide to stop by Bean Haven to see my sister-in-law, Hannah. She owns Bean Haven, Aspen Ridge's only coffee shop and bakery. I swear, she was born with coffee and sugar flowing through her veins. She creates the most amazing baked goods, and her salted caramel lattes are to die for.

As I approach the door, I see my oldest brother trying to get Ms. Nettie's pint-size dog to release his pant leg. Hannah's grandmother looks up at Sawyer like she's annoyed by his presence, which I find hilarious. Her dog, Winnie, is the sweetest thing, but for some reason, she hates my brother.

"Hi, Ms. Nettie, my brother bothering you?" I greet as I crouch down and pet Winnie, her tiny teeth releasing the torn fabric of Sawyer's slacks, causing me to chuckle.

"He's a nuisance. Always getting Winnie riled up."

"That thing is a nuisance, Ms. Nettie. Minnie needs to be kept on a leash."

"Sawyer Hayes, you know her name is Winnie. Do not test me, boy." Her threat doesn't go unnoticed by either of us, Sawyer's spine stiffening as he glares down at the little old lady. I have to bite my lip to keep from losing it. Ms. Nettie is a firecracker of a woman, always saying what's on her mind and not afraid of anything.

Sawyer doesn't say anything as he whips open the door and steps inside. I give Ms. Nettie a sympathetic look, putting Winnie back in her lap and following meathead number one into Bean Haven. The cool air blasts me, goosebumps break out on my arms, and I'm so thankful for those pasties. Hannah keeps it way cooler in here than Barrel House.

"Shouldn't you be at work? You said you couldn't hang with me."

"That was yesterday. Ivy's craving apple cinnamon muffins."

"Tell me you didn't knock up my sister already, Sawyer. She just had Grace."

"Not yet, but as soon as her doctor says that it's safe, I will be."

"Jesus. You could, I don't know, wait a few years?"

Sawyer looks down at me like I'm crazy before shaking his head no. "What can I say? I like her pregnant, body growing with my child."

"You're lucky she loves it just as much, or you'd be shit out of luck."

Hannah serves us our drinks and hands Sawyer a dozen freaking apple cinnamon muffins for Ivy. He's so good about spoiling her. After a decade apart and thinking she was gone from his life forever, I know he's making up for lost time.

Once I'm home, I fall against my bed and let the quiet surround me, my mind drifting to Trey's offer to take me to dinner. I haven't bothered trying to date in so long. My last boyfriend was my sophomore year in college, and he was more interested in screwing the girls at one of the sororities then he was hanging out with me. Dinner wouldn't hurt, right? It's just dinner. He was cute. It's not like I have anything else to do this summer, plus, it would be good for me. I'm starting this new life, and that includes dating.

Grabbing my phone, I click on new message and find Trey's recently programmed number to send him a text. This could be good.

> Me: Hey, Trey. It's Kinsey. It was nice meeting you. I had fun at lunch with you two. If you're still up for it, I'd like to take you up on dinner.

His reply comes immediately.

> Trey: Hey, Kinsey. So glad you reached out. I enjoyed meeting you, too. How about dinner, just as friends?

My heart sinks, and I roll my eyes with a huff.

> Me: Of course, definitely.

> Me: My brothers got to ya, huh?

> Trey: They did. I really need this job to pan out. I feel really good about this move and just don't need to get on their bad side.

Trey: Scary fuckers, huh?

Me: I get it, no worries.

Trey: How about Friday night?

Me: You know what, I've got some plans with my best friend that night. I'll text you some free days?

Luckily, he lets me off easy and doesn't press.

Trey: Whatever works for you, Kinsey.

Trey: Just so you know, you really are a beautiful, smart, incredible girl, and any guy would be lucky to take you out

Trey: I'm sorry it can't be me.

Just not incredible enough to stand up to my brothers to actually date me. Frustrated, I close out of the chat and bring up Piper's pinned thread.

Me: I'm swearing off men

P: Haven't they already sworn you off?

Me: Ouch! Too soon!

P: Who hurt you? I will murder them and make it look like an accident.

Me: Finn's best friend, who crashed our lunch today. He's cute and seemed fun, but I didn't feel any chemistry between us. He asked me on a date, I said yes, my brothers got to him, and he backed out. It's not like I felt this deep connection and had some insta-love thing happening.

P: Right...

Me: So why am I disappointed?

P: Because you're used to this happening time and time again.

P: I'm in a lab, I'll video call you as soon as I get back to my apartment

Me: K. Love you, smarty pants

P: Love you KiKi

I spend the entire next day floating around my studio apartment, moving things around the space and making it perfect. Even though I unpacked fully last week, I need to occupy myself before I lose my mind. The downside of small-town living is the lack of options, and right now, I'm going a little stir crazy. A date would have been something fun to do to fill the quiet that I've discovered I'm not a fan of.

My friend situation needs serious work if I'm going to stay in Aspen Ridge. I've only been back from college for a year, and I was so busy getting settled in at my new job at the elementary school that I hardly had time to even think about my lack of friends.

I could call some girls from high school that I was friends with. We've caught up a bunch when we see each other, and they came to my birthday party last December. My own insecurities have forced me to keep them at a bit of a distance. Even though they never outright went after my brothers, I was always on defense because it had happened so many times prior. All of the girls are now in committed relationships, and even though I am far from being in one, I doubt that would make a difference.

I make a mental note to see if any of them are free to grab a drink or even hit up Grace Beach. While it does get hot here, the Pacific Ocean is still frigidly cold, but lying out in the sun actually sounds pretty amazing.

The sun has started to set on our sleepy mountain town, and I consider going to The Night Owl for a beer, but the idea of seeing people today just sounds exhausting. Instead, I pad across my little apartment and open the door that leads downstairs to Rogue. The moment my foot hits the first step, the creaks from the ache in the wood hitting my ears, butterflies take flight in my stomach.

Reid typically works late into the night, which I don't mind at all. I'm such a night owl, and it's been nice to sneak down here and talk to him. Surprisingly, he's not tattooing anyone right now, so I continue through his shop to get to his office. The door was left wide open, the interior room only lit by a lamp on his desk.

I lean against the doorframe of Reid's office, and for someone as big and strong as he is, he seriously lacks situational awareness. Or maybe he's just so relaxed in his own space that he isn't worried about someone sneaking up on him. So, obviously, here I come like a tornado disrupting his peace.

I assumed he'd be in here drawing again, but instead, he's . . . reading. And not just reading anything, like a murder mystery or thriller, or I suppose even a classic. No. Reid is reading pure romantic filth of the absolute best kind. I recognize the cover, *Haunted Love*, about a woman who moves to a haunted manor to work for the Lord of the Manor, who is more mysterious than the grim grounds themselves. It's dark, spicy, and completely delicious.

"Need something?"

Shit. Caught again.

"Just admiring the book you're reading," I say as I toy with my fingers in front of my stomach.

He sets the book down on his lap, the spine widening and making me cringe. It takes all my self-control not to reach over and keep him from cracking the spine so hard. His lips turn up in a sexy-as-hell grin as he reads my face.

"How far in are you?" I ask.

"They just got to the graveyard."

"Mmm. Things are about to get exciting. I didn't know you read."

Reid's eyebrow arches as if he took offense to what I just said, and I immediately blush in embarrassment. "Shit! I didn't mean it that way. It's not that I didn't picture you reading, Jesus, or picture you at all, I just mean I wouldn't have guessed that you were a romance reader." I nervously play with my hair, tucking it behind my ear and trying to keep my hands busy while Reid's intense eyes look at me.

"Kins, relax, it's okay. I read a bit of everything, but I'm a romantic at heart, I suppose. Can't guys read these smutty things, too? Or are they just for women?"

"No. Uhm, yes. Of course men can read them. You're reading it right now. I'm surprised by it, but it's a good surprise. Been reading this genre for long?" I take a seat, pulling my legs onto the big loveseat, making myself at home in his office even though I was invited in. When I look back at his face, he seems quite dejected, almost like he's struggling to answer the question. I think back to exactly what I asked, and there wasn't any room for misunderstanding, so I find myself slightly confused. Maybe he didn't want me to sit? He could have plans or places to be, people to see. *Or do.*

"I can go, if you're busy. I'm sorry for barging right in." I drop my bare feet onto the cold ground and move to stand, but Reid's large hand reaches out and puts pressure on my knee, stopping me. The touch sends shockwaves through my body, just as it did the other day at the gym. Heat rushes to flame my cheeks pink, my heart skipping sporadically in my chest.

"Stay. Please?" His voice is deep and gruff, but so tender and genuine.

I relax into the seat, pulling my legs back up under me, his hand dropping from my knee. I immediately miss the warmth of it.

"Okay. If I'm ever bothering you, just tell me. My apartment is . . ." I don't finish my sentence, unsure about yapping to him and only slightly worried that whatever I say could somehow make it back to Sawyer.

"It's what, sweetheart?"

Sweetheart. God, why does he have to call me that? Is that any better than *little fighter,* though?

"It's quieter than I expected it to be."

"Isn't that the point of living on your own? I thought that's what you wanted."

He's not wrong, and the irony is not lost on me. My life has always been chaotic, living with my big family, living in a dorm room, of course the quiet was what I craved. Now, I don't know why I wanted it so desperately to begin with.

"It was. Is. I've just always been surrounded by noise or other people. I guess I'm not really used to being on my own. It's not bad, but my best friend is on the other side of the country, the boys all have lives of their own now, I'm no longer talking to Harlow after all the crap she pulled, and I'm just not tight with anyone here. I'm kind of floundering now that I'm not teaching for the summer. I don't want to bother you, though, by sneaking down here looking for some company."

"You're never bothering me, Kinsey. I'm used to the quiet, and having you here has been a nice change. I can see how that would be an adjustment for you. I imagine you've never really known peace and quiet before. You're strong, though, making changes is hard, and you're doing it."

My cheeks flame brighter at his praise. He's such an enigma. This giant of a man, so heavily tattooed, with long hair, sitting there looking intimidating to anyone who doesn't know him, is so soft spoken, so sweet and tender. I'm sure there's another side to him, though, the one I can see hiding behind his eyes.

"Whelp, now that that's out of the way, how was your day?" I ask.

"How about you tell me about yours?"

"It was okay, I guess. Yesterday I went to lunch with Finn, and his best friend crashed it. Which was fine, but he spent the entire time hitting on me." Reid's spine suddenly stiffens, and I wonder if I should even bother talking to him if he's going to act all protective and crazy.

"How'd that make you feel?" Not quite the response I was expecting, to be honest. Since when do people care about how I'm feeling?

"Honestly?"

"Always."

"Flattered. But annoyed. He works at the distillery now, and I knew what would happen before it did. After lunch, he asked if he could take me to dinner. I was surprised because I'm sure he got the same spiel every other guy has received from those meatheads. He noticed my shock and insisted that he could handle my brothers. I mistakenly believed him enough that I agreed to a date."

Reid leans forward, his tree trunk legs spread wide as he rests his forearms on his thighs, listening intently like he truly has nothing better to do. I bat away a rogue tear, feeling stupid for crying over this. "It's not even like I was interested in him, Reid. He's cute and suave, but I knew exactly what would happen."

"He cancelled?"

"Of course he did. They all do. Or they take me on a few dates and then run the other way the moment they meet my brothers. I swear those boys find out I'm dating and they're like blood-hounds, sniffing them out and scaring them off."

"I'm sorry, sweetheart. Anyone who doesn't make you the center of their universe is a goddamn fool. If he isn't man enough to take on those four Neanderthal brothers of yours, then he isn't the one for you. Fuck 'em."

A self-deprecating chuckle comes out of me, making Reid smile. "Yeah, fuck 'em."

"Thatta girl. Now, since your dinner plans were bombed, have you eaten? I'm starving."

"You look like you're probably always starving."

His eyes narrow at me, heavily lidded as he looks over my face briefly, it's heated, and my core turns to molten freaking lava.

"I am," he groans.

Unsure what to do or how to respond, I clear my throat, running my hands through my hair. "Me too."

"You up for pizza from the market?"

Is he seriously offering to feed me? My mind wars with wanting him to hang out with me as a friend and not out of pity. But I'm a glutton for punishment, I suppose.

"It's my favorite."

He pulls out his phone, relaxing back into his chair, the book falling off to the side. This time, I can't help myself, I climb out of my seat, reaching over and picking up the book, looking around for something I can set inside to mark his page. With nothing in sight, I remove the thin, soft scrunchie from my wrist, setting it inside his book and closing it gently, placing it flat on his desk while giving him a glare.

"Noted," he mouths to me while he waits on hold to place our pizza order.

Plopping back down in my seat, Reid speaks up, ordering a large pepperoni and bacon pizza before covering the speaker and looking at me. "What would you like?"

"Barbeque chicken, please."

He smiles at me before ordering a second large pizza with my toppings. After he hangs up, his thick fingers rub through his beard, my eyes tracking the movement, making my heart flutter, and warmth pools between my legs.

Does this man have any idea just how ridiculously handsome he is?

reid

"So, I have a question for you," Kinsey says, reaching for her third slice of barbeque chicken pizza. I love seeing her eat. There's something so sexy about a woman who isn't afraid to stuff her face with food. Watching Kinsey enjoy food is an experience. She takes each bite like it's her last, practically moaning as the flavors explode on her tongue. She enjoys it thoroughly, with no rush, savoring every bite and appreciating it. It's hypnotic, almost sensual, and currently taking up all of my focus.

"Shoot, sweetheart."

"Why don't you ever come to Sunday dinner? I know you're asked constantly, but we all really would love for you to be there." I've been best friends with Sawyer for practically a decade now, and I've never once attended their weekly family dinner, except to drop in for a moment. I love their parents, and my lack of attendance isn't personal, although I'm sure it looks that way. I continue to eat my slice, chewing slowly and methodically while I figure out how to explain this to her.

There's a huge part of me that wants to open up to Kinsey, but the other part, the Rogue part, doesn't want her to know.

"I want to be there, Kins, please don't think I don't go because of anything personal."

"I figured. I've never seen you with your parents, so I just wanted to make sure you knew you had a place where you were always welcome."

Another sore topic. My parents would love to see me for their own family dinner. It's not for lack of them trying, either. For my own selfish reasons, I can't bring myself to share a meal with my parents, who still hold out hope that their baby girl is alive and will walk through their front door someday. I can't sit there with a straight face and talk about the weather when I know that Lena's decaying body is resting six feet under on Hell's Heathen property under an Aspen tree.

"I have other obligations that take me out of Aspen Ridge every Sunday."

Her pretty eyes look up from her pizza to meet mine, and I wait for her to ask me to elaborate further, but she just nods her head like she's thinking it through.

"That makes sense. Does Sawyer know?"

"He does."

"Hmm. Well, if your plans ever fall through, you know you're welcome, right?"

"I do," I tell her honestly, the side of my lip lifting upward. She's so surprisingly refreshing. Any girls I've ever known would have pressed. They would have demanded to know where I was going and who I was with. But not Kinsey. She takes my words at face value and moves on. But I need to know why, and for some reason, I find myself unable to let it go.

"You aren't curious where I'm going?"

"Of course I am."

"Then why didn't you ask?"

"Because if you wanted me to know, you would have told me."

There it is. This girl is so fucking perfect it hurts.

Painfully.

After we finish eating dinner, Kinsey relaxes into the leather seat, letting her head fall back against the headrest, her eyes falling closed. I use the moment to look over her unashamedly. She's such a petite little thing and looks so fragile. I know firsthand that is far from the truth, though. She's stronger and tougher than most people I know. I wish her brothers would give her the space to live a little.

I wonder how I could help her with that without jeopardizing my relationship with Sawyer. After some things went down when Ivy returned to town, I don't even want to imagine how he'd feel about me getting close to her sister.

"Do you know what kind of tattoo you want?" I blurt, the thought unable to leave my mind since she first asked me if I would be the one to tattoo her. Kinsey stays relaxed in the chair, her hair fanning out around her.

"I do. I want one single stem along the inside of my hip with some tiny flowers blooming from it. Super fine line and delicate."

Fuck me.

I run my hand over my face and have to bite my lip to contain the primal groan that is fighting to break free, just as my burner phone goes off. Kinsey sits upright, looking around for the source of the noise, my phone clearly sitting on my desk, not making a sound.

Disappointment rushes through me, knowing I won't be able to ignore it. I watch as she tilts her head to the side, then squints at me.

"Got a secret life we don't know about there, big guy?"

If she only fuckin' knew.

"I'm sorry to cut this short, sweetheart. But I've got some stuff to take care of."

"You're fine." She waves at me nonchalantly as she stands from the chair. She stretches her arms above her head, the hem of her shirt lifting and revealing a section of bare skin along her midriff. My mouth salivates once again, wanting to lean forward and trace that strip of silky, smooth skin with my tongue. What the hell has come over me with this woman? "I've got a video date with Piper anyway. See you later?"

"Yeah, Kins. You'll see me later."

Kinsey leaves just as my phone stops ringing and immediately starts back up again. Once I hear the click of the back door that leads to the loft, I close my office door and open my top drawer, pulling out my burner phone.

"Yeah?"

"That's no way to greet your prez, is it, Rogue?"

"It is when I was in the middle of something important."

"Not like you to get your dick wet anywhere but the clubhouse."

"It's not like that."

"Hmm. Doesn't sound like it to me."

"What do you need, Chaos?"

Because if he's calling me, it's not a want.

"Just giving you a heads up. We got a problem. Our message was received loud and clear. But word is that they're coming for you and Malice to retaliate. You've laid low, and they're only gonna assume you're on the compound with the rest of us. But since you're not . . ."

"I need to be vigilant."

"Correct. You could always come home."

"Not gonna happen, Camden."

"You belong here with us. With your brothers."

"I'll be there on Sunday."

"For good?"

I hold the phone away from my face while I release a frustrated breath. It's always like this with him. He lets me live my life separate from the club, but he never lets me forget who I am and where I belong. How long can I really keep living these two lives? One of these days, one is going to catch up with the other. When that time comes, I don't know which I'll choose. Can I go back to Hell's Heathens full time? I'll never be completely free of them, and I don't want to be.

As much as time is supposed to heal all wounds, I won't ever heal from this one. Losing Lena because of my connections to that world will live with me forever. I'm destined to wade through the darkness for the rest of my days on Earth. The weight of it feels too fucking heavy sometimes.

"You still there?"

I bring the phone back to my ear, ready to get this conversation over with.

"Yeah, just thinking."

"We'll see you this weekend. And Reid?"

"Yeah?"

"Watch your back. I mean it. They're out for blood."

"Got it."

I hang up with Chaos, irritation taking over my headspace. I know he worries about me living out here by myself. I knew I needed to be driving distance from the clubhouse, and I got lucky with Aspen Ridge being as close as it is, even if an hour is still far for what Camden wants. I've been so preoccupied, I haven't given much thought to the fact that the Iron Wolves have regrouped after all these years. Being this close to the anniversary of Lena and Lucas's murders, something just doesn't feel right about it. Call it a sixth sense, but there has to be more here than what we're thinking. Chaos either isn't telling me everything, or we're missing a detail. It seems a bit too coincidental.

I stuff my phone in my pocket along with my other one, deciding it's probably best to keep my burner phone with me, in case shit goes south. As I'm closing up my office, my eyes flicker to the copy of *Haunted Love* sitting on my desk. Curious, I open it up, Kinsey's hair tie slipping from the pages and onto my lap. She was so damn cute when she gave me her little evil eye for breaking the spine, the way she couldn't fight her need to correct it and treat the book with respect.

The fabric is soft between my fingers, and I can't help lifting it to my nose and inhaling the lingering smell of her floral shampoo. The scent lightens the heaviness in my chest for a fleeting moment. She's so fucking *good*.

I relax into my chair for a moment before I have to head home for the night. I hate that Chaos interrupted, but he only calls if it's important, and there's no way I was going to turn my back on him. I just wasn't ready to say goodbye to her yet. I had more fun tonight sitting in my office with Kinsey eating pizza and talking than I have in a long-ass time.

A part of me loves that she caught me reading. I'm not embarrassed by it. My sister used to read romance novels, and shortly after she was killed, I wanted a way to escape other than my bike and alcohol, and I found that I could do that with reading. Knowing that Kinsey reads, too? I toy with the idea for a few minutes before I act on it, knowing what I really want to do and not wanting to fight it. I can already picture the look on her face when she sees it.

Moving over to my desk, I open my drawer and pull out a copy of my favorite book. Grabbing some sketch paper, I quickly leave a note for her and stick it between the front pages with the top sticking out so she sees it. Before leaving Rogue for the night, I quietly tiptoe up the stairs to Kinsey's apartment and leave the book leaning against the doorframe. But before I can turn to leave, I pause, resting my hand flat against the door.

I'm falling for this girl. She's right on the other side of the door, alone, probably lying in bed, and hell if I don't want to knock right now and ask to come in for more time with her. I can't have her, but there's nothing wrong with being her friend. I can be that. It seems like we both need it.

After a restless night of sleep, I start the day with only one damn thing on my mind.

Tattooing Kinsey.

I fought with myself on what the right thing to do was, but I just kept coming back to how badly *I* want to be the one to tattoo her virgin skin. Hell, I want all her firsts.

She's made up her mind that she wants a tattoo, and it's only a matter of time before she finds someone else to do it. The thought alone makes me want to rage, pound my chest like a barbarian, and scream "mine," for all to hear. There's no fucking way.

Mind made up, I slip out of bed naked, reaching for a pair of jeans and pulling them on. Kinsey's hair tie taunts me from its new home on my dresser as I throw on a fitted T-shirt, socks, and my boots. After combing my hair and pulling half of it into a bun, I'm out the door with only one thing on my mind.

Kinsey Hayes.

After I send a text to reschedule the only client I had for today, I make the quick walk up the stairs to Kinsey's apartment. I've never been up here with her before, and the same rush of excitement I get every time I see her courses through me. I knock twice and wait nervously.

Kinsey opens the door a moment later, looking so fucking beautiful that I stand there and look at her like a dumbass, love-struck teenager unable to form words. She's wearing a black tank top with thin straps and a layered-looking floral miniskirt that puts her gorgeous, toned legs on display, with my book held to her chest. She found it. Which means she's already opened this door today, and there's only one reason she would have done that.

She was looking for me.

"Reid?"

"Hey, Kins. You, uh," I rub my fingers through my thick beard, suddenly nervous. "You busy?"

"Nope. What's up?"

Fuck, how is she so damn pretty?

"Can I tattoo you?" Shit, did that come out right? Why the fuck am I so nervous? Probably because of the filthy images I've been having of this woman for weeks now.

"Are you serious?"

"Yeah. You suddenly scared, little fighter?" I taunt. Come on, baby, say yes.

She chews on the inside of her lip, twisting it to the side while she contemplates.

"Yeah, you can tattoo me. Please?"

I can't help it. My eyes fucking flutter closed.

Kinsey takes a second to put the book back inside, then pulls her door shut behind us and follows me downstairs. She's fucking barefoot again, and it just does something to me. Something about her lack of shoes makes everything seem so much more domestic, more comfortable than it should be. Even if that's exactly what I want, though I shouldn't.

I wipe down the leather table, sanitizing it again and pulling out a pillow for her to rest her head on. Kinsey climbs up and lies down on her back, her delicate fingers twisting the hem of her shirt. Once she's settled, I raise the table up so that it puts her at the height I need. I'm such a big guy that it makes certain things difficult, and while getting into some weird-ass uncomfortable positions is sometimes mandatory, I do my best to take care of my back, so I'm not hunched over for hours at a time.

I don't make eye contact with her while I glove up and pull out my colored pens. I do my best to never use stencils unless it's needed. I believe in freehanding the artwork on the client and using their natural body shape to make the designs perfect. Kinsey is no exception. I'll be damned if I'm using a stencil when I have all the time in the world to draw it on her before the tattoo.

After I've set up, I finally allow myself to meet her pretty blue eyes. Her expression nearly takes my breath away, looking at me with so much goddamn trust that I don't deserve and have done nothing to earn.

"How are you with pain?"

I laugh as her expression mutates from awe and trust to her lips pursing as if to say "really?"

"I guess I have seen you take some hits from your brothers. But you've never passed out from needles?"

"Never."

"Alright, sweetheart. If you pass out on me, I'm holding it over your head for life."

"I've got this. I can't believe it's really happening."

"Me neither," I whisper under my breath.

My hand reaches up, her skirt resting high on her thighs, and for the first time, it hits me how close I'm about to be to the paradise that's waiting between her legs. Jesus Christ, why the hell am I putting this temptation right in front of me? Just as my fingers touch the hem of the fabric, I pull back.

"Can you, uh, can you pull up your skirt?"

"Oh, yeah, duh, sorry. I guess I am a little nervous after all."

"Totally normal, you're gonna do great." I say the words, unsure if they're meant for her or me.

I'm unable to tear my eyes away as her fingers reach for the bottom of the skirt and she ever so fucking slowly pulls it up. Inch by glorious inch, more of Kinsey's bare flesh is revealed to me. It's not meant to be, and it's clear she's nervous about it, but there's no denying how goddamn seductive the action is.

Her skin is fair and looks so damn smooth, and there's a tiny freckle on the outside of her left thigh that I so badly want to press my mouth against. She hesitates for a moment before lifting up past her center, revealing a thin as fuck, black triangle of fabric covering her obviously bare pussy underneath.

Fuck, what I wouldn't give to be able to press my face against her right now, to inhale her sweet pussy. I'm completely lost to the visual in front of me. My lungs stop working, my palms become clammy, and electricity zings through my body, waking me up after a long sleep. My cock responds, thickening behind my jeans and pressing painfully against the zipper. I want to rub my palm over it to give myself some relief, but the only relief I could find right now is deep inside her virgin pussy.

I've fucked plenty of women—mostly club patch bunnies— and I've never in my life been so screwed up over one. If she weren't off-limits, I would be begging her right now to let me worship her cunt until she's dripping all over my table. But she's Sawyer's little sister, and no matter how strongly I feel that Kinsey is so much more than that, he'd never agree with me.

With that bucket of ice water dousing the flames currently licking at me, I let her finish hiking up her skirt until it's loosely around her waist while I grab my colored pens.

"I'm gonna draw on what I think you want, and then you can hop down and take a look in the mirror and tell me how you feel."

"Sounds good. I trust you."

Jesus, she isn't making this easy on me. Does she have any idea what she does to me? How deeply she affects me on a visceral level?

I take a few minutes to look at her left hip, studying her pelvis and the natural lines and curves of her shape before drawing on a dainty floral stem that curves along the inside of her hip with several flowers, two in bloom, one partially, and one closed. Once I'm satisfied, I cap my pens and help her sit up.

"Mirror is over there," I tell her, pointing to the full-length mirror on the other side of the room. "Let me know what you think. I want it to be perfect, Kins, so be honest. This is on you for the rest of your life."

I love this part, watching my client see the design for the first time, watching their reaction. With Kinsey, I feel it tenfold. When she said what she wanted, I knew exactly what flower to pick, and right now, I'm hoping like hell she loves it, but it won't hurt my feelings if she wants a different one.

"Reid," she gasps, covering her mouth and failing to hide the huge smile filling her face. I walk up behind her, probably too close, but I don't give a shit right now. She smells like fresh flowers and sage, and I'm starting to become addicted to it. Her hair tie only faintly smells of her. Maybe there's something else of hers I could take. Just to borrow.

The thought slams into me intrusively, and even I'm shocked. This is some unhinged shit Malice would do. That's not me. Even if I would love to hold her panties to my nose while I jerk off, the smell of her pussy filling my lungs.

"Yeah?"

"It's beautiful. It's better than I imagined it would be."

Pride fills me as I watch her face in the mirror.

"Good. That's what I want to hear."

"What flower is this?"

"Gladiolus."

"I'll be honest with you, I've never heard of them before. What on earth made you pick it? Seems kinda random."

Shit. Now or never, I guess.

"You, little fighter."

Her eyes flash up to meet mine in the mirror, a look of shock and confusion sliding across her face. "Me?"

"They symbolize strength. Little sword, warrior, or *fighter*," I whisper.

Kinsey turns, and we're so damn close that she's practically in my arms. No longer looking in the mirror, she arches her neck to look up at me, and I swear I've never been so close to saying 'fuck it' in all my thirty-two years on Earth. I've never wanted to kiss anyone as much as I want to kiss Kinsey Hayes right now.

But I can't.

So instead, I allow myself a moment, running my fingers over the soft skin of her brow, tucking pieces of her hair behind her ear. Our skin is a sharp contrast—hers so light and pure, mine calloused and covered in thick, dark ink. It's a stark reminder of how wrong I am for her. Her eyes flutter closed, her chest rising and falling harder as her breathing picks up, and I know I've affected her. Knowing this has to stop, I let my hand drop just as she releases a small sigh.

And because I'm a glutton for punishment and am losing all restraint when it comes to her, I lean down and kiss the middle of her forehead. Her quick intake of air makes my heart beat rapidly in my chest, and I want so fucking badly to see what other reactions I can pull from her.

Taking a step back, I turn and walk over to my station with Kinsey on my heels. She climbs back up onto my table in silence and gets comfortable. I glove back up, setting up my equipment and ink, and steady my breathing as I lean over her, hovering my machine over the newly drawn design.

"Are you ready, Kins?"

"I want this, Reid. I'm so glad it's you."

"Me too, sweetheart."

I swipe her skin with petroleum jelly and then gently place my machine down, getting started on the delicate tattoo. Kinsey's breath hitches as I steady my needle, outlining the blossom of the flower on her hip. I've never been distracted before while tattooing, and I don't know what the fuck has come over me or what I'm thinking putting myself in this position.

I never look at clients as anything more than just hunks of flesh to be used as a canvas, especially not ones who are almost ten years younger than me and the baby sister of my best friend. There's just something so different about her that I can't explain.

Kinsey is something else entirely. Ever since she moved in upstairs and started to hang out more and more with me, I've started to lose sight of how I viewed her before. Instead of being Sawyer's little sister, she's just Kinsey. And right now, she's this sweet, sexy little thing, lying on my table in nothing but a thin pair of panties, her skirt hiked up around her waist while my gloved hands touch her skin. Which has got me all sorts of fucked up.

I can't stop wondering what it would feel like to be skin to skin, how she'd feel wrapped up in my arms. I notice her quick inhales of breath, the way her eyes flutter closed, how her nipples are hard peaks, and how she's pressing her thighs firmly together. I wonder how she would react if I traced her hip with my tongue or pulled her thin panties aside and licked up her juices.

Fuck. I want her. And I know I shouldn't. She's Sawyer's sister for fuck's sake. And right now, my client. This isn't a line I can cross. But fuck. She's so goddamn beautiful, so innocent and sweet. She makes me feel like I'm a good man. That I'm not shrouded in darkness.

"You doin' okay, little fighter?"

"Yes. I—" She cuts herself off, biting her bottom lip, and I wonder if the pain is too much, but she wants to be strong. I pull back and look at her, taking in her flushed face and heavy eyelids. Jesus. She almost looks turned on. But that can't be right.

"You what?"

"I like it."

Fuck me.

I'm going to hell. Right after Sawyer kills me, slowly and painfully. He forgave me once for coming onto Ivy when I first met her and had zero idea who the hell she was; he'll never forgive me for where my head keeps drifting to about his sister. A fantasy I jerked off twice to last night. Images I keep conjuring up right now, so vivid, so fuckin' real, that I almost need it to be so.

"Sweetheart, I can tell how turned on you are. You have two choices. I can clean you up and you can head into my office to use your fingers to get yourself off, or I can follow you and do it for you."

"Wh-what?"

"You heard me." I spray her down with green soap, wipe her clean with a clean paper towel, and cover her with ointment. "What's it going to be?"

"You're serious right now, Reid?"

"Guess I'm making the decision for you then."

I grab her hand and pull her off my table.

"I'm giving you a two-minute head start while I clean up my station real quick. Go in and lock the door. I'll knock twice, and you're going to let me in. I expect your panties to be off. Understand?"

Kinsey looks at me, her beautiful eyes full of uncertainty, but I also see hunger. She nods her head yes, like I knew she would. I pull off my gloves, tossing them in the trash can before gently pinching her chin between my thumb and forefinger, tilting her head up to look at me.

"I need to hear you say it."

"Yes. I understand."

"Good girl," I whisper.

Kinsey walks toward my office as I quickly clean up my station and wash my hands before heading after the girl of my goddamn dreams. I reach my office door and promptly give it two light knocks in quick succession.

A doe-eyed Kinsey opens it enough for me to slip through. I flick the lock and turn to face her. Every time I see this woman, she takes my breath away.

"Let's see if you listened, sweetheart."

I take two steps in her direction before I've caged her against the wall. She's tiny, just slightly over five feet compared to my six foot four. I bend my knees to be more at her level, rest one of my hands above her head, and slide my other up her thigh painfully slow. I watch as her breathing hitches, her eyes dilate, and her lips slightly separate in anticipation. My hand slides further under her skirt, rubbing lightly over her soft flesh until I reach the apex of her thighs. I'm met with skin. Soft, wet, slick skin.

She listened.

Fuck.

And she's so goddamn wet.

"Such a good girl," I praise. "Do you want this, Kins? I need you to be sure."

She nods and then immediately follows it with a hushed, "Yes. I want this. I want you."

My heart bangs hard against my ribcage, my hands shaky but confident. I move my hand from the wall and grasp the side of her face.

"Good. Cause you're going to love it. I'm going to make you feel

so good." Careful not to touch around her fresh, unbandaged tattoo, I press further into her body and finally take her lips with mine. She holds nothing back in return. I slide my tongue along the seam of her lips while my fingers do the same to her pussy. I'm rewarded with the sexiest fucking little gasps.

"Sweetheart, you're soaking my hand already. Is this all for me?" I take her bottom lip between my teeth before pulling away altogether. I keep my eyes on her as I drop down onto my knees in front of her. I rub both hands up one of her smooth legs before pulling up to rest her thigh on my shoulder.

"Reid. What are you doing?" she practically pants.

"I said I'd do it for you. I didn't say how. Now, try not to make too much noise. I don't want anyone else out there to know what you sound like when you come on my tongue. Those noises are just for me."

I push her skirt up and I'm finally face-to-face with her gorgeous pink pussy. I lean forward, press my nose right to her slit, and take a deep inhale of her sweet scent.

Fuck. She's so perfect.

Her hands go right to my hair, trying to pull me closer to where she wants me. I use my fingers to spread her lips open before swiping the flat of my tongue along the full length of her, coating me in her arousal.

"Fuckin' hell, sweetheart. You taste so fuckin' good."

She drops her head against the wall with a thud and combs her fingers through my hair.

Fuck. Yes.

The height difference is a bitch with me on my knees, so I pick up her other leg and toss her thigh over my shoulder. Letting her ass rest in both of my hands, I hold her up to my face.

Hating that we don't have all the time in the world, I take a few more long licks before focusing on her swollen, throbbing clit. She moans so fuckin' pretty for me. It's the best sound I've ever heard, and I want more of it.

"Ohmygod! Reid. Oh. My. God."

"You like this, little fighter?"

"Yes. Please just don't stop!"

I drop my face back to her sweet pussy and suck her clit into my mouth with gentle pulses. Her hips start to buck wildly, and her hand in my hair pulls my face closer into her.

"That's it, baby. Ride my face. Let me have it," I groan into her flesh.

I move my hand to her center and rim her slick entrance. She's so goddamn wet. Her breathing increases as she tries to swallow her moans. Her legs start to tremble, and I know she's close. I swirl my tongue around her clit before sucking it back into my mouth again. Just before she starts to lose it, I drive a finger deep inside of her and curve upward toward her belly and holy shit if she isn't tight. It only takes me a moment to find that sweet spot that pushes her over the edge and makes her see stars.

"Reid! I'm coming! I'm coming! Oh my god!" Her walls clench tightly around my fingers as I curve them upward and rub deep inside her. Her hips undulate as she gasps for air. I lick and stroke her until she comes down from her climax, pulling every wave of pleasure out of her. I gently kiss the inside of her thighs before placing her back down on the floor and adjusting her skirt.

"That was..." She slowly opens her eyes, glassy and full of post-orgasm haze. I grab her hands to make sure she's steady on her feet before noticing that she's holding a pair of black lacy panties. I stand and unclench her fist around them and take them from her, pressing them to my nose to take a deep inhale of her.

"I'll take these as payment," I say before pocketing them. "You better now?"

"I . . . yes."

"Good. Now take a moment and come back out there so we can finish this tattoo."

"Reid?" Kinsey's sweet, soft voice breaks me out of my daydream.

"Yeah, sweetheart?"

"Where'd you just go?"

"Sorry, was just thinking things through. You ready to continue?" I ask, really needing to adjust how uncomfortably hard I am without her noticing. I'm going to goddamn hell.

kinsey

> Me: You busy? I need you.

> P: I'm free. Laying in bed breathing in my eucalyptus inhaler.

> Me: What? Why?

> P: Trying to get the smell of chemicals and decaying flesh out of my nose.

> P: What's up?

> Me: Jesus I don't even want to know

> P: Life of a med student. You do not want to know.

> Me: He's tattooing me right now

> P: No way! Hottie Reid? I don't understand the problem here …

> Me: He's so close to the inside of my bikini line

> Me: Right. Now.

P: Okay??? Isn't that where you wanted the tattoo?

Me: There's a lot of…vibrations going on.

Me: A lot. Help me!

P: *Spitting water out emoji*

P: You're getting turned on? Haha!

Me: Omg don't make me laugh P! I have to stay still!

Me: Talk me off the ledge you bitch!

P: I hope his hand doesn't slip!

Me: Jesus Christ.

Me: The vibrations are. Right. There.

P: Pain plus vibrations…I'd be screwed

Me: Omfg. Help me Piper!

P: I'm no help am I?

Me: Useless bitch

P: Think about the word musk

Me: So gross

P: Yay I helped

Me: Haha idiot

Me: Fucking hell

P: Other than that how's it going

Me: So great! I love it! I'm so thankful he's willing to risk his life to do this for me.

P: Well of course you are. You're about to drop an O!

Me: Omfg Piper. Why am I friends with you?

P: Cause you love me and can't live without me!

Me: Want to bet?

I PUT MY PHONE BACK DOWN SINCE MY BEST FRIEND IS zero help in these types of situations and try to focus on anything but Reid Knight practically lying between my legs, his face so close to my pussy that I can feel each warm exhale he takes.

Things I expected while getting tattooed: pain, irritation, nerves, maybe slight nausea. Things I didn't expect while getting tattooed? Being so turned on, it's hard to breathe. My clit throbs and I'm so wet that I've never been so thankful I put on black panties today. I'm so worried he'll look down and see how he's affecting me, and I'm hoping like hell I'm not leaking down my thighs.

"You still doin' okay?"

"Yeah, I'm good."

"Good. We're almost done."

"That fast?"

"Why? Not ready for it to be over?"

I feel the heat climb up my chest, and I know my cheeks are blooming pink. No, Reid, I'm not ready for this to be over because I can't think of another time that it would be socially okay for your face to be this close to my private parts and your hands on my skin. I quickly ask myself how much I actually like being tattooed and if I could find another one I want—maybe on my boob or ass this time.

"Just trying to soak it all in, who knows if I'll experience this again."

As if Reid realized the underlying meaning of my words, he pauses and looks up at me. The top half of his hair is pulled back in a man bun, the lower half hanging around his shoulders in natural waves. His thick facial hair covers the top of his lip and travels across his strong jaw and chin, and I wonder what it would feel like to run my fingers through the coarse hair. Wonder what it would feel like against my sensitive skin.

Jesus. I'm not going to survive this. Wave after wave of arousal flows through my body like a live wire, a loud hum between my ears as I nearly combust right here on his table without him even really touching me. The vibrations from his tattoo machine continue to send shockwaves directly to my throbbing clit, and the moment he pulls back, setting it off to the side, I release a long, pent-up exhale.

I grip my skirt, ready to pull it down, but Reid's hand shoots out, covering mine and preventing me from covering up.

"Not yet, sweetheart. I've got to clean you up and bandage you first."

"Oh, okay. Sorry."

"Nothin' to be sorry for. Just not ready for you to cover up yet."

Jesus. Fucking. Christ.

Does he have to make everything sound so dirty and sexual? Or maybe that's just my brain crossing the signals and hearing what I want to hear. Based on my near-desperate need to get behind the closed door of my apartment to use my vibrator, I'd say it's a high probability that's exactly it.

Reid sprays me down with some cold liquid, and I nearly jump off the table. His free hand grips my hip, pressing me back down.

"Holy shit, that was so cold!"

"I know, I'm sorry. I've gotta wipe you down now, and this is usually the worst part for some people. It'll sting."

He uses a paper towel and, as gently as he can, he wipes across my reddened, newly tattooed skin. But I don't feel a damn thing. No, all I can feel, all I can focus on, is his hand on my hip, his thumb swiping back and forth on the inside of my pelvis in a soft, barely there touch. I don't think he even realizes he's doing it, but holy shit does it feel amazing.

"Are you ready to look at it before I put a covering over it?"

I nod my head, and Reid surprises me by helping me sit up this time. I swing my legs in front of me to hang off the side, but he doesn't take a step back. Instead, his hands find my knees, not letting me hop down.

"Take a second, sweetheart. I want to make sure you aren't lightheaded or dizzy before you stand up."

He's so close. His body is huge, especially compared to mine, and I love how his presence is so large. He's wearing a short-sleeved T-shirt, and I take a moment to study the tattoos that cover every inch of his skin. Without thinking, I reach out and trace along a long dagger that cuts through the center of a skull.

"Did you do them yourself?"

When he doesn't answer, I look up at his face to find his head turned down, facing where my fingers trace along his skin, his eyes pressed closed like he's concentrating heavily on something. When I look back down, my eyes narrow in like there's a homing beacon shining right from his crotch. The thick outline of his dick presses heavily against his jeans, the bulge would be notice-able from fucking space, and I nearly gasp at the sight of it.

Holy shit, did I make Reid Knight hard? My fucking word, he's packing. I mean, I assumed based on his massive Hulk size that he would be, but you never know about these things. Espe-cially me.

"Reid?" I whisper in question, really wanting him to make a move. I need him to put me out of my misery. I shift on the seat, rubbing my thighs together for some type of friction. Reid releases a rough exhale before speaking.

"You should be good, Kins, hop down and take a look."

He wants me to stand up? Is he actually expecting my legs to work like they're supposed to? I think all he would have to do is brush my clit and I would combust into flames.

On very unstable legs, I slide down from the table and walk over to the mirror. My skirt is held up around my waist by my hand, and I turn to the side, admiring the gorgeous fine line work he did. My skin is red and angry, which doesn't surprise me since I'm so fair-skinned and have always been sensitive.

"Reid, it's perfect. I can't thank you enough for this."

"It looks beautiful on you," he replies, standing behind me again and studying my reflection with a severe stare. His eyes are heavily lidded, his bottom lip pulled between his teeth. Jesus. I need a cold shower and to put some space between us STAT.

"How much do I owe you?"

"Nothing, Kins. Trust me, it was my pleasure."

It was my pleasure.

I trip over my words of thanks like a fumbling buffoon and say goodbye to him as quickly as possible. Once I'm in the safety of my apartment, I slide against the back of the door with my hand against my heart. That was . . . intense.

There's no way Reid wasn't hard, right? Could this have turned him on as much as it did me? I swear, for a moment in front of the mirror, he was considering kissing me. But there's no way. I shake my head clear of the thoughts that I know won't leave me that easily. Instead, I walk over to my full-length mirror and take a quick photo, sending it to Piper.

P: Holy shit, it's gorgeous! What are those flowers? They're so unique.

Me: Gladiolus. They represent strength. He said they mean little fighter or little warrior. He picked them.

P: Are you sure that man isn't into you?

Me: Trust me, he's not. Although…

P: Although what?

I pause my thought process, not wanting to sound inexperienced and foolish, even to Piper.

Me: Nothing, I swear he was just a little off today, but maybe he's just serious when he tattoos.

P: Doesn't sound like nothing.

Me: He was just a little more intense than he normally is

P: Mhmm. I'm ready for you to spill when you're ready to talk

Me: Love you, P

P: Love you KiKi

Later that night, I'm devouring the book Reid left at my door. He clearly didn't want to hand it to me himself, so even though we spent a few hours together while he tattooed me, I didn't bring it up. I hold the note in my hand, looking over his handwriting and rereading his words.

Kins,
This one's my favorite. He's a broken man who finds a second chance at life in her. Pages 77,

149, & 303.
Enjoy,
R.K.

It took everything I had not to flip directly to those pages to see what he wanted me to read. Why those chapters? What's in them? Curiosity got the best of me, so I spent the morning reading. Chapter 77 was the moment the prince realized he had no hope left. He took a crushing blow, and it was devastating to read. His hopelessness, his desperation to always do what's right, even when he's lost himself. Now, as I near page 149, I cave and text Reid.

> Me: This book, Reid.

Reid: You like it?

> Me: I can't put it down. Thank God it's summer and I can stand to lose an entire day and night to a book.

Reid: What part are you at?

> Me: They just fled their kingdom. She didn't have to go with him but it was never a question of whether or not she would.

> Me: She truly loves him and she's strong enough to pull him through it all

Reid: She sets him free, brings him out of the darkness and into the light

> Me: It's so beautiful

Reid: Read it to me?

My phone rings the next second with my heart in my chest. Is he serious?

"Hi."

"Hi, little fighter. They just got to the cabin?"

"They did."

"So read it to me. I haven't read it in a few months."

With my heart in my throat and my voice trembling, I sit further back and start to read out loud.

"The cabin is dark, lit only by the small fire burning in the fireplace. Lennox is sitting at the foot of the bed, defeat written all over his handsome face. Exhaustion has plagued him since our long journey began. I know the fatigue isn't physical—it's deeper than that. An emotional, mental tiredness that has rooted itself deep in the marrow of his bones. I watch him, like I always do, my eyes unable to see anyone but him. Always noticing everything about him. His chiseled arms bracing himself on his knees. His head hanging low, his dark, chocolate brown hair has fallen into his face. It's in that moment that I know I would do anything to heal him. To take some of his burden. Some of his pain. Anything to relieve him of the heavy weight that seems to be pressing down from all sides.

I move in front of him and brush my fingers into his soft hair, pushing his head up to look at me.

"Lennox," I whisper. He responds by rubbing his hands up my legs, reaching my bottom, and pulling me completely between his legs. He moves his hands to the thick leather vest that sits over my shirt and slowly starts to untie it with strong, nimble fingers. Silently, he pushes it off my shoulders, the fabric falling to the floor.

My breath gets caught in my throat as he pulls my shirt from my trousers, lifting it up and over my head."

I pause, nerves taking over. I know where this is headed, and Reid knows too—he's read it—and he wants me to continue anyway.

"Don't you stop there, sweetheart. It's just getting good."

Feeling just like the female character in the book, I can't protest, I don't want to. My heart is practically beating out of my chest, my voice is shaky, and I know without a doubt there's no missing the subtle change in my tone. He has to know what this is doing to me. He's read this book, and the build-up it's preparing for is heated at best. But I don't want to tell him no, so I keep reading.

"Before my shirt hits the dirty wood floor behind us, his mouth has descended on my breasts. Warmth surrounds me, heat increasing between my thighs that I've never experienced before. He sucks my nipple into his wet mouth while his hands massage and squeeze my full breasts. No words are spoken between us. There's nothing to say. If it's a physical release he needs, then I am his. In every way that matters."

I pause for a moment, doing my best to control my breathing. Jesus, is this happening right now?

"My head falls back, soaking in the pleasure and warmth of Lennox's mouth on me for the first time. The heat from the hearth is nothing compared to the fire that he's stoked within me. I want more. I want it all. He releases me all too soon, and his deft fingers pull at the ties on my trousers before pushing them down my legs. I take a hesitant step back to remove them while he watches, his eyes

perusing up my entire naked body in an appreciative look that has my skin breaking out in gooseflesh.

His chiseled jaw is set firmly, his dark eyes are hooded and glazed as he soaks me in with a look that I feel to the tips of my toes. I return between his legs and drop to my knees. Rubbing my palms from his shins to his hips, I work to remove his pants and pull them down, nerves making my fingers tremble with every moment. Taking my time, I release his thick length from the confines of the fabric and grasp it in my hands. Slowly, timidly, I pump him once. Twice. Three times. Watching his face as it turns from wonder to heated pleasure.

Never removing my eyes from him, his eyes never straying from my touch, I lean forward and take him in my mouth. I lick the salty bead from his slit, taking my time to work him deeper into my mouth. "Claudia," he whispers in a near-desperate plea before he's pulling me off him. I look up at my love, my prince, and then he's hauling me up the length of his body, lying down on his back, and forcing my legs to spread open on either side of him."

BAM!

I jump and scream at the loud thud against the window of my apartment.

"Kinsey?" Reid shouts through the phone. "Are you alright? I'm on my way!"

I bring the phone back up to my ear, the book having fallen into my lap when I jumped. I slap my free hand against my chest and heave in a deep breath.

"No, no, you don't need to come over. I'm fine. I think a bird flew into the window. Poor sweet thing," I reassure him.

"If you're sure?"

"I am. It was the window, I'm fine."

"Okay. Sleep well, sweetheart."

"You, too, Reid. Night."

I disconnect the call and scoot further into my bed, throwing my covers over my head. God, I can't believe he just had me read that to him. That was the hottest thing I've ever experienced. Not that I have much to relate it to, but even if I weren't a virgin, that was hot.

Images of Reid from earlier start to appear when I close my eyes, imagining if things had gone further. My pussy starts to throb again as I imagine his hands caressing my body, rough against my smooth skin. The way his lips would feel against mine, the coarse hair of his beard rubbing against my face, the way his tongue would delve into my mouth, demanding and possessive. His smell surrounding me, all leather and cedar. God, that's my favorite scent. His firm body under my palms.

It's not long before I feel the warmth pool between my legs. Knowing that I won't be able to sleep unless I relieve some of the pressure, I lift my butt off the bed to slide my panties down my legs, the fabric setting off goosebumps as it goes.

Slowly, I slide my hand under my shirt, taking my time to get to my breast before twisting and pulling at my nipples until they're hard peaks. With the pads of my fingertips on my other hand, I work myself up, dipping down my stomach until I reach my core. My breaths are coming in short, rasping pants as I slip my fingers down my seam, tracing along the slit until I can slip a single finger inside. A moan slips from my lips at the welcome intrusion.

I'm met with a slick wetness I knew I would find there. A dampness I've become familiar with ever since Reid Knight started spending time with me.

Pumping in a few shallow times, I slide my fingers back up to my clit. Keeping my eyes closed, there's only one man I picture. I imagine it's Reid's hands on me instead of my own, moving in firm circles over my sensitive, aching clit.

My hips start to gyrate, grinding against my hand, a moan slipping from my lips as the pressure builds. I picture Reid kissing my neck while playing with my nipples, rotating between the two, keeping his fingers pumping in and out of me in slow, powerful thrusts. Would he be rough with me? Gentle?

He'd finger fuck me, his palm hitting my throbbing clit in the most perfect way. I can hear his voice speaking in my ear, "That's it, sweetheart, chase it, take what you need. Come all over my hand." I feel the orgasm build and build as my hips gyrate against the ministrations my fingers are making against my throbbing clit, until it takes over completely.

"Reid! I'm coming!" I yell into the empty room. My fingers are met with a rush of wetness as my pussy contracts and throbs. Wave after wave of pleasure rushes through me until I am left with shaky legs, my heart beating rapidly, and my breath ragged. Completely blissed out and spent. As spent as I can be without having the real thing, anyway. I remove my fingers and take a few moments to catch my breath, my eyes flicking to my phone. I'm not prepared for what stares back at me. Reid's name sits at the top, the timer continuing to count upward with our ongoing call still very much connected.

Time stops.

I can't breathe.

Can't move.

Can't even comprehend the severity of what that means.

As if a switch is flicked, my body finally cooperates. I snatch my phone off my end table and slam my pointer finger into the red 'end' button.

"Ohmygod. That did not just happen!"

Well, if he didn't know how into him I was, there's no denying it now.

reid

I'M NOT SURPRISED WHEN SAWYER TEXTS ME TO COME hang out, even if I have been unfairly avoiding him the last few weeks. What I am surprised by, though, is seeing Kinsey standing in a pair of cutoff denim jeans, cowboy boots, and a lacy tank top that shows nearly all of her back in Sawyer and Ivy's kitchen.

She's holding their newborn daughter, Grace, close to her chest, and if my knees weren't weak from seeing Kinsey alone, I can barely find the strength to walk farther into the room at the sight of her holding *a baby*.

Images of a practically naked Kinsey have been on repeat for the last forty-eight hours. I know she was just as affected as I was while I was tattooing her. I could see how wet she was, the fabric between her legs damp, her sweet, musky scent filling my lungs. I've never wanted to taste something so badly in my life and it was pure fucking torture not to have the meal I so badly wanted.

It got exceptionally worse when she didn't realize she hadn't disconnected our phone call. I don't know why I waited for her to do it. I can't explain why I stayed on the line after I heard her rustling around, her heavy breathing, her hushed gasps and moans. No part of me thought someone was in there with her. I know it was me who worked her up, who made her pussy wet and desperate. I'm the man who made her so hot and bothered that she had to give in to the desire to touch herself.

I pulled out my heavy cock and jerked it to images of her. I imagined her legs spread open in front of me, standing above her and pleasuring myself watching her dainty fingers spread open her lips and swirl around her clit. I fucked my fist and could imagine it so clearly. Her little pussy weeping, so pink and ripe, desperate to be played with.

But when she came? It was my name on her tongue. My name she yelled out as her orgasm took her under. She was fucking herself to *me.* That's what took me over the edge and made me spill into my palm. My name on her lips.

Sawyer's hand connects with my back in a friendly smack. Fuck.

I need to get my shit together.

"Hey, man, come have a seat," Sawyer says, and I don't necessarily like his tone. If he's somehow found out about the time I've been spending with Kinsey, or that I've tattooed her, I'd rather the confrontation be in private. Not in front of Kinsey and Ivy. I wouldn't deny it, and I'd have to tell him how I feel about her. But I'm not really down to ruin my friendship with my best friend without having a conversation with Kinsey first and knowing she's on board. Fuck, am I really even considering this right now? He would kill me. She may be attracted to me and want me sexually, but that doesn't mean she wants a relationship.

I take a seat on their couch and wipe my sweaty palms against my thighs. It's then that my second life catches up with me, and a bucket of ice water is dumped on my head. The letters H.H. on my two middle fingers on each hand are reflected back at me. There's no fucking way I'd make Kinsey mine. I'm a goddamn Hell's Heathen. What I want doesn't matter. I won't jeopardize her for anything.

In fact, I need to start putting some space between us so she doesn't continue to get the wrong idea. I know she can tell how she affects me; I haven't been doing a damn good job at hiding it.

But that needs to change. I don't deserve someone as good and kind as Kinsey Hayes. I don't deserve anyone. A life with me would be a life spent always looking over your shoulder, always wondering. That's why only one of my brothers has taken an old lady. He made her his legal wife not long after, but I'm not him. I won't risk it. Not after what happened with Lena.

"Hey, Drogo, you want anything to drink?" Ivy asks me. "You know I mean water or soda or coffee. I know you don't drink alcohol."

"You don't?" Kinsey interjects.

"Nope."

"Hmm." She shrugs, never one to press for more information. God, I appreciate that woman so much.

Sawyer takes a seat in a chair across from me, Ivy walking into the room and bypassing him to sit on the couch. Sawyer's hands reach out quickly, grabbing her by the hips and hauling her right off the floor and onto his lap.

"Where are you goin', butterfly?"

"To sit down so we can talk!"

"Your seat is right here."

Kinsey walks farther into the room with Grace, taking a seat on the other side of the couch from me, and I'm grateful Sawyer pulled Ivy onto him. If he hadn't, it would have forced Kinsey to be right up next to me in the middle. It's bad enough she's within eyesight, that I can smell her.

Get your shit together, man. You can't fucking have her, and the reason why is currently staring you right in the fucking face.

"Alright, before my brother mauls you and puts another baby in you, what's up?"

"We've got something to ask you two, and we wanted to ask you privately before we let everyone else know," Ivy says, fairly ominously.

"Oooookay?" Kinsey stutters.

"Even though we aren't religious, after my parents' unexpected death, we want to make sure we make plans just in case."

"What are you saying?" I question, my heart in my fucking throat.

"That we don't believe in the term godparents, per se, but if something were to happen to both of us, we want you two to take over raising Gracie."

"Us?" I stammer.

"I know it seems weird because you two are obviously not a married couple, but we wanted to pick the two best people we know, and that's you two."

"I'm sorry, what?" I ask, still confused.

"You okay, man?" Sawyer asks, looking at me with concern.

"Yeah, just, you have three brothers."

"I have four. I picked one of them to raise my daughter if I were to die."

"Me?" I ask incredulously. There's no way he picked me when he has Dallas, Liam, and Carter. I had resigned myself to never being an uncle or having kids to love on and be there for that weren't mine.

"When I have kids someday, you're going to be the best uncle. I'm going to force you to move into my house with me and my husband just so they can know you like I do."

"Are you insane? That had better be twenty years down the road, Lena. You just turned eighteen."

"Yeah, but you're already my favorite person in the world, and the best brother, you're obviously going to be the best uncle, too."

"You're crazy. Has anyone told you that?"

"Oh, whatever. Where do you think I get it from?"

"Sure as shit not me."

"Promise me that when I'm a mom, you won't leave my side and you'll be just as awesome to my kids as you've been to me."

"I'm obviously going to be way better to them 'cause they'll be way cooler than you," I tease because I can't help it.

. . .

Grace stirs in Kinsey's arms, and she bounces her slightly to soothe her at the same time her hand reaches out and touches my forearm. It immediately steadies me, bringing forth a gentle calmness that I need in this moment, grounding me, pulling me back into the present.

I look at Kinsey, who is looking back at me with a huge smile on her face before glancing down at Grace, bundled in her arms. Sawyer chose me? His brothers are some of the best men I've ever met, and he chose me?

When I look back at Kinsey, I'm slammed with a massive amount of guilt that makes my stomach turn. He'd feel so fucking differently if he knew what's been going on between me and his sister. Even if we haven't fully crossed any boundaries, the intent is there. The sexual tension between us is palpable, and the connection we have is strong. Fuck. The realization of what a piece of shit I am hits me full force, and I feel an immense amount of shame. This was the wake-up call I needed.

"You okay, big guy?" Kinsey asks, and I nod my head in reply before turning back to Sawyer.

"You sure this is what you want?"

"It is. We've talked about it for months, and we both kept coming back to the same decision. You two. We know that Grace would be taken care of and loved for the rest of her life just as we would love her. We know you both would give her everything she needed plus some."

"Nothing is going to happen to you, though," I say, when we all know that isn't a sure thing.

"You never know. And we want to be sure."

"I don't know what to say. I'm honored, brother," I confess honestly.

"Me too. I love her so much, and I'm honored you would pick me," Kinsey adds.

Ivy speaks up next, "We love you both so much, and you're two of our favorite people—equally. We needed to ask you before all hell breaks loose when everyone else finds out."

Kinsey starts to laugh next to me, throwing her head back and making me smile. Her laugh is infectious, so sweet and pure.

"I cannot wait to hear Dallas freak out, holy shit. That's going to be amazing. You prepared, big guy? Pretty sure he may attempt to murder you in your sleep to get the spot."

"He can bring it. He knows what a punch from me feels like; he had a nice shiner for a few weeks. I'm not giving this role up for anything."

"It's still going to be hilarious to watch him flip out. Carter probably will too. He loves Grace and Charlotte."

"They can take it up with me. They'll get over their shit, they still get to be her uncles," Sawyer affirms.

With my heart in my damn throat, I spend the next few hours hanging out with them, wondering how the hell I started to fall for Sawyer's sister, and how the hell to close off those feelings for good. I can't do that to him, and I certainly can't do that to her.

Instead of going straight home after being at Sawyer and Ivy's, I swing by Rogue to check on things. As I walk up to my locked office door, I see two books leaning against the bottom of it. A smirk toys on my lips as my heavy boots clamber against the hard floor of my shop. I unlock my office door and grab the two books before opening it. My head is spinning as I read the titles. One is the one I left in front of her door, and the other is one she left for me with a note sticking out of the top in the same way I left for her.

Reid,

This one made me fall in love with romance. She's trying so hard to find herself, but everything is preventing her from spreading her wings. In him, she finds her strength to be free and so, so much more.

Chapters 17, 23, and 35.

Enjoy.
Kins

Fuck. This damn woman is going to be the death of me. After checking on everything and grabbing my tablet to work on a design for a client, I lock up and head back outside toward my bike with Kinsey's book tucked into my leather jacket. I should work tonight, but I know I won't. I'll be lost to the words Kinsey chose for me to read. I know this can't go on any longer, but curiosity has the best of me. This pull I feel to this woman is fierce, but I need to make sure that we stay in the friend zone.

For everyone's sake.

CHAPTER 9

Kinsey

THE RAIN BEATS HEAVILY AGAINST THE LARGE WINDOW of my apartment. I love the rain, and we don't get nearly enough of it here. People often mistake Washington State as being the rainiest place in the country, but they're confusing it with our constant cloud cover. Rain gives a perfect excuse to snuggle up with cozy blankets, coffee, and a book, which is exactly what I've been doing all evening.

It was just what I needed to rest my brain from thoughts of the giant, sexy man that have consumed me lately. I sit up from my spot curled up on my bed, surrounded by pillows, pulling my EarPods out, when a loud noise echoes from downstairs.

I'm startled back to reality, pulled from the book Ivy begged me to read, that I clearly cannot come up for air from. I pull out the other one, set my Kindle down, and listen, unsure if I was hearing things or not, but then it happens again, the distinct sound of something crashing downstairs.

Could Reid have tripped on something? Knocked something over? He doesn't typically tattoo on Tuesdays, but maybe he had a late client? Wanting to know if he's okay, I throw a pink tank top over the sports bra I've been lounging in and gently pull open the interior door that leads downstairs to the back of the shop.

Creeping down the stairs with my baseball bat, I hear more slamming around, and fear starts to settle in. All of the air evaporates around me, everything slowing down and moving in slow motion. I'm not prepared for the sight I find as I slink around the corner. My hands shake like a leaf as I take in the sight in front of me. Rogue is destroyed. Furniture flipped, his artwork torn off the walls. I'm suddenly deeply regretting not calling anyone first and coming down to check this out myself. I know better.

My heart stutters, then lurches into overdrive, beating so rapidly it almost hurts. I should turn and run, I should go back upstairs and call for help, but for some reason, fear holds me in its clutches, rooting me to the spot. My ears pound, my pulse a steady thump between them, blocking out any other sound.

I try to grapple with what's happening. Two men continue to destroy the shop, kicking things over, tossing around paperwork and products. They are both wearing battered old T-shirts with thick leather vests over them, a bright red wolf on the back with words I can't make out from here.

"Who do we have here?" one of the men says as he leers at me, causing terror to slither down my spine. He has creepy fucking eyes and a shaved head, a missing front tooth, and a light dusting of facial hair. The way his eyes travel up and down my body clears my head of the fog, and I know without a doubt, I've never been more scared in my life.

I try to grasp onto the reality of what's happening as I sway slightly on my bare feet. This can't be happening. I'm in downtown Aspen Ridge for fuck's sake, there's no way no one will hear all the banging around, and all I need to do is scream and someone will surely come. Right?

"Who the fuck are you?" I snap, doing my best to turn my terror into rage, even if it's only half of what I'm currently feeling. Call it pure shock, adrenaline, or stupidity, but I'm struggling to grasp the fact that this is happening right now—in Aspen Ridge, no less.

"Ooh, we got a snarky one, Roach."

"Roach? What kind of fucked-up name is that? Your parents must hate you."

Roach just chuckles as he walks toward me. I hold up the baseball bat, ready to swing if he gets too close.

"Aww, what are you gonna do with that, sexy? Don't want you to hurt yourself with it. Why don't you put it down and let me and Slug here make it up to you."

A deep, dark laugh bubbles out of me, half sardonic, half fucking petrified of these two creeps touching me in any capacity.

"I don't think so. How about you get the fuck out of here?"

"Why don't you tell us where he is, then, huh?"

"Who?" I ask, playing dumb. It's obvious they're looking for Reid if they're inside his shop, destroying the place.

"Rogue."

Rogue?

"We're standing inside Rogue, you fucking greasy-ass nut jobs. Get the hell out before the police arrive."

The one who looks like he hasn't seen the effects of a shower in this century looks back at me with his big, bug eyes and tsks. "I don't think so. We need Rogue. Boss' orders. And we don't piss off the prez."

This gets more and more confusing as it goes on, but I'm doing everything I can to fight the adrenaline coursing through me right now. I've got this. They'll leave. They have to.

"Whelp. Sorry to disappoint, but 'Rogue' isn't here right now. Try again, oh, I don't know. Never! Get out!"

"What is she on about, Roach?"

"I don't fucking know. Let's take her with us. If she's here, she's probably important to Rogue. It'll force him out of his hellhole."

Oh fuck.

I grip the bat tighter between my hands until I'm sure my knuckles are white. The next moment happens in a blur. "Roach" lunges for me, and I swing the bat as hard as I can, but he expects it, his hands ready, grabbing it and yanking. I jerk forward but release the bat before I'm pulled into his arms. "Slug" takes that as his opening to come at me from the side, but I'm ready for him. I pull back my arm and channel Sawyer with everything I have, praying like hell it's enough. I connect with his face in a sickening crunch. Immediate pain travels through my knuckles up my wrist, forearm, and shoulder. I've never hit someone bare-knuckled before. It hurts so bad I didn't register that the blood-curdling crunch came from the sicko's nose and not my hand until blood pours from his face and he howls in pain.

"She broke my fuckin' nose!"

"Get the fuck over it and help me get this bitch!"

This time I do scream, knowing the chances have to be high that someone is out walking, leaving The Night Owl, on a stroll, fucking something—anything—to help me get out of this.

"I'm gonna enjoy making you pay for this, you stupid whore," Slug hisses, his voice nasally and strained. He spits the blood draining into his mouth in my direction, and I jump backward and scream again. The one clearly in charge here, Roach, tosses the bat to the side, forcing it to clatter against the metal trays already knocked over on the floor.

"You've really made a mistake here. We could have made this good for you. Easy on you. But now you're gonna pay. After Prez is done with you, he's gonna feed you to his wolves, and we're gonna enjoy tearing you apart. Such a shame. You're a pretty little thing. How many cocks you think she can take before she splits in two?"

Bile churns in my stomach, and I nearly dry heave. How the fuck do I get out of this? I can't let them leave with me.

Roach prowls in my direction, and I hold my fists up in front of me, ready to fight back. I'm not going to make this easy on him.

"You're no use to us dead. But that doesn't mean I can't bruise you up a bit before we take you."

As soon as he's within striking distance, I take my shot, pulling my punch back and letting it fly. He expects it and dodges out of the way at the same time he strikes me, the back of his hand hitting the side of my face so hard it sends me careening to the floor. The hit stings, but I use my position to my advantage and kick as hard as I can between his legs. Roach drops to his knees, his hands cupping his balls. I kick again, both feet to his chest, knocking him off balance and onto his back. Slug moves in quickly, but I'm on my feet and running to the door as fast as I can.

Five more steps.

Four.

Three.

Just two more.

Just as I'm an arm's length away from the first door, hands grab my hair and yank me backward so forcefully, I'm positive he ripped out a chunk. I scream again as my back hits a hard chest. I knock my head back as hard as I can muster, barely connecting with what feels like a chin.

"I don't fucking think so, you dumb bitch," he says as bloody spittle splatters against the back of my neck and shoulder. I dry heave while twisting and turning, trying to break his hold. He lifts me backward, picking my feet off the ground as I kick and scream.

"Get her to shut the fuck up! Someone's gonna hear us!"

Calloused, filthy hands cover my mouth, the smell of fuel and grease assaulting my airways as panic takes over, and I work to pull air into my lungs. Fuck, is this how I die? The fight starts to drain out of me as he carries me further into the room, away from my escape.

"Let's get her to the truck."

"How? She won't shut the fuck up."

"We'll make her."

Roach walks over to me with his hands on his belt buckle, starting to undo it as my eyes widen in terror and my heart sinks into the pit of my stomach.

"You're gonna behave or I'll fuck your throat so hard you can't speak for a week. Do you understand me?"

I nod my head yes, and ever so slowly, Slug releases the hold around my mouth, allowing me to take deep lungfuls of breath.

"If you put that thing anywhere near me, so help me God, I will bite it off and ensure you'll never do it to anyone again."

His hands drag down the side of my face and the column of my throat in a slow caress before he grabs my tank top and rips it in half, pulling it off my body and leaving me in just a sports bra and gym shorts. That finally pulls up the contents of my stomach. I lurch forward and throw up all over him and the floor.

"Fuck!" Slug yells just as his fist flies. The blunt force of his punch connects with the side of my head, and I barely have time to register the pain before everything goes dark.

reid

My phone blares from the coffee table while I'm reading, caught up in a book Kinsey chose for me. The sound has me tossing the book to the floor in a hurry to pick up my phone and view what's going on. The secondary alarm to Rogue was tripped, which means the first one was disabled. Worry prickles in my veins as I do my best to remain calm.

I quickly bring up my security system, moving from camera to camera to find the feed cut. I won't be able to pull the CCTV footage until I get on my laptop, but I feel deep down that something isn't right.

My heart starts to race as my head jumps to the worst-case scenario. For too long, I've convinced myself that I'm safe in Aspen Ridge, that no evil will come knocking on my door here, that I could somehow manage to keep my two lives separate.

I should have known better.

I close out of the app as I bring up Kinsey's phone number, hoping like hell it was just her and everything is fine. If there was a power outage downtown, I have a backup generator that should immediately kick on to keep the security system up and running. Unless she managed to do something, there's no reason it should be down.

Who am I fucking kidding? What could she have done to trip the secondary alarm?

I pull on my leather boots, not bothering to lace them up as I race to my room, using my thumb to unlock my safe and reach for my gun. I grab the magazine, checking that it's loaded, before sliding it into place with an audible click. I call Kinsey a second time, cursing under my breath as I throw on my leather jacket and race out my front door, not bothering to lock it up.

I need to get to her.

The bike revs to life under me as I peel out of Lupine Lane. Fuck living out in the middle of nowhere and not being able to get to her as quickly as I need to. I top one hundred as I take the winding roads toward downtown, the roads slick from the rainstorm that just passed through. My heart pounds louder than my engine, blood rushing between my ears. If anything happens to her . . . Fear grips my heart, memories of Lena flashing through my mind. Images of her bruised and battered body, the blood, her cold, marred skin . . . fuck. I can't let Kinsey meet the same fate. She has to be safe. This is just my fear talking. She's safe upstairs or out with her friends. The alarm was tripped. There's an explanation for it that doesn't result in Kinsey being harmed—or worse. But even as I try to convince myself otherwise, something deep and dark inside me roars to life. This doesn't feel like nothing.

I take the fifteen-minute drive in seven, pushing my bike to its limit and blowing through every stop sign on my way. I skid my bike to a stop, kicking the stand down and jumping off. My heart is in my throat as I race up the two steps and wrench open the door to my shop, finding the lock broken. I pull my gun free from behind my back, cocking it to load one in the chamber. I ease further into the building, listening for any indication that she's still here, or anyone else that shouldn't be. Fear clutches me in a vise grip so strong I gasp for air, nerves freezing my veins as cold dread washes through me.

"Kinsey!" I yell as I step into Rogue, my gun held

outstretched toward the ground. The scene in front of me trips up my feet as my boots crunch over shattered glass. The shop is totaled, but it's not my ruined equipment that has me halting. It's the fucking *blood*. A lot of it.

"Kins!" I yell again as I take the steps three at a time to the loft, crashing through her door, the wood splintering as it bangs against the wall, terrified of finding her here dead but knowing death may be wanted if she's been taken.

I race through the small studio, checking under her bed and coming up empty. Her phone is on the counter, her shoes at the front door. She wouldn't have left without her phone; I know her.

"FUCK!" I roar, jogging back down the steps. I hold my phone in the palm of my hand, quickly weighing my options. I know I should call Sawyer right now, but I also know how it feels to be in his position. He's home with his wife and baby, and there's nothing he can do right now. I can't. Fuck. I'll get her back. I'll call him after I get the help I need. The only people who can help me figure this out.

I shove my phone into my pocket, returning my gun behind my back. Just as I'm about to jog out the door, a flash of pink catches my eye, pinned to the wall with a knife. If I needed any more confirmation that someone took her, I got it. A bloodied piece of paper is stuck to Kinsey's pink tank top. I wrench it free, reading the scribbled words.

You weren't home, so we took a new pretty toy instead. You know what we want. Give it to us and you can have it back. Just can't promise it won't be used up nice and good first.

"FUCK!" I scream, the noise deafening, rattling the windows and echoing off the walls. I'm on my bike before I register I've left my shop and started it. My headlights lead the way out of Aspen Ridge and into the quiet stillness of the night to the only place I know that can help. The only people who can help. The reason the sweetest girl in the world was just stolen from right under my nose.

Hell's Heathens.

My brothers.

I'll kill every single one who was involved in taking her, I vow to myself. And I've never meant anything more. Lena may never feel the warmth of the sun on her skin again, laugh, or feel love or be loved in return, but I'll die before Kinsey doesn't. She deserves fucking everything, and I will be sent to hell ten times over before her life is taken from her.

An hour later, the moon high in the sky, I skid to a stop in front of the tall gates of the clubhouse. The gates don't open right away, which pisses me the fuck off. I should have called our president on my way in, but my head is too messed up to think clearly. Every minute they have her is too fucking long. I have to get her back. Now.

"Let me the fuck in or there will be hell to pay!"

A skinny-looking prospect who can't be much older than eighteen hops down off the crow's nest.

"We're on lockdown!" he says, giving me an attitude he's gonna regret. "Prez' orders, dipshit. No outsiders. No visitors."

"I'm a fucking patched member!" I scream, grabbing his cut and shaking him, shoving him against the chain-link fence, pulling my fist back, ready to make him swallow his teeth.

"Where's your fuckin' cut then?" he says in a snarky-ass tone as if I'm not about to break his goddamn face.

"Whoa! Rogue! Hold up, dude. He's new!" a familiar voice

yells from above. I look up to find one of our members peering down at us.

"Open the fucking gates, Rolo!" I yell up to him before turning my attention back on the weasel in front of me, currently lighting a cigarette like he doesn't have a care in the world. "Seems like you've got an angel tonight, prospect. You won't be so lucky next time." I'll be making sure I'm present at his vote. I don't forgive or forget, and he'll pay one way or another for wasting precious goddamn time.

The gates finally open, and I hop back on my bike, spinning the tires on the gravel and flying up the road to the clubhouse. Our club president, Chaos, and our VP, Sin, are walking out of the main house as I'm jumping off my bike and heading in their direction.

"Rolo just buzzed us, what's the goddamn emergency, Rogue? You okay? You look like you've seen a ghost."

"Someone broke into Rogue. Destroyed the place. They took someone important. She was living upstairs. Is. She is living upstairs. Fuck!" I yell as I run my hands through my long hair.

"Kinsey?" Sin clarifies, and I nod my head in answer. "Shit, man."

"Get inside, Rogue," Chaos demands as he turns on his heels. "Church!"

Sin and I are hot on his tail as other leadership members file in. Chaos pulls open the large wooden doors that lead to our meeting room in the center of our clubhouse. This room is sacred to us. You don't enter without an invite. It's where all our important club business is handled. A large, custom-built table sits in the center of the room, the Hell's Heathen symbol burned into the middle of it—a skull with a slanted crown, a dagger slicing straight through the top and coming out the bottom.

I stay standing and push my hair back, only for the damp strands to fall back into my face. Fuck, I'm goddamn sweating. Sin takes his seat to the right of where Chaos will sit at the head of the table, our sergeant at arms, Malice, sits on the other side, Cash and Wrath take their seats next, the table filling out. Two other members, Rolo and Noose—who steps in as road captain when I'm not around—walk in together, looking around the room, assessing everyone.

Chaos takes a seat and nods at me, but I don't sit down. I continue to pace, wondering what the hell they're doing to Kinsey right now. Wondering where she is, what she's feeling. The fucking terror she's feeling right now. If they hurt her in any way . . . fuck. I can't let this be her fate. If I can save her, if I can get to her in time, I'll spend the rest of my life making sure she's safe, that she never spends another moment being scared again.

"Sit the fuck down, Rogue. Don't make me say it again."

Relenting, I yank out a chair harder than I should and force myself to comply, even if every fiber of my being is telling me to get back on my bike and not stop until she's safe in my arms.

"What happened? And don't leave anything out."

After forcing a steadying breath, I give them everything I have.

"Around 10 p.m., the secondary alarm was tripped at Rogue. I have someone renting the space above the shop, and I immediately called her as I grabbed my gun and headed into town. She didn't answer. When I got there, the lock on the back door had been busted, the interior of my shop was destroyed and there was . . . fuck." I pause for a moment, running my hand through my beard and letting my eyes fall closed. "There was a good amount of blood pooled by the back door and some more in the center of the room." I crack my neck from side to side, flexing my fingers, itching to get out there and get her back. "Her shirt was pinned to the wall by the door with this note," I grind those words out through clenched teeth as I drop the crumbled piece of paper onto the table. Sin grabs it first, opening it up and scanning the contents before handing it to Chaos.

"Rogue, I know you don't want to hear this, but if there was as much blood as you're saying, there's a chance—"

He doesn't get to finish his sentence. I stand, the chair I was occupying flipping back behind me, my fists slamming down on the table. "Don't! Don't you fucking say it!"

Chaos's eyes narrow at me as Sin whistles, insinuating that I just crossed a huge line. But I don't give a shit. She is not gone, and I'm going to get her back.

"Out! Everyone out!" Chaos says, his voice eerily calm and collected. Members stand, pushing in their chairs and leaving the room. When the last person is gone and the doors fall closed, leaving the room to just me and my president, I take a deep breath, prepared to do whatever is needed to get her back, even if that means fighting him on it. I'll take him head-on if I have to, but I'll die before I abandon Kinsey.

Camden runs a tight ship here, but he's the most level-headed, confident, secure one out of all of us. His ability to keep his cool while everything around him burns to the ground is what makes him the perfect man for this job. So when I meet his face, I'm not expecting to be met with anger in return for disrespecting him in front of our committee. He may not take any shit as Chaos, but Camden will let some things slide when he knows they're warranted.

"Is she yours?"

Fuck, is she? She can't be. Kinsey doesn't belong to anyone. Her brothers have made sure of that. But, hell, I want her to be mine, even though I shouldn't.

"She's someone important," I settle on.

"To who?"

"Me. She's the sister of someone close to me."

"But is she *yours*, Reid?"

"If you're asking if I'm gonna make her my old lady, *Camden*, then no. I can't. I won't. But I have to save her. If we had been faster, maybe we could have . . . maybe we could have saved Lena and Lucas."

"We can't change the past, Reid. We also aren't prepared for another battle with these motherfuckers so soon after the hits we took during the last one."

"I'll go alone then." I'm fully prepared to do so.

"Lucky for you, we're brothers and you don't have to."

I release a huge sigh of relief. Camden and I share an experience—and loss—that no one should have to go through. I hope like hell between the two of us, we can make sure Sawyer and his brothers never have to feel what Camden and I do. *That I don't have to feel it again.*

Camden gives me a nod in understanding; we're a unified front. Almost as though his personality is split, I watch as his mask is replaced, forcing Camden back down, replacing him with the stony, strong president we have leading us. Chaos pushes the doors open and loudly barks orders to the members waiting for them.

Committee members move back into church, taking their seats and waiting for Chaos to speak. I know he has my back, but we don't go into a fight without the votes of everyone on the committee. We're a team, and we always fight as one.

"Rogue's woman was taken," Chaos states, and a growl works its way up from my chest at the sound of that. He's an asshole for calling her that after I just got done telling him she wasn't. Chaos shoots me a look that conveys for me to shut the fuck up. "It's safe to assume, based on the note and the hit, that it was the Iron Wolves. So we vote."

I wait with nervous breath as each member goes around the table. Wrath readies himself to count the votes, but it's not needed. Every single one of them votes in favor of us going in to retrieve Kinsey.

I release a deep, pent-up breath of relief. But now, we're faced with gathering information on where the hell she is, and time is ticking at a rapid rate. Every moment she isn't with me, she's experiencing a fear so real I would give my life to keep her from it.

"What do we know?" Chaos demands, his voice laced with the urgency I feel.

Malice speaks up first. As our sergeant at arms, he handles

security and internal and external threats. He may be completely unhinged, but that's just one of the multifaceted pieces of him.

"Wrath and I were able to tail the asshole from the house using CCTV footage and the tracker I put on his bike. There's no way it's their compound, but looks like it's one of their hideouts like the one we found the last bunch of bastards at a few weeks ago."

"You mean where you skinned one of them alive?" Wrath interrupts.

"How many times do I have to tell you? I didn't skin 'em!" he argues. "His blood just sprayed out of him with the force of a geyser. Scared the shit out of me."

"Nothing scares you, liar," Noose adds.

"This did, brother," Malice responds with a shiver. "Was about to call my priest for an exorcism but then I thought, eh, it would be easier just to kill 'em, his soul be damned."

"Good call, Malice, proud of you, little buddy," Noose taunts and just as Malice stands and flicks out his knife, his head cocking to the side and his big obsidian pupils going wild, Chaos slams his fist down on the table.

"Shut the fuck up both of you! Sit your ass down, Mal! What else do we need to know?"

Thankful Chaos got this back under control before I slit someone's throat, I perch my forearms on the heavy table and listen to Malice.

"It's an abandoned garage on the outskirts of town. They're staying right inside our boundaries. The garage is located in the old industrial park that teenagers fuck around at. It's long since been forgotten, so it's a pretty solid spot if you want to fly under the radar. CCTV is still solid for the majority of the property, but there's a blacked-out section. So they got someone to fuck with it."

"Wrath, what can you do?" Chaos asks, turning his eyes to him.

"I can get us in close, but then we're going in blind. I don't got their numbers or their security. I'll cut what I can, but they could see us coming a mile away."

"That gonna change anything, Prez?" Sin asks, beating me to the question. We don't go in blind anywhere if we can help it. While we all understand the risks of every run, we never want casualties of our own brothers if they can be prevented.

"No."

"Alright, Wrath, Malice, work your magic. Noose, you're gonna lead this one."

"What the fuck?" I spit, getting another stern look from Chaos.

"You're not in the right headspace. You'll ride in formation, Rogue, but you're not road captain for this run. Trust us. We'll get her back."

I know Chaos and Sin are right, I can't keep us all running tight and safe if my head is only focused on Kinsey's safety, and I'm glad we have the unconventional setup of having two Road Captains, and that Noose and I get along so well. I trust him. All of them.

"Everyone have all the info they need?" We all nod our heads, and then it's what our president thrives in . . . chaos.

Everyone moves quickly, Malice packing duffel bags of guns and ammo, passing them out like a peddler on a street corner while I jog up the stairs to the bedroom Chaos insists I keep here to make the phone call I'm fucking dreading.

He picks up on the first ring despite the late hour.

"What's wrong?" he asks in a hushed tone. There's rustling, and I can imagine he's sneaking out of bed so he doesn't wake up Ivy by talking.

"I need you to stay calm and trust that I've got it under control."

"Fucking talk, Reid, or I'll kill you next time I see you."

"I'm at the clubhouse. Someone came for me a few hours ago. They hit Rogue and found Kinsey."

His roar could shatter glass, my blood curdling from the force of agony and violence that it promises. Of all the news I could deliver to my best friend, I never could have imagined it would be this.

"They took her, brother. I'm so fuckin' sorry. But she's strong and I'm gonna get her back."

"I'm coming. You fuckin' wait for me, Reid! Do you understand? Wait! Let me get my brothers." The desperation in his tone nearly breaks me, and I have to swallow down the emotion caught in my throat. I have to stay strong for all of us.

"There's no time, Sawyer. Stay put. I got the backing of the club; we're all goin' in together. I can't let any more time pass with her in their grasp. I can't—"

"FUCK! You know where she is?"

"We do," I reply with as much conviction in my voice as I can muster, even though I know nothing is a sure thing. "I'm getting her back, Sawyer. You have my word."

"You fucking bring my sister home, Reid. Bring her fucking home!" His voice breaks, and the fear it's laced with matches my own. How can this be fucking happening right now? How did we get here?

There's only one answer, and I'll have to live with it the rest of my life.

Me.

We're rolling out in under thirty minutes, the collective, loud roar and rumble of our bikes echoing around us, my body humming with energy, each member feeding off each other, ready for battle, and ready to get Kinsey out of the hellhole they've taken her to.

We had better make it in time. Failing twice isn't an option.

kinsey

My head lolls to the side as voices stir me from sleep. Pain spreads through my skull as I try to open my eyes against the assault of the harsh light above me. The pain jabs, sharp and unrelenting, like someone's taking an icepick to my temples. Rough rope digs into my wrists as I stretch my fingers behind me, trying to work blood into the extremities. My jaw aches as I move it from side to side, the events of what happened at Rogue rushing over me.

I squint against the light, trying to take in my surroundings. The sharp tang of decay assaults my nose, mildew, mold, and filth, forcing bile to turn over in my empty stomach. I can't believe these assholes took me like I'm a possession. Fear skitters down my spine, and I dig my nails into the palms of my hands. I can't believe this is happening.

"The fuck happened to your face?" an unfamiliar, deep, menacing voice booms through the room.

"Tripped." That voice I recognize. Slug. The piece of shit.

"Liar. Too much of a pussy to admit that a woman broke your nose?" I yell.

"Shut the fuck up!" he spews. But it's not his words that have me falling to the side, my hands curling over my stomach as I dry heave and gasp for air. I barely have time to brace for the second hard kick to my stomach as he yells at me.

"Get the fuck out, Slug! I'll take care of our new guest," the unknown voice snaps.

"Prez said he wants to see her. See if she's worth his time."

"Well, what are you waiting for? Call him, you idiot!"

I hear the faint sound of a video call being made through the blood rushing between my ears. I know I need to pull myself together if I'm going to survive this, and that means I need to be smart. Smarter than running my mouth to a bunch of criminals. Slug squats down next to me, grabbing the back of my hair roughly and jerking me upright.

"Do you have her?" a voice comes through the speaker. It's slimy and all fucking wrong.

"She's right here, Prez. She's a pretty one," he says as he licks the side of my face. I can't control the dry heave that erupts out of me, strong and unyielding, the noise causing him to jerk my head away from him quickly. "But she's fuckin' feisty. She'll need to be broken in."

Slug jerks my head again, this time holding the camera in front of my face.

"What do you want from me?" I ask, the words coming out in a trembling stutter.

"Oh, you are a pretty one. You were at Rogue's while he wasn't, which means you're important. Welcome to your nightmare, pretty. I'm going to enjoy breaking you. I'll film the entire thing to send to him so he can watch as I stretch your cunt with my fist and batter your sweet body."

Oh dear god.

"Wh-whyy are you doing this?"

"Because. He took something from me. And now I'm going to take something from him. Slug! Don't let anyone touch her. I'm going to enjoy this one. I'll feed her to you all once I've had enough. Wait for things to calm down, I'll text you when it's clear for movement, then you'll bring my new little pet to me."

"Got it, Prez."

They hang up the call and stand, looking down at me like they're contemplating actually listening to the orders they were just given. I curl into myself, wishing like hell I had more clothes on.

"He said not to touch her," says the one too far away for me to read his name on his vest.

"She broke my fuckin' nose, so I'm gonna fuck with her."

"You heard the rule, Prez wants to break this one in, then we get a turn till there's nothin' left of her."

"You disgusting pigs. You're not going to touch me!" I scream.

"Want to make a bet, darlin? We're gonna take turns fuckin' that snatch between your legs until you're overflowin' with cum." His hand reaches out, roughly gripping my chin and forcing my mouth open. I try to fight against his hold but he's too fucking strong. He wrenches my mouth open as tears prick my eyes. I will not give these motherfuckers the satisfaction of seeing me cry. They will not break me. No matter what.

"You're gonna be our cum slut. We're gonna fuck every hole. Over and over and over again, and that's after I use my knife and cut up your flawless body. I like my whores dirty and withering in pain while I fuck 'em." His voice is eerily calm, like he's telling me about his trip to the grocery store, not how I was about to be brutally and violently raped by their club.

The sadistic, maniacal look on his face sends the graveness of my situation to take over just as he spits into my mouth, quickly jamming my mouth shut and plugging my nose. I shake my head against his hold, his greasy hands rough against my skin. I dry heave, hard. Gagging as my stomach turns, bile rising to the surface. "Swallow, you dirty slut. This is the least of what you'll be swallowing as soon as you're given to us. You know what it's like to be starved, darlin'?" he drawls as I struggle to breathe. I swallow hard, getting it over with and hoping like hell he isn't about to suffocate me right here. After a moment, he finally releases me, his hand dropping to his side, my head falling back against the headboard as I gasp to fill my lungs with precious oxygen.

"That's what Prez does. He starves his pack. So when we're finally fed, we're rabid, ready to devour whatever is put in front of us. You're our next meal, and some of us haven't eaten in weeks." He licks his lips in a disgusting display that churns my stomach again, before he turns and walks out of the room, the other man following behind. I don't realize I'm crying until the wetness drips down my chin and neck. This can't be the end for me, locked up in some crumbling building to be raped and beaten? Nothing makes any sense. Why were they at Rogue? What the hell were they looking for?

My mind drifts to Reid, and I immediately feel a wave of longing. How long before someone realizes I'm gone? How will they even know where to look for me? Questions rattle me as fear clutches its nails in deep.

How the hell am I going to survive this?

reid

WE RIDE TOGETHER IN A SHOW OF FORCE THROUGH Amberwood. A lethal combination of anger and fear pumps through my veins in heavy doses. I've been on plenty of runs over the last fourteen years as a member and road sergeant of Hell's Heathens, but only two have made me this out of my mind.

I do what I can to push Sawyer's pain-laced voice out of my head, trying not to lose myself to thinking about what could be happening to Kinsey right now. The way they cut up the dancers at our club with people right on the other side of the door would make a grown man sick to his stomach, and they've got my girl alone in the middle of an abandoned industrial park with no one to hear her screams.

My girl.

Jesus, I love the sound of that. But she'll never be my girl, and I need to remember that. There's no her and I. Especially not now. Once again, I've put someone I care about in the hands of some of the most evil scum of the earth. I should have made sure we erased every single one of them from existence, and because of my failure to do that, the Iron Wolves are amassing numbers and strength, pushing back against us after all this time.

I won't make the same mistake twice.

Half a mile out from the garage, we slow to a crawl, slipping onto the shoulder and pulling to a stop. The industrial park is surrounded by a rusted chain-link fence, with newly installed CCTV cameras. If we needed any sign that this was the place they're hunkered down in, we just got it. No one's been over to this shithole since these businesses closed down years ago. It's no compound, but it's definitely a hideout.

"Wrath, can you get all the cameras down?"

"Already on it."

A boom of thunder claps overhead, making a crew of fifteen bikers wince. The rain starts to crash down on us a moment later like a bad fucking omen, and I curse under my breath.

"This is good. We'll have the noise working to our advantage," Chaos reassures.

Several prospects pull out bolt cutters and get to work cutting into the fence. My boots sink into the sodden ground, the stench of wet, damp earth filling my nose as I walk up closer to the fence, looking out into the dark night. I'm so fucking close. Kinsey is in there somewhere, and I know she's alive. I feel it in my bones.

She's strong.

My little fighter.

I'll heal whatever condition she's in. I'll get her through this. I'm the only one who can.

Chaos steps up next to me, his back straight and solid as he always is, but he's calmer, his voice low and laced with concern that is all Camden.

"You ready?"

"Yep," I reply.

"You can hang back, I'll go in."

"Not a fuckin' chance in hell, Cam."

"You prepared for the worst?" His question grates on me, sharp and unyielding, but I know he's not wrong to ask. I just can't let my fucking mind go to that dark place. She's alive. I can fucking feel it in my bones.

"Can we ever prepare for that shit? You know it as well as I do."

"Together?"

"Together."

And then his mask is put back in place as he spins on his heels. I take a second to pull my hair back in a bun, wanting it out of my face as the rain soaks it.

"Garage is on the southwest side of the park, but we don't know how spread out they are. We're going to clear every building as we work our way in. Malice, take half the group and go east, Sin, you take the other. Start on the west. Rogue and I will go center, we'll meet in the middle at the garage. Kill anyone who so much as breathes, but do it as silently as you can. If you find innocents, get them to stay quiet. We'll get them out after we recover Rogue's woman."

There's a brief moment of collective agreement before Chaos speaks up again, pulling his gun from its holster and nodding for everyone to get through the fence. "Head out!"

Everyone moves quickly, half our members going left and the other right, while Chaos and I stick to the center, watching each other's backs as we walk through the decaying land. Burned-out vehicles, crumbling buildings with busted-out windows, and trash littered everywhere make it all look more like a war zone than any part of Amberwood. It's no wonder they chose this place.

The flashlights illuminate a path for us as we come up to the first building, a crumbling cement shack with no clear indication of what it was prior to its collapse. Chaos nods his head as he takes the lead, holding his gun low with a flashlight in front of him. I clear the sides, checking behind us one last time before following him in. I'm eerily calm, adrenaline finally taking over and allowing me to get through this with a level head as I follow him inside. There are only two rooms, and we clear them quickly, no sign of anyone being there in a long time.

Flicking our lights off, we creep through the deserted roads to the next building. I hear the soft murmur of voices floating on the wind and grab Chaos' thick leather cut to pull him back, putting my pointer finger over my mouth to signal him to be quiet, then tapping my ear twice.

We listen, and the unmistakable grunt of someone turns my veins to ice. I follow the sound to the other side of the building, to find a burly man with a bloated gut and balding head brace himself against the wall with his pants around his knees, jerking his tiny dick in his fist.

I move quickly, pulling out my knife and getting the jump on him before he even has time to release his puny cock. I tower over him, covering his mouth and pressing the blade of the knife to his throat, just enough so that blood starts to pool.

"If you so much as breathe too loudly, I'll slit your fuckin' throat right here. Nod if you understand."

The bastard nods in agreement, making this way too fucking easy. It's clear they're patching anybody with no real give a fuck about loyalty. Numbers don't mean shit if you don't have loyalty. Chaos moves in front of him, pressing a knife so low I can't see where, but by the way the man jerks and whimpers, I'm guessing he's just discovered how the pointy edge of a knife feels against your balls.

"Where's the girl?"

So fucking slowly, I move my fingers off his mouth to let him talk.

"Wh-what girl?"

"The girl that was taken. Light brown hair, tiny thing. Where the fuck is she?"

"Prez wants her as his pet. They're holdin' her inside the garage."

Exactly where we thought she'd be.

"How many are with her?"

"I dunno. A few? She's a feisty one. Fucked up a few of 'em when they brought her in, so they're watchin' her close. You ain't gonna fuck her. We don't get 'em until Prez is done with 'em. He's gotta loosen 'em up for us."

I can't listen to another word. I slit his throat from ear to ear quickly, blood gurgling from the thick open wound at his neck and spilling down his front. Chaos jerks away, shaking out his hand and giving me a look that says I'll pay for that later.

"Let's move," I tell him, already following the building to get to her. My boots clomp through the mud, the rain barely a trickle now, and I do my best to stay quiet while walking as quickly as possible with Chaos hot on my tail.

Small floodlights beam overhead, and I feel it in my gut that she's there. I'm so fucking close I can practically feel her warm body heat seeping into mine. I just need to get to her. Chaos' comms go off in a low hum, Sin's voice coming through the speaker.

"We're clear. Took out a few stragglers. She's inside the old garage. Looks like there's a dozen or so scattered in there with a few hanging in the front."

"Malice check-in."

"What's taking you two so long? We're outside the building, ready to go in and party."

"Wait for us. We go in together," Chaos demands. We move quickly, catching up with our brothers on the south side of the building.

"Their security is shit," Malice says as we arrive.

"Just like the last place. They don't seem to have a care in the world."

"Well, we're about to give them one."

Chaos nods, and we all move in unison, fanning out around the building like it's second nature. I come across two men with beers in their hands, and they're so fuckin' out of it, they don't even notice the danger walking right up to them. The one closest to me, a big motherfucker about my size but not in the athletic shape I am, tips his head back with the bottle of beer at his lips, and I figure this is as good a way as any to keep the pig quiet. I grab the back of his head with one hand while I use the palm of the other to slam the bottle into his mouth with full force. He jerks and gags, blood pouring from his mouth as his eyes roll to the back of his head. I slit his throat for good measure, letting him collapse to the ground.

Looking to my side, Chaos has taken care of the other one, his lifeless body slumped against the building in a pool of his own blood. Then I hear it: two rapid-fire gunshots and a piercing scream that have me running toward the front of the compound.

"Rogue!" I hear Chaos calling my name, but I've snapped. They know we're here now, and it's only a matter of time before they have no use for her anymore. It's fucking now or never.

Members of the Iron Wolves file out of the building, and then all hell breaks loose. There are more of us than there are of them, but it's still a fight. One of our prospects takes a hit to his chest, his body crumbling to the ground in agony, the broken gravel below stained crimson as his blood seeps from the fatal shot.

We're pushed back farther from the entrance of the garage as we fight to take them down. Their members are slow, drunk, and too drugged up to put up a good fight, but even firing a gun at random will eventually hit a mark. I take down two more of their men, as my brothers fight around me. Chaos is a ruthless fighter, choosing to use a knife instead of a gun as long as he can. He gets close to his enemies and cuts one after the other down, their throats bleeding them out dry.

I wipe the sweat and blood from my forehead as I do a quick scan of the property, noting that every Iron Wolf either fled or was killed. Chaos nods to me as he reaches my side, ready to head into the crumbling garage. Nerves suddenly fill me as I lunge forward.

"Let me fucking go!" Kinsey screams, and my heart fucking takes off behind my ribcage. Hearing her voice, even in this scenario, is like music. We got here in time. She appears a moment later in the open doorway of the building, my brothers and I standing just fifteen feet away, waiting with guns ready. She's so fucking close.

My relief at seeing Kinsey alive is short-lived as I take in the mean looking asshole staggering out of the house with his hand outstretched, fist clenched into her hair. Kinsey's arms claw at his hand, trying to alleviate some of the pressure he's causing as she stumbles. Rope binds one of her wrists, and all I see is red.

I take a step forward, Chaos' hand shooting out and pressing against my chest, his arm outstretched, preventing me from going to her. A flashback of a similar scenario flashes behind my eyes, and I nearly crumble.

How have I been so fucking stupid? Camden warned me they'd come for me. I never should have left her alone. Once again, my choices have hurt someone innocent. I'm a walking fucking shell after losing Lena, losing Kinsey would put me six feet under to join them. There's no surviving this.

So that leaves me with one option. Losing her isn't it.

"Reid!" Kinsey screams, her voice strong and pissed off, but I can hear the tremble. She's scared shitless. I grip my gun between two hands, contemplating taking the shot, knowing I could take him out without harming her.

"Hold on, sweetheart. You'll be in my arms in less than three minutes."

"That so? You dumb motherfucker! Don't you see? She's not going anywhere! This bitch is ours!" the unnamed asshole slurs, jerking her head around as if to prove his point. She screams in pain, and I swear I will rip him limb from fucking limb for hurting her. My hand clenches into a fist, and the other digs into the grip of my gun.

"Just hand her over, you're done here. Look around, your boys' bodies are scattered everywhere. There's no one here to back you up. Your prez isn't here to save you. It's just you against us. Hand over our woman, and you can walk away," Chaos negotiates.

"Fuck you! Prez claimed her for himself. He gets what he wants. She's staying with me!"

The growl that works its way up from my chest comes from

somewhere deep and primal. No one had better have laid a fucking finger on her. Before I can register what happened, the asshole howls in pain, his head falling backward as blood pours from his nose. Kinsey twists out of his hold, his hand still firmly holding onto her fucking hair, kicking him hard in the junk. He releases her as he drops to his knees, and I've never been so fucking proud in my entire life.

The next few seconds are a blur. I'm moving just as Kinsey bolts in my direction, and within a few seconds, she's launching herself at me, just as two shots go off from next to me. I don't flinch as I catch her midair, the warmth of her body seeping into mine as she collapses in my arms. Her arms wrap around my neck as her legs tighten around my waist. Kinsey's muffled sobs nearly shatter me as she buries her face in my neck, hanging onto me like her life depends on it.

"It's okay, it's okay, it's okay," I whisper, my arm wrapped around her little body, my other threaded through her matted hair, holding her head, trying to fuse her to me.

After a few moments, I pull her back so I can see her face, needing her eyes on me, desperate to see that she's okay. I haven't been able to take full stock of any possible injuries yet, and it's killing me. I need to know what happened to her in there. I won't be able to rest easy until I know every single detail. I have to.

Grasping her face, I drop my forehead to hers, our noses touching. "I've got you. You're safe, sweetheart. I'm here. You're safe. I'm not going to let anything happen to you." I pepper her cheeks and forehead with kisses, gripping her so tight, I'm probably hurting her.

Jesus fucking Christ, she's alive. I'll get her through everything else. My little fighter.

Chaos and other members circle around the property, checking for survivors as I move farther away from the mayhem. I continue to whisper words of reassurance to her, making promises I'll do everything I can to keep.

"Get her out of here!" Chaos barks in my direction. "Rolo, Jesse! Flank him!"

I move quickly, carrying Kinsey tightly with one arm, my other gripping my gun, ready to fight if I need to. No one will take her from me again. Rolo, Jesse, and I make our way over cracked pavement and broken-down vehicles, and the entire time, Kinsey whimpers into my neck, breaking my fucking heart. I'm torn between not letting her go and wanting to turn back to torture every single one of those motherfuckers who dared take her, who dared to scare her or cause her pain.

If it's the last thing I do, I will find their president and I'll make him regret the day he ever revived the Iron Wolves.

Rolo holds up the space we cut open in the chain-link fence, and I holster my gun, holding Kinsey tightly as I step through, careful not to snag her on any of the rusted metal. Kinsey refuses to let me go, and I'm not ready to not have my arms around her. So instead of unwinding her legs from my waist and setting her on the back of my bike, I keep her where she is, adjusting us so that she's straddling my lap. Her tiny body is weightless in my arms as she buries herself against my chest, and I start the bike. It roars to life beneath us, and Kinsey shivers against me.

"Hold on, sweetheart. No sudden movements, I won't let anything happen to you."

"Where are you taking me?"

"Home."

Kinsey jerks up, instantly breaking the one demand I just gave her. At least I hadn't started moving yet, and my feet are still planted on the ground.

"No! No, please, Reid! They'll lock me up! Move me back in with my parents, or worse . . . with Sawyer! Anywhere but Aspen Ridge, Reid. Please. I'm begging you. I'm not . . . I'm not ready. I can't." Her voice chokes on a sob, and my heart can't take her desperation, her fear. After everything she's been through, I can't fucking do it to her. She needs a minute to heal without everyone suffocating her. Her eyes are wild as she pleads, and I never want to make this woman beg me for anything.

So I take her to the only place where I know she'll be safe. The one place I never wanted her to know about.

The clubhouse.

kinsey

I'm safe.

I'm safe.

I'm safe.

I repeat those two words in my head over and over again. Maybe if I say them enough times, I'll start to believe them. I curl further into Reid's big chest, breathing in the warm, comforting smell of rich leather and cedarwood. He's so large that my arms can't completely wrap around his waist, so I grip his shirt where it's tucked under the thick leather vest he's wearing. The thought stirs something inside me because now I'm recognizing the vest as the same type the assholes who kidnapped me sported.

I'm not stupid, I know it means they're members of a motorcycle club, but Reid's not. He lives with us in Aspen Ridge. Yeah, he rides a bike, but that doesn't mean you're in a club. Right? The questions I have give my overworked, tired, terrified brain the reprieve it needs to not have a nervous breakdown on the front of this motorcycle.

My eyes are heavy from exhaustion and terror, but the adrenaline is still coursing through me at an overwhelming rate. I don't know if I'll ever sleep again after what I've gone through. The rumble of Reid's bike under us is calming, the wind whipping my hair around my face violently, but I feel safe tucked into him, breathing in his familiar scent.

Time goes by differently on the bike with him; it could have been ten minutes or an hour, but he starts to slow down after a while, and I take a moment to look around. I couldn't go back to Aspen Ridge right now. Every fear my brothers have has been used as their fuel to be overbearing and overprotective for as long as I can remember, and now? All those fears just became reality. They'll never let me out of their sight again, and even though I just went through the most traumatic experience of my life, I refuse to let it control me. Refuse to let them control me. I won't go back into a cage, especially not one with even smaller walls. I love them more than anything, and I understand where they're coming from, but this is my life, and I'm going to live it how I want.

Tall gates open for us as Reid drives up a long dirt road, dust billowing behind and around us. Without stopping to talk to the people in similar leather vests, he drives the motorcycle up the path toward a huge black building. It stands tall, even against the mountain backdrop it rests against, ominous and foreboding. I guess it makes sense considering who must live here. A motorcycle club.

We slow to a stop in front of it, Reid's legs dropping down to the ground and holding the bike steady with his legs. His hands release the handlebars before rubbing up and down my back, my sides, my shoulders. His hands are everywhere as if he's trying to make sure that I'm real.

I swear I can hear him breathing me in as he leans down and buries his face in my hair. I inwardly cringe, given the state I'm in. I haven't showered in what feels like days, and since I've lost all concept of time since being locked in the dark room with the windows boarded up, it very well could be that long.

"Wh—" I clear my throat, attempting to force it to stay steady and failing miserably. "Where are we, Reid?"

"You good, Rogue?" someone says from behind us.

Rogue? That's what those two men said before they took me. They wanted Rogue. They meant, Reid?

"Yeah, Rolo, I've got it from here," Reid calls back in return.

His strong hands rub up and down my back in a tight squeeze, and I never want him to let me go.

"I need to get you inside, Kins. Are you ready?"

"Where are we?"

"I'll explain everything, but let's get inside first."

I nod my agreement as Reid grips my thighs, lifting me effortlessly up off his lap as he stands with me in his arms. I loop my arms around his neck, my fingers threading through his long hair that's escaped the elastic holding it back.

With one hand under my ass, Reid holds me impossibly close to him. The large front door is opened, and a rush of cool air blasts us. Hushed voices whisper around us, and instead of looking at my surroundings, at the people who are watching a man they all clearly know carry a random woman through their house, I bury my head into his neck.

"Reid, you can put me down."

"Not gonna happen, sweetheart. Not until we're in the safety of my bedroom."

His bedroom? What the fuck is going on? Who is he? I know I should feel a plethora of emotions right now, fear being the most prominent after what I just survived, but I feel anything but while in his arms. He clearly has a hidden part of himself, but instead of being scared, I'm just confused and curious. No matter what he unveils to me, I know with utmost certainty, Reid would never harm me, and that's the reason I stay safely in his arms and don't drill him with questions.

His heavy boots echo off the cement floor as he walks in large strides through a huge open room. I keep my eyes downcast, my face buried in his neck, not wanting to take anything in this way. After taking a flight of stairs, another door creaks on its hinges as he steps us through a threshold. The room isn't as cool as the rest of the house, but the warmth isn't overly oppressive.

Reid gives me one more squeeze, as I feel him take a deep inhale of air before sliding me down his front and setting me on a large bed. I quickly close in on myself, bringing my legs up to my chest, wrapping my arms around them. I'm still in nothing but a pair of shorts and my sports bra, but more than that, I just want the comfort of being held tight.

I miss his warmth and safety already, and it takes all my self-control not to reach for him.

Reid squats down on his haunches at the end of the bed, his hands gripping my hips and dragging me to the edge. Even with me sitting on the bed and him in a squat, he's still taller than me, but it puts us a little more at eye level.

"I need you to know that you're safe here. I would never knowingly put you in danger. This is probably the safest place in the world right now."

"Okay . . . I trust you, Reid."

His hand dwarfs my face as he pushes my hair behind my ear, eyes roaming all over my undoubtedly bruised cheekbone. "Good," he says with a sad smile that nearly kills me.

"I can't believe you came for me," I blurt. Looking into the greenest eyes I've ever seen, eyes I wished to see again, it suddenly dawns on me that Reid saved me. The realization hits me with the force of a tsunami banking the shore, bringing with it a storm of emotions and unanswered questions.

"I'll always come for you, Kinsey. Always."

"But how? How did you find me?"

He just shakes his head, swiping his thumb back and forth against my cheek.

"We're at the Hell's Heathens clubhouse. Have you ever heard of them?"

"No, but in case you don't remember, I've been ridiculously sheltered. They're a motorcycle club?"

"Yes."

"They called you Rogue. That's the name of your shop."

"It is. That's also my road name."

"Your . . . road . . . name," I repeat slowly, processing what I'm putting together. Reid is in the Hell's Heathens MC? How is that even possible? I pull up everything I know about him, and I quickly realize how little I know of his past. Everything I do know, though, doesn't conjure images of a violent criminal motorcycle club member.

"My road name. Do you know what that is?"

"It's clearly a nickname, right?"

"Of sorts, yeah. They're given when you're patched in, and they usually have some meaning behind them."

"And you're in an MC? Hell's Heathens?"

He nods his head slightly, his face full of pain and sympathy as if this is the last conversation on earth he'd like to have. I'm not sure whether or not to take offense.

"Since I was eighteen. As much as I want to talk this through, it's fuckin' killin' me not knowing if you're okay, sweetheart, what they . . . what they could have done to you."

My eyes pool with tears that start to spill over and trail down my face as images replay in my mind of being in that filthy room, the two men who kept coming in and harassing me. The things they threatened and did haunting me in perfect clarity.

"Look at those perky tits. That's the first thing I'm gonna cut up. Run my knife over the tops until they spill with your blood. You see how hard it makes me?"

I turn my head and look away as he grabs his length over his stained jeans.

"No, not gonna look? Fine, darlin', you're just gonna sit there while I get myself off then."

Oh, god, no. Please. I squeeze my eyes closed as I hear the zipper of his jeans slide down and then the noise of him spitting. Please don't let this happen. I dig my nails into the palms of my hands, hoping with all my might that he stays over there, that he doesn't touch me. The noise of him beating his dick echoes through the room, his loud, labored breathing and heavy grunts.

"I'm gonna fuck your ass until you split in two, darlin'. You're gonna be chained down and forced to take all of us. You're gonna look so fuckin' good when your skin blooms with purple and red. Fuck. Oh fuck."

His grunts get louder and louder until they finally stop, and I hear him shuffling around, the noise of his zipper, and then finally the opening of the door.

"You're gonna beg for me when Prez gets his hands on you. You're gonna wish you had never told me no."

I gasp for a breath as I bat away the tears streaming down my face.

"Can I take a shower? Please?"

Reid looks at me with the saddest, most desperate expression I've ever seen in my life. His eyes are pinched in pain, his bottom lip jutting out with a slight tremble, as if seeing me this way is breaking him, too.

"Of course you can. I have some clothes you can wear when you get out."

I nod my head, letting Reid grasp my hand and pull me to stand. Together, we walk to the bathroom, where he flicks on a harsh fluorescent light.

"There's no girlie soap or anything, but you can use whatever is in there. I'll get you some better stuff from Rolo's old lady for you to use next time."

I just nod my head, sure that the adrenaline crash has started, my body becoming very numb, reality setting in. Reid opens the glass door and reaches in to start the shower for me, and then retreats to the doorway.

"Thank you, Reid."

"Anything for you, Kins. I'll get you a clean towel." With that, Reid leaves the bathroom, leaving the door slightly ajar. I strip out of my soiled clothes, avoiding the large mirror in front of me. I can only imagine what I look like right now, and it's the last thing I want to see. I just want to get clean, scrub my body to within an inch of my life to get their hands and eyes off my skin.

I step into the shower, welcoming the spray of hot water as it cascades down my skin. I reach for the soap, pouring some blue gel into the palm of my hand. I start at my neck and work my way down, using the pads of my fingers to scrub at my skin. When that doesn't feel good enough, I start to scratch, leaving heavy red marks down my arms and chest. I heave in a choked sob, gasping for breath as I drop to my knees on the cold tile floor. My cries come out uncontrollably as I roll onto my side, pulling my knees to my chest.

I'm safe.

I'm safe.

"I'm safe."

"Kinsey?" Reid's voice breaks through my sobs, but I can't answer him, I can't think about anything other than being locked up in that room with those evil men leering at me, their hands reaching out and grabbing, their voices in my head, the threats, the feeling of pure terror that stuck with me like a terminal disease. The desperate way I clung to hope that I would find a way out. The anger and embarrassment over being taken in the first place.

"Kins, sweetheart, you're killin' me. What can I do, baby? Tell me and I'll fix it for you. *Please.*"

When I don't answer, the shower door opens, and I barely register it. The next thing I know, I'm being picked up and put into his large lap over his denim jeans. Reid covers my body with a towel as the water jets down on us, soaking him as he sits at the bottom of the shower. He doesn't seem to care as he holds me to him. I curl in as close as physically possible, my arms wrapped tightly around my knees, my head under his chin. He holds me against his massive chest, his hands rubbing up and down over my now towel-covered back.

"Shh. You're safe. I'm here and I'm not letting you go. Do you understand?"

God, I hope with everything I am that he speaks truthfully. I've never felt safer than I do when I'm in his arms. After a while, my sobs slow, my tears dry up, and my breathing comes at a more regular pace.

"Thatta girl. Just breathe for me. Deep breaths, baby. Just one at a time. You're so strong. So fuckin' brave. I'm so proud of you."

I can't bring myself to say anything back, because what is there to say?

"I would hold you in here until you're ready to leave, but the water is getting cold, and I want to get you warm."

I nod my head against Reid's chest as he stands, making it look so easy as he barely jostles me against him. Once the water is turned off, he steps out of the shower with me in his arms, bridal style.

"I just need to switch out your towel, sweetheart, hold on."

Reid sets me on my feet for a brief moment as the towel falls off my body with a wet plop at our feet. Within a split second, I'm surrounded by the warmth of an extra-large, plush towel and pulled back into his arms. It doesn't even cross my mind that Reid has clearly seen me naked now, and I can't even be bothered about it.

Reid walks us back into the bedroom, setting me on the edge of the bed, pulling the towel closer to my body, clearly making sure I'm completely covered. How is this man so genuinely good and sweet? How can this man that I thought I knew be in a motorcycle club?

"I'll be right back, I just need to change out of these wet jeans," he tells me before opening a drawer and grabbing some clothes and returning to the bathroom. I take a second to look around the space; a large dresser stands in front of the bed closest to the door, plain black curtains cover the window, blacking out the world outside. His leather jacket is thrown haphazardly against a chair that sits in the corner. There's no closet and just the bathroom. It's simple and modest and reminds me of a single college dorm room.

He has no photos or real personal items anywhere, and I wonder how much time he actually spends in this room. It can't be often since he's always in Aspen Ridge. Everything just leaves me with more unanswered questions.

Reid returns quickly with a T-shirt and hairbrush in his hands.

He pulls the extra-large T-shirt over my head and makes sure it covers my torso before pulling away the damp towel. I situate myself so that I'm covered, and then he's moving behind me, each of his legs on either side of mine so that I'm sitting between them. He starts at the bottom of my tangled, matted hair and slowly starts brushing, working through each knot with such tenderness, I almost cry.

"You don't need to talk right now, Kins, but you're goin' to someday, and I'm gonna be here for you when you're ready. I want to know what happened in there."

We sit in silence as I sway into his delicate touch. How can this massive man be so heartbreakingly gentle with me? After he's worked through every inch of my hair, he lifts me again, pulling back the blankets and covering me. His calloused hand sweetly touches my face, running his fingertips along the crown of my head and trailing past my ear. He leans down, and my eyes flutter closed as he presses his firm lips against my forehead in the sweetest kiss that has my body humming and my heart flipping over in my chest. I have a moment of panic that he will leave me in here alone, and his next words validate that.

"Get some sleep, little fighter. I'll be next door if you need anything."

My hand darts out, reaching for him. "Please don't leave me." I know my voice breaks, the emotion caught in my throat, but I don't want to be alone right now. Especially not away from him. *"Please."*

"Fuck, I was hopin' you'd say that. I can't stand the thought of leaving you in here alone."

Relief courses through me as I lie there, my shoulders deflating. Reid works his jeans over his hips, pushing them down his legs. I do my best to give him privacy, but I've never seen this man in anything but denim jeans or athletic joggers to box in.

His legs are thick like tree trunks, each one thicker than my waist. Just as I had suspected, every inch of the skin covering them is adorned with tattoos. A mix of black and gray with various colors mixed in. I can't make them out from my position on the other side of the bed and the darkness of the room, but there's no missing that they're there.

He strips his short-sleeved T-shirt next, his chest equally covered in ink. A large skull with a crown falling to the side, an ornate dagger slicing through the top and coming out the bottom fills the center of his body, identical to the one on his arm, with an array of hodgepodge designs scattered around it. Reid lifts up the covers, slipping into bed next to me in nothing but a tight pair of boxer briefs. I lay stiffly next to him, my knees still tucked up to my chest.

"You're gonna be okay, I promise."

"I believe you."

"Can I hold you? I really wanna hold you, Kinsey. *I need to.*"

I bat a stray tear away from my cheek as I answer him, "Please." His hands don't waste any time snaking around my hips, pulling me to him, tucking my body into his. My back lies flush against his front, his large arm bound around me. The warmth of his body seeps into mine, enveloping me in exactly what I need right now—familiar comfort and safety.

I breathe in the rich scent of leather and cedar as my body finally gives in, relaxing against this beast of a man who has become such an enigma to me. Why aren't I more concerned about his hidden identity? His secret life? Why does everything with him feel so . . . right?

I wake for the first time in my life next to another person, and the sudden newness of it pulls me under a tidal wave, threatening to drown me. Fear clutches my heart, squeezing painfully as I struggle to remember where I am. I thrash against the body, a scream piercing my ears as I try to escape my captor.

"Let me go!"

Warm hands grip my shoulders, turning me over in the bed, and I buck wildly in response, squeezing my eyes shut, trying my hardest to kick him away.

"I'm here, Kinsey, it's me, I'm right here." Familiar hands touch my face, so strong but so gentle, and I start to relax, letting my eyes peel open to reveal the man next to me. He's not my captor at all. He's my protector. His hair is disheveled, hanging around his face in a wild mess, his face pinched in a desperate mix of pain and concern.

"There's my girl. You're safe. I've got you. Nothing is going to hurt you."

"Reid."

"Yeah, sweetheart."

"I'm so sorry. I thought . . ."

"Shh, I know, I know. But you're not there anymore. You're at the clubhouse with me, in my old bedroom. You're safe."

"I'm safe."

"Yeah, baby, you're safe."

He smiles down at me, continuing to stroke my hair, running his other hand over every inch of me he can reach, doing his best to calm and relax me. I melt against him, suddenly desperate to be closer to him.

"Thank you. Please keep me safe, Reid. Please."

"Always. Nothing will hurt you ever again."

I line my body against his as close as possible, snuggling further into him and draping my arm over his big chest. He curls around me, letting me use him as a gigantic teddy bear.

Reid's got me.
I'm safe.

reid

FUCK EVERYTHING I SAID BEFORE. FUCK EVERYTHING except Kinsey Hayes. She's mine. Today was the second most terrifying day of my life, and the moment I had her safely in my arms, I knew. For the first time in almost a decade, hope filled my chest. As I held her body close to mine, I could have fused her to me, and it wouldn't have been close enough. Fuck everything else. No one will be able to make her feel what I can. No one will be able to keep her safe like I can. I may have failed to do it once before, but I'll die before it happens again.

I still don't know the details of what went down while she was captive but I'm going to get to the bottom of it, and then I'm going to hunt down every single one of those evil motherfuckers if it's the last thing I do. They'll pay with their lives for taking what's mine.

Mine.

After her nightmare, she practically crawled under my skin, and I would have let her if that would have made her feel safe. She finally fell back asleep, her little hand tracing circles over my collar-bone. After lying restless for a few hours, not wanting to leave her for a moment, needing to touch her for my own reassurance, I forced myself to leave the bed to call Sawyer, who is without a doubt losing his mind.

I'm gutted thinking about how broken and fragile she seems right now. I've dreamed of seeing Kinsey naked a million times, and never in my wildest fantasies did this scenario cross my mind, but there was no part of me that could have walked away from her lying on the bottom of that shower. I responded out of pure instinct and would do it again in a heartbeat. It took all my strength not to scan her body from the top of her head to the tip of her toes to look for injuries, but I wanted to respect her privacy as much as the situation allowed. It's killing me slowly, not knowing what they did to her.

I dial Sawyer's number, and he picks up on the first ring.

"Tell me you have my sister."

"I have her."

"Fuck!" He moves the phone away from his face, clearly talking to Ivy, or whoever else is in the room with him, relaying that she's safe. "Is she okay? When will you be back in AR? Jesus Christ, I can't think straight."

I take a deep, steadying breath before dropping the bomb that I know is going to cause a shit storm.

"Listen, she's okay, she's strong, but she's shaken. Her physical injuries seem to be minor, but the emotional and mental ones? Brother, she's struggling."

"Did they . . .?"

I know exactly what he's asking without having to say it because it's been on my mind since she was taken. Did they rape her? Did they violate her body in any way? I run my hands through my hair and tell him honestly.

"I don't know yet. She hasn't opened up to me, but I'll get to the bottom of it."

"Fuck. I can't believe this happened. How the fuck did this happen? I fucking knew she shouldn't have left Mom and Dad's. We've been going crazy. Now when the fuck will you be home with my sister?"

It's now or never.

"We're at the clubhouse. We're staying here until she feels ready to return to Aspen Ridge."

"The fuck did you just say to me, Reid? You did not just say you brought my sister to the Hell's Heathen's clubhouse. Get her ass home to us."

Fuck. I knew this was going to go this way but it still fucking hurts to not be on the same page as my best fucking friend. But I'm not about to hand Kinsey over to her family when she said that's not what she wants right now. She's the one in control here.

"No."

"No?" His voice is lethal, but this is a fight I'm willing to face. For her.

"I love you, man, but she doesn't want to go back right now, and I'm letting her lead this. She wants a minute to breathe and process. Not to mention, they're still out there. We can't afford to pull everyone off duty to run Kinsey and me back to AR. It's safer for her here right now," I tell him, not lying, but stretching the truth. The compound is the safest place for her right now, but we could leave if we wanted to. After taking the hit tonight, the Iron Wolves will no doubt go into hibernation for a bit to recoup. There's silence between us for a moment while I wait for Sawyer to make his next play. He can be a hothead when it comes to his family, so I'm expecting the worst. It doesn't matter, though, I'm prepared to fight on her behalf until she can fight for herself.

"Okay," he breathes roughly into the speaker, but I catch the words clear as day, and my breath stalls. "I don't like it, but I trust you. She's safe?"

"I'd die before I let anything happen to her, brother, you know that."

"I do. Which is the only fucking reason we're all not driving up right now to pick her up ourselves. What do you need?"

It's not until he asks that I realize what I need, and he's the man who can get it to me.

"I need you to work your magic and get me the names and

information of everyone ever involved in the Iron Wolves MC. No detail is too small."

"Give me a few days max."

"Done."

"Reid?"

"Yeah?"

"Take care of my sister. And when you find them, I'm going in with you."

"Sawyer . . ." I argue.

"No. Ten years ago, you said you owed me, and I brushed it off because I never wanted anything in return. I want this. We bury these assholes together. Promise me."

Fuck.

"Get up."

"Fuck off."

"You're coming with me. We're going to put on some gloves and we're gonna go until you can't lift your arms to bring that drink to your mouth."

"I said fuck off, Sawyer."

He's not having it, though, just like always. He shows up every day, forcing me to eat and drink water, giving me some spiel about getting out of this bed and stopping drinking. But drinking is the only thing that dulls the pain and emptiness of losing Lena.

His heavy footsteps stomp on the concrete floor of the bedroom I'm staying in at his family's distillery, but I don't bother to move from where I'm sitting on my ass with my hands loosely holding the neck of a bottle of whiskey between my bent legs. I don't flinch when he snatches it out of my hand, or when he grabs my face roughly with his fingers, squeezing my cheeks together.

"She's gone. There's nothing you can do to bring her back. This isn't how she'd want you to live."

"There's nothin' to live for anymore."

"Then you wade through the fucking darkness until there is. But

you don't give up. 'Cause someday you're gonna find your light and all this suffering will be just a distant memory."

His words hit their mark, even if I don't fully believe all of them. No light will come for me. But Lena wouldn't want me to live like this, and I need to push through for her, because she can't.

"Okay."

"Okay?"

"That's what I said, isn't it?"

"I expected to have to carry your stubborn ass out of here so excuse me for being a little shocked."

"Whatever. Where are we going?"

"Knockout."

Sawyer forces me to his gym twice a day every day until my arms can't lift the alcohol bottle to my lips anymore, just like he said he would. We train hard, and he takes every single hit I throw his way, fighting my demons.

"Who was she?" I finally ask after a few weeks.

"Ivy. She's the love of my life."

"Where'd she go?"

"She left. No note. No goodbye. We were madly in love, planning our future, and she took off in the middle of the night."

"I'm sorry."

"She'll find her way back to me. I'm not giving up."

"Hope is a dangerous thing, brother."

Brother. The word came out smooth like butter, and I don't regret it.

"Hope is all there is."

"I'll repay you someday for this. Whatever you need, whenever you need me, I'll return this."

"There's nothing I want. Just keep pushing and stay off the bottle."

"I promise."

"Update me later. As soon as she's up and moving, I want to hear her voice. We all do."

"As soon as she says she's ready, I'll have her call you all."

I hang up with Sawyer, a storm of emotions warring for dominance inside me. I assumed he and his brothers would already be on their way here the moment I told them our location, the fact that he's letting me lead this, with one of the most precious things in his life? I just hope he still feels that way once I tell him she's mine now and he doesn't need to worry anymore. If Kinsey thinks her brothers are overbearing and protective, she has no idea what she just hitched herself to.

"How's our new houseguest doin'?" Sin asks, walking into the kitchen and refilling his coffee, his pet bunny curled into a ball in the crook of his elbow. I didn't want to leave Kinsey again, but she needs energy if I want her to heal, and that means food and drink.

"She's strong. I'll get her through it."

"You will, huh?"

"She's mine."

"Singing a different tune today, Rogue, just trying to keep up with what's goin' on."

"Yeah, well, mind your own goddamn business and don't even look at her, Rhys."

He puts his free hand up in defense, like that would stop me from making him choke on his own teeth.

"Small and breakable isn't my type. She's all yours, Rogue."

"The fuck did you just call her?"

"You're taking it the wrong way, buddy. I meant for fucking. I knew she was more than a kitten the moment I met her. You got yourself a lioness, brother."

"Watch yourself, Sin, Rogue seems to be out for blood now that he's got a woman," Malice adds as he joins us in the kitchen for the party we're apparently having.

"Better heed his warning, I'll slit your throat with a smile on my face if you think about fuckin' with her," I warn, my voice thick with violence. He just snickers, leaning his big ass up against the counter, watching me work while he pets his bunny.

"Get that damn thing out of the kitchen or I'll eat it," Malice threatens. Sin moves quickly, his free hand snapping out, fingers surrounding Malice's throat and holding him tightly against the refrigerator.

"Don't threaten Mr. Bun-Buns or I'll cut you from throat to cock, letting your innards spill out while you watch."

"Sounds like my kinda foreplay," Malice goads, and Sin releases him with a little shove.

"You two are insane," I tell them.

"I'm normal. Malice is insane."

"Quite clinically, actually," Malice adds.

Jesus Christ, I need to keep Kinsey locked in my bedroom and away from my dysfunctional family. They'll have her begging to leave, and to my surprise, as much as I didn't want to bring her here, I'm not ready to take her back to Aspen Ridge. Luckily, she's the one calling the shots, and she doesn't seem remotely close to being well enough to head home.

I finish making us each an omelet with bacon and cheese and butter two pieces of toast before leaving my asshole brothers and heading back to my room. I've already been away from her for too long, and my skin is tight, my spine tingling with unease.

I push the door open as quietly as I can, cursing the old hinges and the loud creak announcing my arrival. Kinsey stirs lightly, her hand slapping the bed in search of . . . *me*. Shit. She's waking up alone, and she wants me? My heart swells. I need to get her through this.

"Hey, little fighter," I whisper against her forehead. The bruises on her cheek are so much worse today, and I hate seeing her beautiful skin marred and blooming with blacks and blues. "I brought you breakfast in bed. I need you to eat for me."

"Hi," she squeaks, her voice raspy with sleep.

"How are you feeling?"

"Sore, tired," she groans, and my heart plummets. How the hell do I ask her where she's sore? My hands clench into fists in frustration.

"I've got some pain meds, water, and food. That's gonna make you feel so much better. Will you sit up?"

"Yeah."

I help her sit up in the bed, careful to keep the blankets pulled up around her waist, fully aware and attuned to the fact that she's not wearing any panties under my shirt. The thought should turn me on with the number of times I've thought about taking her in nothing but one of my shirts, but right now it just makes my heart ache painfully.

I grab her plate of food and cut a piece of the omelet with the fork, bringing it up to her mouth.

"I can do it myself, Reid. You don't have to feed me."

"I know you can do it yourself, sweetheart, it's not about what you're capable of. I *want* to do it for you."

"You want to feed me?"

"I want to take care of you."

She gives me the first real glimpse of a smile as it plays on her lips ever so slightly, and my heart jump-starts behind my ribs. Kinsey opens her mouth, her lips closing around the tines of the fork as I gently pull it away.

"That's my good girl," I growl, not meaning for my voice to come out so gravelly but fuck, this woman is so goddamn perfect. I'm done pretending there isn't something between us. Done fighting what's wrong and right. I was a dead man walking until Kinsey Hayes walked into my life, all light and good. She's my beacon, lighting my way out of the purgatory I've been wandering through. She's my salvation.

Kinsey feels like she could save me. If I cling to her hard enough, maybe I can find peace, accept the peace she brings me, and hopefully, in turn, I can do the same for her.

After feeding her a late breakfast, she drinks two glasses of water and takes some pain medicine that Stitch, our in-house doctor, gave me for her. I hold her long after she falls back asleep, until my phone vibrates in my pocket, forcing my attention away from watching her breathe.

Sawyer: She awake?

Me: She woke up to eat and then went right back to sleep

Sawyer: We want to talk to her

Me: Your other two brothers know where we are? I know you told Dallas.

Sawyer: I only told them as much as I needed to

Me: Which is?

Sawyer: That you took her to your old house

Me: So not a lie

Sawyer: But not the full truth

Sawyer: I don't like it though

Me: Then tell them the truth

Me: It's gonna come out anyway. I can't keep these two lives separate much longer

Sawyer: You going back in full time?

Me: No, just need to make some changes

Sawyer: You doing okay? I know this dredged up everything with Lena

The mention of her name reminds me that I haven't been to see her yet. Every Sunday, it's my first stop, and I've been back here for twenty-four hours already and haven't thought to go see her once. Fuck. I'm such a piece of shit.

Me: I'm hanging in there. Lena was next to me the whole time, making sure Kinsey didn't see the same fate

Sawyer: I owe you my life

I hope he remembers feeling that way once we're home and I tell him I'm rapidly falling in love with his sister and that I'm moving her out of the studio and into my house with me. I know Kinsey feels this between us; she just needs me to be all in. I thought I could be noble, I thought I could be strong and resist her, but I don't want to fight *being with* Kinsey. I want to fight *to be with* Kinsey. And I know her brothers are going to put up a hell of one.

Kinsey stirs next to me, and I pull her in close, loving the feel of her in my arms. She's so fucking tiny compared to me, but she's anything but fragile.

"Hi, sleeping beauty."

"What time is it?" she asks groggily as she blinks and lets her eyes adjust to the warm light pouring into the room from the window.

"I've lost track of it, actually. I think our days and nights are flipped."

"I'm sorry."

What the hell could she be sorry for? She's doing exactly what she should be doing—resting, healing.

"Sweetheart, don't ever apologize to me."

"You're too kind, Reid Knight."

If she only knew my history, what I'm capable of, what I've done to balance the tides, and what I'll do to those who hurt her.

"How are you feeling?"

"I'm okay. Tired."

"You feel like talking?"

"Not about what happened."

I don't want to push, knowing that she's never done that to me, but if something happened, I need to get her checked out. I can't be irresponsible when it comes to her safety, even if it pisses her off or crosses a boundary. I have to get to the bottom of it. I have to.

My arm curls tighter around her for a moment before releasing my hold, my hand moving to slightly grasp her chin, forcing her head back so I can see those blue eyes when I speak.

"Sweetheart, we don't have to talk details yet, you don't have to tell me what happened until you're ready, but I need you to please tell me if you were violated." My voice cracks on the next words that I never thought I would need to say. "If you were raped."

Kinsey's eyes bounce rapidly back and forth between mine, and I know she understands why I need to know. I just care about her safety and providing what she needs to heal. Her sweet face shakes briefly side to side, but my heart doesn't settle. I need her words. I need verbal confirmation.

"Words, baby, *please*. Did they?"

"No."

The relief I feel is instantaneous, but only a brief reprieve from knowing that she still went through something traumatic. It doesn't mean that her fear over them possibly raping her wasn't constantly running through her veins. Rage ignites inside me as I start to spiral, my emotions ping-ponging back and forth. I push them out of my mind, instead focusing on Kinsey and being what she needs right now.

"Would you like to read?"

She perks up, the mood lightens, and that spark of hope in my chest gets a little brighter.

"You have books here?"

"I may have had someone smuggle some in for me."

Her smile fills her face, and I feel like I just won a million fucking dollars. I would do anything to see her smile like that every damn day. It nearly takes my breath away.

"Jesus, you're so beautiful, Kinsey."

"You need to get your eyes checked, big guy."

"I'm seeing everything perfectly clear for the first time in a long time," I whisper against her forehead before sealing my lips right under her hairline.

"Read to me?"

"I suppose it's only fair after making you read to me, isn't it?"

"I couldn't agree more. What are my options?"

I reach over and grab the bag that I left on the nightstand next to me, dumping out four romance novels that Rolo got from his old lady for us. I told them they were for Kinsey, and he didn't ask any more questions. I'm not going to hide anything, but I don't need to give those assholes any more fuel to rag on me.

"You feeling regency, Mafia, small town, or rom-com?"

"Did you just say rom-com?"

"Romantic comedy. That's what it is."

"It sounded so silly coming from your mouth, Reid. Your voice is so raspy and deep, and you're this gigantic, burly guy," she laughs, and I'd say I'm winning right now.

"You're a brat, you know that? Rom-com it is then."

Kinsey snuggles back into my chest with a smile on her face as I open the book and start to read. We lay there for hours, until my voice was practically hoarse, but I would have read the rest of the week if it would make her happy. Once she had fallen asleep again, I pulled myself away from her to find Chaos and my brothers. I've been putting off checking in because the storm I feel brewing is a full-blown hurricane nearing our front steps. I expect Sawyer to pull through for us and get the information we need to take the

Iron Wolves down for good, but now I need to break it to Chaos that we'll have an extra pair of hands with us when we do.

I don't like the idea of Sawyer coming with us, but I respect it and won't stop him. Nothing could have kept me from going after Lena's murderers, and even though Kinsey is still breathing, they still took her, they harmed her, shook the very foundation of everything she knew and trusted. I've got my work cut out for me to make sure she feels safe again.

reid

TWO DAYS GO BY WITH THE SAME ROUTINE. SHE SLEEPS the majority of the day and night and only wakes when I rouse her to force her to eat and drink. We've read the books we got from Rolo's old lady, and I've returned them and asked for more. I love reading them to her, even if the sex scenes have started to affect me. Something about holding my woman in my arms while reading those words makes me harder than steel. I haven't acted on any of it, and I wouldn't until I know she's ready, but fuck, it's killing me.

She still won't open up about her time there, and I'm starting to spiral. I talked to Stitch about getting her checked out, but I'm terrified to bring it up to Kinsey. We sleep next to each other every night, and I know I can't ever go back to not having my woman in my bed. But today, I've had enough. She needs to talk; it's the only way she's going to process everything.

"Morning, sweetheart."

"Morning. What is that amazing smell?"

I sit down next to her in bed as she shuffles to sit up. She's still wearing one of my large shirts, even though she's showered once more since that first night. The hem rides up high on her thighs as she scoots backward to rest against the headboard, and I can't fight the urge to track the bare expanse of her silky, bare skin. Fuck, I want to touch her so badly, bring her pleasure, joy, take her mind off everything haunting her. I want to show her that life is worth living.

"See something you like, big guy?"

I allow myself a slow perusal of her body as I lift my eyes to meet hers. She's got a sexy smirk on her face that I haven't seen in a while, her eyebrow arched in question. She's proud of herself for catching me checking her out, but I'm not going to be ashamed. She's mine.

"Very much so, sweetheart."

"Hmm. So you say."

"I don't say useless things. If I say it, you can believe it because it'll only ever be the truth."

She looks up at me, her eyes swirling with confusion, and I swear I see a glimmer of heat behind her irises.

"It's not Bean Haven but we've got a fancy machine in the kitchen, took me way too damn long to figure out how to use it, but I made you your favorite.

"My favorite?"

"Salted caramel latte," I say matter-of-factly. I know damn well that's her favorite because she drinks one almost every day. She takes the tall mug from my hand and brings it to her nose, inhaling the rich, sweet scent of the espresso and caramel.

"I'm nervous. What if it's terrible and you spent all this time trying to make it for me?"

"Then you tell me what you don't like about it so I can try again."

"That easy, huh?"

"For you? Yeah."

Her eyes stay on me as her perfect, pouty pink lips reach the rim of the mug, and she ever so slowly takes her first taste. I know the moment I got it right because her eyes soften and her posture relaxes.

"Ohmygod. Yesssss, Reid. Thank you."

"Fuck me, *that sound,* Kinsey."

"Mmm. I don't even care. This may give Bean Haven a run for its money. Thank you so much, Reid."

"Watching you enjoy it is all the thanks I need."

"You say such pretty things sometimes. It messes with my head," she whispers against the rim of the mug as she enjoys every sip. God, I love watching this woman enjoy things.

"They're all true, baby."

"I'm not in the right place for the fake flirting, Reid."

"There's nothing fake about this, Kinsey."

"Please. I appreciate everything you're doing for me, but you and I both know you're just like my brothers, and this would go nowhere fast."

She struck a chord and my head cocks to the side as I take her in. She has no idea.

"Sweetheart, I am nothing like your brothers," I confess, my words firm and low. She sets the mug down on her lap and meets my eyes just as my hand touches her cheek. I lean in, letting my lips brush her ear as I whisper the next words, wanting her to know how serious I am. "I'm so much worse."

A shiver runs through her, her body breaking out in goose-bumps, but then she scoffs, brushing off my words.

"I don't believe anyone could be worse than my brothers. They take overprotective to the extreme. You can't top that."

"Trust me, sweetheart, I can and I will. They don't feel the way I do, and I'm not ever going to let harm come to you again."

"I'm not going to trade one cage for another, Reid."

"I'd never put you in a cage, Kinsey. You're far too strong for one."

"Well, that's something I haven't heard before."

"That you're strong?"

"Mhmm."

"The strongest woman I know."

Her face nuzzles into my palm, and I slowly lean in closer, ready to claim this woman's lips for the first time. There will be no one who comes after her, and I want to remember this moment.

"Reid . . ." she breathes roughly, looking up at me with so much hope and desire. I know she wants this, wants me, wants us. But she's scared I'll be like every other man that came before me. Never putting her first, never willing to fight for the right to be with her. Kinsey is everything, and I'm going to prove it to her.

"I know, sweetheart, I've got you."

My heart beats frantically in my chest as I slowly lower my head, resting my forehead against hers, sharing air, loving the way her breathing has picked up, the way her free hand has gripped my T-shirt into a fist, as if she's holding me in place, not wanting me to run.

Just as I'm about to connect with her perfect lips, my phone blares from my pocket. Kinsey startles, but I just drop my head in irritation and disappointment.

Reluctantly pulling out my phone, I look at the caller and turn it around to show Kinsey.

"It's your brothers. Again. You need to talk to them, Kins. They're worried about you."

"Just tell them I'm sleeping. I'm not ready to hear them go off on how they knew something like this would happen. All of this is happening to me, Reid. The worst part of coming out alive is that they're all going to look at me differently now. They were insufferable before, and now that everything they said could happen to me, did, it's just going to increase tenfold. So, no, I'm not eager to talk to my brothers so they can prove their point."

"You really think that, Kinsey?"

"Yes!"

"They love you more than anything in this world, and they've been losing their minds over not hearing your voice or seeing you. They don't want to throw anything in your face; they want to hold you through it so you can heal from it. Sawyer hasn't slept. Dallas tore down a barrel house in rage. Liam and Carter haven't been to work; they're all together, waiting for their sister."

"I don't want to hurt them, I'm just scared."

"Of them?"

"Of everything, Reid! I'm scared!" Her voice cracks, and tears flow from her pretty eyes. I take the steaming mug from her hand and set it on the table behind me before scooping her up into my lap, rearranging us so that I'm in the center of the bed and she's lying on top of me.

"Shh, I've got you. It's okay to be scared, baby. But you're so goddamn strong. Look what you survived?"

"I don't want anyone to look at me with pity, or like I'm the reason I was kidnapped."

"No one would think that, so get that out of your mind right now. And if they do, I'll happily straighten their shit out because they're wrong. You survived, Kinsey. You fought. You get to move on and see the light of another day. Are you gonna let it break you and swallow you whole now that you're free, or are you gonna fight back?"

She shakes and sniffles against my chest, and I keep my arms wrapped tightly around her, rubbing my palm up and down her spine.

"Why are you so good to me?"

"Because you're mine, little fighter," I whisper the truth to her for the first time against her hair, inhaling the scent of my soap on her. "And I'm always gonna be good to you."

"You gotta get her outta that room, Rogue," Chaos tells me from where we're sitting at the bar inside the main room of the clubhouse.

"You think I don't know that?"

"She's sleeping way too much. If you know what she needs, then give it to her. Stop treating her like she's broken and push her to be the strong woman you keep sayin' she is."

"Don't tell me what to fuckin' do, Chaos."

Camden slams his hand down hard between us, the slap echoing loudly, demanding my attention away from my phone, where I'm willing it to go off. It's been three days, and still nothing from Sawyer's guy on the information we need to move forward and end this once and for all.

"Watch it, Rogue. You may be goin' through some shit right now, but I'm still your president. Get her out of that room or she's gonna wither away."

My phone goes off, and I give Chaos a few more seconds of silence before nodding my head in agreement. I'm trying to let Kinsey lead this, trying to let her heal the way she naturally wants to, but she seems to be doing the opposite.

Sawyer: Emailed you over everything. Wes got it all. It goes back decades.

Me: Thanks. I'll keep you updated on what we find and when we make a plan

Sawyer: How is she today?

Me: She's getting better every day.

Sawyer: Still won't talk to us?

Me: She just says she's not ready

Sawyer: Did we fuck up that bad with her? That she doesn't even want her brothers to lean on? I thought we were all so close.

Me: You are. Don't downplay what you five have. She's just scared and needs time to process

Sawyer: Tell her we love her, that we miss her

Me: I remind her every day

Sawyer: Thankful for you, brother

Me: I'll update you soon

"We got the info. All of it."

"Forward it to Wrath. We'll get it sorted and figure out what we missed. Their leader has to be someone connected to the OGs. It's too out of pocket for some new asshole to revive a dead club."

"I agree. And this close to the anniversary of Lena and Lucas's death? It's all felt off from day one."

"Go take care of your woman, we'll find the hole. No one is perfect, and there is always a trail, just gotta find the crumb that leads to it."

I leave Chaos and head back upstairs to my bedroom, knowing he's right. It's time I force Kinsey to live a little, remind her there's so much to live and fight for. She's been given a second chance, and I'll be damned if I let her waste it.

CHAPTER 16

kinsey

"As much as I love seeing you in nothing but my clothes, I got you something else to wear. I've gotta get you out of this room," Reid says as he walks into the bedroom. Panic pounds through my chest, my blood turning to ice in my veins as I scramble to sit upright.

"Reid, I'm not ready to go back." Half a demand, half a plea. His emerald green eyes soften as he looks down at me, those tattooed hands running over his thick beard.

"We're not. I'm taking you on a ride. Fresh air and open roads are what you need. It helped me heal once, and I've got a good feelin' it's gonna help you, too."

"A ride?" I ask, even though I know exactly what he means.

"On my bike. You trust me?"

"Yes," I reply instantly. This man hasn't left my side. He's handfed me, washed my hair, held me while I slept, and been everything I could need. I've fallen quickly for him, but I'm so scared I won't be enough for him to fight for me, even if that's what he's already been doing. I know my brothers, and I can imagine the heat Reid has been taking while he keeps them at bay, fielding all their questions and letting me have the time and space I need to process.

171

Reid hands me some clothes as I step out of bed and walk to the bathroom. Once I shut the door behind me, I strip out of his T-shirt, something I've been loving living in, and pick up the denim skirt he handed me. There are tags still on it, and there's no way that's right because he's only left my side long enough to make us food and come back.

I step into the simple panties, and then the skirt, pulling it up my legs to find they're a perfect fit. It's the same thing with the simple white bra and plain V-neck T-shirt. For the first time since getting here, I take a look at myself in the mirror. The bruise across my cheek is awful, and I lean forward, running the pads of my fingers over the spot. It's still tender, but Reid said nothing seemed broken, which is good. My hair has luckily been tamed, thanks to Reid brushing it for me every night. My heart warms at the memory of his touch, how sweet and tender he's been with me.

The best part, though? The unexpected part? Sleeping curled up with this man has been what dreams are made of. He makes me feel so safe, so comforted, and complete. I don't know how I'll ever spend another night away from him after experiencing what it's like to sleep in his arms. After the nightmare the first night we were here, I haven't had one since. The moment I'm wrapped in Reid's arms, I relax and let the world fade away. It's as though my body understands and recognizes, at a chemical level, that I'm safe with him.

I walk out of the bathroom to find Reid leaning against the doorframe of the bedroom. He's looking out into space until he hears me, then his eyes are on me, and there is no confusing the look that's reflected in them.

Heat.

Desire.

Arousal.

"Fuck, Kinsey," he exhales while running his fingers through his thick hair. "I imagined what you'd look like in that, but my imagination didn't come close to the real thing."

"Yeah?"

"Yeah, sweetheart. You're so damn sexy."

Jesus. When he talks like that, it's almost as if he well and truly means what he's saying. I know Reid isn't a liar, I trust him with my life, but will he still want me after he has to come face-to-face with my family? Will I be enough for him?

"There you go again. Saying things that make this seem different."

"It is different, Kins."

"I want to believe you."

"You trust me on everything but this?"

"I trust you, Reid. I'm ready to go if you are."

He doesn't push the topic, which I'm grateful for.

"Yeah, you just need these," he replies, pointing to a leather jacket lying on the bed and a pair of boots on the floor in front of it.

"Let me guess, also my size?"

Reid shrugs, and I can't help but smile. It's unrestrained, and it feels so good. I pull on the black leather combat-style boots that come up to my ankles, and then he helps me into the jacket, batting my hands away as I try to zip it up.

"I know you can do it yourself, but let me anyway."

I watch as he bends his knees so that he drops down several inches to make it easier on himself, and then his large fingers are slowly zipping up the jacket. I watch him the entire time, his eyes tracking the slow slide of his fingers up my body.

Once he's satisfied, my eyes flutter closed as his lips connect with my forehead. Every time he does this, it sends a wave of emotions through me, mostly in my heart, making it gallop and leap, roaring to life at just the press of his lips in such a tender way.

"I'm sneaking you out the back so you don't have to face anyone today. But they all want to meet you."

"I need to thank them for letting me stay here. It's not like me to be so rude."

Reid chuckles under his breath as he pulls the door shut behind us. "Sweetheart, trust me, a bunch of bikers aren't worried about your politeness."

"Hearing it back, I guess it sounds silly. But still, I'm an outside guest you carried in here like a caveman, I should probably say hi and thank you."

"If that's what you wanna do, I won't stop you."

Reid and I walk down the stairs with my hand firmly in the palm of his, and into a massive kitchen where we quickly slip out a back door. The Washington summer air envelopes me immediately, and I tug on the neck of the leather jacket.

"I know it's oppressive right now, but it'll cool off once we're moving."

Reid swings his leg over his massive bike, steadying it between his knees with his hands on the wide handlebars. He's wearing a pair of worn-in jeans, a black leather jacket that fits him like a glove, his thick biceps bulging at the hem of the fabric. His signature black combat boots are heavy against the ground, his jeans pushed up above them. The top half of his hair is pulled back into a bun with wisps breaking free and falling into his forehead and eyes. His looks alone give off strong bad-boy vibes, but that's just skin deep. This man can be the softest, sweetest, most tender man I've ever met in my life.

And I want him.

Badly.

"I've never been on one before . . . well, except for the other day, but I don't even remember how we got here, to be honest."

"Sawyer never took you?"

"No. Said only one woman would ever be on his bike, and that didn't include his sister." I laugh.

"Sounds about right. Having a woman on the back of a rider's bike is a big deal. I get why he'd keep it for Ivy." There's a long pause while I take in that new information and the fact that Reid is asking me to get on the back of his. I understand his need to have me on the front of it the other night, he was rescuing me, for fuck's sake. But this feels different. It is different. "I see the wheels turning in your head. Come here," he demands as he holds out his hand to me.

I obey, my body on autopilot, walking up to him and placing my hand in his. The size difference is drastic. The moment our skin touches, it's like electricity flows through us, jolting me. He tugs me into his space, dropping my hand and wrapping his thick arm around my waist. My hand finds its home on the back of his neck, fingers threading through the hair that hangs loose.

"No one's ever been on my bike but you."

"How is that possible?"

"Like I said, it's a big deal."

I reach out, allowing myself to really touch him for the first time, running my fingers over the coarse hair of his beard, scratching my short nails into it. He leans into my touch, and flames lick at my feet, threatening to consume us both in the heat.

He moves quickly, gripping me tightly and hauling me into his lap. My legs are forced to spread around his meaty thighs so that I'm straddling him on the bike, just like we did when he saved me.

"Fuck the back of my bike, you belong right here, baby," he practically growls, his fingers dipping under the shirt at my back, connecting with my bare skin. Goosebumps break out across my body as electricity crackles through me. My skirt rides up, but he can't see anything from this position. I get comfortable, wrapping my legs around his waist and resting my head against his chest. "That's my girl."

His hand moves down to my ass, holding me practically flush against him as his motorcycle roars to life under us. The vibrations hum through my body, and I brace myself for him to start moving. Instead, his face nuzzles into the side of my neck, lips pressing a light kiss behind my ear that sends chills through my body, despite the hot summer temperature outside.

"I've got you," he whispers, the rough hair of his beard rubbing against the soft spot of my neck. "Relax and trust me."

And then we're moving, the loud engine echoing around us as the tires pick up dirt and loose gravel from the driveway. I cling to him like my life depends on it, the wind hitting the back of my head as I snuggle into his body. I hear the metal cranking of gates being pushed open as Reid slows, and then we're leaving the compound and on open roads, just the two of us.

After a while of silence, nothing but the wind rushing past us and the steady thrum of the engine vibrating through the thick leather seat, I start to relax and let go. The trees zip past us as Reid navigates through the narrow, winding backroads. I have no idea where we are, but I don't care right now. All that matters is the two of us and the road ahead.

Every mile we travel, I can't help but feel lighter, the weight of everything pressing down on me lifting on the breeze, taking with it the ability to haunt me any longer. Reid was right, being out here with nothing but the wind in your face, the roar of the bike, the empty road around us, it's exactly what I needed.

This is healing.

I hesitantly slide my hands between us until I'm gripping the zipper of his leather jacket, sliding it all the way down, and pushing it open. My hands have a mind of their own as I slide them over his taut, muscular waist and grip him tightly. He feels so good under me, and I don't want to let go. I feel the soft rumble of his groans as I daringly dip my fingers under his fitted T-shirt to touch his bare skin. He's so warm, so soft and right. I can't get close enough, no matter what I do. I want him. So badly.

Reid bends his head down, peppering a few kisses to the top of my head, making me melt further into him. I never want this to end. I lose myself to tracing over every defined ab, the light dusting of hair at his chest, his firm, sculpted pecs. Energy crackles through us, a live wire pulsing and electric, making my heart race, my core clench, desire racing through me.

After a while, Reid slows the bike down, pulling us over on the side of the road, nothing but the rustling of the trees around us. We're hidden here, in the middle of nowhere, not having seen a car for miles and miles. I sit up, leaning backward on the front of his bike so that I can look at him. He's so gorgeous. I've truly never seen a sexier man, and while I've always known this, the reasons I've fallen for him far exceed his ethereal beauty. It's in how he treats everyone around him like they're important, how unwaveringly selfless he is, it's in how, when he looks at me, the world around us disappears.

Reid looks at me like I'm the most precious thing he's ever seen, and it's so hard to reconcile that expression and the side of him I know so well with everything I've learned about him in the last few days. I have so many unanswered questions, but I'm not ready to face any of them yet. Mostly because I don't know if I care about any of it. I know *him*. Whether there are clearly two sides to his life or not, he is still Reid.

My legs straddle him on the bike, my hands moving up and down his taught waist, loving the feel of his hard muscles under my touch. His fingers gently trace the outline of my hair, his eyes tracking the movement before finally meeting mine.

"You're so beautiful, Kinsey."

My lips curve upward as I pull my bottom one between my teeth, trying to keep from smiling. His face softens slightly, but the fire behind his eyes can't be missed. His eyes move over every inch of my face in a slow, invisible caress that I feel down to the marrow of my bones. There's so much longing, so much desire behind those bright green eyes, that it's nearly heartbreaking. He looks at me with so much want and reverence, like he's hanging on the edge with barely contained hunger, and I know what I need more than anything. What we both need.

"You going to finally kiss me now?" I ask, done waiting for this man to finally make the move I'm so desperate for him to make. His lips turn up in a sexy-as-hell smirk.

"Yeah, sweetheart, I'm gonna kiss you now."

I ready myself for his lips to finally meet my own, but instead, as I close them, he kisses one eyelid gently, then the other. Another slow, sweet kiss against my forehead, each cheek, and the tip of my nose. Then his fingers are gently tilting my head backward by my chin, those perfect, plush lips of his finally, *finally*, connecting with mine.

Lightning erupts from my body.

Kissing Reid is transcendent.

His tongue gently licks against my seam, requesting access. I open eagerly for him as he slips into my mouth, my tongue meeting his, feeling him out. The moment the connection is made, a deep, primal growl breaks free of him, turning my insides to molten lava.

His hands find my hips, pulling me flush against him, his thick cock bulging against my core, the only separation my thin cotton panties and his denim jeans. I moan at the contact, wanting more of him. Wetness pools at my center, my hands gripping his arms tightly.

Our tongues tangle and caress, and it's the most erotically charged, sweetly passionate kiss I've ever been given in my life. It's the type of kiss that makes your heart fall hard and fast. The type where your soul soars, confident in the match it just found in another.

I'm ruined for everyone but him.

"Do you have any idea what you do to me?" he whispers, voice gruff and gravelly as he kisses my jaw, his breath hot on my skin.

I confidently press my core against him in response. "I think I have an idea."

"Not just that, Kinsey. So much fuckin' more. I'm willing to break all my rules for you. Burn the world down just to be able to look at you. You're perfect. I can't breathe when I'm away from you. And when I'm with you, I feel like I finally have a reason for living."

"Reid . . ." I say, falling rapidly for this man.

"Shh, just let me love on you."

There go the last shreds of my heart.

He descends back down on my lips, kissing me like he needs

me for air. I press harder against him, enjoying the way his hardness feels against my throbbing clit. My hands trace over his strong shoulders, pushing his jacket down to give me more access.

"Fuck, Kins, can I touch you? I need to touch you, baby."

"You are."

His right hand strokes up the outside of my bare leg, dipping under my skirt and tracing the outside hem of my panties, causing goosebumps to break out across my skin. He follows the hem, until the back of a single finger slides up my center in a featherlight touch that has me nearly jumping off his bike.

"Like this, sweetheart. Touch you here."

"Oh, god," I gasp, pleasure pulsing through me at just the faint touch of his finger.

"Let me, Kinsey? Let me make you feel good."

"Y-yes," I stutter. God, I want this man to touch me more than anything.

His hand grips my panties, slowly pushing them off to the side, and then his warm, calloused fingers are sliding through my slit. Electricity zips through me. A sexy, masculine growl of appreciation escapes his lips, and I swear I see stars.

"Jesus. You're soaked for me."

"Mmhmm," is all I can manage in return. He strokes me expertly and exploratorily. Like he's taking his time to figure out exactly what I need. His fingers slide down until one is nudging at my center, slowly pressing inside. I know I'm a virgin, but I've experimented with toys before, so I know what to expect, or at least I thought I did. Because my vibrator has nothing on Reid's fingers.

I shiver against his body, hanging on for dear life as he works me up, pressing a thick digit deep inside and curling. Moans flow freely from my lips as he grinds his palm against my aching clit and strokes something deep inside that I've never felt before.

His free hand gathers my hair at the base of my neck, giving it a tug to force me to arch my head to meet his eyes.

"Just like this. I want to look into your eyes as I make you come for the first time."

"Reid. Oh, god."

My brain nearly short-circuits as pleasure pulses low in my core. His piercing emerald eyes, dark and heavily lidded, gaze over my face, like he's wholly mesmerized by what's happening between us right now. The breath is stolen from my lungs with a sharp gasp as my pussy tightens, fluttering around those thick fingers working me over.

"That's it, little fighter. Give it to me. I want you to come on my hand, my fingers buried in this tight pussy. I want you leaking all over my bike."

"Oh, god, Reid. Don't stop," I pant as I grind against his hand, pleasure winding so tight, ready to snap.

"Not until your legs are shaking and you're screaming my name."

And then I'm coming, faster than I ever have before on my own. My orgasm slams into me, and I do exactly as he said. My legs shake around him as my body convulses, his name on my lips as he fingers me through the best orgasm of my life.

"Fuck, that's so damn pretty. You're a goddamn sight, sweetheart. So fuckin' perfect."

He pulls his fingers free, holding his hand up in front of us as he looks at the proof of how good he made me feel, dripping across his skin.

"Fuck, I hate to let this go to waste, but the first time I taste you, it's gonna be my mouth on your pussy, your cum coating my tongue."

My mouth falls open in shock, and he takes that as an open invitation because before I can protest, he's running those wet fingers covered in my arousal across my lips before dipping them into my mouth. My lips close around them automatically, my tongue swirling around them, my taste exploding on my tongue.

Reid growls in appreciation, a deep, primal sound that fuels me. "That's my good girl."

I moan around his fingers at his praise, and then he's slipping them free, his lips quickly replacing them, tongue delving into my mouth, claiming, pillaging, taking what he wants.

"My god, Kinsey, you're gonna be the death of me."

"I hope not. I want more of that first."

"Baby, I'll give you that anytime you want it, all you have to do is ask."

I'm in love with Reid Knight.

reid

I'm in love with Kinsey Hayes. Having her on my bike? In my arms? Fuck, touching her and making her come? I'm a goner. I don't deserve her, but I'm gonna make sure I do everything in my power to keep her anyway. We rode for hours, wind in our hair, nothing but long strips of empty road in front of us. Her squeals as I turned fast and hard around tight bends will live rent-free in my head forever. I knew she would love it, and pulling back into the clubhouse, I can already tell that whatever was haunting her was left on the open road. We still need to talk through a lot, but I can see the Kinsey that I know again, and that's the progress I wanted.

I steady my bike, turning it off and standing with her in my arms. There's a group of members hanging out on the porch, watching us, and I know it's now or never if she's going to meet everyone.

"Yo, Rogue, woman goes on the back of the bike," Malice teases.

"You sure? Pretty sure I like her ass right where it is, Mal."

"You did not just say that, holy shit." Kinsey blushes and it's so fucking cute.

"Sweetheart, I know you've got a quick mouth on you, so I'm

gonna need you to dig out that wit now 'cause it's the only way you'll survive bein' around these ass clowns."

I stand with her in my arms, turning so that she can adjust her skirt out of their eyesight. I wouldn't want to have to pluck out my brother's eyes for seeing something they shouldn't.

"You good, sweetheart?"

"Yeah, I'm ready."

Kinsey starts to walk, and I keep my arm slung over her shoulders, pulling her into my side, wanting everyone to know that she's taken. I never thought about making someone my old lady someday, but that all changed with Kinsey. It takes a vote, since it's welcoming a new member into the club, so she needs to get to know my brothers.

We walk up to the porch, Malice immediately grabbing Kinsey's hand and bowing like a lunatic. I smack his hand away from her with a violent growl.

"No touching."

His eyes do this crazy thing where they get really big, and he shivers his entire body like he's scared. We both know he isn't.

"Kins, this is Malice, the club's sergeant at arms. Malice, Kinsey. Be nice."

"Hey, nice to meet you," she replies.

"Pleasure is all mine, I'm sure of it."

"Mal . . ." I warn through clenched teeth. If he could just hold his crazy in for a few minutes. He's the one I'm worried will scare her out of here.

"Don't mind him, Kinsey, he's missing a few brain cells. I'm Wrath."

"Hi. Thanks for housing me the last few days and saving me."

"We'd do anything for Rogue, and it sounds like you're an extension of him, so that includes you."

Kinsey blushes and looks up at me with her beautiful blue eyes, and I hope she understands the gravity of what he just said. Once I make Kinsey mine in the club's eyes, their protection will extend to her, they'll take care of her in my place if I can't, they'll die for her if need be. Behind every powerful biker is a queen who has his back and his heart.

"Where's Prez?" I ask the group.

"Doing Prez shit inside somewhere."

I nod and turn to leave, my hand pressed to Kinsey's back. "We'll catch you all later."

"Charming bunch," Kinsey whispers to me once we're out of earshot.

"Malice means well, he's just slightly unhinged sometimes."

Sin is sitting at the bar with Rolo as we walk into the house, and I feel the moment Kinsey registers who he is, her body stiffening, her steps faltering.

"Oh god."

"It's fine, baby."

"I didn't know. How did I not know this about you, Reid?" She looks up at me with panic brewing behind her eyes, and my heart stutters.

"I've kept this part of my life separate for almost ten years. I'll explain it all to you. I promise."

Boys whistle and hoot as Kinsey and I walk further into the room, joining the two at the bar. A new prospect is slinging drinks behind it and nods his head to me in a hello, not making eye contact with Kinsey. Good. He may survive to patch in after all.

"Finally left the bedroom, kitten. It's good to see you."

My hand moves quickly, slapping the back of Rhys' head hard, forcing his teeth to clatter against the rim of the beer that was on its way to his mouth.

"Fuck, buddy, calm down! You almost knocked my teeth out!"

Kinsey giggles next to me before speaking up. "Serves you right. Now don't call me a kitten again or I'll make you actually lose those teeth next time."

A collective "ohh!" roars around us, and I bend down, grabbing Kinsey around the waist and hauling her off her toes to be eye level with me.

"Fuck, you're incredible," I tell her before I claim her mouth with my own in front of everyone. I worship her lips like I have the right to, like she's the only thing that matters. Kinsey is panting when I finally release her and set her back down on her feet, her eyes heavily lidded and lust-filled, a goofy grin on her face. God damn I could eat her alive. Something I plan to do as soon as I get her back alone in my room.

"Kins, you've already met this asshole. This other one is Rolo."

"Hi, Kinsey."

"Hey. Which one of you is the president?"

I chuckle softly as they both smile at her. "Neither of 'em, baby. They'd run the club into the ground if they were in charge."

"He's being a dick, kitten. I'm the VP," Sin says slyly. Kinsey rolls her eyes at him.

"Of course you are. Always second best?"

"Better than last." Rhys gives her a look that almost makes me slam his head down onto the bar top, so instead of breaking my brother's face, I decide it's probably time for us to head upstairs, but before I can do that, Rolo speaks up, making my spine stiffen.

"You gonna see her while you're here?" I know it's an innocent question because he knows I always go there first and I clearly haven't been up there yet, but it pisses me off because I haven't explained anything to Kinsey yet.

Kinsey's blue eyes flash up to me, but she doesn't look a bit jealous, more curious and confused. Anyone else would have heard the word 'her' in relation to another person and gotten jealous, a line of questioning to inevitably follow. But not Kinsey Hayes.

"Yeah, I'll see her when I'm ready," I snap, harder than I mean to.

I usher Kinsey to the back of the house toward the stairs, ready to get her alone.

"You'll meet my prez later, his name is Chaos, and you'll know it's him when you see him." She just nods her little head in agreement, never the one to question me on much.

My hands are all over her as we walk up the stairs and down the hallway to my old bedroom. I haven't spent a night in this place in years because being here dredges up too many painful memories. But being forced to stay here with Kinsey has given me new memories, and being around my club brothers more than I typically am when I pop in for church once a week has reminded me how much I do love them all. We're a family—with somewhat violent tendencies and fucked-up relationships—but we still live and die for each other, and that means something.

I never wanted these two lives to intersect, but now I'm wondering if I can't have both openly, be Reid and Rogue. Hiding one part of me in the shadows only brought my demons straight to my front step.

I kick the door shut behind us, quickly flicking the lock. The tension and desire in the room rises, and there's no fighting that we both feel it. Now that I've touched Kinsey's body, now that I've tasted her lips, it's all I can think about. Kinsey walks further into the room, the only sound our heavy breathing and her soft footfalls. But I want to fill it with her moans of pleasure, her heavy pants, my name on her lips as I make her come and come and come.

My hand curls around the soft skin of her bare forearm, spinning us around and hauling her body up to my level. I swallow Kinsey's surprised gasp with a short kiss. Strong, lithe legs wrap around my waist, pressing her against the back of the door, my hand holding the soft curve of her ass, her crystal-blue eyes blown wide, burning with hunger.

My free hand rubs up the soft curves of her body until I reach her face, running the pad of my thumb across the bruise still blooming there. A feral rage stirs inside me, but I tamp it down, pressing my mouth back to hers instead, needing somewhere to channel this energy thrumming inside me.

She tastes so damn sweet, so simply her, as I drag my tongue along the seam of her lips. I tilt her head back as far as I can and devour her, my tongue spearing into her mouth and finding hers. She gives as much as she takes and it's such a fucking turn-on, kissing me like she's been waiting forever for it and doesn't want it to end. Her hands thread through my hair, gripping and pulling. She swallows every single one of the moans she pulls from me.

My cock strains painfully against the zipper of my jeans as she grinds her little pussy against my stomach. Hell, I can't wait to take her, can't wait to claim her body, teach her how good this can be. There's a quiet voice in the recesses of my mind reminding me to take this slow, that she's a virgin and she's just been through a traumatic event, but I trust my girl and she will have no problem telling me no.

"Fuck, sweetheart, I could kiss you like this for hours."

"So do it."

"There's somewhere else I'm dying to kiss."

Lifting her slightly, I effortlessly shift us so that Kinsey's legs are thrown over my shoulders as I sink to my knees, leaving her back pressed against the door.

Kinsey gasps as my hands move to grip her thighs, spreading them open further and making room for my broad shoulders to fit between her legs. Once I have her where I want her, I lift her to my mouth. Nuzzling into the soft skin of her thighs, dragging my beard along her sensitive flesh.

"Reid, Jesus Christ. You're really doing this? No one's ever . . ."

Fuck, I knew she hadn't had sex yet but she's almost twenty-three, I assumed she'd done other things. What fucking idiots has she dated? I moan against her skin, peppering kisses along the inside of her legs.

I shove her skirt around her waist, leaving nothing but the thin pair of panties between me and the paradise that waits beneath them. I feel feral, possessed, an unhinged need to taste her, to have her scent covering me, to make her come as many times as her body will allow. Gripping her thighs, I spread her wider, dipping my head in and dragging my nose through her center, inhaling deeply. I groan loudly, my fingertips digging into the flesh of her thighs.

Then I do it again.

And again.

And again.

Until Kinsey is writhing beneath me, begging and pleading for more. Unable to deny either of us any longer, I quickly pull her panties to the side, then the flat of my tongue is licking up her center, pushing through her slick folds slowly and purposefully. Her taste explodes on my tongue and it's the sweetest fucking taste I've ever experienced.

"You taste so damn good. No one's ever kissed you here, sweetheart?"

"Never," she moans as she grips the fabric of her T-shirt in her fists.

"Fuck, do you know what that does to me?"

"Tell me," she begs as I lick her again, slow and methodical. I want to taste all of her; I don't want there to be an inch untouched by my tongue. Pleasure spreads through my body like a wildfire, a warmth filling my veins, my heart racing behind my chest, as I devour her sweet pussy. Knowing I'm the first and only man to ever taste her, to hear her sweet whimpers, is pulling me closer and closer to the edge without any stimulation to my cock.

"Shit, Kins. It makes me feral. To be the only man who's ever tasted you?" I shake my head in astonishment before dipping back down.

"Oh god, Reid! That feels sooo goood."

My fingers dig into the flesh of her ass, my mouth pressing wet kisses over her center, switching between long French kisses and deep, slow licks. When her hand reaches down to grip my hair, I'm a fucking goner. I move quickly, carrying her the few feet to the bed and dropping her back down on it, ripping her panties from her body. I'm between her legs a moment later, my thumbs delicately spreading open her lips to look at her pink, dripping center.

Fuck, she is perfect.

My tongue darts out, rimming her wet entrance, collecting as much of her arousal as I can. I want to drown in her. Then I'm pressing inside her warm heat, fucking her with my tongue, winding her tighter and tighter into an orgasm that I want her to remember for the rest of her life. I pull out of her, licking up her center before swirling around her swollen clit, flicking it with my tongue.

"Your pussy is so damn sweet." I lap at her again, torturously slow. "You taste better than I imagined." More licks, pressing harder this time. "I'll never get enough." I rub my hands over her pubic area, over her navel, my thumb swiping back and forth over my ink permanently etched into her skin. I continue my ascent, rubbing between her breasts before I do something that I know will make her see stars, but worried after everything she's been through.

My tattooed fingers wrap around her throat, looking up at her from between her legs. I've imagined what her dainty, flawless throat would look like with my fingers wrapped around her neck countless times, and my imagination didn't come close to the real thing. Kinsey looks down at me, her eyes heavily clouded with lust, her hips chasing my mouth.

"Trust me, little fighter. Take a deep breath and let go."

And then she submits, taking a deep breath just as my fingers tighten, cutting off her air supply at the same time as I suck her clit into my mouth, sucking in quick, gentle pulses. Her mouth falls open in a silent scream as she struggles for air, her hands gripping my arm, nails biting into my skin.

Then it happens.

An orgasm slams through her so hard, I swear the earth shakes below us. I release her throat the moment it happens, her lungs taking a heavy hit of needed oxygen. I swear I see the stars dancing behind her eyes as I lick her through wave after wave, pulling every ounce of pleasure from her tight, little body. Tears leak from the corners of her eyes as she shatters for me, her legs shaking, her stomach contracting.

Pure, unadulterated bliss.

It's the most beautiful thing I've ever seen, and I just became an addict.

I move up her body as she comes back down to Earth, a huge smile on my lips. Fuck, I know her body liked that, but did her head? I'm still so stunned no one has ever had the privilege of going down on this woman. I feel like the luckiest man in the world to be the first and only. Because there's no doubt about it, no one will ever get the chance again.

Her post-orgasm face is flushed with a pretty pink hue, her eyes heavy and glassy, mouth parted slightly. Her hand has fallen over her chest like she's making sure her heart is still beating. She's so goddamn beautiful, my heart beats rapidly in my chest for her.

"I'm obsessed with making you come," I whisper against her lips, leaving behind the glistening wetness coating my own. "Do you have any idea how beautiful you are when you do?"

"Reid, that felt . . . holy shit. Is it always like that?"

God, I have so much to show and teach my woman.

"When you're with the right person and the trust is there? Yeah, sweetheart, it can be."

CHAPTER 18

reid

AFTER I MADE KINSEY COME ON MY TONGUE FOR THE first time, I curled around her small frame and held her close. The feeling of her little body enveloped with mine is an addiction I don't plan to shake. This is where she belongs, this is what feels so goddamn right. For the first time in longer than I can truly remember, I'm at peace.

"Do you talk to your parents?" Unintentionally, her words bring back old wounds.

"I'm going to look for her," I lie. What I mean is that I can't look you in the face, knowing what happened to your little girl. The light of all our lives. That she was brutally raped and murdered because of the life I've chosen to live.

"What? No, Reid, we need you here. It's important that we stick together through this," my mom's voice breaks, and it would kill me if I weren't already dead inside after losing Lena.

"Mom, I can't just sit here, I need to move."

"Don't do this to your mother, son, she's already missing one of her children!"

"Dad, I have to."

"You're going to the club, aren't you? Did they have anything to do with this? Do you know what you've gotten yourself involved in, Reid? I'm a lawyer for fuck's sake! Do you know what that looks like for me? That you're involved with those monsters?"

"I know, Dad. We've been through this before. But the club isn't like the others. They aren't one-percenters. It's a family!"

"We're your goddamn family! Right now, your sister is missing and you're heading off on your bike!"

"Yeah, Dad, I am. I'm sorry, I can't be here."

"We're not close anymore, and it breaks their hearts, especially my mom's."

"I'm sorry. As much as I complain about my brothers, I couldn't imagine life without them or my parents."

"I've always been jealous of how close you all are."

"Have you thought about reaching out to them? Maybe work on repairing things?"

"It's complicated, Kins."

"I understand. I'm here if you ever want to talk about it."

The problem is, I do. I'm just terrified of how she'll view me after she learns the truth, which is why I haven't tried to take things all the way yet. There's just one barrier we need to get through before I let her give that up to me.

"Are you up for a walk?"

We leave the clubhouse, Kinsey's delicate, little hand clasped in mine. I don't want to let go of her. I feel this unmistakable need to be touching her at all times, or she'll disappear. I lead her off the main driveway, through the yard, and around the main building. We walk until the grass becomes tall and overgrown. She walks silently next to me, her free hand outstretched as she lets the grass brush under her palms.

"I like it here."

"You do?"

"It's peaceful."

"You know you're at an MC clubhouse, right?"

She laughs, and the sound carries on the wind. It's the first time I've heard it since before she was taken, and it gives me so much damn hope that she's going to pull out of this.

"I do. Even though Aspen Ridge is small, there's still so much hustle and bustle. But here it's just . . . different."

"Just wait until you see a party and let me know if you still think it's peaceful here."

"Are they wild?"

"They can be. Can't say it's on my list of things I want to take you to, but I won't ever tell you no. You're a big girl and can make your own decisions."

"Why don't you want me to go?"

"Because it's crazy, Kins. As much as I love 'em, my brothers get wild and rowdy. They're drinking and letting loose, they're loud, and they're fucking everywhere."

"Fucking as in . . ."

"Fucking. Having sex."

"Out in the open?"

"Yeah, sweetheart. The patch bunnies don't care, and neither do they."

"Patch bunnies?"

"The women who live here at the compound. They serve the club, and that includes sleeping with the members if they want to. Chaos makes sure they're taken care of and they're here of their own free will."

"Have you?"

I stop and face her, bending my knees so I'm closer to her level, my hands threading through her hair, pushing it out of my view of her pretty face.

"Have I fucked out in the open?" Kinsey bites her lip as a blush spreads across her cheeks. She's so fucking cute. "I'm not gonna lie to you, sweetheart. When I was young, drunk, and dumb, yeah. But I'm not into that. I'm not into anyone else seeing the woman I'm with. I also don't mess around with patch bunnies anymore. Haven't in a bit."

"Okay."

I can't help but laugh. It's such a Kinsey response.

"Just okay?"

"Yeah. What should I say? Tell me more? Everyone has a past; it doesn't change just because you feel the way you do now. What's it matter?"

"You're perfect, you know that?"

"Hardly, big guy. Now, where are we going?"

"I want you to meet someone."

I take her hand back in mine and pull her along, forcing myself to walk at a slower pace since my strides are so much longer than hers. We finally reach the huge Aspen tree at the edge of the property, its bright green leaves swaying in the breeze. Wild lupines are growing in vibrant blues, purples, and pinks across the open landscape.

Lena's headstone rests under the tree, alone and peaceful, and just like it always does when I come to visit her, the leaves quake and rustle.

Kinsey squeezes my hand and looks up at me patiently. I don't even know where to start, so I sit down in front of my sister's headstone and pull Kinsey into my lap. After a few quiet moments of Kinsey running her fingers lovingly through my hair, I open my mouth and let the words fall out as they come.

"Kinsey, this is Lena. My sister. Sis, this is Kinsey. She's important to me, and I needed you two to meet."

I keep my arm wrapped around Kinsey's waist, my other resting on her bare thigh, rubbing my thumb aimlessly over the soft skin there. I swallow hard against the onslaught of emotion.

"Almost ten years ago, I was having dinner with Lena at our parents' house, after I had to head back to the clubhouse for a party. She begged me to take her with me. We were inseparable.

She was my best friend, Kins. There's not much we didn't do together. But I hated bringing her here, and I told her no."

Kinsey listens intently, the light summer breeze caressing her face and whipping her hair around.

"She was secretly seeing Chaos' younger brother, Lucas, and she snuck out to meet up with him shortly after I left her. Later that night, we got a tip that Lucas and Lena had been picked up by a rival club. By the time we got to the house, it was too late. Chaos carried her out of the house and put her lifeless body in my arms."

"Reid . . ." Kinsey gasps, covering her mouth and choking on a sob.

"They raped and beat her to death and left her there as a message to us. I'll spare you what happened to Lucas, but we couldn't retrieve his body to bring it back here to rest with Lena. I died along with her that day, Kinsey. If I had just said yes and brought her with me. If I hadn't joined the club at all, she never would have been targeted."

"Reid, it's not your fault. There is evil out there that you can't control. We can't control other people's decisions, no matter how much we wish we could sometimes."

I release a rough breath as her sweet little hands reach up to grasp my face, wiping away the tears that have started to escape my eyes. I didn't even realize I was crying.

"You need to know what kind of man I am, Kinsey. That club? We hunted them down one by one and killed them all. Their president? I spent days torturing him before his body gave up on him, and he died. I don't regret any of it."

I notice her spine stiffen against me, how her breathing has stopped, and my heart starts to break because I know she's realizing just who Rogue is, the part of me I've kept hidden, what I'm capable of, and while it needed to happen, I wanted to be enough for her, I want to be *good* enough for her.

"That's not all," I say, pausing for a moment. "No one had heard from the Iron Wolves in almost ten years. We assumed we had killed all of them off, or whoever survived went into hiding or joined other clubs. But they've regrouped. They hit us a month ago at one of our businesses, we retaliated, and I went in for the job. I let one of them live to send a message, and because of that, they came for me and took you instead." My voice cracks on the last two words, and my tears flow harder. "It's my fault you were taken."

"Reid, hey, I'm okay. It is not your fault. It's theirs. You saved me. I'm okay."

"Fuck, Kinsey, if I lost you," I choke out the words, my heart fracturing further. "I wouldn't survive it."

"I'm here. I'm going to be okay. I'm so sorry, Reid. But you are not the things you've done. You are the best fucking man I know, do you understand me? You are good."

"Tell me what happened there, Kinsey. It's killing me not knowing what they did to you," I beg her. "My mind is a dangerous, dark place after what I've seen and done. No matter what happened, I'm not walking away from this. Anything done to us in this life doesn't define who we are, and it changes nothing."

She takes a deep, stuttering breath, tears streaming down her pretty face.

"I was upstairs reading when I heard a crash downstairs. It's Aspen Ridge, Reid, it didn't cross my mind that it wasn't you down there, so I went to see if you were okay. I thought maybe you had fallen—anything but what I found. By the time I had opened the door, the crashing and shattering was louder, so I grabbed the baseball bat the boys left me by the front door and snuck down. I have no idea why I didn't call for help or hide. Stupidity? I'm too young and naive?"

"Baby, don't talk about yourself like that."

"It's true! Never in a million years did I think two lowlife scumbags would be trashing your beautiful studio. I was frozen in shock, and then they saw me, and it was too late."

"The blood all over the floor? Was that yours?"

"No." She shakes her head with a devilish smile that makes me so proud. "I didn't go without a fight. I broke one of their noses. Everything else was kind of a blur. I fought hard, and then they knocked me out. I woke up in the shithole you found me in."

"And they didn't touch you?"

She gets quiet, and my heart sinks. I had already had her confirmation they hadn't raped her, but that doesn't mean other things didn't happen.

"Did. They. Touch. You?"

"No. Not in the way you're asking. Only ever you."

Relief floods my veins.

"I'm going to kill them all, Kinsey."

"I know, baby."

A growl works up my chest, shifting her in my arms by her tiny waist. Her legs wrap around me, settling Kinsey's ass right in my lap, her arms curling around my neck. I bend into her, holding her tightly around the waist with my head buried in her neck. I cry for my sister, for Kinsey, for the two pieces of me I've struggled to keep separate for a decade, only to have them forcefully fused together. I've confessed my sins, and I want to accept her love if she'll give it to me after this.

CHAPTER 19

kinsey

REID'S CONFESSION SHOULD TERRIFY ME. IT SHOULD
have me running the other way. But it only made me realize how
deeply in love with this tortured man I am. He's seen and
committed horrible acts, but I'm not going to judge him for
them. He erased pure evil from this world, and I'm not naive
enough to believe everything is always black and white. Learning
his history, what happened to his sister, broke a piece of me that I
left with her. I've always suspected Reid had something dark
inside him that snuffed out his light, but the goodness in his heart
never went away; he just had the inability to recognize all the good
he was doing, past the grief he's been drowning in.

We stayed at Lena's grave for hours, talking and crying. He
told me about what it was like to grow up just the two of them,
how they were best friends and did everything together, how she
wanted to be a midwife someday. He reminisced, and I listened,
soaking in a part of him that I didn't know existed. His fingers
toyed with my hair or rubbed aimlessly over the bare skin of my
legs while he spoke. It seemed cathartic, and I wondered just how
long it had been since he had been able to talk freely about her.

Later that night, we lay in bed facing each other, my fingers tracing over the dark lines of the tattoos that cover his forearm. I don't like to push and ask questions, wanting him to give information freely, but I can't help but think about his parents and what they must be feeling after losing a child and then having a strained relationship with their only living one. My parents would be devastated, and the pain must be unimaginable to live with every day.

"Can I ask about how your parents have coped with your sister's death?"

"They don't know she died, sweetheart."

"How is that possible?"

"The night she died, Camden gave me a choice. We could leave Lena there and call the police after we left, and my parents would know every single gory detail of what happened to their little girl, or I could take her back to the compound with us and bury her. In that moment, Kins, I couldn't let her go. I would have killed any one of my brothers if they had tried to pull her from my arms without a shred of remorse."

I don't know what I was expecting, but it wasn't that. This poor family. This poor, sweet man. I can't imagine the weight Reid has been bearing on his own for all these years. Knowing the truth of his sister's fate and keeping it to himself to protect his family? I honestly don't know what I would have chosen, and I'm not a parent and can't imagine which I'd rather know. Keep hope alive in my heart, or know the truth and have it break me completely?

"I'm so sorry, Reid. I'm so fucking sorry."

"I know, baby. That's why I keep my distance from my parents. I can't face them. They filed a missing persons report, and I even helped look for her, knowing exactly where she was the entire time. It got to a point where one day, I just left. I told them it was all too hard, because it was. They still hold out hope that she's alive, and I know she isn't. I never got to grieve with them."

"Have you thought about telling them?"

"No. My dad's a lawyer, and while he typically only deals with estates and wills, I don't know how he'd react. I have to protect the club, too. I'm in this for life, Kinsey. There's no getting out. It's complicated."

My heart has never felt so heavy. "You carry this all alone?"

He nods his head yes, and my heart shatters. This poor, sweet man.

"You have me, now, and I need you to trust that I'm strong enough to carry it with you."

His hands reach out, pushing my hair behind my ears and grasping my face. He leans in slowly, his eyes bouncing from my eyes to my lips, and I hold my breath in anticipation.

"I believe you, little fighter," he whispers against my lips before he kisses me. It's sweet at first, his lips firmly pressed against mine, his hand cupping my face in such a tender touch that it's almost heartbreaking. But then the energy in the room shifts, heats up as his hands start to roam my body, his tongue pushing into my mouth. I moan at the intrusion, accepting him greedily.

His fingers slip under my T-shirt, slowly caressing my bare skin, sending goosebumps scattering across my flesh. My hands move to his face, running my fingertips through his beard while we kiss like our lives depend on it. He devours me, and I feel every bit of his feelings in every stroke of his tongue, every brush of his lips against mine; it's earth-shattering and life-altering in a way that I never expected kissing someone could be.

Kissing Reid Knight is everything.

He sits up, grabbing the hem of my T-shirt and lifting, my arms moving upward, allowing him to pull it over my head. He tosses it over his shoulder, not wasting any time reaching for the clasp of my bra. With a flick of his fingers, it gives way, falling down my shoulders, my breasts released from their confines. I remove it completely, as Reid sits back on his haunches, watching me. Then he's on top of me again, lying off to the side so he doesn't crush me with his weight, one hand threading through my hair, the other grasping my breast in his palm. I arch into him, trying to press myself against him as much as possible. I'm desperate. I want more of him, I want everything from him. He tore himself open and exposed every dark and gritty part to me, and I want to give him everything in return.

Reid kisses my jaw, licking a trail from under my ear to my chin, and dipping down, peppering open-mouthed kisses, sucks, and bites down my neck.

"I can't get enough of you," he moans against my skin as he reaches my chest and dips lower, lifting the handful of my breast to his mouth and swirling his tongue around the tip. My nipple pebbles for him as he blows a breath of cool air onto it before sucking the tip into his mouth.

My back bows, my hand wrapping around his head as he moans around the bud.

"That feels so good. My god. I want you, Reid. I need you."

"I love making you feel good, Kins, I never want my time with you to end."

He gets up then, gripping my skirt and slowly pulling it down my legs as he climbs off the bed. I'm left completely bare in front of him as he stands in front of me. I've never been naked in front of a man before, and I don't feel an ounce of nervousness lying here in front of Reid. Even though he saw me naked on the first night, this is different.

My heart tumbles in my chest like a shell caught in a crashing wave. Reid looks down at me with so much heat, awe, and reverence. His eyes are heavily lidded, his pupils blown with hunger. I've never felt sexier and more desired than I do when his emerald eyes are on me.

"Jesus Christ, sweetheart. Look at you. You're so goddamn perfect."

My eyes pool with tears. I love him.

"Reid . . ."

"I know. I feel it, too."

Reid answers without my words, always attuned to my thoughts, my needs, sometimes before I even know them myself. We're so chemically connected, it's hard to believe he's never been inside me.

Those large, tattooed hands curl around each of my ankles, dragging me to the edge of the bed before sliding a slow, calloused caress up my legs.

"Do you know how long I've waited to touch these legs?"

I can't take my eyes off him, this huge, strong man being so sweet and tender with me, worshiping me, loving me like I'm the most precious thing he's ever had the privilege to hold.

"I'm taking my time with you, Kinsey. There won't be a single inch of your body that I haven't touched or kissed. I'm going to own you. Your body will only ever know me, do you understand?"

I nod my head in agreement, but I should have known that wouldn't be enough for him. His hands stop their ascent at my hips, his piercing green eyes meeting mine, waiting.

"I understand. But that means you're mine, Reid. Only mine."

His smile is achingly beautiful, his full lips curving at the corners, the skin around his eyes crinkling. My core dampens further, throbbing, pulsing with such a deep need that I'm wanton, feral, my hips gyrating, searching him out as his hands climb up my sides to the outside of my breasts, and back down to my hips—over and over he rubs, his touch getting tighter on each pass as if his control is slipping.

"Kinsey . . ." he says my name on a rough exhale, a plea, desperation thick in his husky voice. "I've never wanted someone as much as I want you. It feels like I can't breathe without you. I've never experienced a need so strongly before, like I'll die without feeling you wrapped around me, your tight pussy pulsing around my cock, the taste of you on my tongue, your body wrapped in my arms."

He drops to his knees then, pushing my thighs apart, dragging his tongue down the inside of one thigh, repeating the process on the other side. My body chills from his touch but my insides are on fire.

"Reid, please," I beg, wanting his mouth at my center.

"You want my mouth, sweetheart?"

"Yes!"

"Tell me exactly what you want."

"I want you to kiss me."

Reid tsks, shaking his head, dragging his rough facial hair over my sensitive, wet skin, driving me crazy.

"Try again, my little fighter. Tell me what I want to hear."

"I want you to kiss my pussy, Reid. *Please.*"

"That's my good girl."

He finally gives me what I want, parting my lips with his thumbs, and with his eyes firmly locked on mine, his tongue dips out, licking a slow path from hole to clit with the flat of his tongue.

A deep, masculine groan rumbles through his chest. His voice is deep and husky, lust-filled and practically feral. "Your taste, baby . . ." Reid's head drops back down, pressing his entire face into my center, moaning against my flesh, the vibrations adding to the sensations he's creating between my legs.

"Everything about you was made for me, Kinsey. I want your scent to coat me, your cum to drench my beard. Fuck, I could stay down here forever."

Holy shit. All of my fictional book boyfriends have nothing on this. I dreamed of what this would feel like, and my wildest dreams didn't come close to the real thing.

My fingers find his head, threading through his long hair, pushing it out of the way so I can watch him pleasure me. Reid eats me out like it's just as much for him as it is for me. It's in the way he takes his time, exploring and figuring out what makes me go wild, it's the way he feels me climbing closer, and he pulls back to not let it end too soon.

Reid Knight is a fucking god at eating pussy.

He settles in on my clit, flicking it ruthlessly. I erupt.

He licks me through my orgasm like he's waded through a barren desert and finally given water, like he'll die without it. And hell, does it feel mind-blowing. Like floating on the highest cloud, pleasure like I've never known before pulses through my body in the most euphoric, addictive feeling. My legs shake, my back bowing off the bed as Reid's hand presses down on my lower belly, forcing me back down on the bed.

"Reid! Oh god, yes!"

He licks me through the waves of pleasure until I relax against the mattress, pulling at his hair for some reprieve.

His green eyes sparkle as he looks up at me, his mouth and beard glistening in the light from my arousal.

"That was one."

"Oh, god," I rasp, trying to catch my breath.

He relaxes again between my legs, his thick finger rimming my pussy. I brace for him to press in, but he just keeps playing, dipping into the first knuckle, using his thumb to spread my arousal up to my clit.

"Reid . . ." I gasp as his tongue replaces his finger, pushing the strong muscle into my core and fucking me with it. His thumb presses softly against my clit, rubbing firm circles and making my legs shake uncontrollably.

"Come for me, sweetheart. Let me have it."

He doesn't stop until I'm a trembling mess, my pussy clenching around his tongue as I give him what he wants. My orgasm rips a scream from my lips that I'm sure everyone in the clubhouse can hear, but I'm too lost to the waves of pleasure crashing through me to care.

"That was two."

"You're going to kill me."

"Never. But I need to get you ready to take me. Our size difference is . . . *drastic*."

"I'm ready," I argue. I'm ready for him to fill me. For him to take my virginity. For him to have a part of me that no one else ever will.

"Have you played with your pussy before, Kinsey?"

His question stuns me for a moment; his eyes are locked onto mine as the tip of his middle finger slowly dips in and out of me.

"Answer me, baby. Have you ever laid in bed at night and played with this sweet little pussy?" He asks again with a devilish smirk.

"Yes, you know I have."

"Show me."

"Show you?"

"Show me how you touch yourself."

"I usually use a toy."

He growls, long and deep, a husky moan, like the thought of me using a toy on myself pushed him over the edge.

"Fuck, Kinsey. You'll be showing me that once we're back home. You fuck yourself with it?"

"Yes. I'm scared to go *too* deep, but yes."

"Jesus Christ. Show me with your fingers. I want to watch."

I comply, wanting to please him, wanting to show him, so I slowly drag my fingertips down my stomach, dipping my middle finger through my slit, finding myself soaked.

"You feel how wet you are? Your pussy comes so good, baby. I fuckin' love the mess you make."

"Oh, god, Reid. Your mouth."

"Get used to it, sweetheart."

I use my finger to dip inside, rubbing my palm against my overly sensitive clit at the same time. My other hand finds my breast, twisting and pinching my nipple while I work myself up. Reid watches me intently, his face so close to where I'm touching myself, the back of my hand bumping his beard and lips.

"That's it, *Jesus Christ*, you're so fuckin' sexy. Look at you. Fuck that little pussy, Kinsey. Make yourself come for me."

"Oh god. Reid."

"Yeah, baby. That's my good girl, work those fingers."

My legs start to shake, my stomach tightening, as the pleasure coiling deep within me finally snaps. Reid pushes my hand away as my orgasm hits me, replacing it with his mouth, and I swear to God, my soul leaves my body.

Reid suctions his mouth around me, gripping my hips and pulling me to his face. My mouth falls open on a silent scream, and I grip the sheets below me for purchase. He prolongs my orgasm, pulling every last drop from my body until I'm spent.

Aftershocks roll through me as I melt into the bed, reaching for him but he just gives me one more wet kiss to my pussy before standing in front of me. I let my knees fall closed, pushing up onto my elbows to watch him.

Reid undresses slowly, and it's only just now that I realize he's still been dressed this entire time. Why is that so hot?

His arm reaches over his head, pulling the back of his shirt up and over his head in a move that is so him and so ridiculously sexy that my mouth falls open slightly as I watch. His hair is lifted with the shirt, finally falling free around his shoulders as he drops the fabric to the floor.

My eyes roam over the expanse of his muscular, rock-hard body. Every inch of him is covered in thick tattoos, and I'll never get over looking at them. I love this man shirtless.

His belt and pants are next, leaving him standing at the foot of the bed in nothing but a pair of formfitting boxer briefs. Unable to stop myself, and knowing I don't have to, I get up, crawling to the edge of the bed and sitting tall on my knees.

My fingers trail across his thick collarbone, dipping down and over his muscular chest, tracing over the outlines of various tattoos.

"You do know how sexy you are, right?" I ask him.

Reid chuckles, deep and husky, as I explore his perfect, chiseled body. My hands dip to the perfect V, fingers tracing over the defined area. My mouth salivates, and I give in to the urge to lick over his Adonis belt. Reid groans long and loud, his fingers threading through my hair as I drag my tongue across his pelvis. His taste explodes on my tongue, salty and manly and all so very *him*.

My fingers dip into the waistband of his boxer briefs, pulling them outward and down, his cock springing free. My mouth falls open at the sight. He's long and thick, and I'm positive my hand wouldn't be able to wrap fully around it. An angry, pulsing vein runs up the underside, leading to a deep-purple mushroom head.

"Like what you see, sweetheart?"

"Reid . . . that," I say, my eyes huge while I take in the tree trunk that rests heavy against his abdomen. "There's no way . . ."

"It'll fit, sweetheart. You were made for me," he reassures me as his fingers massage into my scalp.

"I'm also the size of one of your legs. Reid, you're gonna split me in two."

His hand tilts my head up so I'm looking into his emerald eyes.

"Kins, I would never hurt you. *Ever.* Do you understand?"

"Yes."

"You trust me?"

"Yes," I answer without hesitation. I trust him with my life.

"It'll fit. I'm gonna make this so good for you, and you're gonna take every single inch. Aren't you?"

"Yes."

"That's my good girl."

"Can I?" I ask, my tongue peeking out and swiping over my lips. I want to make him feel good in the same way he's made me. The urge is strong. Nerves are non-existent, even though I haven't done this before.

"Can you what, sweetheart?"

"Taste you?"

"You want to put my cock in your sweet mouth, Kinsey?"

"So badly."

"Jesus Christ," he groans as his head falls back like he's taking a second to collect himself. "Have you ever done this before?"

"Never."

"Fuck, Kins." He grabs his thick dick, holding it out to me like he's about to hand feed me dessert. His other hand moves to the back of my head, gripping my hair. "Open wide for me."

I do as he says, opening my mouth wide for his big dick, hoping like hell I can take at least half of it, if I'm lucky.

"Stick out your tongue, baby. Let me see it."

Reid pulls my head closer to him as he taps the bulbous head against my tongue.

Once.

Twice.

Three times.

Then he's pushing in, and I close my mouth around his dick. He's warm and smooth against my tongue and tastes slightly salty. He pushes in until he hits the back of my throat, and I gag, my eyes watering. Jesus Christ, how am I ever going to make him feel good with this?

"Breathe through your nose and relax your throat for me. Trust me, baby."

I take a deep breath through my nose, urging myself to relax and let him show me how he likes it. He pulls out completely, swiping the tip against my lips, back and forth, before pushing in until he hits the back of my throat. This time, I'm ready for him and know what to expect. I relax my throat, allowing him to slip down, taking him just a bit farther than the first time.

Reid groans loudly, a deep masculine moan that fuels me to keep going, and I reach out, grabbing the base of his cock. He's all rock-hard muscle and smooth skin, and I tentatively squeeze, moving my hand in time with my mouth to give him friction where I can't reach with my tongue.

"Oh fuck, that's my girl. You're sucking me so good. Shit, Kins."

I moan around his length, his praise urging me on, making me feel more powerful than I ever have before. This strong, gentle giant is a moaning, straining mess because of how I'm making him feel. I've reduced him to a puddle, and if that isn't one hell of a heady, intense feeling, I don't know what is. Talk about a boost to my confidence when I don't know what the hell I'm doing.

I suck him hard, going off pure instinct, swirling my tongue around the engorged tip on every upstroke, jerking him with my hand the best I can.

"Damnit, Kinsey, oh fuck. That feels so fuckin' good. Take me deeper, baby. I know you can do it."

I do as he says, taking a breath and relaxing, tilting my head to the side to try a new angle. He slips further down my throat, and tears spill over my eyelids. I gag hard around his length. "That's my girl, goddamn. Don't stop."

I try again, taking him all the way back, and before I gag, I swallow around his length, bringing him back impossibly far.

"Oh fuck!" he yells as he pulls away abruptly, slipping from my lips with a loud pop. I wipe the saliva off my lips and look up at him, confused. His chest heaves, breaths coming in heavy pants, his eyes feral.

"Did I do something wrong?" I ask, suddenly self-conscious and unsure if I screwed this up. His big hands cup my face, tilting my head to look up at him.

"No, sweetheart, fuck no, that was so damn good. I want the first time I come with you to be inside your tight, virgin pussy. You can suck me off as often as you want after that," he chuckles. "But tonight? Tonight, I'm coming with your legs shaking around me."

My mouth falls open at his words, and he takes full advantage of it, bending down and capturing my lips with his. He moves quickly, his big arm wrapping around my waist and dragging me up the bed. He braces himself with one arm so that he doesn't crush me with his weight, his other holding my face cradled in his palm.

"My heart stopped beating the day I lost Lena. Then I was given you. You've brought me back to life, Kins. I don't deserve you, sweetheart. But I'm gonna keep you. You're my salvation.

My light. I'll spend the rest of my life trying to be good enough for you."

Overwhelming emotions race through me like a storm, and tears track down my face. Those three little words are on the tip of my tongue, but he doesn't give me the time to say them as his lips descend on mine, kissing me like he meant every single word.

reid

NEVER IN A MILLION YEARS DID I THINK I WOULD FIND myself back in this room, with Kinsey Hayes lying on my bed looking up at me like I'm deserving of this privilege. I've done unspeakable things, I've been responsible for bloodshed and death, for the loss of my beautiful, innocent sister, I've looked death in the face without a wince, I've seen the bottom of a bottle more times than I can remember, and somehow, I was gifted this perfect, radiant light of a human.

I can't take my eyes off hers as I look down. Gorgeous blue eyes look back at me with warmth and desire I don't deserve. My heart beats wildly in my chest, the selfish desire I've pushed down for as long as I could taking full control. The guilt starts to push through my cracks, knowing the lines I'm crossing, the precious gift she's about to give me. My eyes flutter closed, and I freeze.

Cool hands touch my face, and I open my eyes to find Kinsey looking up at me with concern, my face cradled in her small palms.

"Hey, where'd you go? Come back to me, baby."

My hands move to wrap around her waist, burying my face in her neck, taking a deep inhale of her floral and sage scent.

"Kins, this is gonna kill him."

"We don't have to. I understand. I won't push you. We'll figure this out."

My eyes meet hers and see nothing but genuine understanding and concern reflecting back in them. She's so fucking beautiful it hurts. But her kindness? To feel her affection? Hell . . . her love? I'm crazy about this girl.

"I promise, I get your position with my brother and how hard this is for you. He was there for you at rock bottom. I get it, baby. We'll wait until we talk to him."

I blink back the moisture filling my eyes as she smiles up at me. Her pretty pink lips lift at the corners as she shakes her head, as if this is the easiest thing in the world for her. How is she so inherently good?

"I don't deserve you, sweetheart. You're everything that is perfect in this world. I'm no good for you. I'd snuff out your light with my darkness." My hands move back to her face as I drop my forehead to rest against hers. "I'd never forgive myself for ruining you."

"You could never ruin me, Reid. Let me be your light. Let me pull you from the darkness. Trust that I'm strong enough. Despite what you see in yourself, I see the real you. You are good, you just need to forgive yourself before you can see it."

Fuck it.

Fuck it all.

"You're mine, little fighter. There's no going back for me. I'll burn every bridge if I can have you. Tell me you're mine and nothing else matters."

Her eyes widen in surprise. She truly was content with us not taking this all the way.

"I'm already yours, sweet man. You ready to be the only man who's ever touched me?"

Jesus Christ. She's gonna be the death of me. I'll walk through Hell's gates with a smile on my face, ready to face the sentence for my sins to be with her right now. But maybe she's my salvation. Maybe her goodness can cleanse me.

"The first and last, sweetheart," I vow and hope to hell I'm enough to breathe it into existence. A better man would push her away, tell her to find someone who matches her bright light, but none of them would make her as happy as I can. Could protect her like I can. No one would love her like I do. So I'm going to greedily accept, and I'm not letting her go.

Kinsey's the strongest woman I've ever met. I may not know how to express it to her, but she's already set me free of it all. I push my guilt to the far recesses of my mind. I'll deal with my best friend later. Kinsey is worth it. *I'm worth it.*

I trail kisses down her collarbone, trailing over the protruding bone with my tongue, her nails lightly scratching over my shoulders as I work my way down her perfect body. When I reach her breasts, I take my time worshipping them, sucking on each nipple until they're stiff peaks, gripping the handfuls in my palms and squeezing. She moans softly, each breath coming harder and faster as I go. I kiss over each of her ribs, dragging my tongue down the center of her body until I swirl around the rim of her belly button, flicking at the little metal ring that's pierced there.

"You're so perfect. I love your body, Kinsey."

She moans under my praise, and I love that she accepts it. I reach the paradise waiting for me between her gorgeous, long legs, taking my time to kiss the inside of each of her thighs before pulling them over my shoulders and lying flat on my stomach. I'm face-to-face with her pretty pink, glistening pussy and I take a minute to admire it. I press a firm kiss to her center, swiping my tongue through her lips.

"Mine," I growl before sealing my mouth to her pussy. Her taste explodes on my tongue, and I eagerly lap at it. Moving my right hand between us, I slowly press my middle finger inside, she hums her approval, grinding her pussy into my face.

"You're so tight. Gonna feel so good wrapped around my cock, Kinsey."

I swirl my tongue around her swollen clit, working her over toward another orgasm. I love how responsive her body is to me.

We're so attuned with each other, and I play her body like I've known it for years. I work my finger in and out, her body easing the way with how fucking wet she is. Her arousal drips down to her ass, coating my fingers, and it takes all I have not to lap it all up.

I add a second finger, her pussy fluttering around them as I work her open. I know there's nothing I can do to keep from hurting her since this is her first time, but I want to make her as ready as I can before I impale her with my dick.

We only get one shot to do this the first time, and I want her to remember it positively for the rest of her life. Fuck, I can't believe I'm about to take Kinsey's virginity. Can't believe I'm the only one who will ever get this perfect woman in this way.

I fuck her with my fingers while licking her clit, and I feel the slow build of her orgasm starting, the soft fluttering of her pussy around my fingers, the uncontrollable tremors of her legs on my shoulders. She's close.

The flat of my hand rubs up the center of her body, between her breasts, my hand finding its home around her pretty, delicate neck.

"Take a deep breath and come for me."

She doesn't hesitate, inhaling deeply and letting her eyes fall closed. That's my good girl, I fucking knew she would love breath play. I squeeze just tight enough to cut off her air supply. Watching her body, listening for her cues as I fuck her tight little cunt with my fingers and suck her clit into my mouth.

Her hips buck wildly, her hands digging into the fabric of the sheets below us as she comes. Her cum floods my hand, her walls pulsing around my fingers, making it impossibly tight. I release her throat just as she peaks, her sweet gasp of air filling the room, and she comes and comes.

As she returns to Earth, I watch, enraptured, as I pull my fingers free of her body, soaked in her arousal. Sitting up, I lay over Kinsey, wiping my fingers over her pouting pink lips.

"Suck, baby."

She obeys, sucking both fingers into her warm mouth and licking them clean. I pull them free and replace them with my tongue, chasing the taste of her sweet release. Her hips gyrate, my hard cock slipping through her drenched folds, coating me in her slick arousal.

"I'm trying to be a good man, sweetheart, but the urge to claim you bare is strong. Tell me to get up and get a condom."

She shakes her precious little head no, and I pull back to really study her face. Her hair is fanned out across my pillow, wet whisps sticking to the crown of her head from perspiration, her cheeks flushed pink, eyes blown wide. She looks thoroughly fucked already and I haven't even been inside her yet.

"Take me bare, Reid. I'm yours."

"Fuck, Kins. Are you sure?"

"I don't want anything between us. I'm on the pill for my periods, and I'm obviously clean."

"I'm clean, I was tested after my last hookup."

"Then what are you waiting for, big guy? Fuck me."

The growl that works its way up through my chest is primal, animalistic, and she doesn't realize what she just unleashed. I hold myself up, wanting to watch as I sink inside her for the first time, and notch my achingly hard cock at her wet entrance.

"You ready for me?"

"I've been ready for you for a long time, Reid Knight."

My heart beats out of my chest as I press into her heat for the first time. I watch as she stretches around the very tip of my cock as I slowly start to disappear inside her before relaxing back down flush with her body. Her skin feels so good against mine, her perfect breasts pressed firmly against my chest.

I cradle her head between my hands and gently kiss her mouth as I pull my cock out torturously slow, then start to press back in.

"Are you okay, sweetheart?"

"You're so big, it's not going to fit, Reid," she whines, her soft hands gripping my sides so tight, her thighs trembling around me.

"Oh, it'll fit, baby. Trust me and relax. This pussy is gonna take every inch of my dick. Do you feel how wet you are? You're making such a good mess of us."

I press in slightly more, feeling her stretch around me.

"You're so damn tight, Kins, you feel so good," I whisper against her lips, slowly working my cock in inch by inch. Her breathing is coming in hard pants, and it's killing me that I'm hurting her.

"Reid! God, it burns," she pants, her eyes shining with unshed tears.

"I'm so sorry. You need me to stop, Kins? I'll stop."

"No! Don't stop, just, I need you inside me . . . all of you. I want you to fuck me."

Fuck. Don't say that. Jesus, I don't want to hurt her.

"It's gonna hurt, baby, be sure."

"The pain will fade, going slow is just prolonging it. *Please.*"

Her fingers reach down low, gripping my hips and pulling me deeper. I give in to her wants and pull out almost completely before thrusting all the way inside her tight heat in one fluid motion. I swallow Kinsey's scream with my mouth as her body trembles underneath me. Her pussy walls pulse and contract, and I've never felt something so good in my life, even if my heart is squeezing knowing it's painful for her. I'm a big guy and she isn't just tight, she's fucking tiny.

"That's my girl. You took all of me, baby, a perfect fit," I tell her as I pepper her face with kisses, licking up the tears tracking down her face.

"Oh, god, Reid. I feel so full."

We sit for a few moments, and I take full advantage of being buried to the hilt inside her and not needing to do anything but enjoy her warmth and closeness. I trail kisses along her jaw, working my way back up to her pouty lips, nipping at her bottom one.

"You're so perfect for me, your body was made to take me. My little fighter, so fucking strong."

She tentatively rolls her hips, and I groan loudly, dropping my forehead down to hers, my hair falling forward and creating a curtain around our faces. She feels so fucking incredible, I could come just from her squeezing and pulsing around me. I give her a moment more to adjust around me, watching her face, waiting for the moment she starts to relax and is no longer pinched in pain.

"Move, Reid, please."

I pull out slowly and thrust back in, nudging her cervix and making her wince.

"You're doing so well, you feel so fuckin' good."

"I can't believe you're inside me right now."

"Believe it, because now that I've had you, I plan to spend a helluva lot of time in here."

She starts to rock her hips, meeting me thrust for thrust, her body showing me the pain has at least eased up some. Sitting up on my knees, I grip her hips, lifting her ass off the bed. Her hands move to her breasts, groping them, and it's so fucking hot I almost blow right there.

Her body lies taut in front of me, all long lines and stretched so pretty. She massages her breasts and twists her nipples as I stay deep, pulling her up and down on my cock, rubbing her clit against my pelvis. I finally pull out and thrust back in, keeping my motions slow and as gentle as possible, watching my cock disappear inside her tight little body. My control is teetering on a tightrope. I want to ravish her, devour her entirely, consume her the way that she's consumed me.

"Look at my cock covered in your cum, baby. Makes me fuckin' feral knowing I'm the only one who's ever been inside this tight pussy. I own every inch of you now, sweetheart. There's no comin' back from this. I'll be the only man who's ever and will ever know what it feels like to be inside you."

CHAPTER 21

Kinsey

I DON'T KNOW WHAT I EXPECTED SEX TO BE LIKE, BUT like everything else Reid has opened my eyes to, my imagination sucks. He continues to give my book boyfriends a run for their money. I give up complete control to him, trusting him to learn and know my body's needs just like he's done with everything else when it comes to me.

I rock against him as he picks up his pace, his thrusts turning frantic, coming harder and harder, slamming in as far as I can take him. I swear I feel every hard ridge of his cock, the thick head as he nearly pulls all the way out. Reid alternates from watching where he's fucking me and roaming up my body to look at my face.

I watch with rapt attention as he brings his thumb to his mouth and sucks, coating it with saliva before dropping it between us. He easily finds my clit, pressing down in firm circles and setting my fucking soul on fire. The quivers start low in my belly, a soft ember that he stokes slowly and expertly, until suddenly, it's a raging inferno.

"That's it, sweetheart. Be my good girl and show me who this pussy belongs to. 'Cause you're mine, Kinsey. I'm your first and last. I don't deserve you, but I'm not giving you up. Come for me, my pretty girl."

I come. Hard.

"Oh, god, Reid!"

"That's four, baby," he states, his voice thick with lust and hunger. His thrusts become erratic as I lie below him, his huge body towering over me, his strong, sinewed muscles taut and strained. His tanned, tattooed body glistens with a sheen of perspiration, his brown hair a mess around his face.

He's so fucking hot it hurts.

"Your pussy is making me come, Kins. Shit. You feel so fuckin' good clenching around me."

Reid pulls from my body quickly, grabbing his big dick and jerking it, the tip pointed at my pussy. I sit up on my elbows and watch as he pumps his long length at a brutal pace until he's coming with a loud, sexy groan that I will dream about for the rest of my life.

Pearly white ropes of cum spurt from his slit, coating the top of my pussy with his spend. I thought I wanted to feel him come inside me, but this is so much hotter. Once he's emptied on to me, he drops his still rock-hard cock and smooths his fingers through the mess he made of me, dragging his cum down my slit.

"I want one more," he demands, his voice a deep, husky growl.

He uses his cum as lubricant to swirl his talented fingers around my throbbing, overly sensitive clit, lighting me up again with every perfect stroke. Electricity hums through my veins, my heart pounding at an erratic rate.

"Fuck, you look so good coated in my cum, Kins. So fucking dirty. So sexy."

"That feels sooo good. Don't stop. Don't stop. Don't stop!"

My hands move up to my hair, pulling as I thrash my head from side to side. Pleasure builds and builds, taking me higher and higher. The tremors in my legs shake uncontrollably against Reid's warm body, tears filling my eyes as I watch this sexy beast of a man take me right to the edge.

"Fuck, Kins. You're so goddamn sexy. You like me rubbing my cum into your skin? Feel it, baby. Let go and come for your man."

"Ohhh! Ahh! Reid!"

"That's five. So fucking pretty, Jesus Christ, Kins. I could come just from watching you."

I vaguely hear Reid's words past the blood rushing between my ears. I squeeze my eyes shut as tears spill over, leaking from the corners. There's a high-pitched scream that pierces my ears, and it takes me a moment to realize it came from me. The orgasm wrecks me, and I swear I lose consciousness for a moment as the wave of pleasure pulls me under so deep, everything fades to black. My body vibrates with a warmth that spreads through me, heating me up from the inside out, and I know without a shred of doubt that if I had given myself to anyone but this man, they would all pale in comparison. It would have been sex. Transactional and probably fine. What I just experienced was something else entirely. Reid and I didn't just connect physically; we connected at a cellular level, chemically bonded, like our souls finally found their counterpart.

When I finally open my eyes, Reid is lying next to me, looking down with an expression that exudes happiness and reverence. His eyes are locked onto mine, his thumb running back and forth across my cheek.

"You're incredible, Kinsey. Are you okay? I didn't hurt you too bad?"

"I'm perfect. Going to be sore, but I'm perfect."

"Thank you for giving me that gift. For sharing yourself with me."

"I couldn't have imagined this with anyone else."

After a beat of silence, my heart starts to flip over in my chest. I'm so completely, pathetically, head over heels, unequivocally in love with this man, and I'm terrified that it will all end when we leave here. I understood his inner turmoil when it comes to choosing between me and Sawyer. It's not like with all the other guys I've tried to date or go out with. They had no loyalty to either of us, and they couldn't tell my brothers to fuck off to be with me. How can I expect someone who has a deeply profound relationship with my family to do that?

Reid and Sawyer's relationship is different. I was too young and carefree to know their history, but knowing what I know now about Reid's past and how the timeline matches up, I understand some of it.

While I understand it, it also scares the living shit out of me. How is this genuinely kind, loyal man supposed to tell Sawyer he's going to be with me regardless of what that means for their friendship? How is he supposed to be willing to walk away from a decade-long relationship that runs as deep as blood does in such a betraying way? And there's no doubt about it; Sawyer will take this as a personal betrayal.

There's a tiny spark that flares to life inside me, and I want to hold onto it until it flames brighter than all the worry. Maybe Sawyer will be happy. Maybe he will be relieved that the person he trusts as much as his brothers will spend the rest of his life with his sister, and that he couldn't have picked a better man for me.

But if this all ends here, I need to be on good terms with my family. They're overbearing, but my god, do they love so incredibly hard. I've never spent a day of my life feeling like I wasn't loved. Smothered with it, actually, the bastards.

Reid doesn't stop touching me, his hands running all over my chest, his fingers tracing the lines of my collarbones and over my shoulders, down my arms, and up again. His eyes track the movement like he's trying to etch the image permanently into his brain.

"Are you okay, sweetheart? You're so quiet."

I snuggle further into his big, warm body, hiking my leg over his hip and resting my head on his bicep. His hand moves to my ass, grabbing a handful and pulling me impossibly close.

"I'm perfect. That was perfect. I'll never forget it. Thank you for making it memorable."

"You deserve the world, Kinsey, and I plan on giving it to you."

I hum in response, unsure whether or not it's in agreement or just filling the quiet with sound because I don't have the words to voice my concern.

God, I hope he's right. I want nothing more out of this life than to have Reid Knight by my side.

"I'm ready to call my family," I announce as we untangle ourselves from another round of mind-blowing sex. Reid can't keep his hands off me now that he's had me, and I feel the same. We're insatiable, both of us desperate to cling to the other person and not let them go. It's like we're both fighting the same internal battle without putting it out in the open.

I love him. Plain and simple. Which means that if he has to walk away from me to preserve his relationship with my brother, then I'll respect it. But hell, if I don't want this man to fight for me at all costs.

"Sweetheart, do you have any idea how happy and relieved that's gonna make them?"

"I'm starting to feel so guilty for not wanting to face them, but I also know I needed this time to just breathe and process without external forces pressing down on me."

"Listen to me," he says as he drops down on his haunches in front of me, where I'm sitting on the edge of the bed, hands rubbing up my thighs. "Don't ever feel guilty for putting yourself first. You're a grown woman, and you went through something that no one should ever have to live through. You needed a beat to process, and you took it. Do not have any regrets. They'll understand."

I take a deep breath in and exhale, calming my nerves. He's right, and I needed to hear that. The thought of my family being worried sick over me makes me feel like the worst person on the planet, but I was not in the right headspace to see them all directly after. I know exactly how it would have gone down, and it was the last thing I needed.

Reid somehow managed to know and be everything I needed and more, and gave it to me with zero expectations. He wanted to take care of me in the way that I needed it most.

"Thank you," I tell him, and I mean it with every fiber of my being. "I don't know if I would have survived this without you, Reid." He swipes a stray tear off my cheek with the pad of his thumb before bringing it to his lips and licking it off.

"I don't believe that for a second. You're so strong, little fighter. You can survive anything." Reid stands, pulling my phone from the charger and handing it to me, dropping a hard kiss to the center of my forehead. "Now call your brother."

I look down at the phone and stare at Sawyer's name, my finger hesitating over the green call button before finding the courage Reid's convinced I have stowed away somewhere, and press connect. Sawyer picks up on the first ring.

"Kinsey?"

"It's me."

"Jesus, Kinsey. It's so good to hear your voice."

"Hey, big brother."

"Fuck, are you okay?"

"Getting better every day."

"Jesus, we've been going crazy, Kins. I'm so glad you're okay. You're so damn strong."

"Yeah?"

"Fuck yeah. Reid has kept us all updated regularly."

"I still can't believe he came for me. He saved me, Sawyer."

"Of course he did, Kins. He's my brother. Which means he's yours, too. Jesus, if you only knew his hand in helping Ivy or Blaire, or hell, even Hannah. You're really okay?"

My heart sinks to the pit of my stomach, a large lump forming in my throat, thick with unwanted emotions. He's never going to be okay with Reid and me being together. I clear my throat before talking, but fail miserably at keeping my voice steady.

"Yeah, I'm really okay. I'll be ready to come home soon."

"We're ready for you. I know Reid is keeping you safe, but I still don't like you being there."

"I know, Sawyer. I'll keep you updated. I'm alive. I'm healing."

"Good. I love you, sis. So goddamn much."

"I love you, too, big brother."

I disconnect the call, letting Reid take the phone back to set it on the end table. I can feel Reid's eyes on me as I sit there with what feels like the weight of the world on my shoulders.

"Get out of your head, little fighter."

"Want to take a shower?" I ask, ignoring his attempt to talk about the conversation with Sawyer and how it just fucked with my emotions.

He scoops me up so fast my head spins, the conversation with Sawyer and the worry over what happens next pushed to the farthest part of my mind. I'm going to enjoy this for as long as I have it. For as long as Reid Knight is mine.

Music blasts through the house sometime later, a deep thumping of bass that rumbles through the floorboards.

I look at Reid expectantly, but he doesn't look up from the book he's reading out loud to me. It's a dark, spicy romantic suspense loaded with kinks that sound so fucking delicious when being read from his lips.

"Don't even think about it, Kins. Not gonna happen?"

"Why?" I whine, and how the hell did he know what I was thinking?

"Because you don't want to see one of these parties. Even if they're just the members and patch bunnies, it's wild."

"I kinda do wanna see it though . . ." How many opportunities does one get to see a motorcycle club party? Reid drops the book onto the end table and gives me his full attention.

"They'll be people smoking."

"Okay?"

"And drinking."

"And?"

"And fucking."

A blush blooms across my cheeks, and I know my face is flushed crimson. He's told me this happens regularly here and that no one bats an eye, but is it the worst thing in the world that I'm curious?

"You're curious, little fighter?"

"Possibly."

"Get dressed. You want to go to a party? Let's go to a party. But I'm warning you, if anyone touches you, I will remove their hands."

I balk at him. "You aren't serious."

"Oh, I'm serious. Does that scare you?"

I know my answer before I say it, and that scares me more than anything else could.

"No."

Reid slaps my ass as I scurry off the bed and into the connected bathroom. I have no real clean clothes here, living in Reid's T-shirts and the skirt and plain T-shirt he got for me. The clothes had tags on them, so I know he could have gotten me more, but something tells me he didn't want to give me a reason not to be in his clothes full-time.

I try to fix my hair the best I can, and with no makeup here and one hell of a bruise covering my cheek and a healing busted lip, I look at myself in horror, having a split second of second-guessing whether or not I want to go, self-consciousness creeping in like an evil bitch.

Reid walks in a moment later, standing tall behind me, hands resting on the counter on either side of my hips, caging me in. His mouth drops to my shoulder, kissing it softly.

"You're beautiful. I'm the luckiest man in this building, and everyone is gonna be jealous."

How is he always giving me exactly what I need without me having to ask for it?

Reid takes my hand and leads me out of the bathroom, not giving me a moment to convince myself we shouldn't go. I follow him as we leave the safety and comfort of his bedroom and walk down the stairs, the music coming so loud, the bass thumping through the floorboards.

We quickly reach the large main area, an open concept space that reminds me of a pool hall I went to once in college. A long bar fills one of the side walls, barstools lining the front of it. A guy who looks barely old enough to drink alcohol himself is working on making drinks for everyone behind it, filling cups from a keg, and pouring amber-colored liquid from bottles.

The air is thick with cigarette smoke, spilled beer, and leather, and I don't hate it. Bodies are in every corner, filling up the space with leather vests and half-naked women. My eyes scan the room as Reid leads us over to the bar. Conversation and laughter are a low hum under the loud music, and the entire atmosphere is not at all what I was expecting. It's much more laid-back and much less chaotic.

We find a familiar face sitting at the bar with his forearms resting on the glossy wood top, a beer between his hands. Reid takes a seat next to him, pulling me between his open legs and wrapping his arms around my waist, the flat of his hands low on my belly. I lean into his warm body, allowing him to wrap me in a possessive hold, secretly loving the claim he's publicly making on me.

Rhys turns at our arrival, giving Reid a head nod and giving me a sultry, devilish smirk. He's got the prettiest reddish-brown hair I've ever seen, slicked back and styled at the top, the sides shaved almost to the skin. He has a full beard like Reid that covers part of his mouth, and I'd bet my minuscule teacher salary that this man has no problems with the ladies.

"Glad to see you up and moving. You feeling okay?" he asks in a genuinely concerned tone.

"It's going to take me some time, but I'm getting there. Better every day."

"I'm sure my brother is taking good care of you."

Reid's hands flex over my stomach, reminding me of just how good he has been at taking care of me. In more ways than one.

"Oh, I have zero complaints in that department."

"I don't know, I think I could do better."

Reid pulls me closer, my back flush against his chest now as he practically growls at his friend. I don't want this to end in a fight, so used to how my four brothers handle their issues—with their fists—so I quickly change the topic to hopefully defuse the situation.

"How long have you two known each other?"

"We patched in together."

"What does that mean exactly?"

Reid speaks up this time, explaining how they were both prospects together, doing grunt work side by side, and then when the vote came and they both got through, they became patched members.

"Difference is, I was teaching this asshole everything since I grew up here, and Reid left the comfort of home to go look for something different."

"You grew up here? I can't imagine being a kid . . . *here*. Not that it's bad, but just, wow." I stumble over my words because what the hell? I have so many questions. How'd he become the VP? Is there a rise in ranks like in the military? What is Reid's position here? Do they all live here together in this big compound? My thoughts are jumbled, and before I can ask any of them, a man built similarly to my brother Sawyer walks out of double wood doors in the back of the room with two other men flanking either side of him.

His hair is nearly black, the sides shaved short and the top half long and pulled into a bun, pieces falling loose and framing his face. He's wearing a plain black T-shirt with the same leather vest as every other man here. But he's different from all the rest, and

Reid's words play back to me in my head, "you'll know it's him when you see him," and he was spot on.

This man? This is their president. He exudes an air of confidence that isn't cocky. Each step he takes is with purpose, his presence commanding and sure. Every member he passes nods their head in respect, and you can easily tell that it's a respect that has been earned through loyalty and dedication, not fear. Nerves scatter through my body, setting off chills.

Reid doesn't miss a beat, rubbing his hands up and down my arms, pressing a few quick kisses to my neck and under my ear.

Their president walks behind the bar, nodding to the prospect who takes the rag off his shoulder and hands it to him. The prospect leaves the bar, and then the man is in front of us.

"So, you're the woman who's stolen Rogue's heart?" he says with no preamble.

"She is," Reid speaks up for me, his voice so sure and confident. I've stolen his heart? The man's eyes never leave mine, though, waiting for me to confirm myself, and I feel like a fish caught in a fisherman's net.

"I'm Kinsey. You must be their president?"

"Chaos, but you can call me Camden."

"Thank you."

"Wouldn't expect you to call me by my road name, it's nothin'."

"No, thank you for coming for me with Reid. Thank you for giving me a place to stay. If you all hadn't come, I—" Reid squeezes me closer to him, his lips pressing a firm kiss to the top of my head.

"We take care of what's ours. And sometimes we even step in to take care of what isn't, but it's the right thing to do. I'm glad you're okay."

Wow.

After my first introduction to a motorcycle club with my kidnappers, I assumed all MCs would be similar. Inherently evil, lawless. This is nothing like where I was taken to before. The men

I've met so far here are the opposite of the men in the Iron Wolves.

"If there's anything I can do to repay you," I offer.

"Don't break his heart," he says after a minute of silence, staring at me with his brutally serious eyes. Then he nods to Reid and Rhys and walks away without saying another word. I feel like a student who's waiting to find out if I passed a huge exam or not.

Reid kisses my head again, dropping his mouth to my ear and offering me a piece of reassurance. "You're okay, sweetheart. He's just intense and doesn't trust easily."

I turn my head to the side to look up at him, giving him a half smile. "I'm okay. I'm with you."

"That's my girl." His lips crash down on mine in a heated kiss, his tongue forcing my mouth open to accept him. His fingers press into my hips, and right as I start to turn around and give him more of me, there's a loud slam of a palm connecting with the bar top.

I jerk back to face Rhys, who's looking way too damn proud of himself.

"You're a dick, Sin," Reid says, making him laugh.

"Hardly. I'm practically a teddy bear."

"If a teddy bear likes to play with sharp things."

While the two of them talk back and forth, I take a few minutes to glance around the room, my eyes immediately homing in on the pool table, where a busty blonde is currently bent over the side of it, dress pulled up around her waist, being fucked into it by one of the members.

I've seen plenty of people make out before, even walked in on Piper once with a guy's hand down her pants, but fucking? Out in the open with a room full of people? Never. Nor did I ever think this was something I would see. People move around them like they aren't there, talking and playing darts, another game of pool happening at the table adjacent to the one that's currently being occupied to fuck against.

I've read plenty of smutty books that have public play, and I know how it made me feel reading it, but to see it? Completely different ballgame. Am I surprised to feel myself getting wetter? No. But I don't know how Reid will feel when he finds out that this is turning me the hell on. He said he wasn't into public play anymore, and I know I couldn't do what they're doing right now, but surely there's nothing wrong with glancing over at them once in a while, right?

I press back against Reid, wanting him to touch me. The euphoric feeling of this man's hands on me will never get old. I'll never stop wanting more.

reid

I wasn't sure what bringing Kinsey down here tonight would look like, but the party is tamer than I remember them being. Could be because we're on lockdown right now, or maybe everyone's just chilled out some.

Kinsey chats with Rhys like they're old friends, and I'm torn with how I feel about how comfortable they are with each other. This is probably exactly how Sawyer felt with me and Ivy. Something about the girl made me feel like I had known her forever, and while I'm convinced my past has made me super aware of the broken pieces in women, I saw hers immediately and wanted to fix it.

Rhys is similar to me in that regard, and if Kinsey is making a new friend, I want to respect that. This is what she's been craving after all, something outside of Aspen Ridge, to meet new people from different walks of life. I trust Rhys, and I want Kinsey to make friends.

"Wanna dance, kitten?"

Never mind. I'm going to kill him.

"You wanna die, Rhys?" Kinsey threatens, making me relax slightly. She's got this. I've got to let her fight her own battles; I'll just be behind her when she needs me.

"Your boy won't kill me. Hurt me? Probably. But, nah, he doesn't want to bury a brother."

"Who said anything about him?"

Fuck, I love this woman.

Rhys is asking for trouble with the way he's been flirting with Kinsey. He'd be blind not to be attracted to her, but I know he's doing it to get a rise out of me, and it's not a line he would ever cross.

I adjust her body so her fine, perky ass is sitting right on my rock-hard dick. She wiggles slightly, pushing back harder against it, making me groan. I know I told her I had grown out of having public sex, but fuck if I'm not tempted to lift her skirt just enough to slip inside her tight little hole. Don't even need to fuck her. Just want to be inside her at all times. I still can't believe this perfect woman is mine. Mine to love on. Mine to protect and comfort. Mine to support and encourage. Mine to fuck and dirty up. And fuck if she doesn't like me to have my way with her.

I lean my head down and bite the lobe of her ear as she slides her ass back and forth again.

"Keep rubbing that ass against me, I'll be fuckin' it later."

She turns her face, looking up at me, an image of pure innocence as she bats her pretty, long lashes at me, feigning cluelessness.

"Don't tempt me with a good time, big guy."

My fingers move to the bottom hem of her jean skirt, slowly starting to lift the back of it. We both know she doesn't have any panties here since I ripped the only pair, so she'd be sitting right on my lap, bare assed.

"Or maybe I'll just fuck you right here on this barstool. Let every brother and woman here know exactly who you belong to," I whisper.

She has the audacity to challenge me, raising her eyebrows, her lips turning up in a sexy-as-fuck smirk. She doesn't stop me as I lift the back of the denim so half her ass is out. My hands stay along the sides of her thighs so no one can see how far it's hiked up—not that anyone would give two shits. Hell, a few guys are already fucking some of the patch bunnies right now.

Her focus goes back to Rhys and the prospect slinging drinks, while mine is focused solely on her. I can't believe she's mine. Every few minutes, she rocks her ass against my hard dick, reminding me who's calling the shots right now, but I've had enough of her games. My cock throbs against her ass, leaking precum into my jeans.

"Let's go for a ride."

"Steal me away, Reid Knight."

"I'm gonna do more than steal you, Kins. I'm gonna devour this pussy that's leaking all over me."

"It is not," she argues.

I pop her up off me, slipping her skirt back down over her ass. She turns quickly, looking down at my crotch, her eyes going wide, mouth dropping open into a pretty little 'o' as she looks at the visible wet spot darkening the denim fabric. It's sexy as hell and makes my dick throb with growing need to be deep inside her again.

"What do you call that then, sweetheart?"

"Serves you right. Your big dick was rubbing against me."

"Baby, you know how hot it is that you're dripping for me? I'll wear it proudly. Now, let's get out of here before I fuck you for all to see."

Kinsey lets me drag her out of the clubhouse and to the side of the building, where we parked the bike. The night is dark, the moon low, casting just enough light to see where we're going. I snatch her up by her waist, wrapping her legs around mine as I straddle my bike. Voices carry from the people outside on the deck, alerting us to how close we are to others. We're shrouded in enough darkness that no one could see anything if they walked around the corner, but I'm not letting that stop me now.

. . .

She presses against me, rubbing her wet, desperate little pussy over me as her arms circle my neck. I'm so hard it's painful, and I want inside her tight heat badly.

"Jesus, Kins, you're so fucking sexy. I need you. Let me have you."

"Right here?"

"Right fuckin' here, little fighter. Let. Me. Have. You," I demand, her eyes wild, matching my own. The pretty blue irises are sparkling with heat and excitement. I saw her watching Wrath with a patch bunny. I noticed every time she thought I wasn't paying attention, and she looked over at them. I felt every time she pressed her thighs together in search of friction. Doesn't bother me in the slightest she got turned on, how often are people fucking in the same room as you?

"Take me, baby. Let me feel you," she says in a sweet-as-fuck, sultry voice, incinerating any amount of restraint I was holding onto.

I'm such a fucking goner for her.

I move quickly, yanking up her skirt as she works open the button of my jeans, sliding down the zipper and pulling my cock free. She strokes me from root to tip, her little fist unable to close around me completely. I drive two fingers roughly inside her, pumping a few times before staying deep, curving them inward toward her belly and doing a come-hither motion.

"That's my girl, you're fuckin' drenched, Kins. You always gonna be primed and ready to take my cock?"

"God, yes. Give it to me, Reid. I need you inside me," she begs, and I don't waste another moment. I pick her up, holding my dick with one hand as she uses my shoulders to help lift herself enough that I can notch at her entrance.

Then I'm slamming her down on me, impaling her in one swift thrust, nothing but slick, wet heat sheathing me. Her head falls back with a loud moan, stretching her pretty neck out in front of me like a fucking temptress. I drag the flat of my hand down her throat, loving how small and delicate it is. Captivated by how it looks with my tattooed hand wrapped around it.

With my other hand, I hold her hip, keeping her exactly where I want her body as I fuck into her from below. Her pussy clenches around me, sucking me in with every thrust, her arousal leaking out of her, dripping down my length and coating my sack. I hope it reaches the bike seat. I want her essence everywhere. Me. My bike. My bed.

My hand closes around her throat, pulling her up so she has to look at me.

"You like it when I choke you, little fighter? Like having your life in the palm of my hand?"

"Yes."

"Yes?"

"It makes me feel powerful, giving up control to you. Trusting you with my life. And it feels so fucking good when you make me come."

Jesus.

Fucking.

Christ.

Could this woman be any more perfect for me? I couldn't have written her a cue card with a better answer. I love breath play for the same reason. I fucking love having the power, knowing she's giving it to me willingly, trusting me to know exactly what her body needs and when it needs it.

"Fuck, yeah. You ready to come?"

"God, yes!"

"Deep breath, little fighter, you're about to feel so fucking good."

She does as I say, and I close my hand around her throat, cutting off her air supply. I fuck into her from below, grinding my pelvis against her clit, staying nice and deep, nudging her cervix and giving her that bite of pain that enhances her pleasure.

Her eyes are wide and wild, glassy and looking every bit royally fucked as she is. She doesn't take her eyes off me as I bring her right to the edge of that cliff. It's the longest we've ever gone, and my woman doesn't even flinch or fight me, trusting me completely. I thrust hard and grind.

Once.

Twice.

Her pussy starts to flutter around my dick and then she's falling. I release her throat as she gasps for air and screams. Birds fly from the trees at the sudden noise, her pussy clenching so goddamn tight around me, and I'm right there with her.

"Fuck, baby, you're making me come," I tell her, my voice thick with lust.

My orgasm starts at the base of my spine, spreading like wildfire through my veins. My cock jerks inside her tight heat, filling her with spurts of cum. Our combined releases leak around me and the thought is so fucking hot that I need to see it.

I lift Kinsey off me, leaning her back against the front of my bike and stepping off quickly. Her legs are spread wide, our juices weeping from her swollen cunt. I don't hesitate to bury my face in it, my tongue delving between her legs, licking her puffy lips, coating my tongue in our combined releases. I lick into her center, gathering it up. Right as I'm about to swallow, Kinsey is pulling me up to her face, her hand on my T-shirt, the other around the back of my neck.

Her lips meet mine, her tongue diving into my mouth and tangling around mine, tasting the two of us. It's the hottest thing she ever could have done, and I almost blow another load right then and there.

"Mmm. My dirty girl."

"I used to be so innocent. You've corrupted me, Reid Knight."

"No regrets. I fuckin' love you like this."

After fucking Kinsey on my bike, we came back to the clubhouse to head to my room for the night, only to find Malice pacing the front hall, his head downcast, his mouth moving, only a breath of a whisper audible. Great, he's talking to himself again. Fucking psycho.

"Malice, you good, brother?"

His head shoots up quickly, his body bracing for a fight. He was so lost in his damn head he didn't hear us coming. It's rare to get the jump on Malice, so something is clearly taking his focus.

"Yeah, all's good. Prez is waiting for you in church."

"Now?" I ask as I look down at Kinsey.

"Yep. He's pissed he's having to wait. Said to tell you not to make any detours, get your ass to church," he relays in a mock tone that doesn't sound anything like Chaos, his hands moving around animatedly.

"I'm taking her to my room first."

"I can do it for you. Right, Kinsey?"

"I'm fine, Reid. I don't want you to make him wait, it sounds important."

"Are you sure, sweetheart?" I say as I cup her face in my hands, loving how fucking small and sweet she looks when I hold her this way.

"Go! I'm fine!" She pushes me back with her hands flat on my chest, but I grab her wrists, bringing each of her hands up to my mouth and dropping a kiss to them.

"I'll be up as soon as I can, I . . ." The words are on the tip of my tongue, and they've never felt more right in my life. But I'm not telling her that I love her for the first time like this, not as I'm walking away from her. "I'll see you in a bit," I finish, dropping a hard kiss to her forehead, taking a deep inhale of her scent, missing the floral and sage, but loving how she smells like me.

Mine.

Malice follows Kinsey through the room and to the kitchen to head upstairs, while I take measured steps in the opposite direction toward the two large doors. I knock twice before pulling one open, Chaos nodding his head at me to come in. The door falls closed behind me with an audible click, and I walk into our meeting room to take a seat across from Sin with Chaos at the head of the table.

"We're getting closer, and I need you here."

Fuck. I knew he was going to try to pull some shit to try to get me back here full time. It's not going to happen, especially now that I've got Kinsey. She'd never leave Aspen Ridge, and I'm not starting our life together here at the clubhouse when I have a home I want to move her into.

I start to shake my head, running my hand through my hair and pushing it back.

"Not happenin'. Especially not now. Not after I've finally been given a reason to truly live again, Chaos. I can't. Don't ask me to, I'm begging you." And I would. There's nothing I wouldn't do for Kinsey, and that includes dropping to my knees and begging my president to continue this arrangement we've had for the last decade.

"Fuck off with that, Rogue. You need to get her home, then get her settled, because once we narrow this down, we're going for them, and you need to be available. She may be your woman, but you haven't made her your old lady. She can't stay here if you're gone with us."

I know he's right.

"And if I make her my old lady?"

"Does she know that's what you want?"

"I hope to fuck she does. But this is all too new to her, I can't drop that shit on her with everything else that's goin' on. I'll take her back to Aspen Ridge. She'll be safe there with her brothers. I've looped Sawyer in."

"I'm sure you have."

"Don't start with that jealous bullshit," I tell him.

"Fuck off, Rogue. Get her home, be ready. The battles have been one thing, but it's time for war. I want them obliterated from Earth."

I nod my agreement and turn to leave, walking away with nerves heavy in each step that leads me closer to Kinsey. Would she let me make her my old lady? Would she want that? How the hell is she going to react when I take her home?

Kinsey's pretty blue eyes light up as I enter the room, her face brightening into a smile that steals the breath from my lungs.

"Hey, sweetheart."

"Are you okay?"

Jesus. Not any of the other thousands of questions she could have asked: what happened? What did he want? No, her first thought was to check on me. I don't deserve this perfect woman. After everything she's been through, she's still such a bright light . . . my beacon.

"I'm with you, of course I'm okay."

"Good. That's all I care about."

"Baby, you aren't going to ask me what he wanted?"

She looks up at me, all bright blue eyes and innocent face, and purses her lips. "If it was any of my business, or you wanted me to know, you'd tell me. I'm never going to pry information from you, Reid. You're allowed your privacy. I've always known you to keep things close to you, you're the silent type, and I love that about you. I'm here when you're ready to talk, and I know you believe I'm strong enough to handle whatever you need to lean on me for."

"Sweetheart, you are so goddamn perfect. I swear I was wandering around in the dark, waiting for you to show up."

"You would have found your way out without me, Reid. I wish you could see yourself the way I do. Selfless, loyal, loving . . . the most caring man I've ever met in my life. Your innate ability to know what people need before they do, the way you would do anything for someone who needed help. You are not gloom and darkness, you *are* light. Your heartbreak just kept you from seeing it."

I drop down to my knees in front of her, wrapping my arms around her waist and pressing my forehead to her chest.

"We have to go back to Aspen Ridge."

"I know. When?"

"Tomorrow morning. I'm not ready to give you up yet."

I feel her shoulders sag, and I regret my word choice immediately. I don't want to share her.

"I've enjoyed this while we had it, Reid. You've given me such a gift, you've healed me and given me so much hope."

I sit back quickly to see her face, not liking the sound of that at all.

"Sweetheart, why the hell does that sound like a goodbye?"

"Everything will change once we're back in Aspen Ridge. We both know that. I don't want to leave this experience on bad terms."

Fuck, she really doesn't get it. She really expects me to walk away from her like every other dipshit man she's had in the past. I could kill those brothers of hers for making her feel this way. I love them like they're my own family, and after everything I went through with Lena, I've always related to how controlling and protective they've been of her.

But Kinsey is strong as shit and she can handle herself. She needs someone who will fight for her, but more than that? She needs someone who believes in her ability and worth and stands behind her while she fights for herself.

The last thing I ever wanted to do was hurt Sawyer, but Kinsey is the love of my life, and I'm going to always put her first. The rest is in Sawyer's court. I thread my fingers through her hair, pushing the silky strands out of her face before cupping her cheeks to rest in the palms of my hands. I angle her head back so she's forced to look up at me, her beautiful blues meeting mine.

"You're everything, Kinsey. Here in this room? At this club? You're mine. Yeah, I'm fucking terrified of what will happen when we return to Aspen Ridge, but don't you dare think for one moment that I'm not keeping you when we leave here. Everything will be different when we return, except for us. You're my ride or die, little fighter. I want you in my life, on the back of my bike, in my shop, my house, in my bed, here or Aspen Ridge . . ."

"Reid, don't say—"

"You're mine, Kinsey. And I'm yours. I love you. Nothing is changing. Do you understand?"

"You have no idea how badly I want to believe you because I love you, too. So fucking much."

"I'll prove it to you. You're my woman. My life starts and ends with you."

CHAPTER 23

Kinsey

REID AND I SPENT THE ENTIRE NIGHT TANGLED UP WITH each other. I can still feel him between my legs—the rough hair of his beard on my thighs and my neck, the delicious ache from being fucked so deep, his rough hands that never stop roaming my body. He's obsessed with making me come, and after too many orgasms to count, he showered both of us, carrying my too-relaxed, limp body under the spray and washing me from head to toe with the precision of someone who truly, deeply cares. I never imagined love would feel this way.

The morning light came through the single window in Reid's room, and I gripped his forearm tightly around my chest, not ready to leave the safety and comfort we've found here. So much happened and changed within these four walls, and I can't imagine saying goodbye to it.

"Here, sweetheart. Wear these," Reid says as I'm brushing my teeth in the bathroom. He sets a pair of black denim jeans and a navy tank top on the counter, complete with a pair of panties and a new bra. "Didn't want you to return home in a skirt or one of my T-shirts."

"You think of everything, thank you."

"Anything for you, my love." *My love.* "I'm going to go talk with the men for a few minutes, make sure everything is good for us to head out. Are you alright in here alone?"

"Of course. Do you mind if I use your phone to make a call?"

"You can use anything of mine, take your time. I'll be back in a bit."

Reid drops a kiss to my forehead and walks out of the bathroom, his heavy footsteps retreating until I hear the soft click of the bedroom door shutting. I get dressed in the clothes he left for me, pulling them on and not surprised when they fit perfectly again. It's simple and gets the job done, and I'm actually thankful to show back up in Aspen Ridge in some clean clothes. I know my family will be waiting for me to arrive.

While Reid's downstairs, I grab his phone from the top of the dresser, knowing I need a few minutes with my best friend before everything gets crazy. I plug in Piper's number and connect the video call, hoping like hell she's not in class or at the hospital.

"Jesus fucking Christ, you goddamn fucking bitch," she snaps as she answers the call.

"That's a lot of cuss words for a future doctor; do you talk to your patients with that mouth?"

"Kinsey fucking Hayes. I've been losing my fucking mind! I had to literally beg your brothers to tell me what the hell was going on!"

"Who finally cracked?"

"Carter, of course."

"Sounds about right. Liam would have been my second guess."

"Are you okay? Jesus, it's so good to see your face."

"I'm okay. So much has happened, and it feels like that was some sick, twisted dream."

I spend the next ten minutes filling Piper in on being kidnapped, being locked in that room, and Reid coming for me. Her mouth hangs open the entire time like she's watching some intense thriller documentary on TV and not her best friend's real life.

"Holy fuck, dude. I'm so sorry, KiKi. I wish I could hug you right now," she says as she bats tears off her face.

"Me too. You live stupid far away."

"I know, it's truly a hardship. So the sexy giant came to save you like a knight in shining armor?"

"More like a sexy giant biker in a leather vest?"

"What the hell is that supposed to mean?"

Not wanting to spill Reid's secrets but not wanting to keep my best friend out of the loop, I tell her that he has friends in certain places that helped him get to me and gave us a safe place to hide out instead of going right back to Aspen Ridge.

"All Carter would tell me was that you were safe and Reid had a place an hour north that you were holed up in until you felt ready to come home. So . . . anything else you want to share?"

"Like?"

"Like how you lost your virginity and look thoroughly fucked."

"Okay, I've heard that saying before and always thought it was bullshit."

"Definitely real, my girl. You've got the glow. Not the pregnancy one, but the freshly fucked by a man who knows his way around the female anatomy glow."

A deep, much-needed laugh bellows out of me. "Oh, he knows his way around. That man made the men I've read about in my books look like fumbling amateurs."

"It's more than that, though, isn't it? You found your person."

"You're my person," I argue, not wanting her to feel replaced, even though I know she's happy for me.

"You know what I mean. He's the one."

"Yeah," I tell her honestly. "He is."

After my phone call with Piper, I busy myself by cleaning up his room, wanting to leave it the way we found it. I strip the bed of the sheets, dropping them into the hamper before shaking out the top comforter to fold it. The fabric snaps at the end, knocking over my glass of water sitting on the end table.

"Shit."

I quickly snatch a towel from the hamper, soaking up the spilled water. I open the drawer, dabbing at the beads of water, when the contents at the bottom give me pause.

A framed photo of Reid, two older people, and a very pretty brunette looks back at me. Reid's hair is much shorter, shaved at the sides and slicked up at the top. His face is missing the long beard he has now, but there's no mistaking it's him. His arm is slung over the young girl, her face lit up in a huge smile that reaches her eyes. Her hair is a mess of waves around her face, the wind blowing it off to the side. She's beautiful and looks so much like Reid. Which leads me to believe the couple standing with them is their parents. My heart aches painfully in my chest at what they've all had to go through, for Lena and the pain and fear she must have experienced before her life was stripped from her.

My next emotion hits me like an atomic bomb. Anger. It isn't until this moment that I understand Reid's desperation for vengeance on these vile humans who have no appreciation for life. I suddenly want Reid to end them. Not for me, not even for Lena. But for every single woman out there that they'll hurt after us.

The bedroom door opens, and Reid steps through the threshold, looking down at me sitting cross-legged on the floor with the frame in my hand and tears in my eyes.

"I wasn't snooping, I promise. The cup fell over while I was cleaning, and I wanted to make sure nothing got wet inside the table."

"You think I mind if you snoop? I have nothing to hide from you, Kins. Snoop all you want."

"Is this Lena?" I ask hesitantly, a lump forming in my throat.

Reid swallows hard, his face soft and solemn, and I so badly want to smooth out his features, heal his heart completely. He sits down on the floor in front of me, his big legs stretching out on either side. His hands reach for my legs, dragging me across the wood floor, closer to him. I watch as he takes the photo, running the pad of a finger across Lena's face.

"Yeah, this is my sister."

"She's beautiful. Looks so much like you."

"She was the most beautiful girl I'd ever seen. Everyone was in awe of her. She was pure light, but hell if she didn't have an adventurous side and an innate ability to find trouble."

"I wish I could have known her."

"She would have challenged you, and I'd love to see the two of you fight over me," he says with a laugh. "But I know in the end you two would have been good friends. Sisters even."

"I think so, too. So these are your parents, then?"

"Yeah. Jack and Cindy."

"They look like good people, Reid."

"They are. I miss them."

"If you wanted to see them, I'd go with you if you wanted me to."

"It's so hard, Kins," he says, his voice breaking. "It just got to be too much to look into their eyes knowing what I know."

"I can't imagine what that must be like for you to harbor that weight and protect them from that kind of pain. I won't ever push you to do something that you don't want to do, but I can tell how much you miss them, and I can only imagine how much they miss seeing their son. Just think on it? I'll be whatever you need me to be. I can be strong for you, baby, lean on me."

"I love you, Kinsey."

"I love you, too."

The ride to Aspen Ridge starts off somber, as if both of us are lost in our heads over the anticipation and unknown of seeing my family again. My hands press against the warmth of Reid's skin, my fingers lightly scratching over the light dusting of hair he has above where his jeans are slung low. Every so often, I run the very tips of my fingers under the waistband, his growl vibrating through my chest and face where I'm resting against his back.

Reid lets go of his handlebars with one hand and slides up the back of my thigh, giving it a firm squeeze. Feeling confident and a little reckless, I sit up straight and hold my arms out at my sides, feeling more alive and free than I ever have in my life. As the wind whips around us, the trees blur past us, and the engine hums under us, I understand Reid's need for riding his motorcycle and his attachment to it. It's this weightless feeling where nothing else exists.

His confident handle on his bike and my unwavering belief that he'll keep us safe allow me to lean into it and just feel. I close my eyes and let the world wash away—the pain, the worry, the anxiety—I just exist with Reid and nothing but the open road and freedom in front of us. He was right, being on the motorcycle with him helps, and it's not something I plan on giving up.

An hour later, as we're reaching the very outskirts of Aspen Ridge, Reid slows his bike down and pulls off to the side of the road, cutting the engine and tapping my leg to hop off as concern washes over me. He steadies the motorcycle before climbing off after me, looking at me with an expression I can't decipher.

"Is everything okay?"

"I just needed to remind you."

"Of what?"

He takes a single step into my space, his massive body blocking out the sun. Half of his hair is pulled back in a bun, the bottom half hanging loose around his shoulders in straggly waves. His face is deadly serious, his eyes dark and almost concerned, as if he's pleading. It makes my heart trip over itself behind my ribs, beating wildly and out of control.

"That I love you. That this is real. That I'm not going anywhere, and I'll be damned if I let you leave."

"Reid . . ." I gasp on a rushed breath.

"I love you, little fighter. I'll do anything to be yours."

"I love you, Reid. I'll do whatever it takes to keep you."

Reid and I pull up in front of my family's distillery in Aspen Ridge. Not long later, the sun beats down on our backs, the light breeze from the coast kissing our skin. My brothers jog out of the large barn building as we come to a complete stop, all four of their big bodies rushing out like a pack of feral hyenas.

"Thank fuck, Kinsey," Sawyer yells as he pulls me into a massive hug, his strong arms bounding around me, followed by Dallas, Liam, and Carter. Ivy, Blaire, Hannah, and Finn all wait on the wraparound porch, and out of my peripheral, Reid lifts off the bike and steps aside. The last thing I want him to do.

"You're never leaving our sight again," Dallas mumbles against my hair.

"Never," Liam adds.

"I'm fine, I promise, you big oofs. Let me breathe!" I yell as I try to squirm out of their tight collective hold.

"Alright, alright, give her some space. She's been through a lot," Ivy demands as she starts to pull my brothers off me one by one. As they step aside, I'm left looking at my sister-in-law, her long black hair flowing off to the side in the wind, looking every bit the gorgeous, radiant girl I used to follow around when I was little and she was dating Sawyer. "Hey, you. Better?" she asks as she grabs my hand and pulls me up the steps to join the others and give my brothers a minute to talk to Reid.

"Thanks. They have one mode, and it's suffocation."

"You're not wrong about that. But it's because they love us so hard, they don't know how to control their barbaric behavior. Just want to smother us in love and obsessive protection," she says with a playful eye roll. "Come inside, Hannah and I brought food. Did Drogo feed you?" she asks, pointing to Reid.

"I know you can do it yourself, sweetheart, it's not about what you're capable of. I want to do it for you."

I feel the blush spread across my face as I remember just how well Reid fed me the last few days. "He did," I answer. Ivy's head cocks to the side as she looks at me, Hannah's eyes squinting into slits before the two of them look at each other.

Fuck.

I lasted an entire two minutes before they figured it out. At least having them know ahead of time will allow them to help with the fallout of my brothers finding out. The ten of us shuffle into the huge, open tasting area that Blaire has created. She's dating my brother, Dallas, and is also the event coordinator at the distillery. Even though dating seems like an insufficient word for what they have.

"How long?" Ivy whispers as she loops her arm with mine.

"Feelings started before everything went to shit. Everything else happened after."

"You look happy, Kins."

"I am, Iv. He's endgame."

Ivy sniffles, and I give her a gentle hip bump to tell her to pull it together.

"You're perfect for him, Kinsey. He's one of my closest friends, and his trauma goes deep. I don't know much, but he needs someone like you to help him heal," she whispers. "I'm just happy for you two."

"Why is my wife crying?" Sawyer demands as he pulls Ivy into his arms. He's so openly affectionate with her, and I can't wait to have that. I so badly want to curl up on Reid's lap right now for this little reunion.

"Because I was worried about her, psycho. And my hormones are all over the place still!"

"I'm sorry, butterfly. I know this is emotional. She's safe, she's home with us now."

I take a seat by myself while everyone else sits with their partners. Reid stays silently stoic, sitting relaxed in one of the leather chairs. His legs are spread, his body hunched forward with his forearms resting on his knees.

"What do Mom and Dad know?" I finally ask.

"That you went with Reid to visit an old friend from college and you lost your phone," Liam says.

"Okay, so not too bad. Good job," I praise.

"How are you really?" Dallas asks, concern etched deeply into his features. My heart aches looking at him. His typical light-hearted persona is missing and replaced with a man who has seen true evil this year and now had to face this stuff with me.

"I promise, I'm okay. Everything is very diluted at this point, like waking up from a nightmare and trying to remember the details. It's fuzzy at best. I'm okay. Ready to start living again and moving forward. It's good to be home," I offer.

Dallas' face relaxes, and Blaire rubs her hand over his forearm in comfort. "Believe her when she speaks, she's a big girl and isn't going to lie to save your feelings," she tells him.

"I know, baby girl. Just want to make sure."

"Fuck, we missed you, sis," Carter says after a beat of silence.

"I missed you all, too." And I mean it. There was once a time I thought I loved my siblings more than anything in the world, until I fell in love with Reid Knight and realized that was no longer true. I will walk away from all of them if they can't get on board with Reid and me being together, but it doesn't mean it won't kill me to do it.

reid

WATCHING KINSEY REUNITE WITH HER FAMILY IS emotional. The five Hayes siblings are beyond close, and while I feel so much gratitude that my woman is surrounded by siblings who love her fiercely, it makes me miss my sister that much more.

After things settled down, Sawyer nods at me, signaling that he wants to talk privately. I stand and wait for him as he whispers something to Ivy and walks in my direction. Together we step into one of the smaller offices on the main floor, not far from where everyone is sitting, but far enough away that we can talk privately.

"She seems good."

"She is."

"A little surprising though, considering what she's been through," he says warily, like he's speculating and isn't quite ready to call me out on it yet. Too bad I'm about to beat him to the punch on this one.

"She's strong."

"It's more than that, brother. She's different somehow. Lighter, happier. Like she found a piece of herself that was missing."

"She did."

Sawyer looks at me, arching one of his brows and running his hand across his beard, waiting for me to elaborate.

"Me."

I brace for his reaction to cut me deep when his head bounces back like I sucker punched him.

"You're gonna need to repeat that," he says, his voice ruthlessly calm, his eyes darkening.

"I'm in love with Kinsey. She's mine, and I have no plans of that changing."

Sawyer is a straight shooter and it's better to get it all out in the open, point blank, rather than pussy footing around the truth of the matter.

"You're telling me you're in love with my little sister?" Sawyer balks at me, and I brace myself for whatever physical attack is coming.

"Are you fucking with me?"

"No. We didn't mean for it to happen. She's too fucking good for me, man. She's everything that is bright and good. She saved me. She's my light. I'm not walking away from her."

Sawyer steps into my space, and for the first time in our decade-long relationship, I can't meet his fucking eyes, terrified of seeing his disappointment, his anger. He handles everything with his damn fists and even though I'm bigger than him, he's a better fighter, and I'd take anything he throws at me. Fuck, I deserve it.

The last thing I'd ever do intentionally is hurt him. I meant what I said, Kinsey and I didn't mean for this to happen, but it did and it's the best goddamn thing I've ever experienced. I'm braced for whatever is coming from him, but what he does next nearly brings me to my knees.

"Get out."

"What?" His words are somehow worse than any punch he could have thrown at my face.

"You fucking heard me. I trusted you with her life!" he screams, his face red with palpable fury.

"Then you should know I wouldn't be with her if she didn't mean the absolute fucking world to me!" I yell back, matching his temper.

"I can't believe a word that comes out of your fuckin' mouth. I trusted you! What? You couldn't have Ivy, so you went for my baby sister?"

"Low blow, brother and you fucking know it! I came on to Ivy one goddamn time before I even knew who she was. You still holdin' on to that shit? It was a year ago! And your sister is not a fuckin' baby. She's a strong, grown-ass woman who can make her own decisions, and she chose me." I take a step in his direction, pissed that this is how it's going to go down between us. "Let me make something crystal clear, Kinsey is *mine*, and anything—anyone—who tries to stand in my way, will lose. She is everything to me, and I will take on anyone to be with her—*even you*. If that doesn't tell you how strongly I feel about her, then you aren't the man I thought you were."

Sawyer continues to look at me like he doesn't recognize the man in front of him, and it breaks my fucking heart after the decade of history we share. But I meant every word I said. Kinsey comes above all else.

"Fuck you, Reid!"

I ignore his words and turn on my feet to leave when I find Kinsey standing in the doorway with her hand over her mouth. She looks at me with a swirl of emotions behind her eyes, and I know she heard every single word. She blinks, and in an instant, it's gone, replaced with rage and anger as she turns to face her oldest brother.

"Everyone can hear you screaming, you loudmouth!" she yells as she storms up to him, her hands balled into fists, all five foot two of her looking up at him like she's about to knock him on his ass. "So now you know!"

"That you're fucking him?"

Kinsey's head jerks back, and I take a step in his direction, ready to knock his teeth out because I didn't say that. To Kinsey's credit, she knows it, and doesn't even look back at me. She knows I wouldn't talk about her like that to anyone, even if she hadn't heard the majority of our conversation.

"Oh, so now you can talk about me fucking? Yeah, I'm fucking Reid, Sawyer. Get over it. It's also so much more than that! Did you not hear a word he said to you? He's willing to ruin your friendship to be with me, and that isn't enough for you? That doesn't speak volumes to you?"

"Do you have any idea of the shit that he's into?"

"Do you mean the MC or in bed? 'Cause I know everything. There aren't any secrets between us, and I trust him with my life. Up until five minutes ago, you felt the same way."

"This is not what I wanted for you, Kinsey!"

"Well, it's not for you to decide!"

Her brothers flood into the room, and she throws her hands up in the air in frustration.

"The fuck is going on in here?" Liam demands.

"Did we have to move in here to fight? There's way more room next door," Dallas asks, making Kinsey throw her hands up in the air in frustration.

"Ugh! You are all ridiculous! Reid and I are together. Get the fuck over it!" she screams at all of them and then turns to face me, marching right up into my space with her shoulders held high. I brace myself because I know exactly what my little fighter is about to do, and I'd never deny her. She stretches up on her tiptoes, grabbing the back of my neck, pulling me down to her level, and capturing my lips. My arms curl around her waist, forcing her back to arch as I curl over her and kiss the living hell out of her.

The room disappears while she claims me in front of her brothers. It's over just as quickly as it started, and I don't break eye contact with her as she looks up at me with all the love in the world.

"Take me home?"

"Yeah, sweetheart."

"Kins—" Sawyer starts, but Kinsey spins quickly and points her finger at him.

"No! We're done here. I warned you! I told you if you didn't back off, I would leave. You want to lose your sister *and* your best friend? Think about your shit, Sawyer. We're leaving."

Kinsey grabs my hand, and I follow her out of the distillery, so proud of my woman for fighting for herself and what she wants.

She marches over to my bike and waits patiently for me to swing my leg over and steady it before she slips in behind me, her arms bounding around my waist, lifting up my shirt so her fingers can touch my bare skin. She's just as addicted to touching me as I am her, and it makes my chest fill with pride.

Instead of going straight to my house, I decide to take a detour and drive into town so she can get things from her apartment to hold her over at my place. As I slow my bike and take the turn down the small alley to park in the rear of Rogue, I feel her grip on me tighten, her body stiffening. Cutting the engine, Kinsey takes off her helmet and jumps off, swinging on me, the anger from the distillery simmering just behind her eyes.

"I don't want to be here."

"Sweetheart, no one's gonna hurt you ever again."

"I'm not ready to be away from you."

Wait, what?

"Are you scared to go in there because of what happened?"

"No, I've gotten so used to spending all my time with you, with sharing a bed, with waking up to you, I'm not ready for that to end."

My smile must reach my fucking eyes because Kinsey stands, hands on her hips, looking every bit confused, irritated, and cute as fuck.

"What the hell are you smiling about?" she snaps, making me chuckle under my breath.

"My violent little fighter," I tell her as I grab her face with my hands, dropping a hard kiss to her mouth. "You think you're ever sleepin' away from me again?"

"Isn't that why you brought me here?"

"No, baby. We're packing whatever you need for at least a few days until I can find the time to pack the rest of it. You're moving in with me."

"What?" she practically whispers, and I can hear the relief in her voice.

I bend my knees to be down at her level. "I told you. Mine," I whisper against her lips before biting the pouty bottom one. She hisses, her fingers moving to touch the sore spot.

"C'mon then, big guy, let's get me packed. I want to see my new home!" she sings as she turns and moves toward the back steps, as if she weren't just ready to fight me like a little demon spawn.

In two large strides, I'm grabbing her around her tiny waist, turning her around so her legs wrap around me. My favorite fucking place for her to be. Her hands find my face, delicate fingers scratching lightly at my beard as she tilts her head down and captures my lips with hers.

She squeezes herself around me as she kisses me, her tongue licking the seam of my lips, demanding that I open for her. I comply quickly, loving when she's desperate like this. I hold her close, running my hands up her back and down over her plump ass, gripping and kneading my fingers into the flesh.

My heart sinks as we push open the door. I was expecting to have weeks' worth of cleanup to do, but it's already been cleaned and put back together. The walls are filled with my artwork, held by new frames, the floors scrubbed, and the furniture replaced. It looks like it did before those assholes came in and trashed it— better even. It must have taken thousands to repair all of the damage, not to mention the time over the last few days.

"Holy shit," Kinsey gasps, and her hands cover her mouth in shock that matches my own as we take in the condition of my tattoo shop.

"You okay, sweetheart?"

"Yeah, just . . . wow. I can't believe they did all this."

"I can," I admit. "Your family is one in a million. They're the best people."

"They'll get over this, right? They just need a minute to process. I know they want us to be happy."

"They will. I know just how to handle it, too."

"Shit. I want no part of that."

"This is between me and them now, baby. I'm going to keep you and save my friendship with them. Even if we have to beat it out of each other."

Kinsey and I make our way upstairs to her apartment so she can pack. I take a seat on her bed, noticing the book she was reading last, the one I gave her, which reminds me.

"Kins, don't forget to pack your vibrator."

The pretty blue of her eyes gets wide, her tongue peeking out and swiping against the corner of her lips in a sexy, sultry move that has my cock bucking against my jeans again. Fuck, she's gonna kill me.

Instead of bending her over the bed, I force myself to focus on fixing things with Sawyer. I pull out my phone and start a group chat with Sawyer, Dallas, Liam, and Carter.

> Me: Dom's 8pm. I don't give a shit what you're doing. Be there.

I couldn't bring myself to leave Kinsey, terrified of her being alone. The Iron Wolves were still out there, and my nightmares of her being taken again were too real. She agreed that she wasn't ready either, so after dropping her things off at my house, I brought her to her brother's so I could go to Knock out. Finn said he has zero interest in watching the five of us beat the shit out of each other, so he stayed back to hang with Kinsey.

Carter has surprisingly been the one most chill about all of this. He's been more and more supportive of Kinsey since summer started and he met his boyfriend, and that seems to be true even now as he shows up in a pair of khaki shorts and an Aspen Ridge Distillery sweatshirt. He puts up his hands in a defensive gesture when he sees me.

"I'm not looking to fight you, Reid. You love her?"

"More than anything," I answer honestly.

"Then that's all that matters to me. Nothing changes between us unless you break her heart."

"I'd die first."

"For some reason, I actually believe you're crazy enough that you would," he says as he pats me on the back. "I'll stick around to make sure shithead, dipshit, and spunkrag don't kill you. Probably would take all three, but they'd try."

"Those nicknames are seriously fucked up, man. Thought Dallas was dumbass?"

"I guess it was. Wait, I think it's dickhead now." He shrugs. "I like dipshit better." Carter pulls out his phone, and I know he's texting their sibling group chat to update Dallas' nickname.

Within another few minutes, the other three are walking through Dom's gym, Sawyer walking in front and Dallas and Liam flanking him on either side. Sawyer drops his gym bag at my feet and faces off with me.

"This is how you want to handle it?"

"Ten years ago, you forced my ass here to work through my shit. You and your brothers all do the same. Whether you believe it right now or not, you're my fuckin' brother, Sawyer, so we're gonna fight this out in the ring until you've worked through your shit," I tell him, turning to face Dallas and Liam. "Same goes for you two."

"Fine," Sawyer snaps. "You want to work through this shit? Let's work through it."

We both tape up our hands, sliding our gloves on and stepping under the ropes. The hum of the fluorescent lights and our even breathing are the only sounds, the gym luckily empty at this time of night.

I've known Sawyer a long-ass time, and I've only seen him this angry one other time—when Ivy was kidnapped last year. I never thought I would be on the receiving end of his temper or rage, but if I was going to be, at least it's for something worth fighting for. I know his anger is a combination of betrayal and my association with the MC. I know he blames me for her being taken. But nothing he can feel hasn't already been felt by me tenfold. This is how he wants to handle his issues; this is how we're going to get over ours.

There's no tapping of gloves, no nods of our heads, no warmup. Sawyer circles me on the balls of his feet, his body tense and rigid. He comes at me hard, his typical finesse missing, replaced with rage fueled by a deep sense of betrayal. I dodge his first right hook, one of his signature haymakers that will rattle your brain. But I'm too slow to miss the second, his glove clocking my temple.

The hit forces me to stumble back, but I don't go down, Kinsey's pretty face flashing behind my eyes, reminding me why I'm here. I'm not Sawyer's punching bag, I'm not asking for permission to be with her, I'm here to fight for her so they back off and let her live the life she wants to live.

I swing on him hard, his glove taking the first hit, his ribs taking a hard jab I throw at his side. He grunts in pain, the reverberations of the hit slithering up my wrist to my elbow.

Sawyer cracks his neck from side to side while bouncing on his feet, his eyes squinted into slits as he stares me down.

"Say something!" I yell.

Instead of responding, he comes at me, throwing two quick jabs to my face that I barely manage to block. I return with two hard shots to his ribs again, and I can hear the wind as it leaves his lungs. We go round and round, taking turns throwing hard punches, neither of us pulling a single one.

"She's not a fling, she's not temporary. She's everything to me. I killed for her. I will kill for her. I'd fucking die for her!"

"She's my fucking sister!"

"She's the love of my fucking life!" He hesitates for a moment as my words hit him, finally breaking through a crack. "I never touched her until she was wholly mine, Sawyer, you know me. I wouldn't risk our friendship unless I was in love with her. You fuckin' know me!"

He stumbles backward, his face falling. "You're right," he says as he drops his gloves to his sides. "You're right. I do know you, and that's what scares me. She's twenty-two, and I'm not ready for her to settle down. I'm scared of everything you're involved in. I'm fucking terrified of her getting hurt again."

"Stop treating her like she needs your permission to breathe. She's strong and she knows what she's doing. I'm not forcing her into anything. I'd die before I let anything happen to her again. You would have married Ivy at eighteen if you were given the chance."

"Yeah." Finally, Sawyer's eyes are clear, looking at me like the best friend I've been to him for the last decade. He walks up to me, and I let my arms hang loose at my sides, letting him lead whatever the fuck he's about to do, hoping like hell I'm not about to take one of those goddamn haymakers unexpectedly.

Instead, he shocks the shit out of me by grabbing the back of my neck with his gloved hand and pulls my forehead against his.

"You hurt her, and I'll kill you."

"I'd beg you to."

"I love you. We're good?"

"Yeah, we're good. I love you, too."

Sawyer releases me and climbs out of the ring, pulling off his gloves. I look at his brothers, waiting on the ropes, and hold out my arms in a 'come and get me motion.'

"You two assholes next?"

"Nah, I think this covers it. I heard all I needed to hear," Dallas says.

"I'm good. But I'm with Sawyer, you hurt my baby sister, you're dead."

"Not gonna happen, but I appreciate the threat."

My burner phone goes off, and I scramble out of the ring, pulling my gloves off like they're on fire.

"Yeah?"

"We've got 'em."

"Where?"

"Halfway between you and me. They've got a compound in Briar Falls."

"Security?"

"They got it, but it's nothing we can't get through. How soon can you get back?"

"Let me get Kinsey sorted and talk with her brothers. We'll be there tomorrow. I want to end this."

"We end it permanently this time."

I drop my phone back into my bag and turn to find Sawyer and his brothers waiting for me to relay the information.

"I've got something to take care of."

"We all know, Reid. Sawyer had to tell us, we all kind of had an idea anyway," Liam states.

"I mean, my guess was Mafia," Carter says seriously. His brothers look at him like he's an idiot.

"You thought he was in the Mafia?" Dallas asks for clarification.

Carter shrugs. "Yeah, it was the silent secrecy, the brooding."

"Definitely not in the Mafia," I clarify.

"Yeah, I got that *now*."

I pull out my hair elastic and run my fingers through it before pulling it back again, taking a minute before I speak.

"Okay." I nod. "My president has the information he needs; it's time to go in after the people who took her."

"I'm going with you," Sawyer states again, reiterating what I already knew.

"I know. And you three?"

"We're staying with Kinsey. You've got your crew and Sawyer; we've got Kinsey here."

"I want her at my house. I have security there that I can be alerted about on my phone."

"Easy. Done," Dallas replies.

"Alright. Let's do this."

CHAPTER 25

reid

WITH NERVES IN THE PIT OF MY STOMACH, I PICK UP Kinsey from Carter's house downtown, her body resting comfortably against mine on the back of my bike. She's the only woman I've ever had in that spot, and it's like I was subconsciously waiting for her to fill it.

The ride from town is quiet and serene despite knowing I have to leave her to go after the assholes who took her. There won't be any survivors this time. If it's the last thing we do, the Iron Wolves will be put down for good. I can't live with myself knowing there are people out there actively harming women, and while we can't chase and take down every evil out there, we can surely make a damn dent. Starting with the club that ended Lena and Lucas's lives and took Kinsey from me.

The cool summer air is a welcome reprieve from the storm brewing inside me, Kinsey's soft hands caressing the skin of my abs under my shirt. My heart rate starts to pick up, my breathing comes heavier as her fingers dip into the waistband of my jeans.

Little tease.

My bike kicks up dust and gravel as I pull onto the long, private road, driving up my secluded driveway to the house I want to share with Kinsey from this moment on. I meant everything I said to her, and I don't care how fast it is. She's wholly mine, and that means in every way. I've been living in darkness for so long, and now I want to live in her light.

My heavy boots hit the gravel driveway as I steady my bike and cut the engine. Kinsey climbs off, waiting for me to follow. Her hand is warm in my palm as I lead her to the front door, pulling her inside with only one thing on my mind. Everything else can wait. We kick off our shoes in silence as she looks around the entryway, her pretty blue eyes full of curiosity.

"I'll explain everything to you after, sweetheart."

"After what?"

I reach for her shirt, and she doesn't fight me, putting her arms up and letting me slide the fabric over her head. I unsnap her bra, the fabric falling to the floor, her tits popping free. I take a second to look at her, standing there topless in front of me, her spine straight, hands relaxed at her sides. Her breasts are just a small handful, but they're perky and so fucking sexy, with petite rosebud nipples that respond so well to my touch. My fingers trace the outline of each breast, her breath catching as she lets me explore her.

I don't know what tomorrow will bring, but I'm spending tonight worshiping my woman. The light of my life. My demons might always be right at my back, trying to pull me back under, but I'm going to bask in her warmth for as long as I have it.

I lift her breasts in each hand, loving the slight weight of them, before dropping to my knees at her feet. Her hands reach up, pushing my hair back and looking down at me, her pretty blue eyes sparkling in the light. With my eyes focused on hers, she pulls my head to her chest, my lips opening and sucking her nipple into my mouth. Her soft moans are so sexy as she holds me tightly. Her back arches as I quickly switch to the other side, my tongue flicking at her tight nipple before taking it into my mouth and pulling hard.

"That feels so good."

"I need you naked, sweetheart," I confess as I unbutton her

jeans and work them off her body, thong in tow. She kicks them to the side and then she's standing in front of me completely naked, her soft skin glowing under the light of the room, so gorgeous and all fucking mine.

I return to her breast as I slide a hand up her toned leg until I reach her pussy. My fingers lightly caress her, not surprised to find her wet and ready for me. I slip a finger through her lips, spreading them slightly and teasing her greedy clit. Her fingers grip my hair tighter, her breaths coming in steady, heavy pants. I slide lower, finding her tight little hole and pushing a single finger inside her to my bottom knuckle, her arousal easing my way in.

"Love how wet you get for me," I growl against her breast.

"Ahh. Yesssss. Only for you, baby, always just for you."

"That's right, Kins, this pussy is just for me."

I fuck her with my finger, dipping in and out before staying deep and curling, suckling on the tight buds of her breasts until their stiff peaks against my tongue. I pop off, sitting back on my haunches and gripping her hips, pulling her pussy to my face. I drag my nose through her tight slit, inhaling her mouthwatering, slightly musky scent into my lungs.

My tongue dips out, swiping through her wet pussy, the sweet, clean taste exploding on my tongue, my control teetering on the edge of a cliff. Fuck, I love the taste of her cunt. I lap at her, over and over, her hands gripping her perky breasts and pulling at her nipples, twisting and pinching as she chases her orgasm. But I've got a better idea.

"Where's the toy, Kins?"

"The bedroom," she whispers, grinding her pussy into my face. I told her the first night we were together that one day she'd show me what she does with it, and that day has come. My cock weeps behind my jeans, and it's taking all my self-control not to snap and fuck her hard against the wall.

"I need your cock, baby. Please fuck me first."

Fuck it.

I quickly stand and shove my jeans down my thighs, scooping

her up so her legs are resting on my forearms, her arms grabbing my neck to hang on. She's so fucking light and tiny and I've dreamed about holding her like this while I fucked her like my own personal toy.

I line up my cock with her soaked entrance and meet her eyes —wild with lust and thrust forward, filling her up with one hard stroke.

Her screams echo off the walls as she throws her head back in pleasure. Her legs flex and she lifts her ass to lift herself off me but I'm not having it. She wanted to be fucked, she's getting fucked. I lift her almost to my tip and then slam her back down. Her moans continue to flow freely, mine matching. She feels so goddamn good folded like this, her entire weight in my arms, wet pussy snug around my dick.

"You like it when I fuck you like this, Kinsey? You like being at my mercy?"

"God, yes! Don't stop. Don't stop."

"Jesus, sweetheart, you're clenching around me so tight, your pussy is strangling my dick. Fuck, you feel so good. So fucking good, baby."

"I love when you fuck me. I love how full I feel with you inside me," she pants, her fingers digging into my biceps.

"That's my girl. You take me so well. Your tight little pussy stretching so good around me. You were made for me and only me, Kins," I grunt.

"Only."

Thrust.

"Fucking."

Thrust.

"Me."

"Oh, god, Reid! Please choke me! I want to come, make me come."

Fuck me. She's begging me to choke her? My hand wraps around her dainty little throat just as she takes her last breath of air, squeezing just enough to cut off her air supply. Just as I do, there's a fresh pool of wetness that soaks around my dick, her pussy throbbing and fluttering around me.

"Such a good girl putting your life in my hands, trusting I know exactly what you need. Your pussy is gushing, baby. Come for me, milk my cock and let me fill you while you come around it."

She combusts, doing exactly what I told her to do, pulling me over the edge with her. Her body shakes in my arms as wave after wave of pleasure pulses through her. My cock thickens, throbbing and jerking inside her impossibly tight center as I fill her with my cum, her name on my lips in a repeated prayer.

"Jesus, that was intense," she says as she tries to catch her breath.

"We're not done, little fighter," I say in warning as I carry her to our bedroom, still impaled on my cock. I kick the door open and drop her to the bed as I look around for where she might have hidden her vibrator.

"It's in my bag still, I didn't know what to do with it," she says, blushing.

I dig through her duffel bag until I find a velvet drawstring bag with a very clear outline in it. I pull it out with a smile on my face, so fucking ready to watch her play with her little pussy. I've envisioned this scenario so many times before. Kinsey laying in her bed alone, her spicy romance novels turning her on, making her core ache, her empty pussy throbbing and needing to be filled while she weeps from her center.

I shuffle out of the rest of my clothes, as Kinsey watches me with an anticipatory stare that's all heat and lust. Her naked body is laid out in front of me like an offering, my eyes tracing over her curves in appreciation, just as she slowly spreads her legs for me. She's bare of any hair, lips puffy and pink from how hard she just took me, our combined releases weeping from her hole.

"Show me, sweetheart. Play with your pussy like you do when you're alone."

"Reid . . ." she moans, and I have a split second of doubt that she'll say no until she reaches out and takes the purple vibrator from me. She turns it on the lowest setting, the buzz barely audible as she drags it slowly through her slit, slipping it up and down between her folds.

"What would you think about?"

"You."

She didn't hesitate to answer, and I know it's the truth. Fuck, all that time she was upstairs I could have been up there with her, playing with her, making her feel good, loving on her.

"Tell me, dirty girl. What'd you think about?"

"You eating me out, your face buried between my legs like you'd die without it."

Jesus. She slips the vibrator slowly inside her, my cum oozing out around it. A deep, feral groan works its way up from my chest, my hands clenching at my sides as I watch her chase her release.

"You should see yourself right now, toy in your pussy, my cum easing its way in. You look so sexy, Kinsey. Fuck yourself, show me how you like it."

She moves it in deeper and pulls out, repeating the process in a slow and steady build-up before she pulls it out completely and returns to her swollen clit.

"Reid!" she moans, her motions picking up pace, her hips starting to thrust against the pressure and vibrations of the toy. It's so fucking hot. I don't register my hand has moved to grasp my cock until pleasure pulses through my balls, my hand sliding up and down my shaft, precum leaking from my slit. I pump my hard dick, my thumb swiping over the tip on every upstroke as I try to burn this moment into my brain.

"That's my girl. Get yourself off."

"I want your mouth. Lick me, please, Reid, please."

Jesus Christ.

"Fuck, yes, my baby."

I push her hand and the toy out of the way and replace them with my mouth, suctioning over her sensitive clit. I suck in little pulses as I shove two fingers inside her, pushing in so deep her body jerks forward.

I eat her pussy like I'm starved, her juices dripping down my chin and soaking my beard. Her breathing starts to come in heavy pants, her moans loud and unrestrained, her hips moving wanton. She's gonna be the death of me. Having my face buried between this perfect woman's legs is an addiction I'll never kick. Her sweet flavor coats my tongue, my hands rubbing up the smooth skin of her thighs, settling on her hips.

"You taste so goddamn good, Kins. I can't get enough," I tell her as I use the flat of my tongue to circle her swollen clit, my hips grinding against the bed, needing some type of friction on my desperate cock. "Come for me, let me have what no man will ever have but me."

"OhmygodReid!" She gives me exactly what I want, her body tensing and shaking as the orgasm rolls through her in waves. Her fingers dig into the bedsheets, her lower back arching as her mouth opens on a silent scream. Watching her come undone nearly takes my breath away. It's like with everything else with Kinsey, it happens with so much emotion and feeling behind it; she lets herself go completely and enjoys every single moment. The fact that I'm the only man who will ever see this part of her awakens the caveman inside me.

I crawl up her sated body, lining my dick up with her pussy and slowly pressing in until I'm flush against her, my heavy balls resting against her tight asshole. A soft, long moan escapes her lips as she arches into me, her hands rubbing up and down my shoulders.

"Reid . . ."

"Sweetheart."

I cradle her sweet face in my large palms. "I love you," I whisper against her lips, before peppering kisses along her jaw.

"I love you, Reid Knight."

kinsey

REID AND SAWYER LEFT EARLY THIS MORNING ON THEIR motorcycles to take the hour drive to Amberwood to meet with Hell's Heathens. He fucked me into the mattress before the sun started rising and as he was dressed and walking out the door, he looked at me in nothing but one of his large T-shirts leaning against the doorway, he dropped to his knees and ate me out until I was screaming his name in pure bliss, making the birds fly from the trees and my voice echo into the still morning.

"I want the taste of you on my tongue while I'm away from you."

My heart was in my throat as I watched him pull away, leaving me behind. Spending last night at Reid's house was so different from being in his room at the clubhouse. Not that we were quiet by any means, but it felt like two people whose lives were frozen in time between those four walls, and now that we've left, everything is moving again. Our life is starting, and there's never been anything I've been more sure about.

Overhearing everything he said to Sawyer at the distillery hit me harder than I ever could have prepared myself for, and any minuscule lingering doubts I had about whether or not he would be able to fight for me and stand up to my brother were obliterated. He truly loves me, and I know there's no coming back from it.

My phone vibrates with a text message notification as I lie in Reid's king-size bed, snuggling his pillow, inhaling his masculine scent into my lungs. I roll my eyes as I pick it up off the end table, seeing the notification for my sibling group chat.

Dallas: Blaire and I are taking the morning off, we'll be over to hang out after we pick up some food from Hannah

Carter: Cool, Finn and I will take the afternoon

Liam: That works for Hannah and I. Kins, we'll come hang tonight? That all work?

Me: You all really don't need to come over. I can occupy myself

Dallas: We know that. Maybe we want an excuse to hang out with our favorite sister

Carter: She's our only sister, dipshit

Liam: I was hoping that one would stick. Dipshit is way better

Dallas: Shut the fuck up spunkrag!

Liam: That one doesn't even make sense

Me: What is wrong with you three? Don't come over. Ivy and I already have plans this morning

Dallas: Too bad, we're crashing it then

Me: I'm sure Sawyer is loving having his phone blowing up while he's trying to focus

Dallas: He put our group chat on DND, duh

. . .

Deciding I'm done entertaining my crazy siblings, I drop the phone back on the end table and decide to take a long, hot shower. The hot water beats down on my shoulders and chest, and I'm suddenly overcome with worry. I hate that they left to take care of this. I hate that we just found each other, and he's out there fighting to end something that started long before I was taken. I hate that Sawyer is away from his wife and daughter. I just want everything to be behind us so we can all move forward.

My tears mingle with the water and stream down my face as I allow myself a moment of weakness, knowing that I don't have to be strong all the time. What I went through was nothing compared to what Lena experienced before her death, what other women have experienced before me, but horrific and terrifying, nonetheless. I'm proud of Hell's Heathens for standing up and ending this. Reid's right, these people have no regard for how precious human life is, so they don't get to continue to live theirs.

After pulling myself together, I unpack some of my belongings onto his bathroom counter, setting up my blow dryer and drying my thick hair. I haven't styled it in what feels like weeks, and the process is actually making me feel a little more human.

The black and blue of my cheek has faded to a light green. My skin is healing, and not so incredibly alarming to look at. I don't bother putting on makeup, and throw on a pair of denim shorts and a tank top. As I'm walking out of the room, I see Reid's plain black T-shirt lying on top of the hamper. Picking it up, I lift it to my nose, inhaling him deep into my lungs. The oxytocin hit it gives me is exactly what I needed, and without giving it further thought, I pull it on over my tank, bunching it around my waist and twisting the fabric into a side knot.

The house is quiet, and as comfortable as it is to be in his space, I'm eager to fill it with the noise of my siblings. I thought I would want to be alone, but it turns out that's the last thing I need right now.

I wander aimlessly around Reid's house, making my way through the rustic yet homey living room and taking a seat on the couch. In the center of the coffee table sits a single book, with Reid's handwriting on a piece of paper lying on top of it. I pick up the note first.

My little fighter,

I didn't want to leave you with nothing to do for however long I'll be gone, so read this and think of me. Chapters 24, 36, and 42. You mean the world to me, Kinsey, and I'm coming back to you. You're my whole heart, the reason it beats in my chest, the reason I pull air into my lungs. I will come back.

This is your home now, I dare you to snoop.

I love you, sweetheart.

R.K.

Can a heart melt? It feels like it can melt. This man. What did I do to deserve him? I pick up the book he left me with shaky hands, running my palm over the top of it. But before I can open it to read, my eyes flick back to the coffee table, and my mouth falls open.

Looking back at me are several sheets of drawing paper, the first one is so blatantly and realistically me that it feels like I'm looking in a mirror. With trembling fingers, I pick up the stack to sift through.

In the first one, I'm sitting on the leather couch downstairs in his office, my legs crisscrossed in the seat, looking forward with a smile on my face. I remember that moment, it was when he asked me to stay for pizza. I didn't want that night to end.

The moment I realized you were something more to me. Your smile made me forget the constant pain for the first time in ten years.

The second causes tears to sting my eyes and my heart to catch in my throat. It's me lying in his bed at the clubhouse. My hair is fanned out across his pillow, the blankets covering the majority of my body, my hand outstretched to reach for something, my face pleading and desperate. It was the first night there, and I asked him to sleep next to me. It was the easiest thing I've ever asked for because I had never wanted or needed anything more than I needed to be wrapped up in him. He was safety. Comfort.

The moment I realized I was in love with you. My heart started beating after being dead for so long.

The third and last is of me completely naked, lying sensually on my back in the center of his bed at the clubhouse. My hands are stretched out above my head, gripping the bedsheets, head turned to the side, eyes closed. I look beautiful. My eyes flick to the bottom of the sketch, reading his words, my breath catching in my throat.

The moment I realized you were wholly mine and I'd do anything to keep you.

In each one, I realize, it's how he saw me in those moments, his point of view. With tears in my eyes, I hold them to my chest, sending up prayers to whoever will listen to please bring my man and my brother back to us.

Dallas, Blaire, and Ivy pull into the driveway one behind the other, an hour later. Ivy jumps out of Sawyer's huge, red Ford truck that he's been driving since our grandfather gave it to him when he got his license. I know it's sentimental to both him and Ivy.

"Hey, sis. You doing okay?" Dallas asks me, his arm draped over Blaire's shoulders as they walk up the small porch of Reid's house.

"I guess? Pretty sick to my stomach knowing what I know and where they're going. I'm terrified of something going wrong."

"They're smart, and they both have something precious on the line; they'll come back."

"You're really okay with me being with him?"

"Look, Kins, am I thrilled that you're not our baby sister anymore? No. But I trust Reid with your life, with Blaire's . . . and I don't say that lightly. He's the type of man who won't back down from a fight and will always do what's right. He's the best of all of us. So, yeah, I'm okay with it. I know you'll be taken care of, and I can relax a little."

"Wow," is all I can manage to say.

"He's right, Kins. And it's not just about him taking care of you, I hope you know that. Reid was there for me since the day I showed up in this town. I don't know what they are, but he has demons. Like attracts like, and I'm a firm believer there's a reason why I bumped into him first. His soul is broken, and you're healing him. *You* are perfect for *him*."

We're perfect for each other, is the only thought that comes to my mind.

Baby Grace wiggles and coos as I take her from Ivy's arms and snuggle her into mine. I rest my lips against the top of her head and breathe in a deep inhale of her sweet, clean baby scent. She has a head full of dark hair just like her mom's, crystal-blue eyes just like her dad's, and is the sweetest, most chill baby I've ever met. My nerves immediately relax, that newborn baby magic consuming me.

Ivy stands in the driveway and looks around. The cul-de-sac has two houses, separated by wild lupines and two dirt paths. The house she inherited from her late parents sits on the opposite side of Reid's, tall and foreboding against the Sitka spruce and the view of the Olympic Mountains behind it. The house was purchased by an unnamed investor early this year, and it's been sitting vacant ever since. Still, it houses deeply rooted trauma for Ivy and Sawyer.

"I haven't been back here since everything happened with Brooks."

"Are you okay?" I ask her, nudging her side with my shoulder.

"Yeah, it's just emotional. He almost took everything from me. I had just gotten what I wanted most in the world back, and it was almost gone in an instant. This stuff with you has definitely set Sawyer spiraling."

Unwarranted guilt settles in my stomach. I know deep down none of this is my fault, but I'm positive my kidnapping and Reid's involvement with the MC have aided in his lack of support of the two of us being together.

"It was no one's fault but the men who took me, I know he knows that, and I'm sure he just needs an outlet for his rage."

"And that's Reid," she says. "He told me last night they

hashed out their shit, but it's going to take him a beat to be okay with it."

"I know. It's his issue to resolve. I just hope we can all move on at some point. Reid isn't going anywhere."

"Do you want to know what I think?"

I look up at my sister-in-law, someone I spent my childhood years wishing I could be just like. I'm so thankful she found her way back to us, even if the circumstances surrounding it were dire.

"Tell me."

"I'm happy for you, both of you. You're two of my favorite people in the world, and we meant everything we said the day we asked you two to be Grace's Godparents. Everything is going to work out. They'll be home to us before we realize it."

Her last sentence is whispered, and I don't know if it was to reassure me or herself.

reid

"So, who is it?" I snap. Chaos lets the demand slip, but it isn't without a warning glare. Sawyer and I are sitting in Chaos' office since he refused to bring Sawyer into church. It wasn't something I was going to push him on. That room is reserved for the members who've shown their loyalty and dedication to the club. Sawyer doesn't fit that. Chaos doesn't like outsiders, and he doesn't trust easily, so even though he expected both of us this morning, he's still not happy about it.

"Damon had a son. He was fifteen when we murdered his daddy dearest."

"There's no fuckin' way, Cam. We checked and went after everyone."

"He didn't get his last name. Mom had only just told Damon about him within the last year." He pauses and looks at Sawyer. "Hope you pay your man well, 'cause he knows his shit. If he's open to it, I'd like his contact information. I don't typically work with freelancers and prefer to keep things within the club, but he may be the exception, especially if he's this discreet and good at what he does, and this wasn't a one-off."

"He's the best there is. I'll ask him and get you his info. He also likes to keep to himself and his wife. He's the quiet, stalker type."

Chaos nods his head and moves on with the conversation, giving us the information we came for.

"Proud new daddy was just starting to step into the role for Tyson, even bought him his first motorcycle. Apparently, he wanted Tyson to take over the Iron Wolves someday, introduced his new heir to the club, and had a lavish party where Damon gifted the boy three unwilling women. Tyson brutally beat and raped them—to death. I'll spare you the details, but we're dealing with a truly twisted fuck."

Bile turns in my stomach. *"Prez wants her for himself."* Kinsey was almost in this piece of shit's clutches. I'm guilty of murder. Of torture. All my brothers are. But there's a line you don't cross, and women and children are firmly on the opposite side. Unless there's extreme circumstances, any man who can harm a woman —especially rape her–doesn't deserve to breathe. Anger courses through my veins. I'm going to kill him, and he's going to beg me for it.

"What's the plan?" I grind out through clenched teeth.

"We're all goin' in. Leaving enough here for security, Malice has the plans, and we'll go over them, but I wanted to meet you two first. I'm gonna give it to you straight, boys, doing runs with someone not in our club isn't something we do. I've got committee members not on board with this. We have to do an official vote."

"Fuck that shit! This is my sister they took."

"Yeah? And they killed my brother," Chaos states, venom laced in his voice. "After torturing his woman in front of him for fuck knows how long. Then they lit him on fire and let him burn to death while they raped and murdered her. So don't think for a fucking second you have any say here."

It's rare that Chaos loses his cool. He easily controls the room, and that's just one of the many reasons he's so good at what he does. Leading us. I know there's a sting of jealousy when it comes to Sawyer. Camden let me go, and in his eyes, I replaced my family with Sawyer's.

He doesn't trust easily, and he doesn't let outsiders in. In his eyes, Sawyer's a threat.

"You think I don't know that shit? You think I don't know every fucking thing that went down in vivid detail? I may not have been there through it, but I was there after. It kills me what Reid went through, and that extends to you. I'm here for my sister as much as I am to fight for him," he yells, pointing at me. "You don't have to like me. You don't have to like the situation. But I'm not going anywhere. I'll respect your rules, I will follow your lead. But I'm fucking going and we're going to end every single one of these assholes."

Chaos sits back in his chair and crosses his arms over his chest, aura of calm and collected firmly back in place as he studies Sawyer's face.

"Okay," he finally states. "Reid trusts you, and I respect you. I don't know you, so I don't like you, but we can do this together."

The three of us stand to leave his office, Chaos leading the way, shouting out orders and calling for Malice and Wrath.

"You ready for this?"

"Yep."

"We're in Chaos' wheelhouse now. Get ready, there's a reason that's his road name."

"He seems pretty stable and straightforward," Sawyer says.

"That's just one side of him. The other? You'll see . . ."

Malice is waiting in the hallway with Wrath, the patchwork tattoos that I've inked on him over the years on full display under his cut.

"Don't you own a T-shirt, Malice?"

"What fun is that? Only wear jeans 'cause Prez tells me I have to."

"What the fuck?" Sawyer asks, shaking his head.

"Brother, no one here wants to see what you got goin' on between your legs. Keep that shit in the dungeon."

"The dungeon?" Sawyer repeats.

"You wanna see it?" Malice asks, his eyes glinting with mischief, and I know I've gotta shut this shit down before he has Sawyer cuffed to his Saint Andrew's cross.

"Fuck off with that shit, Mal. What's the plan?"

Malice flips a switch, going into the details of the Iron Wolves compound and the plans to get in. Sawyer falls in line, listening intently and taking stock of how we're going to execute this as efficiently as possible with little to no casualties on our side. There will be no survivors from theirs.

"Reid, you and Noose will tag team as road sergeant. Figure it out with him, don't give a shit how you two do it, just get us there safely."

"Done," I reply.

After I connect with Noose and set a game plan we both agree on that gets us there without alarming the public or local police, I nod at Sawyer to follow me to the armory. Pulling out a handgun, I load the magazine, pressing each hollow point into its slot until it's full, popping it into the well.

"You ever used one of these?"

"Not in a bit, but I remember the gist."

"Safety's built in. Rack the slide as soon as we get there, like this." I pull back the slide, pulling a bullet into the chamber. "Point and shoot. Aim to kill, brother. We take no prisoners, except for one."

"Got it."

"You sure you want to do this? I never wanted this for you."

"I would have taken care of things that night in the woods if you hadn't."

"I didn't want that stain on you. I don't want it now. It's not too late to walk away, and it doesn't make you any less of a man to do so. It actually makes you a better one."

"You've carried this burden long enough on your own. I'm with you."

"Then let's take care of this shit and end it."

The rest of the morning and into the afternoon is pure madness. Club members prepare for war, packing their bikes with weapons and ammo, closing up the clubhouse, and leaving a skeleton crew to hold down the fort while the majority of us go in.

I find Malice leaning against the doorframe that leads outside, his boots crossed at his ankles, whistling while flipping his knives around in his hands.

"Is that one okay? Like, upstairs?" Sawyer asks while tapping his head.

Sin laughs at the question, answering, "Malice? Yeah, he's just got a couple screws loose. He had a fucked-up childhood that gives him a little unhinged edge, but he loves hard."

"Yeah, when you get past the barbed wire," I add.

Chaos' voice shouts out over the voices around us like a knife, plunging the room into complete silence.

"We move out in ten. They'll expect to be hit at night under the veil of darkness, we want them to be surprised, so we're hitting them midday. Stitch, if anyone, women or god-for-fuck-ing-bid, children, are found, you take your pick of prospects and bring them with you to help get them out. That is your only priority. Everyone else goes down. Leave their president to me. Sin, Malice, Wrath, and Rogue will be on comms with me. That's it. Everything else is free game. Who's ready?"

There's a collective cheer as Chaos nods his head.

"Then let's go fuck shit up!"

The energy in the room is palpable, everyone ready for battle as we head outside to our bikes. The roar of engines is deafening as I nod to Sawyer to stay with me. He's never ridden formation before, but he's about to learn real quick. We ride through Amberwood in a massive show of force, keeping it slow and calm to not put a blatant red flag on our asses. The rumble of our bikes and the heavy scent of motor oil fill the air, giving us away. Hell's Heathens has always been based out of Amberwood, and we've always stayed within the boundaries of the law . . . except when we're provoked. Then we're like a pack of wild beasts who've been cornered. We operate as a family unit, owning and supporting legitimate businesses in Amberwood and contributing to the community. The people here aren't scared of us, but those who threaten to harm us or our territory? They're about to find out what happens when you fuck with a Heathen.

Thirty minutes later, we're pulling up a mile down the road from their compound in the middle of fucking no-man's land, while a prospect and two members move forward on their own in a nondescript truck. We sit on our bikes, adrenaline pumping through our veins. My old companions, anger and vengeance, fuel me. I attempt to push everything else out of my thoughts, hyper-focusing on getting in there and ending Tyson and the club he's brought back from the dead. But in the recesses of my mind is something bright and beautiful tugging at me, balancing the two sides of my life.

The explosion echoes on the wind, Sawyer's head snapping in my direction.

"Chaos."

Go time.

Bikes surge forward as we enter their compound, sliding our bikes to a stop and pulling guns from holsters. The air is thick with dust and smoke as we move in quickly, our heavy boots crunching over broken glass and shattered wood. I'm laser-focused, attuned to every sound, every movement at the edge of my vision.

The compound looks like another junkyard, which seems to be fitting for the type of filth it's harboring. It sits wedged against long-abandoned train tracks, the cars covered in graffiti, worn down in places, crumbling completely in others, the original logos faded into oblivion. We're assuming the main clubhouse is the shipping container in the center, a large rust bucket covered in grime and the devil himself knows what else. The perimeter is surrounded by sagging barbed wire that's more rust than metal.

Members flock out with guns in their hands, and shots are

fired as we barrel forward. Chaos, Sin, Sawyer, and I run to take cover against the side of a boxcar.

"Keep quiet, let's get in there from the back," Sin says as we follow him along the line of the crumbling cars next to the shipping container. Just as Chaos and Sin slide between the two buildings, a gnarly looking asshole with a green mohawk jumps in front of us.

I lift my gun to shoot him between the eyes as Sawyer steps forward, throwing a punch to the assholes face, blood pouring from the crushed bone in his cheek. He doesn't waste a moment, pulling his arm back and letting another one land. The flat of his hand uppercuts him right under the nose, pushing the cartilage into his brain, killing him. His body crumbles as Sawyer pulls out his gun again, giving me a look that conveys he didn't break a sweat.

"Took care of that pretty easy. Show-off."

"You said to keep it quiet, what was I supposed to do?" He shrugs.

We follow Chaos and Sin, quickly rounding the house and breaking in through the back door. The house reeks of piss, stale cigarettes, mold, and shit as we step through the threshold. The walls are covered in more graffiti, furniture torn and sagging. Beer bottles, cigarette butts, needles, and other garbage litter the floor. How the fuck can people live like this?

The building has been gutted, minus two makeshift rooms, closed off with plywood and steel sheets. Sin lifts his foot and kicks the first one down, the wood and metal clattering to the floor as a small, weasel-looking man with eyes as round and beady as a tarsier jumps backward with shaky hands and knees.

"Where's your president?" Chaos demands as he descends on him, Sin moving to his front and Chaos to his back, pinning him in.

"In-nn-in the back room. His office."

"You can't force loyalty," Chaos states with mock disappointment as he grabs the guy's forehead and chin from opposite directions and twists at an ungodly angle. The man crumbles to the floor in a lifeless heap.

"Let's move." Sin, Sawyer, and I flank Chaos as we move down the hallway.

Two shots are fired out of the second room, the sound nearly making my ears bleed as it echoes off the metal. Luckily, both shots miss the four of us as we duck down against the wall.

"We know you're in here, Tyson. Don't you know you're supposed to lead your men? Protect your women? They're all bleeding out in your shit lawn while you cower in here like the pathetic piece of shit you are," Chaos taunts.

I steady my gun and wait for the dumbass to do exactly what I know he will, fire at us again, and the moment his arm sticks out of the doorway to shoot, I pull my trigger. His wrist practically explodes, his gun dropping to the ground as we stand and push forward, his howls sounding so much like the little baby wolf he is.

We find him behind his desk, his back against the wall, holding his wrist to his chest in pain. Chaos and Sin flank the doorway as Sawyer and I walk toward the man who was responsible for taking Kinsey. The love of my life.

"This one's mine," I snarl. Sawyer takes a step back, giving me space as I grab the man by his shirt, hauling him and throwing him into the chair. His hands come up defensively to cover his face and head, as if that could protect him from what's about to come. What he fucking deserves.

"So you're the sick fuck Damon created? Should have stayed with your mommy, Tyson." I look down at his leather cut, reading his name patch for the first time. "Reaper?" I laugh. "Well, that's ironic since I'm about to cut down every single fuckin' part of you until there's nothing left."

"You don't know who you're dealing with, Rogue."

"Does it look like you're in a position to think I give a shit?" Pulling my knife from my pocket, I hold it up in front of his face, the light hitting it just right, making the reflection in his eyes almost shimmer. I watch as he takes in the gravity of the situation. Of how well and truly fucked he is.

"You took what was mine. Did you think you'd get away with it? That you could take her from me and get away with it?"

My rage overflows when he ignores me. My fist connects with the side of his face, an audible crunch of bone shattering beneath his eye. "Answer me!" I yell. His head lolls to the side as he looks at me with a sick fucking grin that has me seeing red. I'm lost to it.

"You took him from me, Rogue! You and your band of heathens! So I was going to tie up your girl and fuck every single one of her holes until she was so washed up, she'd be of no use to me. Then I was going to give her to my men until they tore her apart."

I slam my fist into his hard flesh repeatedly, my knuckles burning and splitting open. I don't stop, pounding into him like my own personal heavy weight bag, the sound of flesh on flesh reverberating through the room.

I beat him like he's done to so many innocent women. Just like he wanted to do to Kinsey. Just like his fucking father did to Lena. The darkness starts to close in on me, pitch black surrounding my eyes, hate and vengeance filling my bloodstream, innate savagery taking over, tightening its grip on me.

Then Kinsey's pretty face flashes behind my eyes, pushing through the haze of my destruction. My light, pulling me from the darkness threatening to drown me.

"Fuck!" I roar, my blade slicing his throat from one ear to the next in a deep gouge that quickly separates as the rush of blood pours from the opening. Tyson gurgles, his eyes wide in horror and pain as life slowly drains from him. "Fuck you! You'll never hurt any of them again!"

I stand there unmoving, unblinking, watching as he chokes on his final breath, the life finally leaving his body. He deserved a long, slow, torturous death. I'm frozen to my spot, watching the heap of evil bleeding out onto the floor, the red color staining like spilled paint. Anger still thrums through my veins like a live wire, rage creeping in around the edges of my sight. I can't look away. His eyes are lifeless, looking up unmoving into the abyss, his body nothing more than a shell. I can hope the devil himself pulled his soul to the underworld for an eternity of torment.

Sawyer comes up and clasps his hand around my shoulder, causing me to jerk, grounding me.

"It's over. Let's get the fuck outta here."

We pull up to the clubhouse and park our bikes out front. How we didn't lose anyone is a feat worth celebrating, and I know that's exactly what my brothers plan to do. Adrenaline still races through my bloodstream, amping me up with energy to keep going. It's over. The Iron Wolves are finally no more, and while threats will always lurk in the shadows, at least this one is gone for good.

Now, I've only got one thing on my mind—Kinsey. Her beautiful smile flashes behind my eyes. Chaos slaps his hand against the thick layer of my cut on my back, pulling my attention to him. "Stay the night, Rogue. You and Sawyer can bunk here and leave in the morning."

"I'm washin' up and heading home," I tell him sternly, not leaving room for argument. He may be my president, but I'm going home to my woman.

"Same, I'm not going to stay away from my wife a moment longer than I have to," Sawyer adds. The two of us walk side by side through the clubhouse, climbing up the stairs to my bedroom. I pull out two towels and extra clothes for each of us. The door falls closed behind us, shutting out everything else and leaving Sawyer and me to face each other.

"You really love her."

Surprised by his statement, I turn to face him. His hair is a sweaty mess, pushed up and out of his face, his lip is busted, and his shirt is covered in blood. Jesus, if Ivy could see him right now she'd lose her goddamn mind.

"Yeah, brother. I really love her. More than anything."

"What you did . . ."

"He paid for it less than his father did for what he did to Lena. I meant to prolong it. I wanted it to last days. I wanted him to feel every ounce of fear that Kinsey did. He got off too easy."

"Because you have something more important to focus on than prolonging his death."

"Yeah. I finally have something to live for."

"Camden still going to let you live under the normal arrangement?"

"Yeah, the devil would have to leave the underworld himself to drag me back here full time. I can't ever leave for good, Sawyer, you know that. But she'll always be protected. She'll always come first. Old ladies are valued and worshiped here."

"And that's what she'll be? Your old lady?"

"She's my everything. Call it whatever you want—old lady, my woman, my wife. They're just titles. Kinsey is my everything. Period."

"I get it. I trust you . . . brother. I'm proud of you. For everything you've overcome, for never giving up on life, for still having love inside you to give to everyone around you. You've saved more of us than you give yourself credit for. Now you're making my baby sister happier than I think I've ever seen her in her entire life. You're a good man, Reid, and I'm proud to call you family. You deserve her."

I swallow hard against the knot in my throat and blink away the rogue tear that spills over my lashes. *I deserve her.*

"You told me to keep going when I wanted to give up, that I needed to wade in the darkness until my light came. She's my light, Sawyer."

"I know. Now you're gonna need to figure out the Sunday thing 'cause my mom is going to expect you at dinner. She's put up with you missing for a decade now, and that shit is not gonna fly once she finds out about you and Kins."

I chuckle under my breath 'cause I know he's right. Amy

Hayes is not one to be trifled with when it comes to Sunday dinners with her family.

"Yeah. I'll talk to Cam."

With all of that put to rest, I take the first shower, letting the water wash the blood off me. I watch as it swirls down the drain, and with it, all the darkness I was holding onto. It's time to move forward, to forgive myself and finally live. Lena would want me to. I may have disappointed her for the last ten years, but I'm not going to any longer. I've been a broken man for too long. All it took was Kinsey putting me back together and giving me a reason to.

Part of me wonders if she knew all along. The day on the side of the road when Sawyer found me and the skies parted, her lost, broken brother, wandering through the storm alone. I almost didn't go with him. If it weren't for her sign from above, I never would have ended up in Aspen Ridge.

I wonder if she knew Kinsey would complete me all along.

CHAPTER 28

kinsey

THE RUMBLE OF A MOTORCYCLE BRINGS BOTH RELIEF and fear in equal measure. Instead of running outside, instead of at least checking the window to make sure it's Reid, I stand frozen in the living room, my hand on my heart, a knot in my throat. Liam and Hannah left an hour ago, and I've been a nervous wreck ever since.

Heavy footsteps climb up the stairs of the deck, leading closer and closer to the front door. My hands start to shake as the door-knob turns and is pushed open, revealing Reid's giant silhouette against the dead of night behind him.

"You're home," I rush out, tears streaming down my face.

"You think I'd leave you so soon after finally getting you?"

Then I'm rushing to him, running across the room and into the arms that bring me so much happiness, I don't know how I ever survived without feeling it. My legs wrap around his waist, my hands pushing his long hair out of his face. One of his hands holds my ass tightly against him, the other dwarfing my face, angling my head down to capture my lips. His beard is rough against my skin as my mouth opens for him. We kiss like it's been a year rather than a day. It's all-consuming, altering my brain chemistry in the most life-changing way.

"I missed you. Never leave me again," I demand as I pepper kisses along his face and jaw.

"Fuck, sweetheart, never. Life starts now."

"Promise me. Promise me, Reid."

His hand clenches around my face, gripping my chin and forcing inches of space between us. His eyes are narrowed and severe, but so full of heart, like he's about to deliver a vow, the promise that I begged for.

"I don't know what the future will bring, Kins, but I do know that I will spend every day of my life working to be good enough for you. I'll do everything in my power to see you smile, hear your laugh, and make you the happiest woman alive. I will never do anything to intentionally hurt you, and if I fuck up, I'll bust my ass to make it right. You're the light of my life, little fighter. You're stuck with me now."

My heart combusts, a euphoric feeling of pure bliss floating through me

"Goddamn, I love you, Reid Knight."

"I fucking love you, Kinsey Hayes."

Everything becomes frantic in an instant, fire flooding our veins, our hands pulling at each other's clothes in a desperate attempt to connect.

"I need you inside me."

"Fuck yes, sweetheart," he growls as he rips the large T-shirt over my head and throws it to the side. His lips press against my collarbone, licking a line across the protruding bone from side to side. "You're skin, mmm, how are you so perfect?"

"I'm not, I'm just yours."

"Mine."

Reid carries me with one hand toward the bedroom, his hand squeezing my small breasts in his palm, fingers twisting and pinching my nipples, forcing moans to escape from my lips. Pleasure zips down my spine, my clit throbbing at the ministrations. He kicks the door closed behind us with a loud slam, his mouth never leaving my skin.

Before I can register he's done it, I'm falling onto the mattress with a bounce, his hands gripping the sides of my panties and dragging them roughly down my legs. Once I'm bare, lying on the bed, everything slows down. I look up at his naked torso from my place in the center of his mattress, completely naked. His large tattoos fill his chest—the Hell's Heathen crest, a large skull with a crown, and a dagger—taking up the majority of the space. I'll never get used to seeing this man naked. Chiseled abs, defined Adonis belt, strong pecs, and thick, rounded shoulders. My eyes rake up his gorgeous body until I meet his piercing green eyes when I realize he's doing the exact same thing I am—drinking me in.

"You are so fucking sexy, sweetheart. I can't believe you're mine."

My cheeks flush, a warm heat spreading over my cheekbones. Without taking his eyes off me, he kneels on the bed and reaches for my foot, bringing it to his mouth, pressing a chaste kiss to the soft spot right above my ankle. My breath hitches as I watch him, this huge man, treating me like the most precious thing in the world with the most tender touches.

His mouth trails kisses up my leg, slowly, methodically, as if there's all the time in the world and he intends to take full advantage of it. My heart rate ratchets up, emotion and pleasure pulsing through my body from head to toe.

He repeats the process on my other leg, taking his time, kneading his thumb and forefinger into my flesh as his lips drag up my leg. He alternates between soft kisses, nips, and long licks up the length, giving special attention to the tattoo he marked me with at my hip.

"Goddamn, do you have any idea what you do to me?" he says, his words deep and gruff.

"Show me, baby. Come make us both feel good."

I love watching this man go down on me almost as much as I love the feeling he gives me when he does it. His eyes stay on me the entire time, holding me hostage while he licks me from ass to clit. I squirm in his hold, my legs already shaking around his head.

"That feels so, so good, holy shit."

"Damn, Kins, I fuckin' love eating your pussy. You taste so good."

He feasts on me, licking me over and over, then spearing his thick tongue into my center, plunging inside me.

"Oh, fuck!" I scream, legs shaking, orgasm building, but before I get there, he's pulling back. I let out a desperate whine of protest.

Reid grabs my hips, flipping me over onto my stomach, positioning me exactly how he wants me, with my cheek on the bed and ass in the air. My legs are close together, with his spread around me, making him lower to fit with our size difference.

"On your knees, my little fighter. You think you're ready to take my big dick like this?"

"Jesus Christ, Reid, YES."

He swipes the thick crown of his length through my center, toying with me, coating himself in my arousal. I brace myself as he grips my hips tightly in his grasp and pushes forward. He feels so much bigger in this position, and I swear I feel every inch of him as he thrusts forward, hitting my cervix.

"Goddamn, you're so tight, Kins, I barely fuckin' fit like this, Jesus."

He pulls out and pushes back in, hard, slow thrusts, a moan spilling from his lips every time he fills me. Rough hands squeeze my ass, fingertips digging into my flesh before rubbing over my hips and up my spine. He leans forward, curling around me, licking up my back as he goes. His hand grips my hair, pulling it and forcing my head to arch back. His breath is warm on my ear as he whispers.

"I love you. Your heart. Your soul. Your body. I love you, Kins."

He pounds into me in deep strokes, making me scream against the bedsheets. My pussy clenches around him, throbbing and pulsing as he withdraws and lurches back in. Then he's pulling out, flipping us so that he's on his back and I'm lifted right over his face, my knees on either side of his head.

"Ride my face, sweetheart, don't stop until you make a mess of me."

Energy crackles between us as I hover over his lips, his tongue slipping out and tracing through my slit—back and forth, back and forth. Pleasure zips down my spine. Blood thrums between my ears. My knees shake. Gripping the headboard, I ease myself down onto his waiting mouth, my eyes rolling to the back of my head as we connect. His mouth opens for me, his tongue swiping back and forth, eating me like he always does, as if he's starving for me.

Strong hands on my hips guide me, urging me to move. So I do, rocking back and forth on his mouth, the coarse hair of his thick beard rubbing against the inside of my thighs, stinging and rubbing me raw, as the warmth of his soft tongue dips in and out of my pussy, stroking my clit repeatedly until pleasure nearly blinds me.

I come hard, my stomach tightening, my fingers digging into the headboard, my head thrown back as my orgasm barrels through me. Wave after wave, it takes me under until I'm gasping for breath.

Reid wastes no time, picking me up by my hips and notching his dick at my center. My legs spread impossibly wide to accommodate him in this position, but then I'm sinking down onto him until we're flush, long, drawn-out moans escaping both our lips.

"Fuck, you're so beautiful," he hisses, voice gruff with barely restrained desire as his big palms grab my breasts. He pistons his hips up into me, fucking me with abandon. His motions are frenzied, his control long gone, driving us both to the edge of release.

"Reid, I'm close. Ohmygod! I'm coming!" Mind-numbing pleasure slams into me. Like a bomb was detonated inside me, I fall forward as it completely wreaks havoc on my body.

"Baby, your pussy is clenching around me so tight, you're pulling me with you. Goddamn, Kins, you're making me come."

Reid's thick cock twitches deep inside me, ropes of warm cum painting my insides as he falls off the edge and into pure bliss. My name is on his lips in a long, extended moan, his eyes squeezing shut as his hips stutter.

After we're both spent, I stay on top of him, his dick softening inside me, with no desire to move at all. The world could burn down around us, and I wouldn't have any interest in moving from this spot right here.

He presses kisses against the top of my head while his hands rub over my body, holding me impossibly close to him. After a while, Reid slides out of me and shifts so that we're on our sides facing each other.

"Sawyer is okay?" I ask, assuming he is, or things wouldn't have gone the way they did when he got home.

"He is. Home with Ivy and Grace."

"Are you two okay?"

"We hashed out everything we needed to. We're all going to be okay."

After a bit of silence, my mind is lost to what could have happened while they were gone. If the threat is gone, if everyone in Hell's Heathens is okay. Reid speaks up, reading my mind.

"I know you won't ask, sweetheart, but I want to spare you the details. I will tell you that everything is over. The Iron Wolves are gone. We won't have to worry about them again."

"Are you okay? Really okay?"

"Kins, I'm better than I've been in a very long time."

My fingers trace aimlessly over the Hell's Heathen colors on his chest. "Why do they call you Rogue?" I ask, something I've been curious about since I heard someone call him that at the clubhouse.

"Originally, it's because that's what I was to Chaos. A loaner, even among the club. He said I was always here, but always had one foot out the door. Now, it's because I'm a beast, living away from my herd. Not to mention, how I react when cornered."

"And how is that?"

"Brutally."

"It's hard for me to believe you could hurt anyone."

"I would never hurt you, sweetheart."

"It should scare me. Terrify me."

"But?"

"It doesn't. The opposite actually."

"I never wanted the two parts of me to collide. Never wanted them to be one."

"They've always been one, baby. And I love all of you."

kinsey

"Come on, big guy, let me buy you a coffee. You feeling okay about going to Sunday dinner later?"

"How about we go grab barbeque chicken pizza from North Pass and we eat naked in bed instead?"

"Reid Knight, are you nervous?"

"I don't get nervous, my violent little fighter, you trying to start somethin'?"

"I'll lay you flat on your ass, baby, so try me."

"Oh, sweetheart, you know I'd love to see you try."

"Mmm. Maybe later, first coffee, then my parents' house for Sunday dinner."

Reid's grip tightens around my hand ever so slightly, a soft twitch letting me know how he feels about our Sunday plans. It took some serious convincing and pleading, but Reid got Camden to agree to every other Sunday and—much to my mom's dismay—she agreed to the same. Now we split our Sundays between the clubhouse and my parents', like two children whose parents are sharing custody. Reid always wanted to keep his life in the MC hidden from everyone in his day-to-day life here in Aspen Ridge, but that was never going to be his reality forever. It's as much a part of who he is as the tattoo artist, the boyfriend, the son, the best friend, the brother. I love every facet of him, and I wouldn't change a piece.

Reid and I walk up the cobblestone sidewalk toward my sister-in-law's coffee shop and bakery. Ms. Nettie sits outside Bean Haven at a table for one, watching us as we walk in her direction.

"So the last one is paired off, huh?" she says as a greeting.

"What do you mean, Ms. Nettie?"

"You and beast here. You're holding hands, lookin' like you're on the set of a *Beauty and the Beast* remake."

"Very cheeky, Ms. Nettie. Yes, Reid and I are together."

"You deserve each other. Not so sure about that big brother of yours, Ivy's too good for him."

A laugh bursts from my chest. Ms. Nettie and Sawyer have never gotten along. Even her little dog, Winnie, hates him.

"I'm sure Ivy is just fine with her decisions. And they have baby Gracie now. They're very happy."

"Mhmm," she mumbles as Reid opens the door for us. Bean Haven is the only coffee shop and bakery in Aspen Ridge, and Hannah is constantly slinging drinks. She's the hardest worker I know and is such a good mom. She and Liam worked so hard to redecorate this place when Hannah's grandmother let her take over running things a few years ago. It has Hannah's boho vibe in every corner, and it's one of the most welcoming places Aspen Ridge has to offer.

We walk inside, finding Hannah behind the bakery counter with her sister, Hailey, hands over her tiny baby bump. I sidle up to the counter with a huge smile on my face. "Hey, you two."

"Hey, Mrs. Knight," Hannah teases. Reid straight up growls next to me. A deeply primal, appreciative sound that goes right between my legs. So, he likes that, huh?

"How are you feeling, Hailey?"

"Morning sickness has extended into the second trimester, which has been glorious, let me tell you."

"Buck up, buttercup!" Hannah playfully teases her sister.

"I've heard it can be rough. I'm sorry. Let me know if you ever need any help with anything. I have a week before school starts up again, but even then, I'm there if you need anything."

"Really? I'd love to hang out. Lily and Emma would love to see you. I know we've all been so busy, but we miss you."

Her words nearly make me choke with emotion. The four of us have gone to school together our entire lives, but we were never close. In the last year, they've each settled down into relationships. Lily even got married a few months ago in a secret ceremony to her ex-boyfriend's dad, and Emma is in a relationship with not one but three men who all share her in one big house. I would love friends here in Aspen Ridge, and it's something I've been desperately craving since moving back from college last year.

"I would love that. Just let me know when you all are free, and we can meet up somewhere."

"Sounds good to me! Hannah, I'm going to go see if Mila is done at the bookstore. I'll catch up with you later." We wave our goodbyes as Hannah looks at us with big heart eyes.

"What?" I ask.

"You still want a tattoo? I found a guy for you in Briar Falls," she says with a playful lilt to her tone. Reid's animalistic growl rumbles through his chest, making Hannah throw her head back in a laugh.

"Damn, dude, you're really taking that protective boyfriend thing seriously. I don't know what those Hayes boys are worried about, you're worse than they are."

"She's not being inked by anyone but me," he states with finality.

"Plus, he already did it," I add, making Hannah's eyes go wide. My sister-in-law is covered in tattoos that Reid has done over the years. She has an entire sleeve of fine line floral that extends from fingers to shoulder, and her entire hip and thigh are done to match.

"Let me see it! Where?" she gasps.

"Sorry, sis, another time, it's on my hip and I'm not pulling up my dress in the middle of Bean Haven.

"Mr. Knight, such a rebel! I'm proud of you. I really am happy for you two. You both deserve to be happy."

"Thanks, Han," I tell her as I look up at Reid, who's already looking down at me with all the love in the world. "You coming to dinner later?"

"Yeah, just need to wrap things up here in a few hours," she replies.

Reid orders his coffee and my salted caramel latte, then we head out of Bean Haven and onto the streets of downtown Aspen Ridge. His muscular arm wraps around my shoulders, keeping me tucked into him as we wander up the street to Rogue. This past week, Reid successfully moved all of my things out of the studio and into his house. There's no such thing as rushing when you know without a shred of doubt that you've found your person. There's no way I would willingly sleep away from this man after knowing what it's like.

Once we reach Rogue, we take our drinks inside and head to his office. I immediately kick off my sandals, pulling my legs into the large leather chair that I claimed the first time I was in here with him. Reid's eyes immediately track the movement, looking at my freshly painted pink toes.

"You ever goin' to listen when I tell you to wear shoes down here?"

"Probably not."

Reid makes a tsking sound and slowly shakes his head. Instead of taking a seat across from me like I expect him to, he sets his coffee down on his desk and walks to the other side of it. I sip on the smooth latte, missing the way Reid made it for me while we were staying at the clubhouse, when he steps directly in front of me. My eyes trace up his thick thighs, the visually erect outline of his huge cock pressing against his jeans until I see his hands in front of him. He's holding a book I've never seen before, and as he drops to his knees in front of me, he sets it in my lap.

"New one?"

"Read to me?" he asks.

"Now?"

"Yeah, baby, right fuckin' now."

Excitement courses through my veins, and I quickly set my to-go cup down on the floor beside my chair. As I pick up the book, Reid's fingers grasp my ankle, pulling it off the chair. I gasp as his lips press firmly against my skin on the inside of my ankle.

"Chapter 18. Start reading."

Reid's lips trail kisses up my leg slowly as I open the book to chapter 18. Pleasure zings through me, anticipation ratcheting up to the highest peak.

"Ace tastes like cool peppermint and danger as his tongue delves into my mouth. It's brutal and possessive. A claim. I'm putty in his arms as the hand wrapped around my throat tightens ever so slightly. My core clenches, squeezing against nothing, wanting him to touch me, to fill me."

My voice stutters and pauses as I read the lines, my brain not processing anything but Reid's hands pushing up my dress until he reaches my hips. He grips me roughly, dragging my ass to the edge of the seat so I'm dangling off. His talented mouth moves to my other leg, repeating the process of kissing a trail up the length. Once he reaches my inner thighs, his kisses alternate between nips and licks, his teeth sinking into the fleshy meat of my inner muscle.

I do my best to focus on the words, reading the erotic scene he's chosen for this moment, but my mind is a hazy, lust-filled mess as Reid reaches my center.

"Don't stop reading, Kins, it hasn't gotten good yet."

Jesus Christ, he's going to kill me.

"Ace's fingers move quickly, flicking the button of my jeans, working them down over my hips with swift movements, his mouth

never leaving mine. Once they're down my thighs, his hand is at my center, rubbing over the thin cotton fabric of my panties. I moan into his mouth at the contact. I know he's discovering just how wet kissing him has made me, and my cheeks flush with heat."

Reid presses his entire face into my core, taking deep inhales that send me into overdrive. After pulling my underwear down my legs, strong, calloused hands dig into my thighs, picking them up and pushing them over each armrest so I'm spread extremely wide for him.

"Oh, god," I moan as I'm stretched open, completely bare in front of him and on full display. The book shakes in my hands as my fingers tremble.

"Fuuuck, Kins. This pussy is so damn pretty. Look at you, weeping for me. You're so pink, so wet." His words are strained, feral, borderline unhinged as he stares between my legs. His tongue sticks out as he licks the flat of it up my center, hole to clit. "Jesus, you taste so fuckin' good. You were made for me. This pussy was made just for me."

"Yes, Reid. Lick me, baby. Make me feel good, the way only you ever have."

He looks up at me from between my legs, this huge man on his knees, face inches from my pussy. His eyes darken at my words, a growl releasing from his lips as he dives in. I don't need anything to compare it to, to know how good he is at eating me out. I love this man's tongue buried in my pussy almost as much as he loves it. Almost.

He licks me just like he always does, as if he's starved and I'm his first taste of food. The book falls to the floor, long forgotten as my hands thread through the long, soft locks of his hair, holding his face to me. I grind my hips against his face, chasing the orgasm he's driving me to.

My legs burn and shake as his tongue swirls around my clit, and when his hand reaches up to wrap around my throat, cutting off my oxygen, his mouth suctioning my clit with little pulses, I shatter.

The world dims around me as I climax, his fingers releasing my throat and precious air filling my burning lungs. He licks me through it, long laps up my center, letting my release coat his tongue.

"Fuck. That was . . . just wow," I ramble.

Reid sits back up, his hand wrapping around the back of my neck, his mouth finding my own, tongue spearing into my mouth so I can taste myself on him. I eagerly suck his tongue into my mouth as his free hand makes quick work of his jeans, pushing them down just enough to free his huge cock.

He's driving into me a moment later, filling me completely. He fucks me hard and possessively, driving into me at a brutal pace. I cling to him, hanging on for dear life. My legs burn in this position, but it feels so fucking good.

"Fuck, Kins, I'm not gonna last. You're so fucking wet, so tight. You're pussy is squeezing me too fuckin' good."

"Good, baby. Come for me. Let me feel you come," I beg, my lips against his ear. My teeth scrape against his lobe, nipping at him. Reid readjusts us, pulling my legs to drape over his forearms instead. He hauls me up so I'm suspended in the air, my hands wrapped around his neck as he lifts me up to his tip and then drops me back down. He continues that way, bouncing me up and down on his length, the head of his dick hitting that sweet spot inside me that has me floating away.

I come with a scream, my pussy clenching hard around him, and his movements stutter, as if it's harder to move inside me.

"Oh shit, that's my girl, milking her man, pulling the cum from me."

His deep, masculine moan reverberates through his chest as his orgasm pulses through him. His eyes don't leave mine as he fills me up, hot splashes of cum hitting my insides. I love every single minute of it.

"Jesus Christ, Kins, you're so fuckin' good. It's just so damn good. You've made me an addict."

"Likewise, baby, likewise."

. . .

The sun starts to set as we get on the bike and take the drive to the opposite side of town to my parents' house. I'm eager to experience having him there with me, but slightly nervous to see my parents. They're the most supportive, loving people on the planet, and I know they both already love him. But to love him for me is an entirely different story.

We pull up to the open property, wild lupines lush with pinks, purples, and blues leading the way. My parents are already on the deck waiting as Reid brings us to a stop, steadying the bike with his feet on the ground so I can climb off first. I can feel the weight of their stare as I wait for Reid to join me, his leg swinging over the bike, his big hand clasping mine.

"Reid Knight," my mom says with all the love and heart in the world as she walks right past her only daughter with her arms stretched wide. Reid doesn't miss a beat, his arms wrapping around her.

"Hi, Mrs. Amy," he says as he bends way down to give her a hug.

"I was hoping it would be you," she says as she releases him, her hand reaching up to cup his face. Reid visibly stumbles backward at her words.

"Mom?" I ask, looking back and forth between the two of them. Reid's expression is pure shock, his eyes welling with unshed tears.

She points at his chest with her finger right above his heart. "You are perfect for my daughter. I hope your heart is healing after everything you've lost."

"Lost?"

"You all may have been too young or too preoccupied to pay attention to the news, but I remember. I've always known about your missing sister, but knew you needed space to heal in your own way. I also know wherever she may be, that she would be proud of you and would want to see you finally living and to be happy."

"Mom . . ." I gasp, putting my hands over my mouth, Reid's tears finally falling over the rim.

"That means more to me than you'll ever know, Mrs. Amy."

"You've always been a part of this family, Reid. I'm happy to make it official now that you've fallen for my daughter."

"I agree," my dad says. "You're a damn good man." He reaches out to shake Reid's hand and then pulls me into the best, fatherly hug. I take in a deep inhale of his sweet, woodsy scent that reminds me so much of a rickhouse. Like the whiskey barrels have permanently soaked into his body and are as much a part of him as he is them.

My mom reaches for Reid again, hugging her with all the love and strength that only a mother can. My mom grabs his hand and pulls him behind her into the house. I follow, my heart in my throat.

The noise hits me before I see them all. Sunday dinner at my parents' house is complete and utter chaos. Which is exactly how it has always been, and I would expect nothing less. My niece, Charlotte, comes barreling through the house, nearly knocking Reid out by the knees as she skitters across the hardwood floors in her socks, her dog, Billy, hot on her heels.

"Aunty Kins!" she squeals as she wraps her arms around my waist.

"Charlie! How's my favorite five-year-old?"

"I'm the best! Dad said we couldn't bring Sewer, and I said that was rude. 'Cause now she's lonely at our house by herself, but we couldn't leave Garbage—"

"Charlotte Sidney! What are their names?"

"Garbage and Sewer!" she yells back with the sweetest giggle, her hand clapping over her mouth. Liam stands from his stool at the bar and quickly snatches her off her feet, flipping her upside down.

"Okay, then! Remember, you brought this on yourself,

munchkin!" he tells her while she screeches and squeals. "Listen up, everybody! This one thinks it's funny to name things where they were born or found, so effective immediately, Charlotte Sidney is now to be known as . . ." He pauses and waves his hand for us to fill in the blank. We all collectively holler, "KITCHEN!"

Everyone laughs and goes back to their conversations as Liam flips her back upright in his arms. "Alright, Kitchen, go find Pappy!"

"You're crazy, Dad. I'm gonna go find out where you were born and change your name now."

I laugh as I steer Reid further into the wild and crazy house I grew up in, walking through the main parts and pushing open the back porch doors that lead to the large deck. I close them behind us and pull him to sit, his hands automatically pulling me into his lap.

"Hey, big guy. You doing okay?"

"Yeah, we've only been here two minutes. I've known your family a long time, I'm good, baby."

"I mean about the heart-to-heart with my mom."

"It was unexpected, but I suppose I should have guessed. Lena was all over the news for a long time."

"I love you, Reid. I hope you know how worthy you are of a beautiful life with good things."

"I'm starting to, sweetheart. All because of you."

We return inside, finding Sawyer and Dallas in a heated debate over whether or not he and Blaire can share an office at the distillery. I don't know how these four boys have managed to work together and successfully run a massive distillery. It's surprising one of them hasn't been murdered and put in a whiskey barrel, never to be seen again.

"You know why, dipshit! You already use your office as a playground when I've told you to knock it the hell off!" Sawyer spits.

"I thought we already established we all have done that . . ." Carter interjects, my eyes going wide.

"Wait! Wait a freaking minute. You're telling me all you four freaks have banged somewhere in our family's distillery?" I yell. The four of them look at me like kids with their hands caught in a cookie jar.

"Wow. Real classy, you guys."

"You mean to tell me you've never hooked up at Rogue?" Finn says, my brothers' heads snapping in his direction. My cheeks flush, but not in embarrassment. Reid's arm drapes over my shoulder, pulling me in front of him so he can rest it around my collarbone. I relax my back into his strong build and watch as my brothers lose their minds over their precious little sister not being a baby.

"The fuck did you just say?" Sawyer practically growls, making Finn hold up his hands.

"She would never!" Dallas yells.

"How dare you. Our sister is a fucking saint!" Liam adds. Reid makes a choking sound that he quickly clears with a cough. Heads snap back to us, and my hand slaps over my mouth, hiding my smile. Four sets of eyes practically bore a hole into me as my chest starts to shake.

"I assure you, she is no such thing," Reid says, and I lose it. My laugh erupts out of me, a deep belly laugh that I can't control.

"Oh for fuck's sake!" Sawyer says as he throws his hands up in the air. Ivy quickly swoops in, laughing.

"Wow," I say, wiping the tears from my eyes. "I needed that. I've been listening to your stories for so long, and it feels good not to be on the outside looking in. I'm an adult, fuckers, so stop treating me like a baby, or I'll make sure we make you all real uncomfortable, real quick."

All four of them nod and give their agreement, and I turn in Reid's arms, looking up at my man.

"I love you."

"I love you, sweetheart. It'll be worth the haymaker he throws at me later."

I smirk at him just as my mom's voice echoes through the house, signaling it's time to come eat.

Dinner is wild, and Reid joins right in like he's been here all along. It helps that he's had a solid relationship with every single person at the table. When I dreamed what it would be like to bring a man home to my family, I never could have imagined the sense of pride I would feel to have him next to me. But then again, I never in a million years thought that man would be Reid Knight.

reid

"ARE YOU READY FOR THIS?" KINSEY ASKS ME AS SHE climbs off the back of my bike in front of my parents' new house in Seattle. They moved here over a year ago, wanting a fresh start, and I haven't visited once. Guilt eats away at me, but like Kinsey says, we have limited time in front of us, and we need to live in the present while we have it.

"As ready as I'll ever be. I'm glad you're with me."

The door to my parents' house opens in front of us while Kinsey and I stand in the center of the small driveway, my arms wrapped tightly around her. My heart pounds in my chest as the front door opens and falls closed.

My mom stands in the doorway with her hand clasped over her mouth, looking every bit stunned, as she has the right to be. Emotion slams into me at the sight of her. Lena looked so much like her that they could have been twins. My mom's hair is still dark, beautiful silver greys coming in like highlights. She has the same green eyes Lena and I do, and I wonder what it's like for her to look in the mirror, if she sees her beautiful daughter looking back at her. I know I see Lena every day in myself.

While we've spoken over the last year, I haven't been to see them since before they left Amberwood. The weight of my decisions, the silence, the guilt, the pain of what we all lost squeezes my heart in a vise grip as I look at her.

"Ohmygod! Reid!" my mom gasps from the doorway.

"Hey, Mom," I reply, walking toward her with shaking legs as she rushes down the steps and wraps me in a hug that pulls all the emotion I was holding at bay to the surface. Her familiar, comforting scent engulfs me, forcing the guilt to rush through my veins. She clasps my face in her palms, her eyes roaming all over my face like she's trying to re-memorize my features, as if she's looking for everything she's missed. I can't imagine her pain, and she felt it all without me to mourn with. Tears spill over my eyes as I pull her into another hug.

"I'm so sorry I haven't been here."

"Don't you dare. Don't apologize."

"But I am, though. I'm sorry I've spent so much time away, it was too . . . difficult to be with you."

"My sweet baby boy, I understand. We all grieve in different ways, and while I wanted to hold you tight through it, I've always understood your need to process things on your own and in your own way. She was your best friend as well as your sister. You loved her more than anything."

It's strange hearing her talk in past tense. Two years ago, my parents petitioned to have my sister declared dead. After nearly eight years of no updates on her whereabouts, no communication, and no new leads, it was granted. While I know hope will always live in their hearts, I at least know they've gotten some type of closure without the details that would surely break them if they knew.

"I'm so glad you're here. This is the best surprise."

"I'm sorry we didn't call first."

"We! My gosh, I'm so sorry."

"Mom, this is Kinsey, she's . . ." Shit. What is she? I suddenly can't think of a word strong enough to describe what she is to me. "The love of my life," I finally settle on. My mom's face beams with happiness and maternal pride.

"Kinsey, it's so nice to meet you. Please, come inside. Reid, your father is in the kitchen."

We follow my mom inside, my nerves settling slightly as Kinsey reaches for my hand, giving it a strong squeeze and reminding me that I'm not alone. That she's here with me.

We walk into their new home, and I don't recognize a single thing except for their signature warm scent. It's sad but also refreshing. One of the reasons I avoided visiting them was that every time I stepped into their home in Amberwood, it was like walking into a time capsule where life completely stopped. Lena's presence was everywhere. Her things, her scent—even if it was all in my head. It was a painful reminder that I couldn't bear anymore.

"What brings you here?"

"I miss you." The words are out of my mouth before I have time to think about them.

"We've missed you, Reid."

Footsteps get louder and louder as we stand in the entryway, removing our shoes, and those nerves kick up, making my palms sweaty.

"Son?"

I turn at the sound of the voice, my father standing at the edge of the room.

"Hi, Dad."

He's about my height and looks healthy and in shape, even if I can see the weight of how life turned for him behind his eyes. He takes three large strides in my direction, his arms pulling me into a huge hug.

"Welcome home, son. You look good."

"Thanks, Dad. You do, too. The house is beautiful, I'm happy for you two."

"It's been a nice pace of living, we're enjoying being in the city. Amberwood was just too . . . remote."

"Yeah, I get that."

The four of us move into the living room, my mom serving us

all water and lemonade to cool off from the blazing heat outside. We catch up on their jobs, how they both plan on retiring next year, how they've taken up boating. I fill them in on my studio, how Kinsey and I met, and how we just moved in together. We leave out the evil parts and stick to the safe topics and our life in Aspen Ridge. They don't ask about the club, or marriage, or children . . . even though based on the way my mom's eyes keep bouncing between Kinsey and me, I can tell she wants to. Once Lena and I became legal adults, she would talk about how she couldn't wait for us to settle down and give her grandchildren.

Kids weren't something I ever thought I would have after I lost Lena, but an image of Kinsey's stomach swelling with our child makes my heart ache. She's given me a second chance at life, and if kids are in our future, I would be on board with it. But I know deep down, the only thing I need to be the happiest man in the world is her. Everything else is extra.

My mom pulls out a photo album, sitting between Kinsey and me, and flips through photos of my childhood. Lena and I dressed up as Batman and Robin for Halloween, the time my mom was shampooing the carpet on the stairs, and we took laundry baskets to use as sleds. Lena broke her arm that day, and I can still remember how she and I laughed our asses off after the fact at how mad our parents were.

For the first time since Lena was taken, I relax and enjoy the time with my parents with nothing but love and enjoyment between us.

I've gone back and forth on telling them the truth about what happened to her that night, but at least for right now, I can't bring myself to do it. I know it's unfair to make that decision for them, but I was twenty-two and have to live with my decisions. Maybe it's the coward's way out, maybe it's a selfish part of me that doesn't want to be the one to break their hearts, whatever the reason, today, I just want to enjoy having parents.

After a few hours, Kinsey and I say our goodbyes, with promises to see them soon, and walk out of their house hand in hand. I straddle my bike, holding it steady for Kinsey to climb on and get comfortable, but before she does, she walks into my space, her hands grasping my cheeks, pretty blue eyes looking at me with so much damn love my heart trips over itself in my chest.

"I'm so proud of you."

God, this woman is so good. So perfect. So selfless.

"I love you, sweetheart. I couldn't have done that without you, Kins."

"That's where you're wrong. All I did was open your eyes to how strong you are, to your worth. It's been there all along."

"My little fighter. My ride or die. I'm going to spend however long I have on this Earth making you happy."

"As long as you're by my side, that's all I need."

kinsey

AT THE END OF EVERY SUMMER, ASPEN RIDGE HOLDS AN end-of-season party at Grace Beach. There are vendors with food, drinks, games for kids and adults alike. Once the sun goes down, there's a huge bonfire that rages for hours on end, lighting up the sky with its blazing heat, little embers floating around on the wind.

I've come here every year for as long as I can remember to celebrate the end of summer, to get excited for the school year, or to welcome fall, which is right around the corner. For the last few years, especially, I've come here and found friends paired off, watched my parents snuggle on driftwood in front of the fire, and craved having someone of my own. Someone who would fit in with my family like a sibling, but love me like I was the center of his world.

It's hard to believe it was only a year ago that Sawyer brought Ivy here after she had been gone for ten years. I watched as the two of them walked over to us, her hands rubbing together in front of her body, nerves written all over her face. Sawyer reached for her hand, grounding her and settling her into her skin, silently reminding her that she can take up space, that even though she hurt him, that she was welcome back into Aspen Ridge—back into our family. I watched them, and my heart ached to feel that for myself.

In the last year, all five of us have found our soulmates in the most unexpected ways, and as I stand here and look at my brothers, lost in their own little worlds, completely wrapped up in the person they've found their match in, I'm grateful.

Grateful to have such a large, loving family that puts each other first. Grateful to be suffocated by their overbearing love, grateful they brought me three sisters and a new brother. Grateful to live in a small town that feels like a warm hug.

Reid drapes his arm over my shoulders as the bonfire ignites, tucking me into his side like he always does. It's such a possessive move, but it brings both of us so much comfort—to touch, to be close. It grounds each of us in different ways, and I thrive knowing I'm his and he's mine.

The waves crash hard against the shore, the night lit up by the moon and the blazing bonfire. Everyone is lost to chatter and letting loose. Wes Draven walks up to us, slapping his hand into Reid's, giving him a solid shake, then promptly returns his arms to wrap around his wife, Lily. I can't help but admire how happy she looks, ethereally glowing next to him. Her midnight-black hair and bright auburn highlights remind me of a goddess.

Lily gives me a smile, but then she looks back up at Wes, completely consumed by him. I can relate. It's exactly how I feel with Reid, pulled into his vortex and utterly devoured by it.

"My president sends his appreciation for what you pulled for us. We couldn't have done it without you. If you're interested, he'd like your info in case he needs your services again," Reid tells him.

"It was easy. As long as nothing takes me out of Aspen Ridge, I'm down. You can pass it along."

Reid nods. "We appreciate it. I'm sure he'll be in touch sooner rather than later. There's always something."

"I know how that goes, except I've never been busier than this last year—your brothers are my biggest return clients, Kinsey."

"Well, I hate to break it to you, Wes, I think the craziness has finally died down. Now, we all need to find our new normal."

Wes and Lily wander off, leaving Reid and me semi-alone.

"You doin' okay, sweetheart?"

"I've never been better. What about you, big guy?"

"I've got my woman in my arms, and my soul finally feels at peace. I have nothing to complain about."

"Such a Reid answer."

My parents join us not a moment later, followed by all my brothers and their partners.

"I need a photo to mark the occasion! All my babies are grown up. I'm so proud of every single one of you five and the people you've chosen to spend your lives with. All your father and I ever wanted for you was to be happy and to love hard. You're each doing that in your own way. I couldn't be prouder, and I couldn't be more grateful to be your mom and have the honor and privilege to be in your lives and watch all the brilliant things you do." Her voice cracks, a few tears spilling over the rims of her eyes. "Now crowd in, I want all ten of you in there!"

Sawyer pulls Reid into his side, throwing his arm over his shoulder as Reid pulls me in front of him with his hand wrapped around my waist. Dallas and Blaire fill in next, followed by Liam and Hannah, and Carter and Finn. We've all been through so much the past year, but at the end of it, no matter what happens, we have this. We have each other.

Family.

epilogue

KINSEY ONE YEAR LATER

I SNUCK OUT OF THE CLUBHOUSE WITH MALICE'S HELP, even though he was supposed to be with everyone else; he's just crazy enough to cross Reid and help me instead. Reid was in church for an impromptu vote, and I know I was supposed to stay in the room or downstairs with some of the girls, but I had someone I needed to talk to, and it was long overdue.

The Aspen tree starts to sway its bright yellow autumn leaves at my arrival, and I smile up at it. I know it's her way of saying hi. Taking a seat on the grass next to her gravestone, I lay my flowers down and wipe some of the leaves off it. Emotion gets lodged in my throat as I touch the cold stone, as if it's my hands running over her head instead.

"Hey, Lena. About time I came to see you alone. Your brother is hard to shake when I want a minute of privacy. I know he means well, but I had to come see you, and sneaking out was the only way. Thought it was time we had a little girl talk." I swallow hard against the knot in my throat, tears filling my eyes. "He's going to be okay, Lena. I've got him now, and you can rest. He's spending time with your parents, and they've all gotten so much closer since they were reunited. Every day, he seems to relax more and more, that little ember I saw so long ago finally burning brighter. I love him more than anything. I promise I'll take care of him, that I'll fight for him—even if that means fighting for him to be kinder to himself. He's healing still, but he's getting there. We're going to carry you with us, keep your memory alive, but I wanted you to know that I can take it from here. I want you both to rest. I know we never met, but I need you to know I love you. I love you for everything you are to Reid, for having the kind of sibling relationship people dream of, for opening my eyes to what I have with my brothers, and for never taking it for granted. So, sweet Lena, rest. He's going to be okay."

"Kins?" Reid's voice breaks through the quiet stillness of sitting up here with Lena. I quickly bat away my tears and stand.

"Until next time, sister. We love you," I say as my parting words, turning to find Reid walking toward me. His eyes are a severe storm of concern and frustration, the two warring for dominance.

"Yes?" I say with an innocent smirk.

"You think sneaking out of the clubhouse was a good decision or a bad one?"

"Uhm? A smart one?"

Reid tsks as his legs eat up the distance between us, but before he can get too close, I turn and bolt, running as fast as I can in the opposite direction.

"Oh, sweetheart, fine by me," he growls, his voice floating on the wind as I run away from him. I can hear the rustle of his jeans and the stomp of his boots against the hard ground as he gains on me. My heart pounds in my chest, a laugh bursting from my lungs as his massive arms wrap around my stomach, and then we're falling, rolling on the ground so Reid lands first, flipping us so I'm pinned under him.

"Not very smart, my violent little fighter," he growls into my neck as he flicks the button of my jeans and works the zipper down. I gasp as he starts to shove my pants over my hips.

"Reid! What are you doing?"

"Teaching you a lesson."

"We're out in the open! Someone could see us!"

"We're behind the hill, and no one comes up here but me. Now, are you gonna continue to fight me or let your man fuck you into the grass?"

"Oh god."

"That's what I thought. I bet your little pussy is already dripping for me."

We both know that it is, and when he gets my jeans down my legs, his palms sliding up my thighs, plunging two thick fingers inside me with ease, he groans out his appreciation.

"Oh, my girl, always so ready." He finger fucks me hard, thrusting in deep and rubbing his thumb across my throbbing, desperate clit. Pleasure builds quickly as he hovers over me, watching me as he works me closer and closer to an orgasm.

"Baby, that feels so good, please make me come."

"You want my hand around your delicate little neck, Kins? You want your man to steal the breath from your lungs?"

"Jesus, yes, please!" I moan, my hips wanton, chasing this incredible feeling that's swirling inside me. His hand slides up the center of my chest, fingers grasping around my throat. I know he loves seeing his hand wrapped around my neck, the flawless ivory skin against his heavily inked hand and fingers. It looks like the two don't belong, but we're a perfect match made in the heavens.

My fingers curl around his wrist as his fingers tighten around my throat. I love when he does this, the control, the trust, the euphoric feeling of release as I pull in precious oxygen as my body falls off that cliff into an orgasm.

Reid takes me to the stars every single time.

I'm coming a moment later, my body shaking, nails digging into his forearm as he releases my throat and gives me air. My pussy flutters around his thick fingers, pleasure pulling me under and taking me out to sea. As I come down, Reid is still hovering over me, his lips suctioned around the fingers that were just inside me. It's so sexy to see him do that. To crave me in such a deeply primal way.

"You like playing with fire, little fighter?"

I hum my reply as I use my limbs to climb him like a fucking tree, rolling him onto his back, quickly undoing his belt and jeans, freeing that beautiful cock I love so much. On shaky knees, I line him up with my entrance, swiping his length back and forth through my center, coating him in my arousal.

"Oh, sweetheart, fuck. You are sooo goddamn wet," he purrs. "Did I get you nice and ready for my cock?"

"Yes!" I moan as I drop down, sinking onto his full length in one hard motion. A long, drawn-out groan works its way up his chest at the feel of me enveloping him in wet heat. I'm so desperate for him as I rock my hips back and forth, rubbing my clit against his abdomen.

"That's it, sweetheart, ride my dick. Use me, take what you need."

Reid's grip on my hips is brutal, his thumb swiping back and forth across the tattoo he gave me, as he focuses on my face. I know he's hovering on a tightrope with his self-control, and I love to push him right past it.

"I love you when you're inside me, baby, I'm so full," I moan out the words as I reach backward, grabbing his sack and rolling his balls between my fingers, the pad of my middle finger stroking the soft skin under them.

"That's it. Fuck, Kins, don't stop, you're gonna make me blow. Shit, that feels too good."

"Come for me, baby. I want it."

"I'm gonna fill you up, Kins, my cum's gonna be dripping out of you the rest of the day."

"Give it to me!" I yell as I shatter on top of him. Tremors rattle my body as his big dick thickens, his grip on my hips squeezing painfully. Reid's hips pump into me from below, the tip of his length hitting my cervix, making me scream. I feel the moment he comes, his dick jerking inside me, filling me with warm fluid. After we've both caught our breath, Reid helps me pull my jeans back on.

"Come on, little fighter. I got something for you."

"For me?"

"Do you know any other little fighters?"

"You better not be calling anyone else that, Reid Knight!"

He turns on me quickly, fingers threading through my hair, my face cradled in his big palms.

"You think I could do that?"

"No . . ."

"Good girl. You had better know you're it for me."

I do. The last year together has been unlike anything I could have imagined. Reid is no longer keeping it hidden that he's a member of Hell's Heathens, and I have been going with him to the clubhouse when Chaos calls or for him to attend church. He's opened my eyes to different ways of life, given me a new family through the club, and more freedom than I could have imagined. I love being on the back . . . or front . . . of his bike. Winter was rough without it, but we made do. We take day trips as often as possible, and I don't know how I ever lived a day without knowing what it was like to be connected to him through an activity like that.

I follow him into the clubhouse, my palm clasped firmly in his hand, his strides slow to keep with the pace of my much shorter legs. Once we're in the privacy of his old bedroom, a place we decided to keep in case we need it, Reid grabs my shoulders, guiding me to sit down on the edge of the bed.

He looks nervous, his face slightly pinched, body shifting from foot to foot. Nerves suddenly skate down my spine. Surely, he would have told me if something was wrong before he fucked me in the grass?

"Is everything okay?" I ask hesitantly.

"This is to replace your current one. If you'll accept."

"Accept?"

Reid hands me a leather jacket, and there's no mistaking the property patch on the back. I know the gravity of what it means, and I stare at it with my mouth slightly open.

"The club voted. Everyone agreed. I wish I could have asked you before getting their permission, but I needed to know I have their support before I did. You're my old lady now. My queen."

I chuckle at the demand. A very Rogue thing to do.

"Yeah, baby, I am," I tell him with a sly smile as I stand up. "A Heathen and his queen."

Reid kisses me like he needs to breathe. Fire could be licking at our feet, and he wouldn't stop. His tongue dips into my mouth, tasting, exploring, as if it's the first time and not the millionth. As we break, he presses one last kiss to the center of my forehead before taking a step back and dropping to his knees.

"Ten years ago, I was swallowed whole into an abyss of darkness. For years, I trudged through purgatory, with no light, no hope, and couldn't accept any amount of love anyone tried to offer me. Until you. You and your bright light, your strength, pulled me out and gave me hope, gave me true love. You saved me, sweetheart. I just need one more thing from you, will you please be my wife?"

My eyes well with tears as his words and the desperation and meaning behind them are driven straight to my heart.

"Every piece of me is already yours. You've given me everything I ever could have wanted. Someone who puts me first, who loves me unconditionally, who wants to chase life and experiences. My life is exceptionally better with you by my side. Yes, I'll be your wife. Make me Kinsey Knight!"

Reid stands with a smile that fills his entire handsome face, as he scoops me into his arms and we fall to the mattress. Hidden away inside the room where we fell in love, we remind each other of exactly who holds our hearts.

thank you for reading!

LOVED REID AND KINSEY'S STORY?

Please consider leaving a review! As an indie author, reviews are so important. Thank you so much for your support!

Ready to head to Amberwood? Book one in the Queens and Heathens series is next. Find out how the Hell's Heathens president finds love in All's Fair in Love and Chaos.

acknowledgments

Wow. As I sit here and type the words 'The End' on the final book of the Aspen Ridge series, I am consumed with emotions. I did it. I not only wrote and published a book, but I wrote and published an eight-book series. *Me.*

I did the damn thing.

I am so incredibly proud of the Aspen Ridge series, not only for the stories I got to tell, but for the healing I experienced while writing it. Whether it was Ivy returning to her small hometown and her fears of facing everyone after the way she left, or Blaire's sexual assault trauma and using BDSM to heal from it, or Hannah's focus on raising her daughter as a single mom, Finn's desperate desire to break free of toxic family members weighing him down, or Kinsey's need to live the life she wants for herself—these characters are a huge part of who I am and have healed me in ways I struggle to describe.

I can't begin to thank you enough for being on this intensely amazing journey with me. It has been such an incredible, wild ride, and I hope you'll stick around for everything that is still to come.

To my readers,

Would I be here without you? When I published Unravel Me, I set a goal of reaching twenty people that I didn't know, that would read it. Here we are millions of pages read later, thousands of readers, and I am so blown away and in awe that you pick up my books and read them. What an incredible gift. Thank you for trusting me, for continuing to come back for more, and for sharing your love of this world and these characters. I am so very grateful for each of you.

Michael,

You are so deeply rooted in each of my male characters, and honestly? How couldn't you be? No matter what you have going on, no matter what's on your plate, you have always made me feel like the center of your world. Thank you for showing me what it feels like to be loved. Thank you for juggling both our roles over the last year and a half while I put myself first for the first time in my life and focus on this dream. I'm so grateful for how hard you work so that I can stay home and write full time. None of this would be possible without you. I love you and I'm so proud of us.

My editor, Katie,

I feel like every book I write out 'this one wouldn't be possible without you' but it's honestly the truth. So many people have come and gone over the last year and a half but you've stayed put. As I reflect on all of it, I wanted to say that our relationship started out as editor and author but looking back, I don't think we ever did. It was always easy and instant with us and in you, I found a life-long friend. From titling some of my books, helping with every step of cover design, and decisions, editing, and advising on marketing and planning . . . you are involved and invested in every aspect of my career. Thank you for being there for me on the days where I doubt whether I can keep going, when I fall apart and play the comparison game, for cheering me on when I succeed or am excited. You have made this experience immensely better. I am eternally grateful for your friendship, the education you give me, and the way you have the magical ability to turn my manuscripts into gold. I love you. Thank you!

Mom,

Thank you for believing in me and my writing when I didn't believe in myself. I really fucking did it. I love you!

To Laura S.,

Thank you. You watched me work tirelessly for a very long time on previous projects only to have them ripped away from me by someone who never had my best interest at heart. You pushed me to keep going, to chase my dreams, and start over. Doing that was one of the hardest things I've done when my heart was still so set on the project and world I created that I lost. But you kept at me. As my hype girl, as my confidant, as my friend, and supporter. The Aspen Ridge series exists because you pushed me to keep going. I will be forever thankful for your support, your love, your unwavering belief that I could truly do this. I'm here in a huge part because of you. I love you so much.

Em,

I'm so thankful you've come into my life. Thank you for your constant support of me, my books, and the stories I want to tell. Every check-in message and text, every note, every VM—I'm so thankful to know you and feel your love.

My betas, Britt & Clair,

Thank you for being more like alphas for this one. For answering all my questions, giving your input and advice, and for loving and knowing my characters so deeply. I'm so thankful to have you on my team and by my side.

Samantha at The Smuthood,

Thank you for helping keep me on track, for your support and dedication to me and your authors. I'm so thankful for all you do for me and I'm so grateful to be apart of everything you've created! I love you!!

My cover designers, Melissa at Mel D. Designs and Najla at Qamber Designs,

Thank you for bringing my books to life through these

incredible covers. I'm so proud of them and forever grateful for your time and the work you've done for me.

Destiny,

Thank you for formatting this entire eight book series, for supporting me and being the most amazing human to work with. I'm so proud of these books and of you!!

My ARC/Street Team,

Thank you isn't enough! What a year it's been! I'm so thankful to have felt your support through this publication journey. Every share, tag, edit, comment, DM, and review has meant the absolute world to me. Thank you for taking a chance on a new author and sticking with me!

Harlots,

Thank you! Thank you for your unwavering support, for cheering me on, loving my books, and being the best damn reader group there is!

A special shoutout to, Chelsey, Ginsa, Danielle, Nouha, Shelby, Brie, Meighan, Morgan, Olivia A., Mackenzie L, Susan, Heather, Jen F., Sam, Becca, Christine, Amie, Madalyn, Phoebe, Erica, Amber, Bryanna, Mackenzie S., & Bells, THANK YOU for supporting me!

To every bookstagrammer, reviewer, and blogger,

THANK YOU! Every single post, share, edit, I am blown away. That you not only took the time to read my words and fall in love with my characters, but created and shared graphics to share with others. You hold so much power, and I am so very grateful to every single one of you!

books by jenn plummer

www.jennplummer.com

Aspen Ridge Series

Unravel Me

Crave Me

Love Me

Wreck Me

Complete Me

Aspen Ridge Holiday Novellas

Ready or Not (Halloween)

Sweet Girl (Valentine's Day)

Daddy Issues (Father's Day)

Standalones

Nothing to Fear

Queens and Heathens

All's Fair in Love and Chaos

about the author

Author, wife, mother, lover of reading, overcast skies, chilly
weather, and hockey.
A romantic at heart, Jenn has always been a lover of books and is
constantly dreaming up heart-wrenching stories that will have you
reaching for tissues and make you blush.
When Jenn's not writing, she can be found reading a spicy
romance novel, watching scary movies, and enjoying her quiet life
in New England, living out her real-life romance story.
Follow along for more updates and book news.
www.jennplummer.com
Instagram @authorjennplummer
Goodreads @jennplummer
Amazon @jennplummer
Threads @authorjennplummer

www.ingramcontent.com/pod-product-compliance
Lightning Source LLC
Chambersburg PA
CBHW070600300726
48975CB00006B/1654